A LILY OF FRANCE

"'I was about to ask the name of this most lovely rose.'"

Page 93

From the Society's own Press

To the

Three Companions of my Pilgrimage to the Scenes of this Story

The Friend, the Sister, and the Child

A LILY OF FRANCE

Is Dedicated

To see a man who is willing to die for love, who goes to meet death in the way, who makes a boast of pain and with perfect sweetness and sanity celebrates defeat—that is to be witness of the palpable infinite

—Charles Ferguson

CONTENTS

LIST OF ILLUSTRATIONS

A LILY OF FRANCE

I

THE CLOISTER

PRIME had just been sung in the Sainte Chapelle of the Benedictine Abbey of Notre-Dame de Jouarre.

Two by two the black-robed sisters came out through the south transept door and passed slowly out of sight amid the vistas of the ancient cloister.

Last of all came two children, little girls of ten or eleven years, dressed alike in gowns of coarse white cloth fastened plainly about the throat and falling to the feet, confined at the waist by a girdle. Each wore on her head a white linen coif, from which hung a square of white muslin, forming a short and scanty veil.

While at a first glance these young girls seemed to be habited precisely alike and resembled each other in general appearance, close observation showed significant differences between them. The taller of the two appeared to be the younger, possessing a more childlike contour of face and a noticeably artless and even infantile sweetness of the large and limpid blue eyes. About her mouth, however, lay a strongly marked expression of submission, a curiously pathetic patience. The face lacked altogether the bloom of free and hardy childhood, having added to its natural delicacy of tint the peculiar pallor of the cloister, a characteristic much less marked in the face of her companion.

Despite the traces of a life of constant discipline, the manner and bearing of this taller child were distinguished by a certain unconscious but enchanting imperiousness, a proud little pose of the head upon the delicate neck, a graceful firmness of carriage, while in her friend was to be seen the ordinary *gaucherie* common to her years. The single difference in the habit of the child novitiates was in the girdle which the smaller of them wore simply knotted, while in the case of the other it was fastened by a clasp showing the Bourbon lily richly wrought in gold.

The early morning sun shone down into the recesses of the gray old cloister and the sky above was unclouded and blue as midsummer, although the month was October. The children lingered and looked behind them at the closed door, through which they had just come.

"Do you think we shall see her again to-day ?" asked the younger wistfully.

"Yes, madame said she would come presently and bring her that we may speak with her."

"Oh, joy !" cried the other, clasping her hands with childish delight. "I love her already, Jeannette. Do not you ?"

Her friend, who had a pleasant little face with frank gray eyes and a nose decidedly *retroussé*, looked up with shrewd inquiry.

"If you love her better than you love me, Charlotte, I shall hate her, you know," she answered quite simply.

"*Voilà*, Jeannette ! You are always so simple. As if I could change my friends as I do my dresses !"

"Yes, but you do not change them so very often," said Jeannette reflectively.

At this moment the door of the *chapelle* was pushed open and a woman of slender figure robed in clinging black appeared. Her outer robe, edged with fur, flowed over a tunic of finest white wool, and the furred sleeves fell to the ground. Upon her breast the large jeweled cross, and upon her right forefinger the abbatial ring, gave token of the rank of *supérieure*. The patrician delicacy of face and figure suggested, however, rather the aristocrat than the ascetic, although both bore in some degree the stamp of cloistral austerity.

The lady was leading by the hand a third little girl, apparently a year or two older than the two novices, richly dressed in bright blue velvet with hanging sleeves lined with parti-colored satin, and a chemisette and ruff of finest needlework.

The head of the young stranger was bare, and her dark hair, parted over the forehead, fell in soft, full waves upon her shoulders. Under the straight, fine brows looked out a pair of brown, lustrous eyes ; the nose was fine and small, the lips scarlet, with a half-defiant, half-appealing expression ; the face in tint a clear brunette, with warm color in the cheeks.

It was easy to see that this child had thriven, for her dozen years of life, on sun and wind and untrammeled freedom. The wild joy of living ran in her blood ; the hardihood of outdoor life had given its elastic firmness to her slender but vigorous frame. She looked like a creature of a different strain from the cloister-bred girls, who now stood wistfully watching the astonishing brilliancy of her face and figure.

" The demoiselle de Mousson, my children," said the *supérieure*. The smile with which she spoke would have been winning but for a faint suggestion of mockery which underlay it. Speaking then to the child, whose hand she still held, she added, indicating the younger of the two novitiates :

" This, mademoiselle, is her grace of Bourbon-Montpensier, the Princess Charlotte, of whom the Queen of Navarre has told you many things."

The little maid, with a shy smile of pleasure, dropped upon her knees and kissed Charlotte's hand. A delicate flush tinged the cheeks of the young princess and her face grew marvelously radiant.

"Oh, tell me quickly," she exclaimed, "have you come even now from Béarn? Have you seen my cousin of Navarre of late? Did she send me her greeting by you? Why does she not come to visit me? And how is Prince Henri? Have you played with him often? Tell me all, everything."

"Gently, gently, Charlotte," said madame, with a touch of coldness in her warning voice. "You ask many things in one breath, and time fails now to make reply."

Turning then to the second novitiate, who had stood slightly in the background, she drew her forward and presented her to the new-comer as Jeanne or Jeannette Vassetz.

"We have now two Jeannes," she said with her cold, quiet voice, "for this is Jeanne de Mousson."

"I was named for her majesty of Navarre, Jeanne d'Albret," said the child proudly. "She is my godmother."

Charlotte de Bourbon clasped her hands in a gesture of admiration.

"Ah, but you are the fortunate one!" she exclaimed.

Again madame's gentle smile with its faint shade of mockery. She had herself stood sponsor to Charlotte, who was her sister's child.

"It is hardly possible for you all to enjoy such favor as that," she said softly, and at once led the way through the cloister to the long, low range of buildings on the side opposite the chapel.

Passing from the early sunlight through a long corridor with bare stone floor and dimly frescoed walls, she entered the refectory followed by the three children, Jeanne de Mousson, in her worldly

dress, her unbound hair, and her rich coloring, looking, beside the pale novices, like some tropical bird
of gorgeous plumage which had fluttered down from
the sunshine and alighted beside a pair of caged
and meek white doves.

"You may both take your breakfast at my table
this morning," madame said graciously to the two
Jeannes. Charlotte by reason of her rank always
had her seat at her aunt's right hand.

To the new-comer, as she followed the *supérieure*
down the length of it, the room in which they were
about to break their fast was sombre and cold even
to sternness. The vaulted roof, high and dim, the
stone pillars upholding it, the bare walls and floor,
the uncovered tables forming three sides of a parallelogram, with narrow, unpainted benches along the
outer side, the rows of nuns standing motionless in
their black hoods and robes behind the tables, made
up an ensemble of unrelieved gloom.

Madame de Long-Vic, for this was the name of
the abbess of Jouarre, took her place at the center
of the table which extended across the upper end
of the room and which was reserved for dignitaries
and guests of rank. Standing, while a complete
hush fell upon them all, madame's clear, gray eyes
scanned the rows of sisters. They all stood with
downcast eyes, all faces alike showing the monotonous pallor and the expressionless restraint of the
cloister. An instant's glance satisfied the abbess
that all were in their places and she accordingly
lifted the forefinger of her right hand, a significant
gesture followed by a chant sung in full chorus by
the whole company. As the sounds of the chant
died away, again the forefinger with its symbolic
ring was lifted, and at this second sign all were
seated. Lay sisters now placed upon the tables the
portions of bread, water, and vegetables which con-
stituted the breakfast of the order.

Not one word broke the silence. Jeanne de

Mousson, still unpractised in the convent routine, was about to speak to Jeannette, but was promptly checked by the latter, who cast an anxious look at madame's face as she laid her small, childish forefinger on the red lips of the new and alarming Jeanne.

High up, on the wall facing the table of the *supé- rieure*, projected a tiny balcony furnished with a reading desk, to which a door gave access from an upper corridor. This door now softly opened and a priest in black gown entered the pulpit, and having crossed himself repeatedly, opened a small book and proceeded to read aloud a sermon in Latin in a mo- notonous chanting cadence.

This was Père Ruzé, who for a few months in the year 1558, took the place of confessor-in-residence to the Abbey of Jouarre.

The little Béarnaise, who left her breakfast un- tasted, glanced from Père Ruzé to Madame de Long- Vic, and thence her eyes passed down the sombre rows of nuns. Nowhere was light or gladness or the promise of them. Her glance then strayed aside to the face of Charlotte de Bourbon. She had lived in this drear place all her life and yet had kept that celestial sweetness of look. It was after all, then, a life that could be lived.

II

THE THREE NOVICES

IN the cloister garth, hidden in a dense mass of
laurel and palm, stood a small, marble statue
of the Virgin and child. Within the shrubbery,
and surrounding the figure at a distance of but a few
feet, ran a circular seat of gray stone, weather-worn
and lichen-covered. The place was known as Our
Lady's Arbor.

Here, on the following day, at the hour for rec-
reation after the early convent dinner, came the
three little maids with chance at last to chatter.
Having said each a hurried *ave* before the Virgin,
they perched nimbly upon the old stone seat, the
new Jeanne between the others, who still loved to
look at her bright gown, and found pleasure in
drawing their fingers through the loose waves of
her unbound hair. For not until she had passed
the first term of her novitiate would the young
Béarnaise assume the habit of a *religieuse*, which,
modified to suit their age, the others had worn for
several years.

"This is where we always come," said Jeannette demurely, feeling it incumbent upon her to
enlighten the inexperience of the new-comer. "Do
you not think it is very pretty?"

Jeanne de Mousson looked about her at the stiff,
glossy leaves of palm and laurel rising darkly far
above their heads, at the prim little statue, well-
scrubbed and stony, and shook her head slightly.

"Do you never run? Can we not go out in the
fields and woods and hunt and fish?"

The two convent-bred girls stared speechless for

a moment. Then Charlotte de Bourbon said slowly:

"We can go out in the garden every day, and we are allowed to help gather roses for the perfume-making. That is fine sport," she added almost timidly, as if fearing her mild pleasures would be scorned by her new friend.

Jeanne for answer dropped on both knees on the gray stones which paved the sombre arbor, threw her arms around Charlotte's waist, and buried her face in her lap. The burnished waves of her brown hair were scattered in confusion over Charlotte's white dress, her slender, *gracieuse* frame was shaken by sobs.

"Oh, Jeanne, dear, wild little Jeanne, what makes you do so? You must not cry. Indeed you must not!" pleaded Charlotte earnestly, while Jeannette, drawing near on the stone seat, bent over in deep concern.

"What ails her?" she framed with her lips silently.

Charlotte shook her head pensively for answer.

Then Jeanne tossed up her head, shaking back her hair, and with flushed face and eyes shining with tears, sobbed out:

"Oh, you darling princess! My heart aches when I think that you have never been free. You make me love you too much, so that I cannot bear it that you are so patient, and let them take away all the world from you. To have lived like this always! Oh, it is too terrible!"

"Hush, Jeanne!" commanded Charlotte, with a touch of hauteur, "we have all to obey our parents, or those who care for us in their place," remembering that Jeanne was an orphan child. Then, her lips quivering in spite of herself, she added: "I can go back, you know, once every year, and see my mother and Françoise."

With the name Françoise her own tears came

swiftly to the surface, but dashing them away with a swift, impatient gesture and a bright smile she asked in a voice which trembled slightly :

"Have you been at court, Jeanne ? Because you may have seen my sister, Françoise. And then my brother, François, you must have heard of him ; he is oh, so strong and tall already, and more beautiful than any of the Valois princes. Such a right gallant, soldierly boy ! Monsieur the Duc de Guise already wishes to have him join the army, and he is sure to make a great commander. Is he not, Jeannette ? " and Charlotte glanced at her faithful friend for confirmation.

"Oh, yes," was the reply ; " the prince-dauphin is most noble and debonair. He is like Mademoiselle, only, of course, not so fine."

It was for the sake of this ardently loved brother that the little Bourbon had been placed in the convent in her infancy, that so his estate, unencumbered by any claim for her dowry or support, might the better befit his rank. The Bourbons were poor.

There was a brief silence. Then Charlotte spoke again, noting the anxious faces of her companions.

"I shall not have to be here always," she said with naïve, childish confidence. "Oh, most certainly not ! That would be quite beyond my duty and my will. When François is well established, then, you see, I shall go back to my mother and live at court and be like the rest."

"Oh, Charlotte ! " exclaimed Jeannette, "will you go away from Jouarre, then, and leave your poor Jeannette ? Then you will break my heart. You know I could not live here without you," and tears flowed fast down the good little face.

Charlotte watched her, grieved and pondering, while Jeanne de Mousson, standing before them, looked from one to the other with flashing eyes.

"No, your highness," she exclaimed softly ;

"you cannot leave your two Jeannes! They will follow you wherever you go. They are yours!"

Suddenly then Charlotte smiled with radiant eyes into the ardent face of Jeanne.

"Yes," she cried, with the impulsive ardor of a child, "we belong together. I am yours. You are mine. We go and we stay together. Is it a pledge?" and she sprang to her feet, holding out a hand to each.

"It is a pledge! It is a pledge!" they cried eagerly. "Together we stay, together we go," and they all clasped hands, and then with one accord made the sign of the cross upon their breasts, while their faces grew grave and gentle.

Then Charlotte said to Jeanne, "Now you are no more to call me 'your highness' or 'your grace.' Let us be all alike, for that is as we are before God," with which she gave each a kiss in turn with sweet, engaging grace.

Children as they were their souls knit together for life in that moment. Back again upon the old stone seat Charlotte said:

"But you have not answered me my question, Jeanne de Mousson. I asked you long ago if you had ever been at court?"

"Do you mean at the court of Navarre? For there I have been continually. Or at the court of France? For there I have been once."

"Oh, the last. When were you there?"

"It was last May, and because I was there is the reason I am here," and Jeanne's face grew sober.

"Tell us all about it, as fast as you can," put in Jeannette, "for Sister Cécile will be coming after us and then it will be time for vespers, and then the day is all gone again."

"Her majesty, Jeanne d'Albret, you may have heard, Charlotte, went in a great hurry to Paris last May; the king too, and Prince Henri."

"I do not know what took them there," said Charlotte. "I know my cousin likes far better her own small court at Pau and Nérac."

"It was all about the new religion," said Jeanne, sinking her voice to a whisper. "Oh, there are troubles without end," and she shook her head with mighty seriousness.

"Is it true that my cousin, Antoine de Bourbon, permits heretic preachers in Navarre?" asked Charlotte.

"Yes, he permits them; also he goes to hear them, and bids them to his court, and his majesty, King Henri, grew very bitter in his anger, and commanded that such things should be stopped at once. Oh, indeed, the king made terrible threats, such as to send an army into Navarre to stamp out the treason, for so he calls it."

"What said Jeanne d'Albret? Does she also like heretics?" asked Charlotte, plainly perplexed.

"Not as her husband does; but you know her way. She is light-hearted and free and strong, and likes to have joy all about her. She was not at all afraid of these mighty threats of King Henri, but said she would go to Paris at once and see her good cousin of Valois and make better feeling. And then it was decided that the prince, Henri, should go also, and madame took me with her that I might see the great city and the palace of the Louvre and all the rest. We started the very next day."

"And how did Henri behave at the French court, Jeanne?" asked Charlotte. "I suppose he is a fine boy by this time."

"He is five years old, you know," replied Jeanne, "and bright and handsome like his mother. Every one at the court was charmed with his ways —so bold and yet so winning. Oh, the queen knew very well what she did when she took him to King Henri! His majesty was dark and grim to us all at

first, and it looked like a gloomy time for every-
body, until the prince captivated him so wholly that
one day he gave over all his sour looks and called
Henri to him and took him on his knee, and even
asked him, only fancy it, if he would be his little
son ? "

" What said Henri to that ? "

" You know he does not speak French well yet,
only Béarnais, which I think rather fascinated his
majesty. He pointed to Antoine of Bourbon and
said, ' That is my father,' as stoutly as you please,
shaking his curly head and laughing saucily. He
is so different, you see, from those pale, peaked
Valois youths. The king liked him for his fearless-
ness, and so he said then, and quite as if he meant
it too, ' Well, then, my little Béarnais, if you will
not be our son we shall have to make you our son-
in-law ! ' And to that the prince said, ' Oh, yes,
that I will be, sire, with all my heart ! ' "

" How pretty of him," said Charlotte.

" Was it not ? And it was said all through the
court afterward that the king was in earnest and
that great things may come of this some day.
Every one thinks of the tiny Princess Marguerite,
who is of Henri's age and as bewitching as she can
be. Certain was it that everything went beauti-
fully for us after this at court and every one made
much of us, and of the little de Mousson with the
rest," Jeanne added mischievously.

" But the most wonderful thing of all was how
all the fury about the religion seemed to calm down
presently. It was but a short time before that
King Henri had sent for the Sieur d'Andelot, who
is own brother of the Admiral of France, Coligny,
and accused him of holding the Reformers' faith,
and when he declared it was quite true and so he
did, which certainly was most rash of him, and
small wonder made trouble, his majesty threw a
plate at his head and sent him forthwith to prison."

"Oh, is that the reason that the Sieur d'Andelot was sent under guard down here to Meaux and is now in prison there?" exclaimed Jeannette.

"Oh, yes. He is a terrible heretic," returned Jeanne impressively. "When we heard of this we did not know what might befall us before we got safely back to Béarn, but the king now seemed strangely mild, and said almost nothing about the religion. And no offense was taken even when we walked, all of us, Antoine de Bourbon and the queen and all our suite in the Pré-aux-Clercs and joined in the singing of those psalms of the Sieur Marot which all the world has gone so wild over."

"But you have yet to tell us, Jeanne," said Jeannette, with a touch of impatience, "how it befell that by your going to the court of France you had to come to the convent of Jouarre."

"I am just coming to that. The trouble was," said Jeanne naïvely, "that, alas for me, certain stupid folk at the Louvre took it into their heads that the little de Mousson was good-looking."

At this Charlotte and Jeannette laughed the low, repressed laugh of the convent.

"Worst of all, it happened that her majesty Queen Catharine declared plainly that I would even make a beauty. Now you see my poor mother was one of the ladies who followed in her train when she came here from Italy to be married to the king. He was but the Duc d'Orleans then, you know, and the Dauphin yet living, and who thought that the daughter of the Medicis would ever be queen of France? Ah, how I do run everything together! But Queen Catharine did declare that for my mother's sake and all, she should adopt me as one of her maidens, and by and by make a lady-in-waiting of me."

"Oh, how fine!" exclaimed Charlotte.

"Not fine at all," said the young Gascon, shaking her head seriously.

"Was her majesty quite, quite in earnest?" asked Jeannette, with a shade of incredulity and a measuring glance at the brilliant face of her new friend. She was pretty, to be sure; but there were many as much so, she reflected.

"Alas for me, she was in full earnest, and nothing can shake her when her purpose is once formed."

"But why do you not wish then to become a lady-in-waiting?" said Jeannette half-enviously. "I wish I had such a chance."

"Oh, no, dear Jeannette," returned Jeanne de Mousson, "you would not if you knew what it means. Nothing is more terrible for a young girl than to win the favor of the queen. You do not understand. I did not until Madame d'Albret came to me that night in my little sleeping closet, which was off from her chamber, and talked to me for an hour."

As she said this Jeanne's bright face was painfully clouded.

"Her majesty said it was hard to tell such dark things to a child, and put thoughts of evil and fear into my heart; but I was a motherless girl, and she alone must defend me. Queen Catharine herself "—and Jeanne's voice dropped to a whisper and a slight rustle in the laurel leaves passed unnoticed—"is as cold and as virtuous as madame the *supérieure* here. She looks as if she were cut out of ivory. She has not the sins of others at court, but she helps to make others sin because so she can use them and gain power by them. Madame d'Albret says that the troop of beautiful demoiselles whom we saw always around in the great salons and halls were to the queen just like pawns on a chess-board. They call them the queen's flying squadron. I would rather die, girls, than be one of them! Now you know why I am here. It was my only escape."

Tears stood in Charlotte's sweet eyes.

"How very hard to leave dear Madame d'Albret and your bright, free life in Béarn," she murmured.

"Harder than I can tell," replied the young Béarnaise choking back a little sob. "It broke my heart to leave her majesty; and now that I know what the convent is like, I fear more than before that I never can become a *religieuse*."

"Oh, Jeanne, not even to save your soul?" asked Jeannette reprovingly.

Just then the vesper bell began its slow chiming. With the stroke which called the three little maidens to their feet, the figure of a woman dressed in the black robes of the order, emerged swiftly and noiselessly from the thicket of laurel forming Our Lady's Arbor, and hastened to enter the chapel door.

"*Eh bien!*" said Jeannette, catching a glimpse of her retreating figure as the three came out into the cloister, "there is Sister Cécile now. Did she call us? I did not hear her."

Sister Cécile Crue was the mistress of the novices at Jouarre.

That evening she held a long and secret conference with the confessor, Père Ruzé, who in turn wrote a letter to monseigneur the Duc de Bourbon-Montpensier, father of Charlotte de Bourbon.

III

THE PETIT-MORIN

IN the garden of Jouarre Abbey the beds of thyme
and lavender, of rosemary and bay, were giving
forth their goodly odors.

Late roses were blooming too, in the garden of
Jouarre. They showed brave and red in the October sun, and their odor was sweeter than all the
rest. Between the ranks of the rose-trees an el-
derly nun with a kind, simple face walked slowly.
Over her hands gloves were clumsily drawn, and
she carried a great pair of garden-shears.

This was Sister Radegonde, and she had been the
nurse of the Princess de Bourbon since the day she
was brought, a baby, to Jouarre.

Behind her, with light feet and low laughter, came
the little maid herself, and with her the two Jeannes
holding baskets in which they gathered up the roses
as they fell beneath the shears.

On the southern border of the garden were the
convent dove-cotes, where the doves were peace-
fully tripping about in the sun with their musical
murmuring. To the west lay the massive stone
walls of the refectory and dormitory with their picturesque roofs, their latticed casements swinging in
the warm breeze, their quaint, pointed towers and
gables.

An ancient oak, thickly festooned with mistletoe,
grew just before the wide porch of the cloister,
whose gray columns and delicately carved arches
stretched into a dim and shadowy background.
Beyond the cloister stood the beautiful Sainte
Chapelle, with its graceful tower, and the adjacent

16

chapter house, and yet farther to the east was the cemetery, studded thickly with small crosses. In the midst of these and high above them all rose the tall, imposing stone crucifix, the ancient glory of Jouarre, its arms wreathed with exquisite *fleurons* and bearing its double effigy.

As they lifted their eyes from their roses the little maids of Jouarre looked beyond the tall cross and the low graves about it, beyond the chapel and the enclosing buttressed wall, and saw at the foot of the hill the Petit-Morin flashing between its green banks; saw the fair glebe and the fruitful fields of La Brie stretching beyond, and longed with the wild unspeakable longing of childhood to range freely where they would.

"Now, my good little helpers," said Sister Radegonde, "I have to go into the woods. It is just the day to gather the herbs and roots for our cordials, and I must make haste that I may return for vespers."

"Where are the woods?" asked Jeanne quickly.

Sister Radegonde pointed down the hillslope and the smooth grasslands where the cows belonging to the abbey were grazing. Between these and the river was a stretch of oak forest beginning to change and grow brown and russet already.

"Oh, dear, dear Radegonde, let us go with you," exclaimed Charlotte, throwing her arms around the withered neck of her old nurse with a sudden irresistible impulse. "We need to run and stretch our legs, and we will carry your basket, and be perfectly obedient."

"We will dig the roots for you, Sister Radegonde," cried Jeannette. "We will save your poor back, if only you will take us, and you know how stiff and lame it has been of late."

The sight of the three wistful, upturned faces was too much for the good old soul.

"What harm can it do?" she muttered to her-

B

self; "the saints bless their pretty hearts! Poor lambs, thus to beg for what they ought to be free to do every day of their lives!" and she bent down and patted Charlotte's pale cheek.

"The little Béarnaise there, she has had her fill of sun and air and chance enough to grow strong and sturdy; and Jeannette too has had her turn, but my own sweet child, my little white lily, has never had one free race over the fields in all her blessed life," and Radegonde caught Charlotte to her breast and showered kisses on her head. Hers was all the motherly petting that the princely child in her loneliness had ever known. Nevertheless, a mother's heart yearned unceasingly over her, and while it could not speak, could not be comforted.

Already, seeing Sister Radegonde so favorably inclined, Jeanne de Mousson was darting swiftly down toward the end of the garden where a small wicket gate in the abbey wall gave exit to the fields beyond. This gate, however, was closely locked and barred.

"Softly, softly," cried Radegonde. "What a wild bird you are, to be sure. I do not know what Sister Cécile Crue will say."

"She went to Meaux this morning with Sister Marie Beauclerc to see the bishop, or some like errand," hastily interposed Jeannette.

"That is true," replied Radegonde, plainly relieved; "and madame——"

"Madame would permit it this once," urged Charlotte; "but she would be greatly displeased if you disturbed her at this hour, you know."

"True again, *mignonne*," said the old nun, and she hastened to carry her roses to the low building at the southern border of the garden where the operations of distilling perfumes, cordials, and tinctures were carried on by the nuns.

In a few moments the three children were darting through the gate unlocked for them by Radegonde, and racing like young deer down the sloping pasture toward the woods.

The breathless run over the velvet softness of the smooth-cropped meadow, the sense of unchecked freedom, of throwing her own small person into the liberal spaces whither she chose, birdlike and unbounded, thrilled Charlotte with an unknown ecstasy. The others forgot their own pleasure in watching the motions of her lithe graceful limbs, each motion eloquent of delight, while her face grew rosy and her large eyes brilliant.

"She was born for freedom," murmured old Radegonde to herself. "May I live to see the day ——" but here she bit her lips and looked to see if Jeannette, who was nearest to her, had heard her words.

In the woods all the doughty promises of work were promptly forgotten, and old Radegonde's back was left to take care of itself while the children ranged freely through the underbrush, gathering acorns with the instinctive desire of children to appropriate anything of neat and elegant form, however useless, and quite indifferent to the homely, serviceable herbs for which Radegonde was faithfully searching.

Presently Jeanne de Mousson's trained and eager eyes made a discovery. The woods grew to the edge of a bank, steep but not twenty feet high, at the foot of which flowed the Petit-Morin, hastening westward to reach the Marne. Down under this bank, on the river's edge, tied to a stake, lay a small skiff, bare and empty.

Jeanne de Mousson clapped her hands with delight.

"Come, come quickly!" she cried to the others, and not stopping or caring to tell them for what purpose, she drew them with her and plunged with light, sure feet down the gravelly bank.

Jeannette followed timorously, but Charlotte's

blood was up and she was ready now for any-thing.

Springing into the boat, Jeanne looked at the other two, who stood on the edge of the little river, which was high between its banks, swollen by the September rains. The oars had been removed, the boat was tied. It looked a harmless bit of play.

"Come, step in, Jeannette, and give Mademoiselle the seat in the stern," cried Jeanne. "It shall be the royal seat, cushioned, you see, in crimson vel-vet, with a silken canopy above her head, and a banner flying the Bourbon lilies on a field azure. Hasten, before we hear Sister Radegonde calling! Why do you wait? The boat is tied, surely no harm can follow."

As Jeanne thus challenged them, standing grace-fully poised on the rocking edge of the old boat, her hair flying, her dark eyes shining, her face bril-liant with daring, the two to whom she was no less wonderful than the freedom of the fields and forest, found in her voice the voice of the wild life of nature calling to them irresistibly.

In another instant Charlotte was reclining in the invisible grandeur of the stern, while Jeannette took the bow and Jeanne de Mousson, in the mid-dle, with her brown hands on the sides of the rick-ety craft, rocked it gently up and down, the rope's length only out in the current of the Petit-Morin.

All this was safe and sensible, and even the pru-dent Jeannette forgot her scruples. But full soon the effervescing Gascon spirit of the young de Mousson, impetuous and audacious, broke out in strength and a storm arose. From a gentle motion she changed to one of violence, and the more madly she rocked the boat the brighter shone her eyes, the more brilliant became her smile, for she watched the face of her little princess and caught the inspiration of her kindling joy. In a moment

the inevitable had happened. The rope by which
the boat was loosely moored became untied by the
persistent motion, all unseen by the children, and
before they dreamed of it they were slipping quietly down the river. Jeanne de Mousson was the
first to perceive it. The storm abated then with
startling suddenness and the boat glided smoothly
onward.

"We are adrift," she said quietly, her eyes on
Charlotte's face.

A glance at the trailing rope and the receding
bank showed the statement to be true.

"Very well," said Charlotte de Bourbon, not
moving save to fold her hands with a strange gesture of content. "Since we cannot help ourselves
let us go on."

Jeannette began to cry a little.

"What are you afraid of ?" asked Jeanne with
curling lip.

Jeannette was thinking of madame and Sister
Cécile Crue; also of Père Ruzé and penance. Besides, there was the chance of shipwreck, of which
she had heard terrible things, and a cold grave
among the reeds in the bottom of the Petit-Morin.
As the current grew stronger and the boat increased
its motion these fears intensified and Jeannette
sobbed under her breath.

"Do not cry, Jeannette," said Charlotte with
gentle, unconscious authority, "I like it."

Jeannette looked at her face then and her sobs
ceased. Jeanne too looked and the scorn left her
lips and the bold daring in her eyes grew softer.
The child in the stern was carried quite beyond
their thoughts of doubt and danger, and they perceived it. Her lovely face was lifted, the white
coif had slipped from her head and her golden hair,
thus set free, was blown back from her forehead,
which was calm and pure and royally molded.
The blue eyes were full of a new light, and some

strange inspiration gave a lustre to all her look
such as they had never seen.

She stood then in the stern and looked up into the
blue dome of the sky above their heads ; she felt
the rapid current beneath their frail shell, the swift
breath of the wind upon her cheeks ; she saw the
green meadows of La Brie stretch broad and sunny
on either side. For the first time in her life, with
a wild, breathless thrill, she felt herself free.

IV

THRUST AND PARRY

MADAME LOUISE DE LONG-VIC sat in the hall of the abbess' house awaiting the visit of Père Ruzé.

This hall, which was the private audience room of the *supérieure*, was of ample size and agreeable proportions. The floor, on which leopard skins and rich carpets were laid, was of dark wood, highly polished ; the walls were hung with Cordova leather ; the ceiling, rather low than otherwise, was crossed by heavy oak rafters, curiously carved with heraldic and ecclesiastic symbols, among which the monogram of Saint Columban and the date 634 recurred frequently. At the end of the hall opposite the entrance was an enormous projecting chimney-piece, carved in massive oak, in which was set a dim, archaic painting of Sainte Theodehilde, first Abbess of Jouarre, who died in the odor of sanctity in the seventh century A. D.

Before the chimney, in which a fire of beech logs was burning, filling the room with ruddy light, stood two chairs with ecclesiastical canopies of elaborately carven wood, and a table at a slight distance was set forth with a dainty and sumptuous evening meal. Madame partook of all other meals in the common refectory. The third meal of the day, served in her own hall, was frequently shared by guests of the abbey, and was of a ceremonious and stately character.

From the carved ceiling hung silver chandeliers, exquisite productions of Venetian goldsmiths, filled with wax lights, which were reflected from wall

mirrors fitted in between the panels of darkly
gleaming embossed leather. On a massive buffet,
filling the end of the room opposite the chimney,
were ranged flagons, cups, and "marvelous fair ba-
sons" of gold and silver plate of rich workmanship and design. In fine, the hall of the abbess at
Jouarre, in startling contrast to the ascetic bareness
of the other portions of the establishment, expressed
in itself not a little of the peculiarly sumptuous but
subtle and refined luxury of that Renaissance which
Francis I. had introduced into France from Italy.

Madame de Long-Vic, who had sat watching the
fire dreamily, rose from her seat and began to pace
the hall with slow, noiseless tread.

Her appearance at this hour contrasted even more
strangely with her ordinary aspect than did the
richness of her private apartment with that of the
convent in general. Her conventual habit laid
aside, according to the relaxed custom of the Bene-
dictines of her day, much of the austerity of her
aspect vanished, while its authority and distinction
remained, and the Abbess of Jouarre appeared rather
the stately chatelaine than the watchful-eyed *supérieure*. In fact, Louise de Long-Vic, having enjoyed
for many years the honors and revenues of this
opulent abbey, had found in it a position of worldly
advantage well suited to her mind. Advanced in
mid-life she still retained the delicate grace of face
and figure characteristic of her family, and as she
moved to and fro in the firelight in her flowing dress
of gray satin she bore the unmistakable air of the
grande dame.

A lay sister in attendance interrupted her meditation by the announcement that Père Ruzé was
at the door, and at the word of the *supérieure*, the
priest with an obeisance expressive of admiring devotion entered the hall and presently seated himself
in his accustomed hooded chair, to which a gracious
gesture of madame's hand invited him.

Jean Ruzé, doctor of the Sorbonne and confessor to Henri II., was a man of fine physique and impressive presence, predestined it would seem to a bishopric. He had the imperturbable repose of countenance, the benevolent smile, the slow, impassive manner and speech, and the delicate, chastened gallantry in his bearing toward women which mark the successful ecclesiastic. However, while all these impressive characteristics had been displayed in madame's presence daily for nearly three months, she had confessed to herself definitely within the last half-hour that she did not like Père Ruzé and that she distinctly preferred that he should leave Jouarre. Accordingly, being an adroit woman and accustomed to managing men shrewdly, she received Père Ruzé to-night with a cordiality approaching warmth.

As they sat facing each other over the well-seasoned viands noiselessly served to them by the black-robed sister, and of which Ruzé partook heartily and madame not at all, she remarked in a casual, careless tone :

"Is it two months or three, monsieur, since you came to us at Jouarre ? "

"It is rather more than three, madame," was the reply, spoken in a rich, well-modulated voice. "If you remember it was in the week following the ill-fated battle of Gravelines that I came, directly after the death of Père Boquin left you without a confessor."

"And Gravelines was on July the twelfth."

The priest bowed assent.

"You have been long away from court."

"Yes, madame," returned Ruzé, sighing gently ; "longer than the three months, which I have spent with such unmarred enjoyment in the repose of your charming convent. For nearly a month before I came hither I was almost constantly at Meaux or at Melun."

"Oh, to be sure, in the affair of the Sieur d'Andelot. And are you now quite satisfied with the
results of your mission?" Madame asked the
question with the politeness which betokens indifference to the answer.

Ruzé shook his head with an expression of serious
concern.

"It is too soon, madame, to be confident. The
Sieur d'Andelot most certainly consented to be
present at a celebration of the mass. I myself administered in person and know whereof I affirm.
But since by the grace of his most puissant majesty
freedom has been restored to him, I hear strange,
disturbing rumors. I like it not that he has made
such haste to join Coligny. Madame," and the
priest straightened himself in his chair and struck
his hand with emphasis upon the table before him,
"madame, when once these insidious and corrupting doctrines enter into the heart of a man or woman,
or even of a child, there is no faith nor truth to be
found in that heart!" and crossing himself devoutly Père Ruzé murmured a brief prayer for the
deliverance of the church from these evil snares
and schisms.

Louise de Long-Vic watched him narrowly, as if
to satisfy herself of his sincerity. The attendant
now brought wine and fruit, trimmed the candles,
arranged the fire, and withdrew. When they were
alone madame asked with a shade of coldness:

"Did you tell me that it was at his majesty's request that you came to Jouarre, monsieur?"

Ruzé looked at her with a shrewd, swift glance:

"His majesty was pleased to appoint me to this
pleasing and most welcome service, until such time
as the return of my young pupil, the prince-
dauphin, madame your sister's son, shall make
my presence demanded at Paris. Or, let me add,
until his grace, the Bishop of Meaux, shall appoint
a successor to Père Boquin, whom may God ab-

solve," added the priest with a devout inclination of his head.

Madame drew her chair slightly away from the table and played with the long stem of her wine glass.

"Monsieur," she said presently, fixing her eyes upon the face of Père Ruzé with her quiet, cynical smile, "what are you really here for? Why not tell me?"

Instead of showing surprise, the face of the priest only became a shade more impassive than before. He took a pear from its silver dish and turned it about in his fine, well-kept hand, regarding its blushing and waxen surface with musing consideration for a moment before he spoke. Perhaps, on the whole, it was time to be frank. The orchards of Jouarre were famed for their exquisite fruit; madame was undeniably both a clever and a charming woman. And yet he was getting a little weary of this quiet life in La Brie; court life would not come amiss after three months of hearing these simple nuns patter their petty confessions and their endless prayers.

"Madame," he said, looking up with the winning smile of the courtier in place of the benevolence of the priest, "you asked me a question awhile ago. Will you give me the liberty of asking you the same? How long have *you* been at Jouarre?"

Plainly this was an unexpected shaft, and one which found a weak point in madame's defensive armor. A slight tremor of her eyelids, however, only indicated the fact.

"Does monsieur mean as *supérieure?*" she asked quietly.

"Precisely."

"It is nearly fifteen years."

Père Ruzé appeared to reflect with the seriousness of one approaching an interesting subject for the first time.

"In time madame could even afford to retire," he said musingly. The revenues of the rich abbey of Jouarre were a matter of conjecture rather than of knowledge to outsiders.

A slight flush tinged madame's cheeks.

"Madame is still young, charming, born to command in some larger field of influence. Madame is not, we will hope, without resources——"

Louise de Long-Vic tapped her slender foot impatiently on the floor.

"Why not say plainly, monsieur, the Duc de Montpensier has sent you here to arrange for my withdrawal in favor of his daughter ? I have suspected this before, but have put the thought forcibly from me as monstrous. The child is not yet twelve years old, a frail, innocent little creature ——"

"There was, I believe, an unwritten promise at the birth of Mademoiselle ? " the question was asked with insinuating gentleness.

"But the promise supposed that the canonical age should have been reached."

"Marie de Bourbon became Prioress of Poissy at the age of four," said Ruzé reflectively.

"Doubtless outrages have been committed," said madame slowly ; "but I can assure you that my sister will never give her consent to have these measures forced upon her little daughter."

Père Ruzé shook his head regretfully.

"It is much to be deplored that her grace, the Duchesse de Montpensier, should have no voice in a matter of so much moment."

"What mean you, monsieur ? " asked madame sternly.

"Alas, madame, it is known only to a few, but your sister is at heart a heretic. You cannot fail to realize the necessity of withdrawing these princely children absolutely from an influence so baneful. It is sad, indeed, for monseigneur."

Madame de Long-Vic's color changed swiftly.
She was about to speak when a loud knock at
the door was followed by Sister Radegonde, who
burst rather than walked into the room, wringing
her hands and exclaiming:

"Mademoiselle is lost, and the little Vassetz and
the de Mousson with her! Ah, madame, do with
me what you will! It is I alone who am to
blame!"

Closely following Radegonde came Sister Cécile
Crue, newly returned from Meaux.

"To think," she cried softly, with a curious
mingling of consternation and triumph on her face,
"only twelve hours have I been absent from
Jouarre, and yet this has happened! I shall not
leave my post again, madame, while I have my
reason."

Madame de Long-Vic looked at the mistress of
the novices with a glance of cold dislike, but
turned swiftly to Radegonde and demanded an ex-
plicit account of what had happened. The room
was quickly filling with curious and breathless
nuns. Père Ruzé listened keenly for a moment.
When he heard mention made of a vanished boat
on the river he left the women to themselves,
hastened swiftly from the hall, and by its private
gate made haste to leave the abbey precincts.

Within five minutes he was galloping down the
hard, white road toward La Ferté-sous-Jouarre,
where the Petit-Morin flows into the Marne. A
half-mile short of the hamlet he met what he hoped
to meet, namely, a peasant's wagon. It was an
open wagon, lumbering heavily, driven by a
countryman in a gray blouse and long-peaked cap,
who carried a lantern. In the wagon, on a little
scattered straw, sat three young girls. Père Ruzé
reined in his horse and stood within the shadow of
a high bank to let them pass, then turned, himself
unnoticed, and followed them at a distance. What

he saw did not surprise the priest.   What he heard surprised him much.

In their clear, childish voices, nothing daunted nor dismayed by what might await them, the three little maids, one of whom he recognized, even in the dim light, as Mademoiselle de Bourbon, were singing the psalms after Clement Marot.

"Plainly," said Père Ruzé, riding quietly on between the fragrant and dewy fields, "the time for action has come."

V

THE DUC DE MONTPENSIER VISITS HIS SISTER-IN-LAW

THE bleak gray days of the November of 1558 passed painfully to the little maids of Jouarre.

Père Ruzé having with bland benevolence inflicted the bitterest penance for their involuntary escapade and the most useful which he could devise, namely, the complete separation of the three from each other's company, and having entrusted the accomplishment of this penance to the care of the faithful Sister Cécile Crue, rode off one day in the direction of Paris. In time he would return. As to that, Madame de Long-Vic did not deceive herself. However, a month passed and more.

Then, when Christmas snows whitened glebe and garden and the red roofs of Jouarre, and cold winds whistled through the cloisters and chilled the unwarmed cells of the nuns and novices and made life itself a perpetual penance, then, on such a day, the gates of the abbey swung wide and over the bridge and into the abbey court rode his grace, the Duc de Montpensier, and in his train rode Jean Ruzé.

Now Sister Radegonde was as watchful in her way as Sister Cécile Crue, and, with the instinct with which the hen hastens to gather her chickens under her wings when the hawk is swooping near, she betook herself to Charlotte on the instant, while the porter, on his knees before the great lord, was still murmuring his *benedicite*.

She found the child in the infirmary, where a trifling illness had kept her for a few days. She was lonely and listless, with over-bright eyes and flushed cheeks.

" Ah, my precious one," said Radegonde, " monseigneur the Duc is here and you will soon be sent for. Shall I say that you are ill ; that you cannot go ? "

" How mean you, Radegonde ? " asked the child proudly, while her breath came quicker and the color went and came in her cheeks. " Do you think I would not see my father when he has come so far to see me ? "

It was bravely done, for never yet had the visit of Louis de Montpensier brought aught but added rigor and sadness to the martyred life of his child ; but Radegonde knew what she knew, and as she prepared the toilet of her little princess tears ran unchecked down her face, which was cold and red with the raw December morning.

This did not escape the eyes of Sister Cécile, who was presently upon them, with a mighty air of importance, to make Mademoiselle ready and conduct her to the presence of her august sire.

" *Voilà*, Radegonde," she said coldly, " Mademoiselle will do very well now. His grace cannot be kept waiting for you to weep over his kindness in riding twenty miles out of his way on such a morning simply to show his affection for his child. Come, Mademoiselle."

" Thanks, Sister Cécile," said Charlotte, leading the way, holding Radegonde's hard old hand. " Will you too go with us ? "

Cécile followed, slightly set back. It was after this fashion that the little Bourbon now and again, but rarely, made the women about her feel that she knew herself after all to be of the blood royal.

In the hall of the abbess, before the great buffet, at which he stood to drink a glass of wine, Charlotte met her father and swept him a courtesy to the very ground with the grace of one to the man-

ner born, then lifted a shy, sweet smile of wistfulness which, seeing, the Duc responded to with a
kiss, cold rather than fatherly.

A tall, soldierly man was Louis de Montpensier,
head of the younger branch of the house of Bourbon, peer and prince of France. In his splendid
costume of velvet and miniver, with his proud and
handsome Bourbon features animated by the instinct
and habit of command, he stood the imposing per-
sonification of authority, confronting the small,
white-robed novice in her cloistral shyness. Madame de Long-Vic, appearing to-day in her black
conventual robes and with her abbess face of wan
austerity, watched them from her place apart, and
her heart sank to see the two, so unequally matched,
pitted against one another.

And yet, had Louise de Long-Vic been less a
woman and more a seer, she might have discerned
that in the end, in the long duel of which one bout
was now passing before her eyes, it would be the
weak, defenseless child who would win. For Louis
de Bourbon was by instinct, by habit, by life, a
petty tyrant, and petty tyranny in the end must
always surrender. His fatal fault, as it is the fault
of all tyrants, was his fanatical stupidity, which
could see in human souls no forces greater than he
could mold to his will. Pledged by birthright and
inheritance, by habit and training to the ancient
religion, he had no hold upon the noble and permanent elements of that Catholic faith of which he
was so fiery a champion. It was to the powerful
political and social organization, to the concentrated
authority, to the perfected discipline of the system
that he so hotly adhered, while the vital and spiritual essence informing these mighty energies escaped him. As an engine for the use of despotic
power he found the church supreme and in accord
with his own instinctive bent. Upon those who
swerved from the right line punishment must be

c

swift and summary. Extermination he regarded as the only and sufficient specific. Had he been Protestant he would have made Catholic martyrs. To differ with him in opinion was to be guilty of crime. Like the man whom he adored and upon whom he ardently modeled himself, Philip II. of Spain, the Duc dreaded in the Protestant cult those notes of doom to tyranny, *freedom, inquiry, republicanism*, and with the instinct of his class he availed himself of every means of suppression to a reform whose success meant the fall of monarchy.

But, like Philip in his implacable hatred of independent thought and in his fervent devotion to the notions of monarchy and papacy, Montpensier was unlike Philip in the field in which he exercised his tyranny. Where Philip ruled over a kingdom the Duc ruled over a family of women and children, and even here he was destined to be outwitted in the end. His wife, Jacqueline de Long-Vic, first lady of honor to Catharine de Medici, was a woman of noted personal charm and intellectual ability. Her husband, her inferior in every noble faculty, depended upon her influence at court and her intuitive leadership in matters of State policy. Thus the fact that she was known to be, although not avowedly, Protestant, produced no public scandal or separation between husband and wife. On the other hand, in relation to their children the Duc, with the vengeful bitterness of his baffled will and pride, took the power into his own hands and declared their mother disqualified to have any voice in determining their future careers. One thing was fixed: he would far rather see his children dead than see them Protestant.

Such was the prince, such the father, who looking down upon Charlotte de Bourbon now remarked, with grim gallantry:

" By our Lady, Mademoiselle, you grow pretty. Whence won you such bright eyes, and so bright a bloom in your cheeks ? I have seen them pale and lifeless hitherto. Had you but a dowry we might marry you yet to some cavalier of good degree."

"Is madame, my mother, well ?" Charlotte asked simply, wisely ignoring this line of conversation.

"Madame is very well. She can think of nothing latterly, however, save the marriage of your sister Françoise to the Duc de Bouillon, with which she is highly pleased."

Charlotte choked back a sob. No word of love or remembrance from her dear mother ! Was she then quite forgotten ? So it seemed. Her dearest sister married and she unable to see her as a bride or give her one kiss of farewell ! But with the self-control of long discipline she uttered no complaint, rather asked :

"And my brother, François ? "

"He is still with the Duc de Guise. We shall make a soldier of him." Then abruptly, with a gathering frown, the Duc said :

"Mademoiselle, my time is short for these matters. Let me ask you, then, what is this that I hear of an attempt, awhile since, at running away from your home here at Jouarre ? "

"Monsieur has been misled. There was not such an attempt. There was an accident. No runaway was intended."

"I hear of a little vagabond sent here by Jeanne d'Albret, for the very purpose, no doubt, of corrupting you from the true religion and leading you into all kinds of wild adventures. De Mousson—is that her name ? It was her work, I understand."

"Monsieur has been misled." Again the childish courage ; there was trembling lip, quickened breath, but the heart of her still dauntless. "Jeanne de Mousson did not lead me into this accident. I went, monsieur, of my own good will, and when she and the Vassetz would have stopped the boat sooner, for we had the chance, I would not let them, because I chose to go farther. It was my own doing and my own fault."

"You are bold, Mademoiselle," and the soldier looked with an odd twitch of his lips at the gallant child.

"I am your daughter, monsieur," Charlotte made answer cannily, with another courtesy. Montpensier laughed shortly.

"Is it perhaps within your plans to make further essays in this direction ? You seem well satisfied with your success in this."

"No, monsieur, such is not my thought."

"Have you been punished properly for this wild caper ? "

"Sufficiently, monsieur."

"What has Père Ruzé given you for penance ? "

"*Paternosters* and *aves* without end," sighed Charlotte pensively.

"And is that all ? " and the Duc's brows knit stormily.

"No, monsieur ; I cannot speak to my dear friends, my two Jeannes. I have now *no* joy in life," and Charlotte's lips trembled.

"When Mademoiselle is naughty she can expect no joys. It is only the good and the obedient who are happy," and the Duc glanced at madame as if expecting confirmation of this impressive platitude, but madame's eyes were fixed upon the floor.

"Have you, then, thus far duly discharged the penance assigned you by Père Ruzé ? " he added more sharply.

"Yes, monsieur."

"Very well. I will not keep you longer. I have much to confer upon with your aunt ; but before you go, let me say this," and Montpensier laid a heavy hand upon each slender arm of his daughter and looked with stern, hard eyes into her face : "Père Ruzé is to you in the place of God. You have no knowledge of right or wrong apart from his teaching. If he punishes you, submit. If he praises you, be glad. He is not only in the place of God to you, but also in my place. He is here to represent me, your father. Whatever he bids you, you are to obey him positively, without question or opposition. You have known, hitherto, the lightest, most childish of penances. For those who disobey there are penances which crush out the very heart's blood."

As he spoke those last words slowly and with peculiar distinctness the face of Montpensier became sinister in its ominous harshness, while the suggestion of a fanatical cruelty, with which the sixteenth century was but too familiar, gave to what he said the effect of physical violence.

Trembling through all her slight frame, Charlotte looked up for a gentler word of parting, but it was not vouchsafed her. With a gesture of dismissal and a cold salutation the Duc turned to Madame de Long-Vic, and the child slowly, and as if half-paralyzed, made her way out of the hall. In the ante-room she found old Radegonde waiting to take her in her arms and soothe her like a baby upon her breast, and so carry her through the dark labyrinthine corridors back to the narrow bed in the cheerless room she had left.

"I am hurt, Radegonde," moaned the child, "something aches so here," and she clasped her small hands over her heart. "Something dreadful is coming to me. I feel it and know it, but what it is I cannot understand. Oh, how can I bear any more?"

And Radegonde with her own heart bursting with rage and pain was powerless to gainsay her.

Meanwhile Louis de Montpensier, well pleased with the palpable success of his policy of intimidation, turned to his sister-in-law, and remarked:

"Madame, the times are waxing evil. It be-

hooves us to act circumspectly, with promptness
and prudence.''

Madame de Long-Vic lifted her downcast eyes
slowly, allowed them to rest, cold and unresponsive,
upon the face of the Duc for a moment, and then
withdrew her glance. She was neither a tender
nor an impulsive woman, but at that moment all
her heart was crying out its pity for the bruised and
bleeding spirit of her little niece, and she burned to
pour her scorn upon the fanatical martinet who
stood before her now as self-satisfied as if he had
wrought a high deed of valor and chivalry.

Receiving no response to his sagacious generali-
zation, the Duc now added :

'' You have heard, I daresay, of the death of the
consort of Philip of Spain, Mary Tudor, on the
seventeenth of last month ? ''

Madame had heard of the event.

'' The consequences to Christendom are likely to
be exceeding serious,'' continued the Duc. '' The
base-born daughter of Henry by one of his court
ladies, Mistress Anne Boleyn, succeeds.''

'' So I have heard,'' said madame.

'' The Lady Elizabeth. She is said to be Protestant. All that has been built up in the brief but illustrious reign of Mary and his Spanish majesty is
like to be now undone, and we may see all England
lost to the true faith. Surely this contagion spreads
like the plague itself. Flanders is full of it, I hear,
and insolence and presumption go from bad to
worse. But the king of Spain is preparing to make
short work there, and his majesty of France will
not be far behind in stamping out this *canaille* with
an iron heel.''

'' *Canaille* you can scarce call them of the new
religion, monsieur, since among them can be num-
bered already princes of the blood and such men
as the Admiral of France.'' Madame spoke in her
quiet, measured tones, her face calmer even than

its wont. Her words and no less the chill of her manner stirred Montpensier to an outburst of the passion which had been gathering beneath the surface throughout the interview.

"By my faith, madame," he cried hotly, "I am fain to fear that even the seclusion of a convent such as this is not proof against the poison! Can it be, then, that your sister has already won your ear to the accursed heresy with which she has betrayed the faith and fealty of the house of Bourbon, and made the name of Montpensier a byword and a scorning to its enemies?"

The face of the Duc turned purple, as his fury fired by his own words grew, until great cords stood out on his forehead. Louise de Long-Vic watched him, undismayed; she was prepared now for his worst.

"I shall live and die, monsieur," she said rising, "in the most holy Catholic faith, and in loyal submission to the church of which I have sought to be a faithful though humble servant. But when you speak of my sister, your wife, in terms such as these I must decline to prolong our conference."

"Be seated, madame!" cried the Duc. "This is no time for play-acting. I am here for a purpose. Be pleased to remain until that purpose is made known to you."

For a moment they faced each other, the delicate woman and the harsh, fanatical tyrant, as if they had been preparing for an actual passage at arms, and then, seeing that the crisis might not be avoided, Louise de Long-Vic resumed her seat.

"I am here, madame," proceeded Montpensier, "to cite you to the understanding which was made between us at the time my daughter was brought, an infant, to Jouarre. Our compact provided that she should, in due time, succeed to the position which you have held these many years with full power and privilege, and, as is well known, greatly

to your own advantage. The time is come to act
upon that understanding. Pardon my bluntness,
madame. I am a soldier, not a diplomatist. I strike
from the shoulder when the time comes to strike.
You have my errand."

"Monsieur, may I recall to your remembrance
that the agreement which was unwritten regarding
the succession of your daughter, Charlotte, made
due reference to her first attaining the canonical
age? It was never intended that she should become
Abbess of Jouarre in her childhood. Ten years
hence I shall gladly retire in her favor. To-day,
monsieur, pardon me if I follow your lead, and myself speak plainly—the proposition is preposterous."

" Ten years hence !" and again the Duc's wrath
rose high. "That will give you plenty of time,
will it, madame, to feather your nest with the
revenues of Jouarre fully to your mind? Plenty
of time too, for these infernal heretics to pour their
poison into the mind of my daughter? Plenty of
time to compass the defeat of a father's lifelong
hopes, and make him the butt of scorn in court and
camp! *Mort Dieu*, madame, it is too late to talk of
ten years! A month were better suited to my intent, and would better suit your character as a
woman and as a *religieuse*, and as mother's sister to
my child. Have you really her salvation at heart?
or is it only, as begins to appear, your own worldly
gain of which you take heed? According to your
decision you will be judged," and Montpensier's
eyes scanned her face with scorching intensity.

"And the agreement of monsieur that I should
hold my office until Mademoiselle reached the fitting
age goes for naught?" said madame, meeting his
look with her own unshrinking gaze.

" There was no such agreement," replied the
Duc hardily. "I remember nothing of the kind."

Madame's face relaxed into a slight smile of cold,
incredulous contempt.

"Ah, monsieur," she said softly, "at length I apprehend you. You must pardon the slowness of my perception. Until now I had fancied myself conferring on terms of faith and honor. I have no weapons to use in this species of combat which you have chosen. I leave you master of the field."

With these words, and with eyes that shot their gleams of scorn full upon his face, Louise de Long-Vic swept the Duc de Montpensier a profound obeisance, and so left the room.

Left alone, the Duc walked up and down for a little space, smiling cynically.

"She has mettle," he murmured to himself; "the de Long-Vics have fighting blood, and can set up a stout defense when you press them too hard. She is beaten, however, which for the case in hand is all that can be asked."

A few moments later an attendant was summoned, who was sent forthwith to fetch Père Ruzé to wait upon his grace.

After an hour's conference, to which Sister Cécile Crue was later bidden, the Duc's suite was ordered to remount, and the small but brilliant cortége soon rode out through the abbey gate, and galloped down the road to Meaux, by which they had come.

Père Ruzé alone was left behind.

VI

"CETTE PAUVRE ENFANT"

A HEALTHY self-interest made Sister Cécile Crue an efficient partner with Père Ruzé in carrying out the will and purpose of Louis de Montpensier.

During the long and worldly prosperous rule of Louise de Long-Vic as abbess of Jouarre, Cécile had grown to womanhood with an ever-deepening desire to share the power to which she had so long deferred. Promoted, by reason of prompt and punctilious service, to the position of mistress of the novices, she found that with this she had reached the limit of advancement possible under Madame de Long-Vic. The prospective position of Charlotte de Bourbon at Jouarre was perfectly understood by the nuns, but until these last events no suggestion of a change in the office of abbess for many years to come had been whispered.

With the advent upon the quiet routine of convent life of Père Ruzé, an ecclesiastic of distinction at the court of France and representing as he did the Montpensier interests, the keen perceptions of Sister Cécile detected a possibility of startling and imminent revolution. Plainly he was here for a purpose.

The shrewdness of Cécile at once foresaw in this possible *bouleversement* her own and her only avenue to promotion and power and to a share in the rich emoluments of the abbey. With a child as prioress, a sub-prioress would be an imperative necessity ; and who would naturally be placed in that office but the circumspect mistress of the nov-

ices, already the subtle rival of madame in influence among the sisters of the house ?

Unsuspected for a time by madame, Cécile had
shown herself to Père Ruzé as a supple and useful
tool in the delicate operation before him, and a
quiet understanding had been formed between the
two to which madame's eyes were at last opened.
It was now, however, too late for her to meet plot
with counterplot or to place herself openly or secretly in opposition to the Duc. A more unselfish
woman would perhaps have braved all odds and
fought a generous fight for the helpless child, in
whose defense no champion but herself could now
appear.

Madame, however, loved ease and quietude too
well to enter the lists thus unequally equipped and
do battle for the protection of a child against her
own father, when upon that father's side all the
sentiment and sympathy of her world would be en-
listed. Accordingly she now quietly began her
preparations to retire to the chateau of Long-Vic,
which was hers by inheritance, and with cold and
scornful withdrawal she left Ruzé and Cécile to
work out their own and their master's purposes
with Charlotte de Bourbon.

Thus the new year, 1559, dawned upon the little
princess in strangely ominous loneliness. With
her "two Jeannes" she was still forbidden to hold
intercourse. Her aunt was kind but mysteriously
distant and preoccupied, given, however, to glances
and casual words of pity, a pity more disturbing
than her coldness.

The nuns about her began to watch her with
curious looks and to speak of her as "*cette pauvre
enfant.*"

No word reached her from the outside world.
Neither from camp nor court came any message to
speak of a father's remembrance or a mother's love.
Save for poor Radegonde's humble devotion, the

assiduous attentions of Père Ruzé and the espionage of Sister Cécile, Charlotte was left to herself.

But not for long was she to remain in ignorance
of the step which she was destined next to take.

Père Ruzé approached the subject first in the
confessional, cautiously suggesting that it was now
time for herself and Jeannette Vassetz to complete
their vows and assume the habit and vocation of
the sisterhood.

To this Charlotte replied flatly that she did not
intend to take the final vows nor assume the habit
of the order; in short, she did not wish to become
a *religieuse*. A second attempt was made with the
presence and aid of Sister Cécile. On this occasion
the intention of the Duc that Charlotte should be
straightway exalted to the honors and privileges of
her aunt's position was insinuated, at first with
great caution and then plainly declared. Looking
from one to the other she made answer simply:

"*Mais, mon père,* it is impossible! I am only a
child. How could I direct this great house, and
govern all these women who are so much older and
wiser than I? You must have misunderstood my
father's wish."

They let her go for that time, and she hastened
to Radegonde, crying: "They cannot force me to
make profession, they cannot force me to become
abbess against my will, can they, sister? Never,
never will I consent to such a thing! I know my
mother loves me still, although she never comes to
me or sends me her love and greeting any more.
But I know of a surety that she wishes me to go
back to her, and I am going, Radegonde. I am
going as soon as she sends for me!"

Then Radegonde said plainly: "Mignonne, your
mother will never send for you. That is beyond
her power. You are in the hands of Père Ruzé.
Do not struggle against his will. Remember the
words of monseigneur."

That night, as on many another which followed it, Charlotte cried herself to sleep, and the child-heart within her fainted for fear. But when daylight came her courage returned, and again and yet again she met the advances of the priest with steady, albeit respectful repulse, worthy of the high Bourbon spirit and resolution which were within her.

Then at length Sister Cécile came to Ruzé after compline one dreary March evening and said :

"*Mon père*, behold, we prevail nothing. The winter is over, you perceive, and as yet nothing has been accomplished. Madame is but too well suited and speaks no more of departure. You are content, then, to let this baby outwit you ? Methinks monseigneur will find you something soft-hearted, *n'est-ce pas ?*"

Ruzé looked at the nun with a slow, inscrutable smile. He had that morning received a messenger from the Duc.

"Do not disturb yourself, Sister Cécile," he said ; "something will be done to-night. I must ask you to bring Mademoiselle to matins and remain in the chapel until I can join you."

Cécile looked into the face of the priest with shrewd inquiry, but received for the nonce no further enlightenment.

Under the present régime Charlotte had been removed from the immediate care and oversight of madame and a small carrol adjoining the chamber of Sister Cécile in the novices' house had been assigned her. Scrupulously neat, like all the cells of the nuns, its furnishing consisted of a narrow bed and a chair of unpainted wood, a *bénitier* against the wall, above which hung a "discipline" or scourge, and a rush mat or two on the cold stone floor.

Here, just after midnight, Sister Cécile, candle in hand, fully clad in her black hood and robes,

stood for a moment to watch before waking the
unconscious child. Released from its coif, Charlotte's hair flowed in bright waves over the pillow; her small hands were clasped and nestled
under her chin; her face was exquisite in its
dreamless repose; her very attitude as she lay on
the hard, white bed and the lines of her graceful
though childish form bore a dignity which touched
the sense of the woman beside her with an inde-
finable awe.

*"Take heed that ye despise not one of these little
ones; for I say unto you, that in heaven their angels
do always behold the face of my Father."*

Words like these came to her memory with startling distinctness in the hush and stillness which
held the place and brought with them an inner
trembling. Had this child, then, with her pure
brow and the strange majesty of her innocence,
an angel in silence beholding, invisibly defending,
in sternness witnessing against that which should
be done?

For an instant Cécile, not highly gifted with imagination or with sympathy, drew back and hesitated. Even then the slow chiming of the convent
bell struck upon her ear in the silence, sad minor
tones, but persistent, authoritative, and not to be
withstood.

Laying her hand upon the shoulder of the sleeping child, Cécile held the candle where its rays
struck full upon the quiet eyelids, and called
softly: "Waken, Mademoiselle, you must rise and
come with me to matins."

Charlotte opened her eyes, against which the
light smote poignantly, smiled up into the face of
the nun with the instinctive habit of sweet-hearted
childhood, and murmured sleepily: "But I never
had to go to matins before, Sister Cécile, had I?
That is altogether new; but I shall not mind, you
know," her feet already on the floor and her ten-

der limbs trembling from the bitter chill of the
night.

Quickly dressed, Charlotte took a candle which
Cécile gave her and followed her through the dark,
winding passages which led to the cloister. Spec-
tral figures of nuns, with their long, black hoods
and pallid faces, glided on before them, each with
her flickering candle, each chanting a low, lugubri-
ous strain. Thus they passed through the darkness and rigor of the cold cloister, where a moon as
pallid as the faces of the nuns looked coldly down
upon them through the ancient arches, and entered
the transept door of the Sainte Chapelle.

Lighted only by one dull, misty lamp burning
before the altar, the interior of the church of Jouarre was at this hour like a pit of blackness, in
which Charlotte's eyes presently could discern the
crouching shapes of the sisters kneeling on the
floor. As in a wail of yearning heaviness the
voices, some harsh, some strangely sweet, rose in
the chant :

" *Deus in meum adjuvandem me festina.*"

At the altar, with hands folded over the cross
upon his breast, stood the imposing figure of Jean
Ruzé. Unnoted, apparently, by the others, Cécile
led Charlotte to the deeper shadow of the stone
desk near the choir, where with sharp, observant
eyes, stood the *circa,* to whom belonged the discipline of the nocturnal services.

Dazed and wondering, Charlotte knelt beside
Sister Cécile while psalm and prayer followed in
monotonous course, and when the final words of
benediction had been spoken and she would have
unbent her stiffened knees and risen from the cold
pavement, a touch on her shoulder admonished her
not to leave her place.

Then, all the nuns having passed with noiseless
tread from the chapel, these two still kneeling alone
in the icy gloom, Charlotte saw Père Ruzé, who,

coming from the sanctuary with slow and solemn steps, stood before them and held out his hand.

"Mademoiselle," he said, with his benevolent smile and mellow voice, "I must ask you and Sister Cécile to come with me."

He turned then, and they followed him in perfect silence through the dim choir out into the Lady Chapel and thence by a narrow passage lighted only by their own candles, to a flight of steep, descending stairs cut apparently in the rock upon which the chapel had been built.

Charlotte hesitated here for a moment, repelled by the dark, earthy vapors which rose from below, but a motion of Cécile's eyelids impelled her still to follow, and after a moment of dizzy winding down the steep, spiral staircase they reached the crypt of Saint Paul, the mortuary chamber of the abbey church. At a signal given by the hand and eye of the priest, Cécile halted and remained standing at the foot of the stairs, candle in hand, with downcast eyes and still, impassive countenance, while, taking Charlotte by her hand, he led her forward into the cavernous spaces which stretched before them in thick darkness.

As they advanced, the light from the torch which the priest carried and from Charlotte's faint candle brought out into fleeting sight the weird, fantastic sculpture of the heavy Norman pillars supporting the low vaulted roof, the vague outlines of the old Merovingian tombs, the ghostly effigies of saints rising at intervals between the shafts. When they stopped it was before a central tomb, in which reposed, open to their view, a figure of the dead Christ in stone, startling and dreadful in its verisimilitude.

Until now neither the priest nor the child had broken the silence of the place by a word.

Charlotte had grown paler and a sharp contraction of her throat made every breath a pang; but

49

there was calmness still in the look which she now
lifted to the face of her confessor. It said that she
was perturbed, shaken, and oppressed, but in it
there was still the divine confidence of childhood.
It was a look which searchingly inquired, but
which did not reproach. The eyes of Père Ruzé
were veiled against the look which they could not
meet.

With studied deliberation he now fastened his
torch into a rusty iron socket which projected from
a pillar closely fronting the tomb and its awful figure, then seated himself upon a block of stone
which formed the base of the pillar, gently took
the candle from the hand of the child, extinguished
it and placed it on the floor beside him. Every
movement of Père Ruzé was suave and of a soothing gentleness, and yet, as he now held out his
strong, white hand and drew her to his knee, and
even as he laid that hand as if in blessing on her
head, the child trembled violently, and an irrepressible sob broke from her lips. Still she did not
speak. She left the initiative of this strange colloquy wholly to the priest, who, perchance, found it
not altogether easy.

"My daughter," he said presently, with his
most subduing softness, "to-night a final question
must be asked of you, and your final answer must
be given."

The thick, murky blackness around them swallowed up the red flare of the torch and seemed to
rest palpably upon them in the breathless silence.

"I have even to-day received commands from
his grace, your noble father. We have too long
yielded to your strange unwillingness to take upon
you the holy vows to which you were pledged
in your cradle, to tread the path of sanctity and
peace, to be exalted to the high privilege of the
mother of God's saints."

Still the child did not speak.

D

"I ask you, Charlotte de Bourbon," and now
the voice of the priest assumed a solemnity which
she had never heard before, and an inflexible sternness took the place of the pacifying smile which
usually dwelt upon his lips, "I ask you once
more, in the name of our blessed Lord, whose
sacred, broken body is now before you, will you
obey the voice of your father, the voice of your
father in God, the voice of Holy Church which
has graciously protected and nourished you through
all the years of your life, and perform the duty now
commanded you ? "

"Father, I cannot." Her voice was low, her
breast heaved with piteous sobs ; she stood defenseless, but her steadfastness was unmoved. "I have
no vocation to be a *religieuse ;* something in my heart
forbids me. I want to go to my mother. I want to
be free. If I take these vows it would be without
heart, it would be false and vain."

The short, broken sentences followed each other
with the sharp, gasping breath between. The
priest took the little hand, which hung limp and
nerveless by her side, and laid it on his knee.

"So," he said softly, " do not close the fingers.
Let them lie thus, slackened." And he placed the
forefinger and thumb of his own right hand upon
the small wrist, in which the pulse labored fiercely,
and so continued to hold it throughout the interview.
It would not do to go too far. Even Montpensier
would prefer to stop short of an extremity.

But even with this action, whose gentleness
veiled a purpose beyond the child's innocent apprehension, Ruzé's lips sharpened again to their cruel
sternness, thinly masked in a smile.

"Mademoiselle, you must understand that this
profession, this sacred office, while irrevocably
binding, may lie gently and pleasantly upon you.
You have known confinement and discipline suited
to your years and the term of your novitiate. As

Abbess of Jouarre you will know power, ease, lux‑
ury, wealth, and pleasure. Where you have hith‑
erto obeyed, you may henceforth command. You
will be answerable only to your confessor, and he
will be your dependent. It is a gracious and an
easy task that is set you, Charlotte de Bourbon.
Think well before you reject it, for child though
you are, the church will not forcibly exalt those
who reject her gifts."

But the heart of the little maid was not more
accessible to this appeal than to those which had
gone before.

"Father," she said, "it is not wealth and ease
and pleasure that I want; I want love, I want lib‑
erty. I will die rather than be Abbess of Jouarre."

"You prefer death, Mademoiselle? Death, how‑
ever, may not be so easy. Do you, then, prefer
Fontevrault?"

This word acted upon the child with strange
effect. The small frame shuddered visibly, and
wavered as it stood.

"Mademoiselle has heard, perhaps, of Fonte‑
vrault?"

She bent her head in faint assent.

"Yes," said the priest reflectively, "at Fonte‑
vrault there is a donjon not unlike the donjon at
Jouarre, and a crypt beneath resembling the place
where you now stand. In this crypt, however,"
he proceeded with slow, gentle emphasis, "there
are small cells enclosed in stone walls of unusual
thickness. The door of such a cell is of oak, and
also quite heavy. There is no window, save a
grating in the door.

"The church is tender, Mademoiselle, and nour‑
ishes her children like a mother so long as they are
penitent and obedient. For the rebellious and
hard-hearted, for those who defy their parents and
seek their own foolish will, there remains such a
refuge as Fontevrault can give. Childhood will

not save you, Charlotte de Bourbon, nor rank, nor
tears. Your father has made known his will.
Either obedience or a quiet cell in Fontevrault,
where one does not die, but from which one does
not return."

"*Oh, mon père!*"

With a cry of anguish the child, pressed now too
hard for her endurance, drooped suddenly, and with
closing eyes and relaxing limbs sank upon the
mouldy floor of the crypt at the feet of Ruzé.

Keeping his finger still upon her wrist to satisfy
himself that he had not gone too far, the priest
murmured, "*Pauvre enfant,*" with cold compassion,
and then resting his head against the pillar behind
him, tapped softly upon its stone surface.

Instantly Sister Cécile was at his side. She
stooped over the child, who lay as if dead.

"Leave her a little," said Ruzé calmly. "She
will recover presently."

"How do matters stand?"

"Wait a moment and see."

That moment of waiting beside the unconscious
child in the lurid glow of the single torch and the
dreadful hush of the crypt never faded from the
memory of Sister Cécile.

When, finally, Charlotte opened her eyes, she
was lifted gently and supported in the arms of the
nun. As the color slowly returned to her lips and
the light to her eyes the sense of what had passed
came again to her mind, and she looked directly
into the face of Père Ruzé with a long look, as of
one greatly astonished. Several moments passed
before she could speak. Then she said imperiously:

"I wish to leave this place now. It is enough."

"And what does Mademoiselle answer to the
command of her father?" asked the priest with
unrelenting face.

"You may say to him that I will allow them to
make me Abbess of Jouarre."

Then, after brief pause, she added, drawing away from the supporting arms of Cécile Crue and lifting her head with a sorrowful loftiness infinitely pathetic: "You may say to him that I am no longer a child."

VII

CROSS AND STAFF

O N the seventeenth day of March, in the year of grace 1559, the convent bells of Jouarre rang out a joyful and triumphant peal. Royal banners streamed in the morning sun from every tower and turret, and the deep tones of the organ poured from the open west door of the Sainte Chapelle.

From the neighboring village and from the crofts and manors of La Brie came peasants, knights, and tradesfolk, all in holiday garb, and made gala procession through the abbey gates and across the great green courtyard, streaming into the church. For to-day, with cross and chrism, with solemn sacrifice and exultant *Te Deum*, the ancient monastery is to receive and consecrate as its mother *supérieure* a princess of the blood, a fair lily-maid of the house of Bourbon.

So let the banners wave, the trumpets blow, the organ music roll resounding ! Let the royal virgin receive such welcome as befits her, and let the holy women of Jouarre bow in reverence before their head !

Crowding hard upon each other, even to the doors, the spectators, gentle and simple, saw the solemn procession of priests enter the choir, saw the bishop's chair filled, not by monseigneur of Meaux, but by Père Ruzé, bishop not yet, but soon to be, and noted that he was of presence serene and august, heard the deep voice behind the altar sing :

Prudentes virgines, aptate vestras lampades,
Ecce, Sponsus venit, exite obviam ei !

54

saw then the ranks of nuns pass down the sanctuary, responding in sweet strains of holy confidence,

> Unto the hills lift I up mine eyes
> From whence cometh my help ;

saw not the Lady Louise de Long-Vic, but in her
place Madame du Paraclete, brought hither from her
famous convent at Nogent, the see of Jouarre having been declared vacant.

With candles in their hands, a company of youthful *postulantes*, among them Jeanne de Mousson
and Jeannette Vassetz, pass presently before his
reverence, and with ceremonial full sweet and
solemn, make their profession. They receive the
black robes and veils of the order, still glistening
with the holy drops from the silver *bénitier*, while
the nuns in plaintive voices are singing, "*Adieu
du Monde.*"

But who is this that comes ? A murmur like a
wave of ruth and tenderness sweeps through the
curious multitude.

Led by the mistress of the novices, whose face
alone is cold and stern, with steps that falter,
comes a forlorn and fragile child, robed in deepest
black. A white veil falls from her head ; beneath
it her face shows wan and woe-stricken. She
kneels at the feet of Père Ruzé and trembles visibly
so to kneel. A voice then begs his reverence, if it
seem good in his eyes, to receive and to bless this
young virgin and to unite her in spiritual union to
Christ, and to grant his benediction upon her exaltation to the holy headship of this order.

The deep, sonorous voice of Père Ruzé inquires if
then the priest so speaking believes this young virgin worthy. Receiving the answer, "Yes," he
proceeds to put to her the solemn questions as to
her sincerity and freedom in this action and her full
comprehension of the rules of the order.

Does the child reply ?   Some who are very near
her see tears fast falling as bright as the drops of
holy water, but they hear no voice.

Nevertheless, the stately ritual proceeds.   The
Veni Creator is sung with thrilling power and the
office of high mass is celebrated with much magnificence.   Père Ruzé turns now in full pontificals
to administer to the abbess-elect before all others
the sacred host.   Again she is led to the altar rail
by Sister Cécile, and this time, as she kneels, a
candle is held in one small, trembling hand, and
a white paper in the other, from which she is to
read before the assembly.   This paper contains the
formula, written and signed by herself, of the
irrevocable vows which Charlotte de 'Bourbon,
daughter of Louis de Bourbon and Jacqueline de
Long-Vic, shall now, of her own free will and intent,
make and pronounce.

All ears are strained to catch a syllable of those
vows coming from the white and quivering lips, but
not even the nuns who are nearest her can be sure
that they have heard a word.

And yet it is a vow of singular and unprecedented
mildness, containing, so those who know say afterward, "*paroles douces et fort légères.*"

A murmur goes about the chapel.   The scene is
not altogether of a sort to suit the mood of the
people.   Is this a valid consecration ?   Is it made
with the free will of the *postulante ?*   Even Père
Ruzé hesitates an instant with an irrepressible
frown, but the point of danger is quickly covered.

Madame du Paraclete, acting as abbess, has advanced with the long black veil, the abbatial ring,
and the pectoral cross and staff.   Sister Cécile
Crue has taken the folded paper, with its counterfeit vows, from the hand of the child, to deliver to
the priest, and who but old Radegonde sees that
she dexterously slips it into her own bosom and sub-
stitutes for it another paper ?   On this are written

the full vows of the order, unshaded and unsoftened in their stern import, vows which the unconscious child has never seen but which she has thus taken upon herself.

Veil and ring, cross and crozier, are now duly blessed and sprinkled at the hands of Père Ruzé and given then to Madame du Paraclete. By her, in turn, they are bestowed upon the child-abbess with words of solemn investiture, who turns then with mechanical obedience at the bidding of the priest to face the eager throng. For a moment all behold the childish shape, wrapped now by the clinging folds of the black veil. Against her breast she presses the great abbatial cross in that right hand on which the massive ring weighs all too heavily. The childish face, in the midst of all this pomp of symbol, is white like that of death. The eyes are lifted now ; they are wide and blue and innocent, but with a look tragic and heart-rending. It is a look that sees nothing !

Again the music thunders forth ; the *Te Deum*, with full organ and trumpet, makes the air vibrant through all the precincts of the abbey. The child is seated now in the seat of the Abbess of Jouarre.

But the cross and staff are quickly laid aside, and the Abbess of Jouarre, a child in her nurse's arms, is carried, as the joyous bells ring the people out into the sunlight again, and is laid in a narrow bed in old Radegonde's cell. So she lies with wide-open but unseeing eyes and the murmurs of delirium incoherent and broken on her dry lips. It is so that the mistress of the novices finds her, but she finds also Radegonde barring the entrance to the place, Radegonde, with a stern and wrathful light in her dim old eyes, saying :

"You have had your way with her, Cécile Crue ! Now it is my turn. If she lives, it will be because I shall love her back to life. If she dies, it will be only I who will weep over her."

VIII

LITTLE SAINT SILENCE

THE court was at Vincennes. Henri II. had illustrious guests to entertain and a great hunt in the famous forest was to be given in their honor.

The guests of France were also her hostages.

The war against the aggressions of the great emperor, Charles V., which for eight years had ravaged the borders of France and Flanders had in April been brought to a conclusion.

Charles, from his retirement in the monastery of St. Yuste, in Spain, had watched with irrepressible eagerness the progress of that contest which he had so reluctantly left for his son Philip to carry on. But the old emperor watched no more. In September the programme of death which with his instinct for the spectacular he had so often rehearsed had taken place in stern reality, and the last world-emperor had left forever that motley stage on which his part was played out.

The success of Philip's arms had been barren of permanent results, and had brought but little glow of pride or lust for further military glory to his sombre spirit. Another and a sterner war was in his thought. France too was facing a great internal upheaval and was glad to draw her armies back into her own domain.

At Cateau-Cambresis, on the third day of April, 1559, the kings of France and of Spain annulled the results of the long struggle and made mutual restoration of their conquests on the frontiers of Flanders and of Italy.

58

A new era in the history of Europe opened that day, for in the inglorious treaty which closed a futile war lay, scarcely concealed, the outlines of that monstrous conspiracy against the rights of man and the spirit of the age for which Philip and Henri gladly laid aside all other purposes.

What better than a marriage between the houses of their Catholic and very Christian majesties could seal these acts of diplomacy ? Philip, thirty-two and already twice married was at the moment, and most opportunely it appeared, himself marriageable. Left a widower four months before, he had promptly offered his hand to Elizabeth of England, step-sister and rival of his late bitter and suspicious spouse, Mary Tudor, but having been rejected, he was still free. The eldest daughter of Henri II., Isabella of Valois, was now a girl of fourteen. She had, it is true, been betrothed to Don Carlos, son of Philip, but the first compact was speedily canceled and a fresh one effected with the king of Spain himself as bridegroom elect. The festivities attending the marriage promptly to follow were already beginning, for it was now June.

From Cambresis the French king had brought back to Paris as hostages four noblemen high in the service of Spain, who were to remain at his court for a time as pledges for the execution of the new treaty.

Well pleased with the results of the long conference, Henri showed his satisfaction by lavishing his hospitality upon his guests in royal measure. Fêtes and revelries had succeeded each other in bewildering profusion at the palace of the Louvre, and to vary the gayety by sport of a hardier sort, the court had now made excursion to the ancient chateau of Vincennes for a season of hunting in the famous forest.

The great courtyard of the castle was alive, therefore, on this bright June morning with a bril-

liant company gathered to participate in the hunt
or to watch the departure. The pavement resounded beneath the clatter of hoofs of the horses
led by the bit by their masters' grooms, while the
hounds in leash barking impatiently, the cracking
of whips, the shrill whistles of the pages, and the
loud and merry voices of the pleasure-seekers filled
the air with tumult.

Already mounted upon a blooded chestnut, which
curvetted proudly with arched neck and tossing
mane, displaying her superb horsemanship to advantage, appeared the Duchesse de Valentinois,
better known as Diane de Poitiers.

Her still brilliant beauty and the magnificence of
her figure, invulnerable it seemed to the weapons
of time, still carried every eye to follow all her
looks and motions. In her close black hunting
dress, relieved only by facings of white and a white
panache in the small black velvet toque, looking
the very embodiment of the spirit of the chase,
Diane swept at a gallop around the court. Reining
up her hunter before the stone balustrade which
capped the terrace, she saluted a lady in violet
velvet who stood there with a small group of attendants and who held a little girl by the hand.

Beside her and bending to hear her speak, a tall,
spare man of military bearing was standing, a man
with a stern, cadaverous face, a beak nose, deep-
set black eyes under a high and brazen forehead,
and a long beard flowing over the collar of the
Fleece which adorned his dark, fur-trimmed doublet.

The lady, whose face was of the fineness as well
as of the tint of ivory, a face which in its smooth
impassiveness was a mask to whatever emotions
might fill her mind, replied to the salutation of
Diane in a low voice and with peculiar sweetness
in her smile.

"You never were lovelier, dear duchesse, even
in your youth," she said with an air of artless im-

pulsiveness. "Is it not true, monsieur, that Madame de Valentinois is the brightest ornament of this or any court in Europe?" and she turned with smiling appeal to the dark man beside her. He was one of the hostages from Spain, and one of the greatest generals of his time, being none other than the renowned Ferdinando Alvarez de Toledo, better known as Alva. He bowed profoundly at this challenge, but his gravity did not relax, and his eyes rested upon the brilliant face of Diane with cold neutrality.

"What your majesty says may surely not be disputed," he said in a dull and half-reluctant voice, as if despising the gallantry into which he was forced ; "but where the queen of France can be seen men can hardly have eyes for others, however fair."

Diane flashed a smile of insolent amusement into the bronzed face of the unresponsive warrior, and then sat in her saddle noting for an instant, although with undisguised indifference, the movements of the queen. Catharine de Medici bent now with an action of graceful and becoming modesty and as if to hide a confusion at the grim flattery of Alva which she was far from feeling, and lifting in her arms the little Princess Marguerite placed her upon the broad flat stone of the parapet. The child was of piquant loveliness, and sat looking out at the lively scene before her, her dark locks stirred by the sweet breath of the June morning. Her two brothers, the Duc d' Orleans and the Duc d' Anjou, boys of seven and eight years, were caracolling around the courtyard mounted on small but spirited horses, and the child laughed aloud and clapped her hands as they saluted her in passing with noisy banter and boyish show of daring.

"And where are your *confrères* this morning, monsieur ?" Catharine now asked of the Spanish general.

"They are coming hither even now, madame," was the reply, "or rather Egmont and the Duke of Aerschot are approaching. I have not seen the prince this morning."

At this moment the two Flemish grandees, the gallant hero of Gravelines, Lamoral of Egmont, and the Lord of Aerschot, crossing the pavement below the terrace, advanced to the parapet, and, uncovering, paid their *devoirs* to the queen and her ladies. Both gayly kissed the tiny hand of the little Marguerite, who at once began to coquette with Egmont, to whom she was instinctively attracted, and who received the favor of the royal child with merry and charming deference.

His Spanish colleague, Alva, watched this dallying the while with a curiously bitter severity, augmenting the harshness of his face.

"We were saying, messieurs," said Catharine presently, "that we have not this morning seen your brother in this hard imprisonment to which your lord and mine have condemned you. Is he then not to join the hunt to-day?"

"Madame," said Egmont, looking up from a favor he was dexterously weaving of some bits of riband which little Marguerite had given him and bowing with courtly grace, "if it please your majesty, the prince has gone to mass this morning, if I have been rightly informed."

"*Morbleu!*" cried Diane de Poitiers, lightly laughing, "who would have expected so great devotion from Monseigneur of Orange! It was but last night, moreover, that he came hither, and one would have said he had chance enough for masses in Paris."

"By my faith, Madame de Valentinois," and Egmont turned gayly to Diane, "I doubt greatly whether the prince went so much for the sake of the mass as for the chance to look at the new window of Maître Cousin, that so he could gaze unvexed and unhindered at the charms of its most glorious figure."

Although the notorious Diane was the central personage in the mythological frescoes and canvasses of the French Renaissance, and had been already immortalized as the goddess Diana in the statue of Jean Goujon, it was still matter for surprise and protest, even in the dissolute court of Henri II., when her figure wholly nude, her golden hair encircled by a blue riband, had been introduced into the scene of the Last Judgment in the new window of the apse of the chapel at Vincennes. Hence it was that the glance of bold flattery which accompanied these words of the Flemish grandee called a slight flush to the cheek of the duchesse. Her eyes rested upon Egmont with a curious expression, at once imperious and caressing, and she was about to make some deprecating remark when from the wide-open door of the château behind the company two persons advanced, who at once drew all eyes to themselves, being no less than the heir-apparent to the throne of France and his young wife of a year. A tall, slender boy of sixteen, François was known at this period of his life as the *king-dauphin*, of a graceful, negligent carriage, a figure rather effeminate than manly, and a countenance pallid and heavy-eyed. By the hand he was leading his wife, Mary, "her most serene little highness," the Queen of Scotland, whose lustrous beauty for a moment startled the group on the terrace to wondering silence.

As she approached with buoyant step Mary's fresh rose bloom made the olive Italian face of Catharine de Medici appear strangely worn and sallow. Even the peerless Diane did not care to put her still powerful charms into immediate comparison with those of Mary in this strong light of the morning and so, without further dalliance, she galloped on toward the great gate of the donjon

tower. A gentleman in rich but plain hunting costume, who was riding in at the moment, instantly
dismounted and kissed her hand with affectionate
gallantry. This gentleman was no less than the
king of France, Henri of Valois, whom for twenty
years the unscrupulous duchesse had held in the
chains of an almost insane infatuation.

Catharine de Medici wisely ignoring the further
movements of the formidable Diane, with graceful dignity proceeded to present the Duke of Alva
and the Flemish noblemen to François and Mary.
The latter had arrived at Vincennes the day before,
coming directly from Villers-Cotterets, where they
lived in the retirement prescribed by the etiquette
of the royal family for the king- and queen-dauphin
until called to the throne. On occasions of special
festivity it was, however, permitted for them to appear at court and the approaching marriage of their
sister to the king of Spain had at this time given
ample warrant for their presence.

"You are not of the hunting party to-day, my
son?" said the queen, looking with evident concern at the lack-lustre face of François. "That is
deprivation something severe, I fear, for our daughter." The last words were spoken with a negligent
coldness which she scarcely attempted to conceal,
and an indifferent glance at the young wife, whose
ardent love for all sports and athletic exercise was
well known in the Valois family.

"Thanks, madame," said Mary in a clear, bell-
like voice, in which a thrill of conscious power and
gladness seemed to vibrate, "monsieur is slightly
indisposed, and I do not myself find the hunt amusing when he is not among the rest."

As Mary spoke thus with an arch and roguish
look aside into the face of her boy-husband, she
was so wholly bewitching in spite of a faint trace of
insolence which accompanied her words that even
the hard face of Alva relaxed into a reluctant smile.

Catharine, however, did not apparently yield to the influence of her daughter-in-law's charms, divining but too clearly, with the sharpened instinct of long and bitter experience, that full soon they might be arrayed in potent rivalry against herself.

Never yet in the twenty-five years which had passed since as a girl of fifteen Catharine had ridden into France, the bride elect of the Duc d'Orleans, had she, as princess or as queen, been permitted to rule in her rightful realm.

Completely eclipsed by the Duchesse de Valentinois, to whom she was not even a rival, the devotion of Henri to his mistress had never yielded for an hour to the subtle and persistent attacks of the wife. A queen without a following, without influence, and since the death of her father-in-law, François I., without the affection even of her immediate family ; with the deepest sources of her life embittered by the ceaseless and terrible struggle with Diane, whom she valiantly professed to love, Catharine could only bide her time. But a slight knowledge of human nature would suffice to foretell that if the pent-up bitterness of the heart should find a vent, if the devouring lust for power of the cruel will be allowed to work freely, there would follow deeds such as honest men fear to mention, deeds conformable to the Italian craft and the wholly unscrupulous nature of the woman.

As if to divert the eyes of the cavaliers from the person of the Queen of Scots Catharine exclaimed, looking down the courtyard :

"Ah, at last the knight *fainéant!* My lord of Orange appears to have finished his devotions and to prepare for the day's pastime."

All eyes were now directed to the figure of a cavalier who had newly appeared upon the scene, and who had stopped for a moment to speak with the groom who was leading a magnificent black hunter up and down.

E

This cavalier now turned, perceiving the group of ladies upon the terrace, and hastened to greet them. As she noted his approach Catharine said in a low voice to the first lady in waiting:

"Surely, Montpensier, this is the goodliest gentleman in the king's company."

The lady replied:

"*Un preux chevalier, ce Prince d'Orange,*" and her face, which hitherto had borne a sad and anxious expression, brightened perceptibly.

The Prince of Orange, as he now hastened to do homage to Catharine, was seen by all to be a young man of marked nobility of mien, clean-limbed, well-knit, and graceful. Younger by many years than his fellow-hostages, slender and even boyish, with something of youthful bloom still on his cheeks, he was imposing withal by reason of the impress of profound and penetrating intellect dwelling in each line of his face.

As he removed his cap of black velvet the sun shone full upon the bright brown hair, cut close to the head, upon the clear *brune* skin, the dark gentle eyes, the sensitive well-chiseled lips. The prince was dressed in a black velvet doublet and trunk hose and black silk stockings and wore no decorations save the insignia of the Fleece upon his breast, while his black cap was without panache or other decoration. In his left hand he chanced to be carrying a single white rose. With the right hand, as he dropped upon one knee, he lifted the hand of the French queen to his lips; then rising, responded with a manner of singular and captivating charm to the salutations which were rained upon him from the brilliant group of lords and ladies.

The face of the prince which had at first worn a shade of melancholy, natural in view of the recent death of his young wife and itself a distinction in that company, was transformed as he entered into their airy converse, and he displayed in high degree

the free and debonair complaisance of the accomplished courtier, the facile ease of the man who
"carries a talisman under his tongue." Gay and
gracious, proud yet delicately deferential, the young
knight, at this time the prime favorite of fortune,
seemed to possess and unconsciously to exert that
mysterious magic of personal ascendency to which
all who met him irresistibly yielded.

Turning to the Duke of Alva the Duchesse de
Montpensier remarked aside :

"I have not seen his grace of Orange before. Is
it true that it is he whom the Emperor Charles
brought up as his own son ? "

"The same, madame," was the brief reply.

"The emperor has shown himself a judge of
men," rejoined the lady. "And he, like Philip, is
a widower, *n'est-ce pas ?* "

"Yes, madame."

"A pity such a young and gallant prince could not
have been the bridegroom for our Lady Isabella,"
said the duchesse regretfully, "rather than his fos-
ter-brother, his majesty of Spain, whom, saving your
presence, monsieur le Duc, we French women consider a somewhat sombre and icy gentleman and a
melancholy husband for our pretty little princess."

Without waiting for a reply, which indeed the
general did not seem disposed to give, the duchesse
turned again to hear what the queen-dauphin and
her ladies were saying to the prince.

"Then after all it was not the mass which kept
monsieur ? "

"No, madame," was the reply ; "I cannot claim
to have visited the chapel this morning."

"Ah, then monsieur has been at some mysterious
tryst with one of our demoiselles ! And it is from
some fair hand that he has received the lovely rose
he guards so carefully. Confess now, and tell us
the name of the fortunate lady ! "

For answer the prince deliberately proceeded to

fasten the flower with a small jeweled brooch into his cap, which he then waved to the vivacious maiden with a gesture of gallant grace, but without a word.

"Oh, for shame, Adelaide," cried the Queen of Scots to her young court lady. "Are you then ignorant of flower-language? Have you forgotten that the rose is the symbol for silence?"

A shrill musical blast upon a silver horn rang at that moment upon their ears. The king galloped up to the terrace with a courteous greeting to the ladies and a call to horse to the gentlemen.

"What then really is the mystery of your white rose, Orange?"

It was Egmont who asked the question half an hour later as the two rode side by side through the deep shade of the forest, skirting the Lac Dumesnil. Despite the nearly dozen years disparity in their ages these rival Flemish princes were close friends and comrades-at-arms.

"By our Lady, Egmont, it is in truth a mystery," returned Orange, whose face had now won back the thoughtful expression habitual to it in repose. "It may even be that you can give me some enlightenment."

"Gladly will I if I may; say on," said Egmont.

"At the time when you supposed me to have gone to mass," said the prince, "I had, in fact, withdrawn rather for the chance to stroll in the peace of this rare morning through the garden walks and as far as might be from the shadow of yon gloomy chateau, which, I confess, seems to me more like a prison than a palace. I turned down a long, shaded lane, between the high, clipped hedges of yew which rose above my head, and was pacing forward, my eyes, I believe, downcast, my thoughts certainly far away in Breda with my little motherless children, when I caught sight of a fig-

ure at some distance before me which startled my
attention. Down the long green lane, among the
rows of the white lilies growing tall below the
hedge, stood the form of a child, or rather, perhaps,
I should say of a very young maid, as pure and as
virginal as the lilies. She was clothed from head
to foot in a shining white garment, straight and
flowing, with a veil of lightest gauze surrounding
her like a pale nimbus. Her head was lifted, the
hair which showed about her temples was of the
color of gold, her face was, as it were, transparent
and of a most affecting whiteness, and her eyes,
blue and innocent as an angel's, were lifted, looking up beyond the dark line of the yews, and from
them down her cheeks tears were fairly streaming.
I think she did not know that she thus wept; I
perceived that she had not heard my step approaching. However, I could not choose but go on.
Following her eyes I gained this much, that it was
the flight of a lark which was soaring far up into
the sky which she was so intently watching.

"As I approached her this creature, more like a
vision than a maiden of flesh and blood, seeing me,
dashed the tears off her face with a swift motion
and fixed upon me the gaze of her large, blue
eyes, with a look the saddest yet the most searching that I have ever known.

"Egmont," and the prince showed in the strong
emphasis and the seriousness of his tone that he
had been profoundly moved, "if you have ever
seen a child weep, not from childish vexation, from
fear or from pain, but from deep, unspoken sorrow,
you will know the strange pang with which I met
this look. It was a look as of an angel shut out of
heaven who will not murmur nor upbraid; a look
of utter, hopeless, but most patient sorrow, and on
the face of a child who ought to know nothing of
life yet but its joy and sunshine."

"Did you speak to her?" asked the count.

"I asked her, in good sooth, if I might serve or help her and pledged myself so to do in faith and honor if she would tell me her trouble. At first she made no answer. Near her now, I had a chance to note the fineness of her person, the grace of her bearing, the traces of sore illness which had left her face so sadly wan and transparent, the fact that on her breast she wore a large cross of rarely fine workmanship, and that it was a clasp of Bourbon lilies in gold which fastened her girdle."

"All these signs bid fair to tell a tale of passing significance."

"Surely. There was much to arouse a peculiar curiosity and reverence, for if ever I saw a holy and yet most unhappy child it was she. When I pressed her to speak she said at last, with no confusion, nor bashfulness, as might have been with her years, that her troubles could not be told but to increase them, and that she must learn silence, and so begged me to excuse her and let her go her way. I stood aside then, and passing me she smiled, and by my faith her smile did move me yet more deeply than her tears, so forlorn and so sweet was it. She had in her hand two or three of these June roses, and after she had passed me she stepped back and quite timidly, and yet in a something stately fashion, bestowed this one upon me, but did not speak. Then said I, 'Farewell, little Saint Silence,' and waved my hand, the rose in it, whereupon she said softly, '*Au revoir*, monsieur,' and so sped swiftly and gliding like a shining shadow down the alley."

"In truth a very curious history," said Egmont as the prince concluded his narration, and they rode on for a little space in silence. Then presently he added:

"The Duc de Montpensier is riding toward us; I know him by his height and by his white horse. What say you, shall I inquire of him concerning

this mysterious little maid ? He knows all the fam-
ilies who consort with the court and could surely
give us cognizance. I am fain to think that this
seemingly forsaken child, by the lilies at her belt
and the bearing you describe, may even be a princess of the blood. What say you, shall we inquire
of Montpensier ? "

"Nay, Lamoral," said Orange quickly, "least
of all of him. The man is little to my mind.
Something harsh, metallic, and cruel, even in his
most flattering words and ways, grates upon my
spirit. Ask nothing of him nor of any man. In
the end I choose rather to keep the vision in its
present semblance in my memory. What can it
profit to know more concerning it ? "

"That shall be as you say," said his friend, and
the Duc de Montpensier joining them they put
their horses to the gallop, making speed to join the
royal party.

When the sun of that June day was sinking in
the west, the prince rode homeward from the hunt,
and beside him and alone in the darkening glades
of the forest rode the king of France. Then and
there in free and lordly confidence his majesty dis-
coursed to the young prince, his guest and hostage,
on the all-controlling purpose for which himself and
the king of Spain had closed their long warfare. It
was then that the prince heard proposed as a prac-
tical measure, and one shortly to be executed in
his own country, that fateful dogma of the sixteenth
century, " *To exterminate heresy it is only necessary to
exterminate heretics.*"

With ardor Henri dwelt upon the searching work
already begun in Spain by the first *auto-da-fé* of
Valladolid a few weeks previously and which to his
sure knowledge his royal son and brother Philip
would now prosecute without fear or favor until
the "accursed vermin" were purged from the land

forever. The same measures were to be employed
in the Netherlands by means of the magnificent
machinery of the Inquisition set in motion and sustained by the Spanish army still quartered there.
In his own realm the king admitted the problem
was a more difficult one, since some of the chief
men in his kingdom and even some princes of the
blood had declared for the new religion. But " he
hoped by the grace of God and the good understanding that he had with his new son, the king of
Spain, that he would soon master them."

Thus his Very Christian Majesty, taking for
granted in hearty and undoubted confidence that
this right royal plot was already in its general outline familiar to a prince who was the favorite of
the father of Philip, and was the most powerful
Catholic prince of the Low Countries.

Neither by word nor look, breath nor motion, did
the prince betray the consternation with which he
was filled by the revelation of a plot wholly un-
dreamed of by him until that hour.

Perchance the king observed that his companion
grew somewhat silent and did not discuss with enthusiasm the details of that " excellent purpose,"
which was presently to convulse Europe from one
end to the other. Certain, however, is it that not
for one moment did his majesty of France dream
that the man beside him in his grave, attentive
courtesy, being " deeply moved with pity for all
the worthy people who were thus devoted to
slaughter, and for the country to which he owed so
much, wherein they designed to introduce an Inquisition worse and more cruel than that of Spain,"
in that brief hour received the impulse which,
slowly maturing, was destined to make of him in
after years the champion of his people and of the
spiritual liberties of all Christendom.

Soon king and prince with all the brilliant cavalcade returning from the forest, mingled in a rout of

royalty and nobility in the salon of the gloomy chateau and questions of kingcraft were for the time apparently forgotten.

A month from that day the hostages had returned to their own country ; Catharine de Medici no longer queen, but queen-mother, had become the mother-in-law of Philip of Spain ; Diane de Poitiers, whose proud device had been, "I have conquered the All-conqueror," had been scornfully dismissed from the court of France ; François of Valois and his young Scottish wife were king and queen of France, for a greater than Diane had conquered and Henri II. was dead, dead of a chance sword-thrust in a tournament.

Meanwhile and many days ere this, torn again from a mother's yearning love, the lonely child-abbess, the "little Saint Silence" had returned to her nuns of Jouarre.

IX

THE WHITE ABBESS

A GAIN the scene is the cloister garth at the Abbey of Jouarre, and on a summer afternoon in the year 1565, we find the three maidens, Charlotte de Bourbon, and with her the two Jeannes, sitting as in an earlier time, upon the old stone seat of Our Lady's Arbor.

The arbor is unchanged. The leaves of laurel and palm are still lustrous in the sunlight and give their sombre, enclosing shade ; the little Virgin in the center of the circle is stony and prim as of old ; the massive seat still surrounds the figure unaltered save for the gradual encroachment over its surface of the fine gray lichens. But while the scene remains the same, the three who again enliven its cold severity are no longer the chattering *insouciante* little girls who once came hither, but three full-grown maidens.

The six years which have elapsed have witnessed the death of François II. His fourteen-year-old brother, Charles IX., is now king of France, and, as regent of France, Catharine de Medici has the long-coveted power at last in her hands. The first religious war has been fought to a close and the peace of Amboise has run through two years of its fitful and uneasy course.

The Abbess of Jouarre at eighteen is tall and fair and stately, clothed to-day according to the habit which she adopted on first assuming her office, wholly in white. Her robe and coif, veil, and ornaments are all of the prescribed monastic cut and character, but like the Cistercians, she prefers white to black, and this preference has met with no opposition in the convent, it being obviously suited to her years, and a distinction which her princely rank suggests. As the young abbess bends over her embroidery frame her face and figure in their bloom and symmetry show that the years have brought reconcilement and surcease of the agonies to which her childhood was subject. No longer held under strict discipline and kept in the narrow and rigid limits of those early years, firmness, health, and elastic grace have succeeded to the earlier piteous pallor and weakness. Nevertheless, the expression of the Bourbon princess is characterized by a peculiar languor, the look of one who does not despair, but who no longer hopes, a look which gives a mysterious and pathetic charm to her youthful beauty.

Bending over the same frame, her head almost touching that of Charlotte, is Jeannette, clad now, as is also Jeanne de Mousson, in the full conventual robes of the order, the soft, clinging black garments, the clear white linen caps, from which flow the black veils, concealing their youthful grace of outline. But despite this melancholy habit, the two Jeannes have little of the aspect of cold, superimposed quietude of the conventional nun, but a wholesome, sunny contentment. Jeannette is still small, even insignificant in stature, and her face is simple, honest, and affectionate as ever. Jeanne de Mousson, who paces slowly back and forth reading aloud from a small missal, is as tall as Charlotte, and has a figure which even under its jealously concealing garments can be seen to be instinct with spirit and lissome energy. Her clear, dark skin has not, for all the years of her convent life, wholly lost its vivid color; her dark eyes flash with their old luster and her lips have still their proud, impetuous curves.

Old Radegonde could now be seen approaching

the arbor as if on an errand of great importance.
Her brown, hardy face was but a trifle more
wrinkled by the six years which had elapsed since
the consecration as Abbess of Jouarre of her adored
princess.

It had been her loving devotion alone which had
brought the exhausted child through the fierce
fever which had followed that ordeal. This season of suffering had knit the heart of the royal
child to the heart of the humble old woman forever.

As she crossed the cloister Radegonde was intercepted by the sub-prioress, whose slender figure
had been noiselessly passing and repassing beyond
the stone pillars for the past half-hour as if on
guard. To her keen questioning, Radegonde but
replied :

"I will tell you presently, Sister Cécile. My
word is first of all for my lady."

Radegonde's head now appearing in the narrow gap between the laurel bushes which served
as entrance to the place, Charlotte de Bourbon
looked up from the parti-colored tapestry upon
which her fingers were employed, and smilingly
asked a quiet question :

"What is it, Radegonde ? "

"Madame, her majesty of Navarre, Madame
Jeanne d'Albret, has at this moment arrived at
Jouarre with a small escort, and awaits your high-
ness even now in the hall."

A bright color rushed to Charlotte's cheeks and
an exclamation of joy broke from her lips, which
was echoed with delight by Jeanne de Mousson.

Charlotte dropped her embroidery frame into
Jeannette's lap, and taking the young Béarnaise
by the hand, the two hastened from the place with
Radegonde, Cécile Crue furtively following afar
off. A moment later they entered the beautiful
hall of the abbess and were clasped in the warm

motherly embrace of the Queen of Navarre, who
stood there awaiting them with two ladies, who had
attended her on her journey hither.

Still bearing the potent charm of her young
womanhood, despite the perils and adversities of her
stormy life, the royal matron seemed by her presence to exert instantaneously upon these motherless and lonely girls a strangely energizing influence. Noble in person and in dress and of an
unconscious majesty of demeanor, the beauty of
the daughter of Marguerite de Valois was far beyond that of the conventional, artful beauties of
her day ; hers was a spirituelle, eloquent sweetness, the clear light of a puissant spirit and an invincible heart. Power, confidence, and freedom
seemed to flow from her and animate every one in
her presence.

Jeanne de Mousson showed the influence of the
queen, her godmother, yet more notably than did
the young abbess. She was transformed from the
grave monastic demureness which had characterized her but now as she had paced the sober little
arbor. Her dark eyes fairly flamed with joy, her
cheeks glowed with excitement, she held herself
with new and spirited grace, and it was not difficult to see in her a reflection of the heroic temper
and brilliant leadership of that queen who had been
called through all her girlhood, "the darling of
kings."

But the time was short and much must be said
between her majesty and the Abbess of Jouarre
alone. With quick perception, the young Béarnaise proposed that she should accompany the
ladies-in-waiting to the guest house and establish
them there in the apartments set aside for guests
of their degree, while the young *supérieure* should
enjoy a tête-à-tête with the queen.

The two were now accordingly left alone while
old Radegonde took her place outside the door of

the great hall to keep watch and ward over the privacy of her beloved lady. The sub-prioress had disappeared.

The sumptuous room was unchanged since the days of Louise de Long-Vic. The dim old picture of Saint Theodehilde still looked down from the great carved chimney; the Cordova leather of the walls gleamed richly in the afternoon light falling through the deep-set windows; the brave array of plate upon the great buffet alone had suffered loss, much of it belonging to Madame de Long-Vic, who had removed it with her when she went to the chateau which had become her residence.

Jeanne d'Albret now, taking Charlotte's hand in hers, drew her to a seat in the embrasure of one of the high lancet windows.

"Ah, my little cousin," she cried in her full, resonant voice, "how lovely you have grown in these four years since I have looked upon your face!"

They spoke long and tenderly then of the death of Charlotte's mother, which had taken place four years previously. The lonely girl had been summoned to her mother's death-bed only in time to receive her parting words and her last fervent prayer for herself.

With uncontrollable emotion Charlotte cried to her friend :

"Oh, dear madame, can you, can any one, tell me why it was that I was never permitted to be alone and at liberty with my dearest mother, never once in all those years ? I know that she loved me." And with that sobs made speech impossible.

"Do you not know, then, that your mother for many years before her death was Huguenot ? " Jeanne d'Albret asked, looking earnestly into Charlotte's face, which changed swiftly as she listened. These were bold words.

A slight, hardly perceptible tremor, as of dismay,

passed over the painted figure of the first abbess of Jouarre in its frame above the chimney.

"No, madame," replied the young girl. "I knew that she was wholly without the desire to persecute the Huguenots which animates my father. That she was herself Protestant I never knew. If this be so it explains many mysteries!"

"It explains, perchance, even more than you think, my little Charlotte. It explains the undue haste with which your investiture with your office of abbess was precipitated. Your father feared the influence of your mother upon your Catholicity and sought, ere it was too late, to bind you by irrevocable vows to fulfill his purpose."

Charlotte clasped her hands with a strangely pathetic gesture of hopeless submission.

"Ah, madame," she breathed, as if her voice was smothered by her sense of wrong, "I have not been fairly dealt by!"

"Most unfairly and cruelly have you been dealt by, to my sure knowledge!" said the queen, the sense of outraged justice giving her face a noble sternness. "I speak thus plainly because I know how your faithful and loving heart has been torn by questions concerning the seeming neglect and coldness of your mother. Ah, my child, even you will never know, no one not a mother can dream, of the agonies which the noble Jacqueline suffered concerning you, and which she could never permit herself even to hint to you, since the result could only add to the sorrows and rigors of your lot."

"Even when I was at court," said Charlotte, her tears checked, her face still and white as if cut from marble, "we were kept apart, or watched while we were together, and many a time I have gone away by myself alone to hide the tears which I could not restrain for longing and the crying out of my heart for the tenderness and confidence which even in her presence were denied me."

"Oh, Charlotte, my little maid, the blight and burden of this cruel time have fallen over-heavily on your young years! God help us, for I greatly fear me there is worse yet to come."

"Can there be worse for me, madame? I think I have nothing left to fear," and again Charlotte's sweet lips trembled.

"For you, it may not be. I cannot tell, yet even in this quiet convent there may be forces at work of which you do not dream."

As she spoke these words the Queen of Navarre chanced to lift her eyes to the ancient painting above the chimney. Could it be that it shook? Was the old first abbess of Jouarre, in her straight black robes, coming down out of her frame to fulfill the words? Absurd and impossible, Jeanne d'Albret thought, and turned again to the young, white-robed living abbess before her, whose blue eyes were fixed with wondering intentness upon her face.

"Madame, I hear that you have yourself joined the Huguenots, and that you do not permit now the celebration of the mass in Béarn. Is that true?"

"Yes, *ma mie*, it is quite true," and the queen smiled at the dread and anxiety plainly to be read in Charlotte's face.

"And now that monsieur my cousin is dead, can you alone sustain so great a change?"

Jeanne d'Albret cast about her for an answer which should be true and which yet should not convey the whole truth to the mind of Charlotte. For Antoine de Bourbon, a man faithless even for that faithless age, had been recreant to every pledge either to the new religion or the old, childish in his fickleness, the sport of all parties.

"We will do our best, little cousin," she said with a tinge of sadness in her look, which was yet full of conscious power. "But we wrestle in our little realm against masterful foes. The powers of Rome and of Spain have both of late been arrayed fiercely against us.''

"And you fear not to set yourself against such mighty odds ? " cried Charlotte, gazing with breathless admiration at the queen. " You alone, of all women of France, should have your name written forever with that of Jeanne d'Arc. Like her, you are high-souled and fearless ; like her, you have the soul of a soldier in the body of a fair and delicate woman," and Charlotte covered the beautiful hand of Jeanne d'Albret with kisses. " But, is it true that you have defied his holiness, Pope Gregory, as men say ? "

" Not quite that, I hope. So at least I have not purposed ; but his holiness has been greatly aggrieved at the measures which I have taken in Béarn, and has proposed to enforce obedience among my subjects by means of the Inquisition. Think you I would permit that atrocious tyranny among my leal and true people ? " and the eyes of the queen flashed her indignant protest.

"I made answer to Cardinal d'Armagnac : '*I receive here no legate at the price it has cost France. I acknowledge over me in Béarn God only, to whom I shall render account of the people he has committed to my care. I shall do nothing in my kingdom by force. There shall be neither death nor imprisonment nor condemnation, which are the nerves of force.*'[1] That letter, Charlotte, which God gave me, a weak woman, the heart to write, has been printed and scattered throughout the land, by whom I know not. Thank God, I hear that the hearts of his fainting saints have been cheered by it. But the consequences which followed its reception by the Holy Father bade fair to be full serious. You have, even here, doubtless heard of the bull against me ? "

---

[1] In this volume the authentic original utterances of historic persons are indicated by Italics.

F

"Yes, truly. I heard it with utmost dread and amazement."

"I was cited to appear before the holy tribunal of the Inquisition at Rome itself to clear myself, if I could, from the stain of heresy."

"But you did not go?"

"Nay, indeed I went not," and Jeanne d'Albret laughed frankly. "The queen-mother this time espoused my side of the quarrel. It suits not the majesty of France to permit his holiness to carry matters with too high a hand, and particularly to order about those of the blood royal. So Gregory was fain to give way, and Catharine stood me in good stead for this time, whatever have been our troubles in the past, or may be in the future."

"I know it is said of her majesty," said Charlotte, "that she is neither friend to any person nor foe to any, save for her own ends."

"That is said but too truly, I fear me," was the reply. "But no sooner, my Charlotte, was Rome silenced than his majesty of Spain began to proceed against me after his own peculiar fashion. In good sooth, I think not the Holy Father himself so good a Catholic as my neighbor Philip!" Upon which they both laughed lightly.

Madame d'Albret proceeded to recount her thrilling escape from the plot of Philip to abduct herself and her two children from their castle at Pau and carry them by a force of armed men into Spain, there to come before the Inquisition. From this murderous plot the Queen of Navarre had been saved only by the timely warning sent by Philip's wife, Isabella of Valois.

"So this time, *ma mie*," she concluded her narrative, "we are safe; but it is only for a time, for all signs portend that sterner scenes are before us than any we have known."

"But why say you so, *chère cousine?*" asked Charlotte. "Surely the land of France is now in a state of rest. I have heard much of this royal progress which the king and the queen-mother are making through the southern lands. That, at least, would seem to befit a time of peace."

"Ah, but, my child, wheresoever they go they carry with them new and harsher oppression for the new religion," returned the queen earnestly. "They profess to protect it, but to lure our people into a deadly security, while in reality every measure which they dare they take against us. Last of all, and most ominous, we have had this illustrious conference at Bayonne, hardly yet concluded."

"Were you at Bayonne, madame?"

"Nay, not I, Charlotte, but my brave boy, my Henri, was in the train of the queen-mother, with Calignon and others of my council, his tutors and attendants."

"It has been told me that the queen-mother has a great liking for the prince."

"Yes, it is even so. She seeks to have him about her whenever it is possible, saying that his high spirits greatly divert and fascinate her. I trust she intends honestly, but who can tell?"

For the first time a cloud of anxiety rested on the strong face of the queen.

"Sometimes," she continued more slowly than she had been speaking, "I misdoubt me that Catharine fears my boy more than she loves him. But why should she? Hers are long, long thoughts, but even the longest should not reach Henri. She has a son of less than twenty years now on the throne of France, and besides him yet two sons to take up the succession should Charles lack issue. It would seem impossible, save for that old tale of the vision shown her by the astrologer. That, it was said, gave twenty-four revolutions of a magic wheel for my Henri, which was supposed to prefigure so many years on the throne of France. But that was long ago and perchance but idle gossip," she cried, as if interrupting herself, "and at best it was a superstition better forgotten. I was speaking of Bayonne.

"You know, perchance, that Philip came not thither to meet Catharine, as had been expected, but sent Isabella, my defender, and with her his ferocious favorite, Alva, the deadliest foe of freedom and the cruelest in the world to-day. What could such a conference bode save ill to the cause of liberty and toleration ? "

"I hear that my father accompanied the king to Bayonne," said Charlotte anxiously.

"It is true; my cousin Montpensier was most eager to show his devotion to Philip and to Catholicity. You must know Alva made bold to challenge the loyalty of the court of France to the papacy. All the French princes and nobles present thereupon protested their devotion to the Church and Spain and monsieur the Duc, your father, exclaimed, I am told, that he would be cut in pieces for Philip's service. He even embraced Alva, declaring that if his own body were to be opened at that moment the name of Philip would be found imprinted on his heart ! "

A slight groan escaped Charlotte's lips.

"While he was at Bayonne," proceeded the queen, " Henri overheard Alva and the queen-mother earnestly discussing various plans for ridding Europe of heresy. Alva, it seems but fair to think, was urging that the first step and the most important would be to cut off by violence the Protestant leaders in each nation. The rest would follow easily. Without leaders the common herd could easily be shocked into obedience. 'For, madame,' said the duke,—and this Henri distinctly noted, while they thought him too much a child to heed their words,—'the head of one salmon is worth the heads of ten thousand frogs !' That gives the key to what we may expect, little cousin, for I cannot doubt, from the temper of Catharine, that in the end such counsels as these will prevail. Calignon sent an account of this conversation as Henri repeated it to him, in cipher by a special messenger to me in Béarn, not three weeks since."

At this moment the vesper bell from the chapel tower was heard ringing and Charlotte rose at the summons.

Calling Radegonde, the young abbess directed her to conduct the Queen of Navarre to the suite of rooms now prepared for her in the guest house across the abbey courtyard, where she would find her ladies. This done, with a tender *au revoir* Charlotte hastened to the chapel.

From the vesper service, it was noted by the *circa*, the sub-prioress, Madame Cécile Crue, was on that summer evening absent.

X

MAÎTRE TONTORF

"MADAME, we have spoken of the Catholic leaders; who are the master spirits to-day among them of the new religion?"

Charlotte de Bourbon asked this question of the Queen of Navarre as the two paced slowly together the walks of the convent garden the following morning. The flowers seemed kindlier, her majesty fancied, than the decorations of the hall.

Mass had just been celebrated in the Sainte Chapelle, at which the queen had not been present.

"My journey at this time from Paris," she replied, "will take me for conference with the greatest military leader our cause has to-day in all Europe, the admiral of France, Gaspard de Coligny."

Jeanne d'Albret spoke the name with enthusiastic reverence.

"Madame is then on her way to Châtillon? This I did not know, because, in sooth, I had not stopped to inquire. Ah, how good you are thus to come out of your proper road to see your little lonely cousin!"

Charlotte's eyes brimmed with grateful tears.

"It is a mere trifle out of my way, little one. I was glad, moreover, to tarry a night at Meaux, where I have a good friend I wish some day to make your friend also, the Sieur de Minay. To continue with the leaders of Huguenoterie,—which to-day is no longer solely a spiritual temper, a religious conviction, but has become a great and powerful political party, for all Europe is divided

86

now into two great camps,—next to Coligny I should place your cousin, brother of my husband, the Prince of Condé."

"Yes, that is as I supposed," said Charlotte.

"But around Coligny there is growing up a little group of young cavaliers, men of like temper with him, knights of pure life and holy purpose, *sans peur et sans reproche*. These men are deeply de-voted to the admiral, men like the Chevalier de la Noue and young Teligny and many another."

"I would I could once see the admiral," cried Charlotte longingly.

"Ah, my child, he stands almost alone now for the old chivalry of France, a gentle and perfect knight, though so great a soldier. If I could but take you with me to Châtillon! There you would see not only Coligny but Charlotte de Laval, his wife, surely the sweetest saint and the bravest in France to-day! But to continue. Like women ever we range everywhere rather than cleave to one narrow path.

"Jean Goujon, Ambrose Paré, and many other Frenchmen of genius and fame, have now declared for the religion. In England, you know, they have at present a Protestant queen, who," Jeanne d'Albret added with a touch of sarcasm, "when she can be fully persuaded and remain persuaded over a night that it is for her own material interest to aid the cause, has been known to dole out a few ships and men."

"That sounds, dear madame, as if the English queen were not unlike the queen-mother of France."

"Charlotte, allowing for the differences of race, of family, and of education, Elizabeth of England and Catharine de Medici are like enough to each other to be sisters! Neither has a heart which can be touched by tenderness or by religious devotion. Policy and self-interest rule the Englishwoman as they rule the Italian. They will outwit Catholics one day and Protestants the next, if it serves their purpose, and in my own heart I believe they despise both alike, being unable to conceive the sincerity of either. Nevertheless, the Queen of England is counted in the Protestant camp.

"Then we have many German princes, most notably the Elector Palatine, Friedrich der Fromm, whose court at Heidelberg is a haven of refuge for those who flee from France, being persecuted for their faith. In the Low Countries, where the conflict between the two religions bids fair to be a fierce one, there is as yet no great Protestant leader; howbeit I have many hopes myself of what may come from the influence of my friend, the young Count of Nassau, Louis, brother to the Prince of Orange."

Charlotte de Bourbon glanced up at the queen with quickened interest.

"The prince, although himself Catholic, is married now to a Protestant princess, Anne of Saxony, and is known to stand stoutly against the introduction of the Inquisition into the Low Countries. Ah, he is a noble and a puissant prince; if we could but count him among us!"

"How chances it that these brothers are so diverse in name and faith, the one a Prince of Orange, the other a Count of Nassau; the one Calvinist, the other Catholic?" asked Charlotte.

"It is quite a tale to tell," replied the queen, "and goes back a generation. The Nassaus are, as you perchance know, a German not a Flemish family; but having vast estates in Flanders, one branch of the house has ever held the German and the other the Netherlandish possessions. These are known as Nassau-Dillenburg and Nassau-Breda, in token of their great baronies. Young Réné of Nassau, a generation ago the head of the last-named house, by his maternal inheritance became also Prince of Orange, the small estate in Avignon,

small and yet a free sovereignty. This Réné was
a gallant soldier and a great favorite of the Emperor
Charles. By special favor the emperor permitted
him to name as his heir his young cousin of the
German branch of the Nassaus, William. Then,
about twenty years ago, at the battle of St. Dizier,
Réné was killed; and this youth, but eleven years
of age, who had been brought up in the German
and Protestant home of the Nassaus at Dillenburg,
succeeded to his princedom and to all his titles and
possessions.

"The emperor liked the boy, who was at once
taken to the court at Brussels,—from the first, and
brought him up as his own son and, it needs not to
say, as a Catholic. He was given the best education that a prince of sovereign rank could receive,
and peculiar privilege and training in all matters of
diplomacy and State, for which he is said to have
extraordinary talent.

"Thus you see, my child, while John and Louis
and the other young counts of Nassau have grown
up in their ancestral castle at Dillenburg simply
noblemen and Protestant through and through, the
eldest son, this William, has grown up at court ; he
has had the training of a Catholic prince and of a
son of the great emperor. Moreover, he himself is
of sovereign rank and enormous wealth and influence. Have I answered your question ? "

"Yes, surely, and it is a matter of much interest.
Are the Prince of Orange and Philip of Spain then
right fain and brotherly together ? " Charlotte had
listened to the queen's recital intently, with a delicate flush in her cheeks.

"Nay, far from it, *mignonne*," cried Jeanne
d'Albret. "That dark and bitter Spaniard has had
from boyhood, it is well known, an unquenchable
jealousy, an inborn suspiciousness toward his grace
of Orange. Probably the old emperor liked him too
well. Surely he might be pardoned if he took

greater pleasure in his gracious companionship than in that of a son who, men say, was never known once in his life to laugh heartily.''

" And this brother Louis, madame *ma cousine*, of whom you have such hopes, you speak of him as your friend. Have you seen him, then, frequently ? ''

" Yes ; yet I would have seen him far more frequently if I could. He has come to our court at Pau more than once from Geneva, where he studied for some years. Ah, Charlotte,'' and the queen glanced at the young abbess with arch raillery, "if you were not a *religieuse*, Louis of Nassau would be the cavalier I should wish to see win you if he could ! So gallant, so debonair, and withal so religious a young knight have I never seen. He is irresistible ! I could even fall in love with him myself, I, at my age,'' and the merry, unconstrained laughter of her majesty rang out upon the still air, a most unwonted sound in those precincts.

Charlotte glanced instinctively up the garden walk to the deep, shadowy portal of the cloister beyond the ancient oak tree. What could be more natural than to see a black-robed figure silently vanishing through the dim vista beyond ? And yet it was an hour when the nuns were not wont to be walking at will in the convent's cloisters and courts.

Jeanne d'Albret's keen eyes had also perceived the figure in its clinging draperies, with its bowed and hooded head and its noiseless step.

" Madame Crue, *n'est-ce pas ?* '' she asked dryly.

Charlotte assented.

They turned again and walked on.

" My child,'' said Jeanne d'Albret after a moment's silence, " there have been times since I came into this beautiful old convent of yours that I have even envied you its secure repose. It seems to possess a most sweet and holy atmosphere, so protected and so peaceful. I love those gray and ancient cloisters and that dim, vaulted chapel and your old stone cross yonder among the quiet graves. Your nuns are like those doves in their mild, meek ways. They go quietly about their pleasant tasks and every nook and corner, every bit of brass or piece of linen shows their exquisite care. The roses are marvelously sweet; the voices of your choir make holy music; I listened while you were within the chapel during mass and they stirred me strangely with those most affecting strains, 'O God, make haste to help me. O Lord, make speed to save me.' In faith, Charlotte, that music melted me to tears, and I weep not often. For a moment, as I said at first, I could have wished that my lot like yours had been cast here, far from the noise of camps and the glare of courts, sheltered and sure."

Greatly surprised at these words from her energetic and high-spirited friend, Charlotte awaited eagerly what should follow.

"But, little cousin," the queen proceeded with lowered voice, "when I see the scarce hid espionage, when I observe the face of your sub-prioress, those hard, watchful eyes, that cold mouth, and when I note on all the other faces that chill restraint which tells of life and energy suppressed, then I long rather to flee from the place, fair and peaceful though it is, and take you and all these companions of yours with me into freedom. Loving you as I do, Charlotte de Bourbon, I would rather see your heart burn itself out with the fire of devotion to faith and country in these fierce times, than to see that heart crushed out by the benumbing weight of this infinitely petty world of Jouarre!"

Carried beyond her own judgment and intent the queen had spoken with the impetuosity common to her when deeply stirred, and she looked with quick compunction at the profound sadness of Charlotte's face.

"And yet I should not have spoken so hastily," she quickly added. "There is another aspect to this case ; you are in an exalted place of influence, with power to lead many to God. You are absolute in your own realm and you rule that realm with wisdom. I have marked the spotless order and I have seen the clock-like regularity with which the day's work and worship are discharged. You are a woman now, my Charlotte, gentle, just, and wise like your dear mother——''

"Madame," cried Charlotte de Bourbon, interrupting her majesty and speaking with a mournfulness, and yet with a power which had not hitherto appeared in her almost languid gentleness, "madame, I am, alas, not a woman. I am not what you think me. I am what they have sought to make me here—*a cipher.*"

"How mean you?" asked Jeanne d'Albret watching the significant change in the lovely girlish face with earnest interest.

"I mean, madame," replied Charlotte, with the same serious emphasis, "that whether it be with good intent or ill, all these women about me have conspired to keep me a child, satisfied with a show of power ; petted and pampered, made to be the princess and the *grande dame*, but in all spiritual and actual influence—nothing. Oh, yes," the girl went on, her cheek flushing, her lips proudly, sadly smiling, "why is it I have never seen before what I see so plainly to-day ? It has been something magnifical to the old Abbey of Jouarre to name as its abbess a Bourbon princess ; and so they have been fain to keep me here ; I have been a pretty ornament—a decoration like a rose of gold, or a corbel of marble for the altar, without use or energy ; all they have asked of me is to be nothing more than this, that so unhindered they may rule this little world to suit their own will and purpose."

"This can hardly be true of all the women about you, my Charlotte. It may be true of one," said Jeanne d'Albret significantly.

"And since Cécile Crue rules all the others," returned Charlotte under her breath, "what matters it ? The same end is reached. Did you fancy, madame *ma cousine*, that I ruled in Jouarre ? Hardly could you have been wider of the mark. Like yourself I am a guest here. But unlike you I must remain even to the end."

Charlotte spoke each word slowly as if weighing for herself rather than for the Queen of Navarre its full significance.

The latter turned, fully facing her, and taking both her hands in hers, which were strong and supple and satin smooth, she said very low : " Madame Crue is coming down the walk, we may not again be alone together. This remember—never to despair ; never to forget your high heritage. More than all, in faith and true humility rise without fear to your rightful place and rule your realm as true woman and true Christian. Ah Sister Cécile," she said in a lively tone, the nun having now reached them, "Mademoiselle and I have had a happy little family visit here among your famous flowers. I was about to ask the name of this most lovely rose ? " and she bent and lifted the exquisite creamy head swaying in the sunlight on its glossy stem.

Cécile Crue knew that roses had not long been occupying the royal mind, but her part was pliable, obsequious deference and she proceeded to fill her part.

In the evening the Abbess of Jouarre entertained her royal cousin at a banquet in her own hall, served with something of stately splendor, as befitted the rank of her guest of honor.

With Jeanne d'Albret came her ladies, while Charlotte de Bourbon was attended as usual by her maidens, the two Jeannes. Present besides by reason of their office were the sub-prioress of the abbey and the priest in residence.

The Queen of Navarre had assumed a state costume in honor of her hostess, and was magnificent in a flowing robe of black lace worn over a closely fitting suit of white and silver brocade, a fashion of attire famous in the day under the name "transparencies."

Charlotte, as she advanced with maiden grace to meet her majesty, looked not a whit less royal than her guest. She was dressed in spotless white as ever, but with a long embroidered silken train, and with her golden hair, which was full and of waving luxuriance, tastefully disposed and covered only by a wide meshed net of gold thread, studded with pearls. Her color was deeper than its wont tonight, her eyes were full of a new light, soft and yet proud, and on her lips was a firmness of resolution in contrast with the charming yet pathetic languor which had hitherto been their most familiar expression.

As she led the Queen of Navarre across the brightly lighted hall and placed her at the head of the table at her own right hand every eye in the room followed the two, and those who had known her longest, marked with surprise the bearing of the youthful abbess, whose dignity and charm seemed rather augmented than overshadowed by the presence of the renowned queen.

The sub-prioress and the two Jeannes appeared of necessity in their conventual robes, but the rich dresses of the court-ladies of Navarre counterbalanced the mournfulness of these, and the scene at the table was brilliant and imposing.

The banquet was nearly at an end when Sister Radegonde entered the hall and crossing to the head of the table spoke in a low voice to the young abbess. After the exchange of several questions and replies, Charlotte turned to the queen and said :

" Madame, the sister tells me that a lace merchant from Brussels, a man of worthy and reputable appearance, has arrived at the abbey, accompanied by his servant. The curious circumstance is that he was on his way with his wares to visit your court at Pau, having been commended to your majesty's favor by a friend of yours. At Coulommiers he heard by accident, but most naturally, that you were at Jouarre on a visit and accordingly he has made haste to come hither. What say you? Would it be your wish to see the man now?"

Jeanne d'Albret heard this account with a somewhat indifferent countenance.

"I know not that I care to buy laces while on a journey of such length as this," she said carelessly. "And, moreover, why cannot the man wait till morning?"

One of her ladies bent over and reminded the queen that their own party would leave Jouarre early the following morning.

"Very true," was the reply, but with a doubtful and unconvinced accent.

"What have you there, Radegonde?" asked Charlotte.

Radegonde now handed her a small sealed note, which, marking its address, Charlotte passed on to the queen.

Opening it, still with a countenance expressive of slight and casual attention, Jeanne d'Albret read a reverential greeting of herself, followed only by these words:

I trust it may seem good to your majesty to receive the lace merchant, Tontorf. I believe his wares will please you.
LOUIS OF NASSAU.

Jeanne d'Albret dropped the missive carelessly into her lap, her face unchanged even to the curious eyes of Sister Cécile, which scanned it narrowly.

"How is it, *ma cousine*," she said lightly, smiling

at Charlotte, " have you holy maids of Jouarre use
for such trifling gauds and fangles ? The man
comes well commended, but the time seems to me
a thought inopportune."

" We need new lace, if it please you, madame,"
said Jeannette timidly to the abbess, "for the
altar."

" That is true, dear Jeannette," said Charlotte ;
" and moreover it will be a chance to while away
an hour for these noble ladies who I fear find the
monotony of our abbey dull and irksome. Yes,
Radegonde, if her majesty agrees, send the merchant in hither presently."

" Of a surety," said Jeanne d'Albret pleasantly ;
" I can always find pleasure in good lace, even if I
care not to buy."

As they rose from the table the queen crossed to
the fireplace where a few embers smoldered as
the August evening had chanced to be cool, and
seemed about to toss the note which she had just
read into the fire. As she bent to do this something
caused her to change her mind, and unnoticed, she
slipped it into her bosom.

Even as Jeanne d'Albret turned from the fireplace
and stood looking down the fine old vaulted hall so
unwontedly full that night of light and color, the
door was again thrown open and a man of somewhat striking aspect was ushered into the presence.

As this man passed slowly up the hall, followed
by a man-servant clad in drab moleskin hose and
jerkin and carrying a pack enclosed in brown leather,
he was seen to be upward of fifty years, a man
with a clear-featured and clean-shaven face which
contrasted not unpleasantly in its firm lines and
ruddy color with his hair, which was absolutely
white. There were lines as of thought and study
about brow and eyes of the man, and a singular,
brooding thoughtfulness dwelt in the latter which
made the face one not soon forgotten. For the rest,

the lace merchant was of goodly port and mien, well though slenderly built, dressed in doublet and trunk hose of fine cloth of a dark claret color, with long black stockings and with broad, delicately embroidered ruffles at throat and wrists.

Charlotte de Bourbon had crossed to her cousin's side, and led by the nun, the merchant advanced and knelt in dignified but humble obeisance before the princely pair, kissing the edge of the robe of each. Then rising at the bidding of Jeanne d'Albret he received permission to present his wares, which the servant now proceeded to unfold and produce from his leather pack.

While this was going forward Maître Tontorf stood in a respectful but composed attitude at a slight remove from the royal ladies, while from time to time his eyes strayed around the room with a glance peculiarly swift and searching.

A table had been drawn up upon which the laces were now laid, Tontorf stepping forward and displaying them, handling them with marked dexterity of touch.

Five minutes sufficed to bring the heads of all the ladies present together over the table, for the dealer's wares proved to be of rare and exquisite quality, and even Sister Cécile could not withstand their attractive power.

Ten minutes passed. The interest in the laces was noticeably on the increase. Several pieces surprisingly fine and cheap had been produced. There was food for much discussion and the ladies proved eager to discuss and compare values. Very quietly then Maître Tontorf withdrew from the little group by a few paces and standing before the chimney-piece seemed to study the fading figure of old Saint Theodehilde in the ancient portrait with marked interest.

This action on the part of the dealer did not escape Sister Cécile. From the group of chatter-

ing women her eyes cautiously and steadily followed him. His earnest scrutiny of the historic
portrait began to prove annoying to her. A sense
of uneasiness concerning the man's action displaced
that of short-lived interest in his wares.

Presently she moved noiselessly nearer to the
place where Maître Tontorf stood. Turning his
eyes, without otherwise moving, and seeming
neither startled nor disturbed by her silent approach the lace merchant said in a strikingly well-
modulated voice:

" Rather an interesting old portrait, madame, but
I should advise her grace the Abbess of Jouarre to
have it presently more securely fitted to its frame.
Do you notice a considerable space," and Maître
Tontorf pointed with one finger, " at the right, between the portrait and the oakwood of the mould-
ing ? "

He turned as he spoke and fixed his eyes in a
direct gaze, mild and musing upon the pallid face
of Sister Cécile. A deep, dark flush rose slowly
and suffused her cheeks and even mounted to the
temples. An instant later she clasped her hands
beneath the long black folds of her sleeves, and
turned with downcast eyes as if it were not permitted for a *religieuse* to hold longer converse with
a man.

" Possibly you are right," she murmured coldly.
" It is a matter for the house carpenter."

XI

THE DAUGHTER OF A KINGLY LINE

O N the twenty-fourth of August, being St. Bartholomew's Day, a scene of singular interest was enacted in the ancient Abbey of Jouarre.

The ringing, solemn and prolonged, of the chapel bell at an unwonted hour called all the nuns, servants, and retainers together to the chapter-house, but for what purpose all inquired in vain.

As they waited in wondering silence the bell ceased tolling. Then in the full habit of her office and order, her white veil fastened about the head by a slender circlet of gold, her tall crozier in her hand, Charlotte de Bourbon, Abbess of Jouarre, walked alone and slowly into the lofty ecclesiastical chamber.

So stately, so imposing, and so noble had they never seen her, and yet there was something of the shy and gentle modesty of her youth and of her natural habit in the slight droop of her head upon the slender neck, and in the appealing sweetness of her mouth; but in the blue eyes, under their level lids, dwelt a light of conquering courage at which all her world marveled.

Until this day their abbess had been among them as a child, a princely and a well-beloved child, but as she herself had said, destitute of power and without energy. What signified this strange scene? Surely this was not enacted at the instance of Cécile Crue, for hers was the blankest face and the most perplexed in the company, and yet heretofore for many years hers had been the operating mind and hand in every event of importance at Jouarre.

Charlotte de Bourbon, crossing the wide, octagonal chapter-house chamber, now mounted to a
raised and canopied stone seat, and standing before
it, lifted her right hand, pronouncing in a clear voice
the words :

"In the name of the Father, and of the Son, and
of the Holy Ghost, Amen."

Every person in the room had risen and stood
now with eyes fixed upon the young abbess, listening with eager ears for what should follow.

Without tremor or hesitation she proceeded to
address the chapter, the nuns, the novices and servants in words of affectionate greeting, and all
marveled greatly at the authority with which she
spoke.

"I have called you together," she said, "to cite
you to the past, imploring your pity for what I have
suffered and your pardon for my neglect, my ignorance, and my faults. I have not been your
head ; I have been scarce better to you than a play-
thing or an ornament. I have not been a woman,
but a child.

"Dear sisters of our holy order, I have this to
say to you in few words, as I have no gift of speech
to hold you long. I was made your abbess in my
childhood, against my will and my most earnest
protests and prayers, and only because it was my
father's wish. With bitter tears and a broken
heart, being driven by cruel threats and heartless
menaces, I came into your presence, scarcely conscious, such was my confusion and anguish, yielding only because my childish feebleness had been
overborne by the force of tyranny. Thus I received my sacrosanct investiture as abbess of this
house.

"But how was this holy office solemnized ? No
bishop bestowed the benediction, but an unqualified
priest. The good Bishop of Meaux would not have
consented to such a mockery, and his presence was

not desired. Madame du Paraclete, who gave me the veil, was not herself an ordained abbess, and consequently could not make my profession lawful ; the written paper from which I read my vows was a counterfeit, a travesty on the real vows, smoothed and altered to pacify my childish fears.''

As Charlotte de Bourbon continued, recalling and recounting these circumstances of her consecration, a scarlet spot burned on either cheek, a high and imperious light flashed from her eyes, her voice rang through the vaulted room fearless and firm. She was every inch the daughter of a kingly line.

"So then, by force, by fraud, at an uncanonical age, and without benediction of a bishop, the child was made your abbess. These facts are known in part to all of you, in greater part to a few of you. To Madame Cécile Crue and to Père Ruzé they are known wholly, to every last heart-throb of the child's agony. To-morrow, in this room, in presence of a notary I shall require the signatures of such of you as were knowing to these facts to a document clearly stating them which I conceive belongs of due right in the archives of this monastery as well as to myself.''

At this declaration the countenance of Cécile Crue had become fairly livid, while the amazement of all the other nuns and novices at the sudden transformation of their maiden-abbess kindled to a passion of adoring loyalty. Was this the pathetic, languid child of Jouarre ? Nay, rather, they saw at last a right royal and worthy head, an abbess of holy heart and of power commanding, such a head as Jouarre had never known. Through all the company ran a murmur of sympathy and devotion.

"Holy Mary, Mother of God, blessed art thou ! The child is a woman and has come to her own,'' whispered Sister Marie Brette to old Radegonde, while the two Jeannes clasped each other's hands with adoring glances.

"To-day, sisters beloved," continued Charlotte de Bourbon, "I declare myself, in spite of all that is past, your present head. I have now attained the age of eighteen and I wish to enter upon my full charge. No longer among the small number of our sisterhood is the office of sub-prioress required. According to the power and authority vested in me, I now and herewith, in presence of you all, declare that office vacant, this to be confirmed, if it be your will, by the chapter in session following.

With softer looks and a voice which trembled now with deep emotion the young abbess continued:

"It shall now become my ceaseless effort in all humility, obedience, and love, to grow up into a worthy headship, to be among you as a true abbess, guiding, purifying, and upbuilding the flock, fulfilling the will and commands of our blessed Jesu, Son of Mary, spotless Lamb of God," with which words the abbess and all present bent the head in reverent devotion, making the sign of the cross upon forehead and breast.

After a solemn chant and the benediction pronounced by the breathless and astonished confessor, the now self-consecrated abbess, for such she seemed to all of them, crozier in hand with slow steps and noble humility of mien, walked from the place, a look of high, angelic devotion resting upon her face.

The day which followed witnessed the formal signature of the document which the young girl had framed in due form with the assistance of Maître Bonnard, advocate, of Jouarre. It set forth in full, without extenuation or malice, the conditions attending her consecration in the March of 1559.

Without a dissenting vote the chapter next proceeded to carry out the action proposed by their abbess, which declared the office of sub-prioress abolished. In cold and envenomed bitterness of spirit Cécile Crue asked and obtained permission to be transferred to a neighboring convent, to which she presently departed.

Quietly but with firm purpose and energy the girl abbess now began to carry out her new purposes in the selfish and petty life of the little community. A new spirit of consecration and of outgoing charity took possession of the sisters of Jouarre, and a new and broader activity quickly stirred to life.

Then, when peace and charity seemed to have begun their reign, the shadow fell again, for the influences set in motion by Cécile Crue had been working, and into the abbey court on Saint Benedict's eve rode Jean Ruzé, hard set to do his worst.

Thus it fell out that the bishop-elect of Angers, author of the famous treatise, " *La verité et anti-quité de la Foi catholique* " once again sat at her own table *en tête-à-tête* with an Abbess of Jouarre.

As the priest glanced from time to time at the face and figure of the stately golden-haired maiden opposite him, the contrast between his present hostess and his hostess at this same table eight years before, recurred to his mind forcibly. In spite of the antipathy and fear which she felt toward her guest, the frank innocence, the bright bloom, and the exquisite gentleness of Charlotte de Bourbon were sharply set against his memory of the cold, repellent, mocking worldliness of Louise de Long-Vic.

But although Jean Ruzé was quite capable of admiring youth and loveliness in a woman he was, as prelate, capable of ruthlessly crushing every instinct which might have led him to chivalrous and manly protection. The purpose of his presence was soon disclosed. His coming was the slow fruitage of seed sowed by Cécile Crue at the time of the visit to the abbey of the Queen of Navarre.

Rising from the table at the close of the meal, Charlotte turned with resolute initiative to Ruzé, feeling as if the hated presence of this man had turned her to steel, and said :

"Monsieur will be so good as to explain his mission here speedily, as my duties at this hour are many and pressing."

Surprised at the clear unflinching courage of her looks and the note of authority in her demand, Ruzé bowed repeatedly with his wonted suavity before he attempted to reply.

"I ask simply as representing his grace, the Duc your father, Mademoiselle has made some changes at Jouarre, *n'est-ce pas ?* "

Charlotte bowed slightly in assent.

"I note the absence of Sister Cécile Crue. I hear that Mademoiselle has deposed her from her position as sub-prioress of this convent. Was she then not a faithful and diligent servant ? "

"Faithful to herself," replied Charlotte steadily ; "incomparably diligent in your service, monsieur. For mine there was something to be desired. I do not employ women to listen behind doors nor to secrete themselves in the crevices of walls to overhear the private converse of others. Furthermore, I do not choose that such things shall be done where I am mistress. Madame Crue showed herself no longer capable of serving the sisterhood acceptably in a position of trust and honor. Is this answer sufficient ? "

It was a bold and dangerous challenge and Ruzé felt his blood tingle with the sense of encountering a foe worthy of his steel. Still smiling coldly he now remarked :

"It is commonly rumored that Madame Jeanne d'Albret is at present the actual, albeit invisible, head of Jouarre, and that it is her purpose, by insidious and underhanded operations, to turn it, little by little, into a seat of heresy."

"If such rumor exists elsewhere than in the imagination of monsieur I will give him full authority to contradict it. Insidious and underhand action is impossible to the Queen of Navarre, however common to her enemies. It is wholly, contemptibly false."

Jean Ruzé glanced aside at Charlotte's face with genuine amazement. What had come over this girl, that she so fairly and fearlessly defied him ? He fancied he had broken the strength of her will while she was yet a child. Did she then know that he had power to lay again a fearful weight upon her spirit ?

" Madame d'Albret however remains in constant correspondence with Mademoiselle, I believe," he said after a little pause, "and her majesty is still, it is supposed, as obstinate a Huguenot as ever, even to the defying of his holiness himself."

Charlotte made no reply.

"It will not escape Mademoiselle," Ruzé continued with his crafty blandness, "that some slight suspicion may be aroused in the mind of the holy father regarding her own Catholicity if she continue in intimacy with so rebellious and troublesome a heretic as Madame d'Albret ? "

" I hardly flatter myself so far as to fancy that his holiness takes cognizance of the motions of a demoiselle so insignificant as myself," replied Charlotte simply.

" Then allow me to assure you, dear lady, that no event nor action of yours of any importance passes without cognizance of the humble servant of his holiness, else would he be indeed a faithless under-shepherd."

" Monsieur refers to himself ? "

Ruzé bowed and proceeded :

" Let Mademoiselle not deceive herself. Innovations and changes have been already brought about in this convent which are fully known by his holiness. If matters take on a shade deeper tint, if by any means the Abbess of Jouarre secretly or openly wavers in her allegiance to Holy Church, there are means swift and sufficient to bring her back to duty or to put an end to an influence not conformable to the church's high interests.''

Charlotte's color changed perceptibly, but her voice did not tremble.

"Monsieur Ruzé doubtless has reference to the agencies of the Inquisition.''

Ruzé again bowed, glancing with remorseless avidity at the face of the young abbess to note the effect of this suggestion.

For a moment the young girl turned from that look of malign menace. It was as if she were taking time fully to face the ominous crisis, fraught to her perchance with life and death. But if for a moment she faltered, faith conquered in the end, for it was with look fearless and stern and high, the look of the saint and the martyr, that she turned again to the priest.

"Monsieur Ruzé," she said, with incredible calmness, "long ago, when I was but a weak, defenseless child, you threatened me with the terrors of the church as you come to threaten me now. In the crypt of Saint Paul, on one certain night you wot of, my free childhood lay slain before you, slain by your own hand. Summoning to aid you every source of dread and peril, with a cruelty which to this day seems to me beyond belief, you intimidated me to do your will and the will of my father although, in the event, my life itself was well-nigh crushed and was saved only by the devotion of one old, humble woman. For what you did then you must one day give an account before God.

"To-night you come again, bringing with you the mysterious menace of a terrible force wherewith you again hope to chain and overwhelm my spirit which is seeking God in simplicity and truth. I tell you plainly that you come in vain. I am true and loyal to the holy Catholic Church and hope ever to remain her dutiful child; but it is for love of her holy truth that I adhere to her, not for fear of such threats as these. I shall obey the voice of God, not the voice of men. If the time should ever come that the machinery of the Inquisition should be sought to be used against me, as born of the house and lineage of Saint Louis, I shall appeal with confidence to the majesty of France; but as a child of God I shall appeal with a far greater confidence to my heavenly Father. If death comes, believe me, I can die."

A change, little by little, had come over the face of Jean Ruzé as he listened to these words of Charlotte de Bourbon. He stood as if overawed, unable to remove his eyes from hers, while his own face grew strangely pallid and he was seized with an inner trembling. It was he this time who was overmastered. His sharp and poisoned weapons had fallen harmless before the divine faith and courage of this maiden, and his own seared conscience was pierced by the memory of the spiritual violence he had done her innocent childhood.

Murmuring a few half-intelligible words of apology he withdrew in strange haste from the hall and betook himself to the guest house, where he passed a night of mental torment.

The following morning he was, to his own surprise, summoned to the presence of the abbess.

Gently, but with something of imperiousness, Charlotte de Bourbon laid before him the parchment on which was written the true and authentic description of her consecration as Abbess of Jouarre by force and fraud.

"*Voilà*, monsieur," she said coldly; "better than these women whose signatures follow, you are acquainted with all that befell on that night, and by what manner of device I was made *supérieure*. You will be so good therefore as to append your signature here," and bending she touched a space on the parchment, her eyes fixed full and steadily upon the face of the priest which showed in this morning light, in its wan and sunken aspect, as the face of a craven coward.

He glanced over the words of the document with strong effort to regain the mask of composure and of judicial deliberation which he usually wore so successfully.

"It is not necessary for you to take time to read the paper, I think, Monsieur Ruzé," said Charlotte; "Madame Crue has already made you familiar with its import. You have simply to sign."

Strange reversal of the relation of these two, the man of the world, the facile Jesuit, the experienced court ecclesiastic, and this simple cloister-bred girl!

As if acting without volition Ruzé took the pen and signed, then precipitately left the hall, called for his horse and his escort, and rode away from Jouarre with all haste.

XII

THE HOUSE IN THE LANGE DELFT

ON that same Bartholomew's Day in which the youthful Abbess of Jouarre came to her own, two hundred miles to the north of Jouarre the sun was shining broadly over the streets and squares of the Zeeland capital, Middelburg, the proud "city of the center." Center, indeed, was the rich and stately old town of its island of Walcheren, center also of the commerce of all the North Netherlands, and the center of Middelburg was its ancient Gothic abbey, See of a bishop, and scene of many a brilliant gathering of Knights of the Fleece and great ecclesiastic lords.

Important, powerful, opulent, and jealous of its rights, Middelburg possessed in the time of which we write a cosmopolitan reputation greater perhaps than any of its sister cities, by reason of the foreign commerce which drew to it in force the trade of England and Scotland, of Italy, France, and Spain, and which made merchant princes of its burghers. While the trade of Bruges had already begun to decline, that of Middelburg was still increasing.

But the inhabitants owed their wealth and their privileges to a circumstance which bestowed upon Middelburg a prestige greater and more enduring than that gained by its commercial prosperity. To the citizens of Middelburg had been granted in 1217 the earliest charter or *Keure* in the Dutch language, the first charter ever issued in the provinces of Holland and Zeeland for protection of the rights of life and property of its citizens and defense of their liberties against tyranny of kings or emperors.

The sober dignity of the burghers of Middelburg, hospitable to strangers, and yet reticent and even impassive, the subdued splendor of living of the heads of its powerful corporations, notably the great wine lords (Wijnheeren), the judicial gravity of its magistrates, and the picturesque pomp of its bishop, all comported well with the appearance of the city itself.

Circular in form, it was builded around the great abbey which enclosed a square of enormous proportions, approached like a fortress on all sides by a labyrinth of narrow, winding passages and feudal arches. The primitive moat, drained and filled, had been converted into a street which described a perfect circle around the outermost fringe of the abbey limits, and was known as the Lange Delft, or long ditch. Outside this was a series of streets constructed in concentric circles, the last circle being the stout city wall, with the wide blue waters of the canal surrounding all and permitting the largest ships afloat in those days to approach the commodious, busy, thronging quays.

The great market place of Middelburg, not far removed from the abbey precincts, unshaded and of enormous dimensions, was upon the afternoon in question flooded by the August sun, whose beams scintillated from the numberless airy pinnacles of the Gothic Stadthuis and brought out into bold relief the richly canopied statues of its magnificent façade. High into the blue of the summer sky rose the graceful belfry, pierced by mullioned windows and flanked by slender turrets. The clock on the belfry showed the hour of five and on the stroke the clear carillon of the Stadthuis chimes, familiarly known by the name of "*Gekke Betje*" (Giddy Betty), pealed out merrily upon the heated air.

The market place was almost deserted, the burghers preferring the coolness of their shops to the heat of the afternoon sun, but a tall, young fellow of eighteen, who was just turning into the Lange Delft, glanced up with a half-smile of indulgent derision at the clock in the belfry.

Distinctly seen from the square, lifting its lofty spire far above the red and clustering house roofs, rose "*Lange Jan,*" the tower of the abbey church. The moments passed and still no sound could be heard from its belfry. In dignified silence it stood there, its fine proportions arrayed, it might almost seem, in grave rivalry with the exuberant Renaissance elegance of the Stadthuis.

Five minutes passed and then rich and deep, with full sonorous tones the chimes of *Lange Jan* for five o'clock were heard ringing out over the old abbey roofs, over the silent market place, and the substantial houses of the burghers. This interval between the voices of *Gekke Betje* and of *Lange Jan* occurred according to an unbroken custom, upon which the younger and more romantic Middelburg folk built many a fanciful tale, hinging usually upon a love affair between the noble and stately Jan and the frivolous and impulsive Betje.

Several minutes before the abbey chimes had caught up with their impetuous neighbor, the youth whom we have seen turning from the market place into the Lange Delft had reached and entered a mansion of a rich and soberly imposing exterior. Like all the burgher dwellings of the day this house stood immediately upon the street, but unlike many of them it was approached through a large portico. This portico in itself gave marked distinction to the dwelling, being built of dark oak deeply paneled in the style which immediately preceded the Renaissance, and entirely covered with rich and delicate carving. Among the various devices of the significant ornamentation the initials A. H. gave token to the owner's name. For the rest the house possessed a wide façade of quartered stone, with panels of fine carving set in above the windows of the ground floor, while quaint and graceful arabesques capped the rows of windows, until the fifth and highest was crowned by a small tower of elegant design flanked by the steep battlements of the roof.

Passing through a hall lined with massive chests and cabinets, Norbert Tontorf, for this was the youth's name, opened a door opposite the one which gave entrance from the Lange Delft, and stepped immediately into a broad sunny courtyard paved with round cobblestones and surrounded by buildings of brick, of solid and regular structure two stories in height, the famous printery of Mijnheer Nikolaas Tontorf.

The red gabled roof with its dormer windows shone warm in the sun ; beneath it the walls were covered thickly with a luxuriant grapevine of ancient growth, interspersed with the darker leaves of the ivy. The rows of casement windows stood wide open, the shutters with their painted quarterings swung in the light wind ; voices came from the interior, and figures could be seen as they moved to and fro, or bent over their work. A vaulted passage gave entrance to a narrow side street, and here several heavy carts stood awaiting their unloading.

Men and boys, laborers and apprentices, at work around the carts called to each other in loud and cheerful voices ; a flock of pigeons flying down from the roof surrounded a charming girl of twelve, who had corn in her hands which she scattered abroad for them. The whole scene was fraught with busy life and contented activity.

Crossing the courtyard with an occasional salute to the apprentices, who doffed their caps as he passed them, Norbert Tontorf was not sorry to escape the force of the ardent sun as he stepped into the shadow of a species of loggia, where an open flight of stairs gave access to the offices of the second story.

The stairway was massively built of oak and the handrail terminated in two Zeeland lions rampant with gilded manes and tails. At a little distance was a well from which young Tontorf paused to draw a draught of sparkling water in a shallow iron cup swung from the pump by a rusty chain.

In every motion of his well-knit limbs as well as in the frank, sunburned countenance, and in the steady gray eyes which now looked out over the edge of the broad drinking cup, the sturdy independent character of the lad could easily be read. A shock of curly yellow hair showed under the small student cap he wore, cropped close to a well-shaped head. As he dropped the cup to go swinging on its chain he called to the young girl across the courtyard, in a ringing, masterful voice:

"Heh, Jacqueline! that black pigeon is none of thine. A shame to entice away our neighbor's fowls to fill thine own flock!"

Not waiting for the answer which the girl looked up with a merry defiance to call back, Norbert sprang up the oak stairs, pushed open a door, and entered a low-ceiled room of considerable dimensions.

At a table near an open window, through which the sunny air was streaming, sat a middle-aged matron of dignified yet winning aspect, and beside her a slender girl with long flaxen braids of hair, strongly resembling Norbert.

Both Vrouw Tontorf and her daughter Helma were bending over small printed folios on which they were illuminating by hand initial letters and borders of brilliant colors and lacelike delicacy of design.

A feminine orderliness and refinement were plainly perceptible in all their appliances, while both mother and daughter wore a certain patrician aspect in no way interfered with by their artistic handiwork.

H

"Welcome, Norbert," said Vrouw Tontorf, looking up from her work ; "where hast thou been all
these hours of the afternoon ? "

"Why dost thou ask, mother ? " said Helma
Tontorf, "since Norbert is sure to have been at
the Rouenische Kade watching for an incoming
galleon."

" But none came ? " asked the mother with falling
cadence as of repeated disappointment.

" Nay, but Piet Blaeser said the *'Fleur d'Auxerre'*
might arrive to-night. I shall therefore go down
again to the Kade after supper. It is surely high
time that letter or message reached us from my
father."

Vrouw Tontorf's face betrayed a wearing anxiety,
but it was Helma who spoke.

" It is now two months and more, is it not, since
my father left Middelburg ? and many weeks since
aught of tidings has reached us."

In silence Norbert crossed to his mother's side,
placed his arm affectionately around her shoulder,
and bent to kiss her cheek.

"Dear little *moeder*," he said softly, "I am not
uneasy ; oh, no, that is not at all what takes me to
the Kade——"

At that moment a footfall was heard on the stairs,
and the young Jacqueline, the loose waves of her
light brown hair blowing behind her, her dark eyes
fairly blazing with excitement, burst into the room,
exclaiming :

"The father has come ! he is here, safe and
sound ! Hurry, hurry, and greet him ! He is
awaiting us in the Gossaert-Saal ! " and without
further pause Jacqueline bounded down the stairs
again.

Vrouw Wendelmutha Tontorf was the eldest
daughter of Adolf Hardinck, thirty years earlier a
prominent burgher of Middelburg and Master of the
Rolls. He had been architect and householder of

the fine old mansion, and it was his initials which were still to be seen carved in tracery in the panels of the oak portico.

Suspected, with more or less reason, of the Lutheran heresy, and in the form considered most opprobrious, that of the followers of Menno and Hoffmann, Adolf Hardinck fell a victim to the edict of the tenth of June, in the year of grace 1535, having been put to death by order of his imperial majesty, Charles V., in the fierce persecution wherewith he sought to root out the first growth of heresy from the Netherlands with fire and sword.

For what caprice of carelessness or pity the records fail to show, the lives of the wife and children of the Master of the Rolls of the free city of Middelburg were spared, and their stately house escaped confiscation.

By the industry and genius of the husband of Wendelmutha, a prosperous printing establishment had been developed, to suit the needs of which the house had been enlarged until its present proportions had beeen reached. The family residence, however, as it stood fronting the Lange Delft, remained unchanged in its general aspect since the day of Adolf Hardinck's death.

The great drawing room at the left of the entrance was known in the family as the Gossaert-Saal, from a notably fine portrait of the Master of the Rolls, by the famous Mabuse, which was rightly held as its chief glory. Albeit after a sober sort the room was splendid and stately, for in the refinements and luxuries of domestic life the people of the Netherlands at this time surpassed all their contemporaries.

The walls were hung with Flemish tapestry and richly wainscoted in black oak; the windows were blazoned with the arms of the Hardincks and Tontorfs; the furniture consisted of massive tables of old walnut of deep, warm hue, and substantial

carved chairs covered in leather. Many family portraits besides the Mabuse adorned the walls. Cabinets of Dutch oak, and also of inlaid ebony, held
rare vases and jars of old *faience* and curious goblets
of Venetian glass and of *repoussé* silver.

In front of the great carved chimney piece in the
coolness and dim rich dusk of the room stood, waiting to receive wife and children, Nikolaas Tontorf,
Dean of the Printer's Guild of Middelburg, who,
as the lace merchant from Brussels, visited Jouarre
scarce two weeks before.

Here in another moment he was found and welcomed home with overflowing gladness.

Having refreshed himself with the delicious food
and wine brought him by a servant-woman in
snowy cap and kerchief, whose delight in her master's return seemed as great as that of his family,
Mijnheer Tontorf announced himself ready to recount certain experiences of his journey.

"I shall tell you first of all that which took place
last of all," quoth the quondam lace merchant with
his grave smile at the eager and affectionate looks
fixed upon him. "It is freshest in my mind and it
will explain why I have returned so much earlier
than I looked to do.

"You will recall my prime purpose—to convey
the Bibles and the letter of Count Louis of Navarre
as speedily as possible to her majesty of Navarre.
As on former journeys, I provided myself with laces
to produce for sale as an ostensible object; and,
pursuing my way southward toward Nérac, I had
gone so far through the fertile province of La Brie
as the ancient walled town of Coulommiers. Here
I had purposed spending the night, when an incident occurred which caused me to retrace my steps
with haste.

"In the public house to which I had betaken
myself, Fritz fell in at the table with a varlet
from the Abbey of Jouarre, which we had passed

on its green hill above a little river on our way from Meaux.

"The fellow appeared to me a kind of confidential servant of the establishment, and overhearing him make mention of her majesty of Navarre, I joined myself forthwith to the pair of them, and sent for a bottle or two of red wine, with which they drank my health cheerfully.

"It soon appeared that this varlet, Lambinot by name, had been sent post-haste with a letter of great importance from the sub-prioress of the convent at Jouarre to a priest by the name of Ruzé, at Angers.

"Little by little I gathered from the fellow, who was very willing to show his familiarity with the affairs of his abbey, that its nominal head was a demoiselle of but eighteen, a princess of the blood; while the sub-prioress, Madame Crue, in reality held everything in her own hands—the affairs of the young abbess with the rest.

"It further appeared that the Queen of Navarre herself was even then on a visit to Jouarre, and that following a long *tête-à-tête* between her majesty and her cousin the abbess, in her great hall on the preceding afternoon, he, Lambinot, had been very early that morning summoned by the sub-prioress and sent on his present errand.

"'Oh, you can lay a wager,' said the fellow winking cunningly, 'that Madame Crue lost not a syllable of what their serene majesties and royal highnesses had to say to each other! Pretty rich stuff it was too, I'll venture to say. The Queen of Navarre is the worst heretic in France.'

"'Does the sub-prioress listen at doors then?' I asked with feigned carelessness. 'I suppose that is the fashion of women in these convents. What else have they to divert themselves with, poor things?'

"To this he replied with coarse scorning: 'Nay,

then, master, you must think Madame Crue a
clumsy, common sort, little better than a serving
wench! Ha, ha! *Ventre-saint-gris!* She has a
trick worth two of that, and it's Loys Lambinot
who served her to it too. Nothing can escape her,
I'll swear to that.'

"I need not tell you that before the man was
well out of Coulommiers our horses were ready and
we on our way back to Jouarre Abbey, hoping to
be in time to have speech of the queen and to deliver into her keeping the letter of Count Louis.

"I found a noble and ancient monastery and a
kindly reception. With little delay I was ushered
with my lace pack, the other being left in safe hiding, into the abbess' hall, where I found the Queen
of Navarre herself and other ladies."

"Oh, father, pray tell us what the queen is
like!" cried little Jacqueline with childish eagerness.

Mijnheer Tontorf looked into her bright eyes with
a fond smile.

"The Queen of Navarre is a right royal lady,
with eyes almost as bright as thine, little maid, and
a gracious and noble mien; but I think if thou
couldst have seen both, thy eyes would have dwelt
longest upon the white abbess, as many call her,
for among a group of beautiful women she was indeed fairest."

"Tell us more of her, father," said Norbert,
keenly interested.

"The Abbess of Jouarre is a lily-like maiden,
tall, graceful, and, although commanding, of an
exceeding gentleness withal. She has large shining eyes of a most heavenly azure, a proud and
yet a tender mouth, glinting golden hair and a fair
delicate color. She was clad—they tell me it is
ever her custom—all in white, with little of the
nun about her garb save a quaint severity of cut.
She has a low, quiet voice, and a smile which begins

in her eyes like a dawning. But you see I have not the right words! For there was a something well-nigh celestial and yet strangely wistful and pathetic in the whole aspect of her. She was made abbess at twelve years, I learn, without her mother's consent and wholly against her own will."

"Oh, how terrible!" murmured Vrouw Tontorf.

"I found at once," continued her husband, "that the sub-prioress, Madame Crue, was present—a pale-faced, ascetic woman, with thin lips and sharp eyes. While the ladies amused themselves with the laces I took my chance to observe the room. The walls were solidly lined with Cordova leather, and from the nature of the situation did not seem to me to furnish the particular coign of vantage from which I doubted not Madame Crue must have gathered the substance of her long letter to the priest, Ruzé.

"My attention was soon drawn to the projecting wooden mantelpiece sheathing the chimney, as does this one, and reaching even to the rafters above. Here was built into the framework an ancient portrait of some early patroness or founder, I cared little who, but noted at once that the picture did not quite fill its frame, a narrow gap intervening on the right. Convinced that I had discovered the trick of which Lambinot had made mention, since a space with scant doubt existed between the portrait and the chimney, I purposely drew the attention of Madame Crue to my scrutiny. I believed it would be possible to discern by her countenance, when taken thus unaware, if this were her listeners' gallery. Her changing color and evident uneasiness were full proof to me of this, and I believe the poor lady was most unhappy as she presently perforce left the hall with the nuns and ladies-in-waiting."

"Oh, father, how could you have been so bold?" cried Jacqueline.

"What less could I do than come to the succor and protection from her enemies of so lovely a creature as this white abbess?" asked her father.

"Left alone with these two royal dames," he continued, "I assisted her majesty in bringing to light the contents of the letter of the Count of Nassau, which being writ in sensitive ink she had well-nigh missed. Then as she read I said plainly to Mademoiselle de Bourbon, since time failed for many words:

"'Madame, you are watched.'

"'Yes,' she made answer quite simply; 'I have been all my life.'

"Then I spoke of the man Lambinot and of my conjecture as to the hiding-place of Madame Crue on the previous evening, and was straightway confirmed by Madame d'Albret, who had noticed a motion of the ancient picture while they conversed. A hasty examination of a disused chamber and loft beyond the hall showed a ladder so placed as to give ready access to the niche between canvas and chimney. A few boards had been sawed away and a listeners' gallery easily formed.

"'All that we said yestereven has been overheard, then, by Madame Crue!' cried Mademoiselle, as we returned to her hall.

"'Yes,' said her majesty, whose face showed deepest anxiety, 'and not only so, but it is now in substance on its way to Père Ruzé in Angers.'

"Mademoiselle de Bourbon turned white as death. This priest Ruzé has a cruel power over her which he has cruelly exerted in times past at the will of her father, who is perhaps the harshest bigot in the Catholic ranks. Cécile Crue forms the connecting link between the young Abbess of Jouarre and, I fear with little doubt, the Inquisition itself. Madame d'Albret, with her knowledge of the powers at work, had good cause for anxious looks."

Norbert Tontorf rose from his place and strode up and down the great room with compressed lips and a flash of indignation in his eyes.

"By my troth," he cried, "I believe I will myself make my way to that same Jouarre, if so you call it, and offer my services in the defense of its lorn and lovely lady. Shame upon us if we leave her thus defenseless with those geires swooping down upon her."

"Young cavaliers are scarce welcome in convents, my son," said Vrouw Tontorf with a smile, in which motherly sympathy for the impulse of the youth and amusement at its irrelevance were mingled. "Continue, my husband. Your tale is of strange interest."

"The position of the demoiselle is not, Norbert, wholly without support or defense," said his father gravely. "The Queen of Navarre has, as I had heard full often, but now saw for myself, a high-hearted courage. 'Fear nothing, little cousin,' she said, 'our God will defend us and we will trust ourselves quietly in his hands. Friends like Coligny and Condé will aid me if need be in your defense. And who knows? Perhaps it is even full time for you to break wholly and boldly with this woman, so evil and malign, and yourself be mistress of Jouarre, bringing to naught with your own holy and maiden bravery the counsels of the enemies of our Saviour. For myself, I have met dangers far greater than this, unscathed. Shall I fear priests, who have escaped the hands of popes and kings?'

"With great calmness she then said to me: 'I learn from the letter of my friend, the young Count of Nassau, that it is you who have printed my letter to the Cardinal d'Armagnac. I learn also what precious wares you have brought me, according to my great desire, other than these laces which have to-night so well served your purpose.

Have you not even now with you one of those same Bibles that you so courageously continue to print in Middelburg and scatter through France and Flanders in spite of the bloody edicts ? '

" I drew from my inner pocket that volume which thou, Helma, hast so carefully illuminated. She praised its beauty, and then, kissing the young abbess on brow and lips, and placing the little book between her hands, said : ' Now, dear child, let the word of God comfort and lead thee, and may the Lord himself defend thee with his own right hand.' "

The face of Helma was radiant with exalted pleasure.

" How beautiful," she exclaimed, her eyes filling with tears, " that the lovely, lonely young princess in that far-away convent has my own dear book upon which I worked so long ! Did she appear to prize it ? "

" Yes, truly. She pressed it to her lips, and then hid it in her bosom, and I thought a change came over her face ; something of the fearless spirit of Jeanne d'Albret was reflected there, and her tears flowed no more. We spoke then of my mission to Nérac, and the queen gladly accepted the further care of conveying the packet of books thither by her own people. They were to continue their journey on the day following by way of Châtillon in order to have brief conference with Admiral Coligny. The letter of Count Louis of Nassau contained much matter of importance to the Huguenot interests, and most opportune it seemed that this should have reached her majesty before her visit to Coligny. She then and there hastily wrote a reply which I am presently to deliver. I hear the count is just now at Spa, drinking the waters for his health, and holding conference with Brederode and other patriotic gentlemen for the health of the country.

" But for the matter in hand! Having thus un-expectedly discharged myself of my undertaking, and being saved the journey across all France, to return to you and home suddenly became a joyful possibility. Accordingly I set out not much later for Meaux, which Fritz and I reached, tired men with more tired beasts, at cock-crowing of the morning.

"Here, by the favor of the queen who sent a letter by me, I was hospitably received by a Hu-guenot gentleman, the Sieur de Minay, a serious and God-fearing man, and one well learned in the precepts of Maître Calvin. The morning after we journeyed on to Rouen, and by happy chance found the '*Fleur d'Auxerre*' ready to set sail. And now what is new here? Are the placards enforced? Is the regent still vacillating? Ah, what is it, Hen-drika?" for at this moment the servant appeared in the doorway.

"Shall I bring Mijnheer Droust in?" she asked. "He asks to see you, master."

Nikolaas Tontorf rose with an emphatic assent, and advanced to meet a man of tall, meagre figure, who now entered the room. This person, whose garments were of black and of great plainness, but whose worn, gentle countenance bore the stamp of highly developed spiritual faculties, was saluted with great respect and affection by all the family. He was, indeed, the pastor of the secret congrega-tion of Middelburg Protestants, known to its mem-bers under the mystic name of the *Fleur-de-lis*, which held its nocturnal meetings in an upper room of the Tontorf printery.

"I heard at the Kade," said the pastor, "that Mijnheer Tontorf had returned, and so hastened hither. May I have private speech with you if it be not an unkindness thus to withdraw you for a half-hour from these happy people?"

Mijnheer Tontorf at once led the pastor out

through the house and across the dark courtyard, for night had fallen, to his own private office. This occupied the space behind the loggia, where the stairs ascended to the room in which Vrouw Tontorf and Juffrouw Helma carried on their dainty handicraft. It was in that same upper room that the secret meetings of the *Fleur-de-lis* were held.

The pastor and his host held long and earnest conference regarding the rising tide of religious persecution. Throughout the summer, during which Nikolaas Tontorf had been absent from the Netherlands, the oppressive measures against Protestants had increased in cruelty, until the agitation among the common people was approaching frenzy.

"Here, my brother," said Pastor Droust, "is a placard which touches you something nearly :

" '*It is forbidden to write, to print, or to cause to be written or printed, any book whatsoever without permission of the bishop. If any one does so he shall be put in the pillory ; the executioner shall brand him with hot iron, or he shall pluck out one of his eyes, or cut off one of his hands. For printing Bibles the scaffold or the stake is the penalty.*' "

"Nevertheless," said Tontorf, lifting his hand to call attention, and smiling soberly, " you hear that sound ? "

While the pastor had been reading a vibration of the floor of the room where they sat had become perceptible, and with it from beneath could now be heard a rhythmic beating sound.

The pastor looked steadily with a question in his eyes at Tontorf.

"Nevertheless, we shall print Bibles by night," said the latter quietly, "and scatter them by day."

"That being so," said Pastor Droust, with a dry smile, "I would like half a dozen to take with me now."

Without reply Mijnheer Tontorf stepped into a small, inner room, closing the door behind him.

Stooping, the printer pushed away a pile of dusty boxes, and touched a spring in the wall near the floor. Immediately, without noise, a panel slid back, disclosing a small closet piled high with books. A rack of shelves sliding on strong ropes could be drawn up into this place from a similar closet in the subterranean pressroom, which was likewise to be opened only by a secret spring in an invisible panel.

The existence of this depository was known only to Nikolaas Tontorf and his son Norbert and to the head bookkeeper, the trusted right hand of the great printer.

A moment later Mijnheer Tontorf returned to the side of Pastor Droust. He handed him the desired number of small, well-bound Bibles. No word was spoken by either until the pastor, having hidden the volumes within his black surtout and reached the outer door, said :

" And to-morrow night the *Fleur-de-lis* will meet in the usual place ? "

" Such would be my desire."

" Good-night."

As the pastor emerged upon the narrow lane from the vaulted entrance to the courtyard of the Tontorf establishment, he looked cautiously up and down in the darkness. No one being in sight he drew from his pocket a bit of chalk, and on the rough surface of the wall, with three swift motions of his hand, drew a cross enclosed with a circle, and went his way.

This was the signal by which the Protestants of Middelburg were summoned to their secret and perilous worship.

Secrecy, silence, and apprehension of betrayal ruled the day in every condition throughout all Christendom, for alike over convent and court and peaceful burgher dwelling in that year of grace, 1565, there brooded a thick cloud of darkness and doom.

XIII

NASSAU-BREDA

WITHIN the vast parallelogram of the castle of the Nassaus at Breda, in the magnificent inner court, stood young Norbert Tontorf in the sunshine of an April afternoon.

The young Middelburger, taller, sturdier, more deeply bronzed by the two years which have passed, gazed about him in admiring wonder at the Tuscan colonnade surrounding the spacious court, at the gilded medallions and lacelike tracery of the freestone arches, at the imposing octagonal towers flanking the angles, all of which possessed in high degree the harmonious beauty of the best period of the Renaissance. Norbert, who had until now seen no castle finer than that of the abbey at Middelburg, no domestic interior richer than that of his father's house in the Lange Delft, was keenly alive to the princely grandeur of his present surroundings, and for a moment he had well-nigh forgotten the purpose of his coming.

A liveried retainer, one of a dozen who loitered about the court, approaching him with a question, the young fellow collected himself and with marked, albeit modest, self-possession made known his desire to have audience of his excellency, the Prince of Orange, if he were minded to receive him, as he brought a paper which he had been commissioned to deliver into his hand.

Informed that his excellency was still in Antwerp, Norbert asked if it were known whether he would be likely to come to Breda within a few days.

The servant made an evasive answer and suggested that the jonkheer should leave his paper with him to deliver. Declining to do this, Norbert had turned on his heel to depart, when a sharp tapping on the window of a room beyond the opposite gallery caught the attention of the servant, and bidding Norbert remain where he was yet a moment he hastened to cross to the point from which the sound had proceeded.

The casement had been hastily pushed open, and from his place Norbert could now see the head and bust of a woman who appeared at the window. Something bizarre and striking in the effect of this personage awoke in him the liveliest interest. The face seen from this distance was marked by a pair of flashing dark eyes, and features irregular but animated, the mouth being full, flexible, and expressive of pride, impatience, and impetuous will. A richly jeweled coif and a broad ruff turned away in a point from the throat completed the picture framed in the window.

Greatly to his amazement Norbert now heard this lady soundly rating the servant in a harsh, metallic voice.

"What mean you, you fat-witted clown, by sending away messengers without consulting your mistress? I will have you discharged if such a thing happen again. Who is yonder dammarel? He is of goodly bearing, and I would fain have speech with him and learn his errand. What say you is his name?"

"Your excellency, I do not know the young man's name. He is a stranger in Breda, and as I think by his speech, from the North," said the servant respectfully.

"Which means that he is a shade worse churl than if he were from the South," returned his mistress. "In any case, send him in hither, Joost. He may amuse me, and i'faith there is scant amusement in this dreary place."

The servant hastened back and now conducted Norbert through the colonnade, its walls resplendent with rich gilding and brilliant escutcheons of the great seigneuries of Breda, Orange, Holland, Zeeland, and others of which the prince was the lord. From this cloister the youth was led by a second lackey into the castle and through a series of galleries of royal stateliness in which groups of gentlemen and ladies were listlessly lounging.

Passing down the length of a salon which glittered in crystal and silver, they reached at last a small boudoir separated by hangings of magnificent tapestry from the salon and decorated wholly in gold and crimson.

Stepping under the hangings the servant now ushered Norbert, whose heart beat hard with excitement, into the presence of the Princess of Orange, and left him alone to sustain an interview for which he had neither taste nor training.

Reclining in a great arm-chair sat the lady whom he had seen but now in the window and who was, as he had already concluded, albeit with great amazement, none other than the wife of the prince, the daughter of "the great elector," Maurice, of Saxony.

Dressed in a gown of vivid green satin with bands of rich embroidery much soiled and fretted, her small feet crossed upon a footstool in a careless attitude, her dark eyes half veiled now by the lids, a green parrot perched upon her shoulder, a fan in her hand which she flirted nervously at the parrot, the princess made a yet more equivocal impression upon the young Zeelander, than when seen from the distance. Accustomed to the most delicate orderliness in dress, and the most demure propriety in bearing among the women of his own household and acquaintance, Norbert was almost bewildered by the fantastic freedom of the great lady.

" Come hither, jonker," she cried, now abruptly

"why stand you bowing there on the threshold
as if you were afraid of me ?   I am only a young
woman after all, and since I have sent for you,
you can e'en make bold enough to come hither
and kiss my hand," and she laughed shrilly.

Accordingly Norbert now advanced, knelt and
kissed the hand outstretched to him for the purpose, and as he rose he received the unexpected
comment:

"Very fairly done, jonker, for a country lad!
You may make quite a gallant if you remain long
enough in our court here in Breda."

"Your pardon, madame," said Norbert, looking
down respectfully on the princess, but with a little
flush of distaste showing in his sun-burned cheeks,
"but I am no jonker, but the son of a good burgher
of Middelburg, Nikolaas Tontorf, dean of the Guild
of Printers."

"Oh, that is unlucky.   How do you come by so
elegant a shape, young Sir Printer, and so possessed
a bearing ?   In good sooth I have hardly seen so
knightly a figure since I came among these Flemish
boors," and she flashed a smile of flattering coquetry at the young man, whose amazement increased with every word.

A flask of wine in a silver standard, together with
a bowl of white sugar broken in pieces, and several
crystal goblets, stood on a small table near the
chair of the princess.   She rose now and going to
this table filled two glasses.   Norbert noted the
curious awkwardness of her shape, and of her halting gait which had not hitherto been apparent to
him.   He waited uneasily for what would follow.

Holding out one of the glasses which he took
from her hand perforce, she said:

"I will not send you away unrefreshed, my lad,
though you have the ill luck to be the son of a
printer.   What is your errand to my lord ? "

As she carelessly asked the question the princess

I

was dipping a piece of sugar into her glass of wine with which she proceeded to feed the green parrot on her shoulder, unheeding the syrupy drops which trickled down on her gown and fingers.

"I have a paper, so it please your highness, to deliver into his hand," replied Norbert.

"I trust it is none of these tiresome petitions and manifestoes wherewith we are fairly flooded," said the lady lightly. Then with a sudden sharpness she asked : "Are you a Protestant ? "

"Yes, madame," replied Norbert sturdily.

"The worse luck for you," answered the Protestant princess, turning to the parrot and adding non-chalantly, "let me tell you, now while you are young and it is to be hoped not so stubborn as you Dutchmen come to be when you are older, get rid of all this nonsense about Protestantism and Catholicism. The quicker the better ! It's all a miserable mish-mash. It makes no difference which you are in the end. Be what is easy to be and change as often as it is necessary. Above all things, don't get this foolish notion of dying for your religion into your head."

The princess leaned back, tapping the beak of the bird on her shoulder with her fan while she lux-uriously sipped the delicious wine and glanced over the edge of the goblet with a satirical smile of en-joyment at the evident perplexity of Norbert.

"Madame," said the young fellow, who liked his company less and less and yet found a curious fascination in the lady's bright smiles and caressing glances, "if it please your highness to excuse me, I have matters yet to attend to ere nightfall—— "

"Go to, go to, now, my young Tontorf, if that be your name ! you like not my rede overmuch, I see, and find the society of the castle unlike that of your bourgeois gossips. You must learn to wait upon a lady's pleasure and never to anticipate her dismissal. But, hark ! What is that ? " and hastily setting her glass, which was now empty, upon the table, the Princess of Orange crossed to the window overlooking the courtyard.

Norbert stood where she had left him, biting his under lip in vexation and wishing himself well out of the presence. Sounds of hoofs on the courtyard pavement without now reached him, giving token of the arrival of a considerable company. Anne of Saxony turned toward him from the window and nodded blithely :

"Forty horsemen at least, I should say," she cried. In another moment she turned again :

"Yes, boy," she said, laughing, "run along now. It is my lord himself, ridden all the way from Antwerp, and he looks vexed and gloomy e'en now. What might he say should he discover that I was *en tête-à-tête* with a handsome young gallant? Do thy errand another time. My lord will be in no mood for thee to-day, that I see plainly."

Norbert, waiting for no second bidding, made haste to leave the apartment and to reach the courtyard. Crossing this he caught a glimpse in passing of a gentleman just dismounted of commanding figure and presence, with face grave and preoccupied, whom he surmised to be none other than that exalted personage to whom the document in his pocket was addressed as :

Lord and Baron of Breda, Burgrave of Antwerp, Governor General of Holland, Zeeland, and Utrecht, Count of Nassau and Catzenellenbogen, etc., etc., in fine, the puissant Prince of Orange himself.

At the outer entrance to the castle court Norbert encountered the retainer who had been his guide. The man greeted him with the question :

"Holloa, Master Middelburger, how came you off? Did my lady kiss you or curse you?"

"Neither the one nor yet the other," Norbert made laughing answer.

"You are the lucky man, then," was the rejoinder, and Norbert went his way back into the town, where he was lodging with his sister, Jacqueline, in the house of their father's sister, Vrouw Van Marle.

The commission on which he had been sent by his father and other patriotic citizens of Middelburg to the Prince of Orange, was one of more than passing importance, and the young man was himself deeply imbued with its purpose.

The year 1567 was one of greatest crisis and upheaval in the Netherlands. The Inquisition, now thoroughly established, was spreading its terrors everywhere, but the iconoclastic fury of the Antwerp mob and the petition of "the Beggars," showed the king of Spain that the spirit of revolt was stirring alike the high and low. In boundless rage, Philip resolved upon a fearful and summary punishment.

In pursuance of his plan, an army of splendid organization and discipline, veterans of Spain, under the merciless Alva, was even now marshaling at Genoa and preparing for its long march across Europe into the Netherlands. Alva was to supersede the Duchess of Parma as governor general. The black death itself could not be dreaded as a more awful scourge than were Alva and his army.

A personal and immediate test of the absolute fealty of the Netherlandish nobles, and of their willingness to uphold the Inquisition, was meanwhile made by Philip in the following oath of allegiance, which every Knight of the Fleece was imperatively required by his sovereign to sign:

"*As the king, our sire, in consideration of the troublous times and of the rebellious spirit that is abroad in the land has charged Madame, the Duchess of Parma and Governor General of these lands in his Majesty's behalf, to demand a declaration from every person in office as to his intention to carry out his Majesty's will without limitation or restriction,*

*I ——— ——— Knight of the Order, etc., hav-
ing received the said command, now declare by oath
that I am ready to serve him and to carry out his
orders to all persons without limitation or restriction."*

It had become known to Nikolaas Tontorf that
the Prince of Orange, at the time representing the
regent in Antwerp, which was a very hotbed of
troubles, had refused to take this oath, had resigned
his commission, and had withdrawn his young
daughter, Marie, from the court of the duchess at
Brussels.

Although Catholic and supposedly attached to
the government, the profound penetration and mod-
erate views of Orange, his enormous popularity
with the people, his great political power and vast
wealth made him the only man who by any possibility could lead the patriot forces of the Netherlands in a revolutionary movement against the intolerable tyranny of Spain.

Fired by the hope that the prince might at the
moment be accessible to such a proposition, Tontorf and certain of his fellow-patriots in Zeeland
had addressed a fervent letter of appeal to him to
place himself immediately at their head and, in the
four months which must yet intervene before the
arrival of Alva, to organize and train the forces of
the opposition.

Such was the letter, such the appeal which young
Tontorf had come to Breda to deliver to the Prince
of Orange.

Meanwhile the prince, having retired to his private apartments to refresh himself after the dusty
ride from Antwerp, appeared presently in the grand
salon of the castle, where with looks alert and ex-
pectant the gentlemen and ladies of his suite were
gathered, awaiting his coming.

Eight years have passed since that June which
saw the prince the hostage and guest of Henry II.

at Vincennes. The brilliant youth has become the powerful diplomat, the foremost statesman of the Court of Brussels, the man of all men in the Netherlands whom the King of Spain must reckon with.

Dressed now in a court costume of blue and silver, with a broad, transparent ruff, his orders on his breast, his face somewhat grave and careworn by the sleepless anxieties of the present time, but still gracious and commanding, the prince turned from one to another with a brief word to each, the courtly grace of his manner, the winning sweetness of his expression exerting the same spell that had been so potent in his younger years. Every lady was eager to commend herself to his notice by the brightness of her smile, every gentleman of his suite sought to hold himself with the knightly firmness of his lord, and thus a sudden revival of energy and animation possessed the company, but now so dull and lack-lustre. The prince did not linger long, however, but hastened on to present himself to his wife.

As he entered the boudoir at the end of the salon a motion of his hand summoned a servant, who at once dropped a heavy curtain until now drawn aside, thus indicating the desire for privacy. The salon adjoining was then quickly forsaken by the ladies and gentlemen in attendance and the prince was left alone with his wife. She sat where she had sat to receive young Tontorf, nor did she rise from her seat to receive her husband, but he advanced unheeding this and bent to kiss her with words of gentle solicitude for her health and comfort.

The wine flask on the table stood empty now. The green parrot had retired to a perch in the corner of the boudoir, where it sat with filming, stupid eyes and ruffled plumage.

"What excitement have you in Antwerp this

time, monsieur ? " asked the princess coolly, the first greeting over ; " fresh riots and insurrections ? You are at least alive, it seems."

" Antwerp has been quiet," returned the prince, "and I have had leisure more than I liked even to confer with the regent's secretary."

" Oh, then, you have consented to see Master Berty again ! I hope you will tell me that this time you have listened to reason."

The prince smiled slightly, but did not reply.

" For heaven's sake, monsieur, answer me ! " cried Anne, her voice shrill with sudden excitement. " Have you at last taken that tiresome oath and ended all the coil ? "

" No, dear child," said Orange gently, " I cannot take an oath which might oblige me to use harsh measures first of all against my own wife because she is Protestant. You hardly wish me to do that, I think ? "

As he asked the question the prince was standing before his wife, looking down into her face. He noted with a dull pang the careless, wine-stained dress, the flushed face and unsteady hands, more than all, the coarse defiance on the full, sensual lips. Never had her aspect been so heedless or so repellent to him as at this moment, when he was at a crisis of all his worldly fortunes, which should have appealed supremely to her sympathy and solicitude.

" You are aware, my wife," he said slowly, repressing his distaste for further converse, " that soon now we shall have the Duke of Alva to deal with in place of the Duchess of Parma."

" What do I care for Alva ? " cried Anne, with a toss of her head, " let me have just one chance at him and see who will win ! I would like nothing better than to try my hand with a man of his mettle. He would be game worth hunting," and she laughed with absurd complacence.

The prince looked at her in grave wonder. Was she in very deed so infatuated as to suppose that her charms were sufficient to subdue the iron duke and to turn aside from her his fanatical purpose? Or was all this bravado the effect of the wine she had been drinking?

"Has Aerschot taken the oath?" she now asked abruptly.

"Yes."

"And Berlaymont and Mansfeld—have they?"

"Both, madame."

"Ah, by my faith, then they are less fearsome than my lord!" with which taunting comment she rose from her place and began to pace the room with her halting, irregular steps, Orange standing the while, his arms crossed upon his breast, his eyes fixed straight before him, his lips slightly compressed.

"Egmont—he was not faint-hearted, I'll wager. He was ever a soldier. He signed, of course?"

"Egmont has taken the oath, madame," was the steady reply, the insult passing unmarked.

Anne's face grew crimson, and her eyes flashed stormily.

"I'll warrant he has!" she cried, her voice rising almost to a scream, for her jealousy of the wife of Egmont amounted well-nigh to mania. "My Lady Egmont then can brave it out at court more gayly than ever, with no one to give her the lessons she needs for her brazen impudence."

"I greatly fear me, madame," said Orange, wholly unimpassioned but with a deeper seriousness than he had shown before, "that the Countess Egmont will have but brief time for gayety. The court of Alva will be something grim methinks, and the shadow may fall soonest on the lightest hearts."

"Oh, prate not to me of your fears and doubts!" cried his wife, who stood now confronting him with fiery eyes, her hands unconsciously opening and closing her fan with incredible rapidity. "I have heard enough of monsieur's fears. Have the goodness to let me hear his purposes. Where am I to be taken, since we are now to play the part of cowards and run away from the new régime?"

"We shall all depart within a week for Dillenburg," said the prince as quietly as before. "My dear mother and my brother John have large hearts and hospitality, and have bidden me make their castle our home until the troubles are over."

"Dillenburg!" shrieked Anne, and burst into a wild volley of derisive laughter. "Dillenburg! The daughter of the great elector is to take her place now forsooth as a guest on sufferance of a family of commoners! On my honor, my lord, this is carrying things too far! Not a step will I go to Dillenburg! I did not marry a petty squire of Nassau. I was made to believe at least that my consort was a sovereign prince, and I, poor gull, fancied in him the heart and courage of a prince," and almost beside herself in her paroxysm of envenomed fury, Anne tore the fan in her hand in twain and broke the slender sticks to slivers.

The prince watched her for an instant with speechless sadness. When her rage began to abate in part he said, sternly:

"Madame, to confer with you is impossible. Much as I regret it I am forced instead to command. You will prepare yourself and our children for the journey, and give such orders in the household as are necessary, looking to our departure a week hence. Adieu," and he turned and left the room.

No sooner had the curtain fallen upon him, than Anne threw herself in a passion of tears into the arm-chair. She was subdued and controlled at last by the strong mastery of her husband's nature, the nobility of which was at all times a source of irritation to her by reason of its contrast with her own

petty and sordid selfishness. Hating him in some
moods, there were others in which this strangely organized woman could gladly have thrown herself
in servile fawning at his feet.

As he passed through the great salon adjoining
his wife's boudoir, a young girl, tall and slender,
with the deep brown eyes and the aristocratic grace
of person of the prince, advanced swiftly to meet
him with a smile of radiant sweetness.

"Ah, little daughter Marie," he said low and
fondly as he kissed her, "thou hast returned to be
sure. What a heart's ease is the sight of thee to
a weary man!"

No word told of the heart-sickening reception he
had encountered at the hands of Marie's stepmother, but the child had weathered full many a
storm of like nature, and understood.

"We go all together to Dillenburg in a few days,
Marie," said the prince, holding the young girl tenderly against him, and pressing his lips upon her
forehead, as if the contact with her delicate purity
were a source of refreshment to body and spirit.
"Will the change be irksome after the gay life thou
hast led in the attendance upon the duchess?"

"Nay, father dear," cried the maiden, "I am
most joyful to think that at last I shall see my dear
grandmother, and all the uncles and cousins of
whom I have heard so much and seen so little.
Dillenburg will be far, far better than Brussels. I
have never liked the court overmuch, and as for
the duchess——"

The prince placed his finger on her lips and shook
his head in playful warning.

"Nay, little daughter, speak not over freely of
those in authority. Silence is safest," he said, and
smiled.

A little later, in the princely banqueting hall of
the castle, William of Orange took his place at the
head of his table, surrounded by the gentlemen and

ladies of his suite. The absence of the princess was so common an occurrence as to pass without remark. The supper was served with more than royal magnificence on gold plate of marvelous richness, while the cookery was a miracle of perfection. The attendants were exclusively pages of noble birth, one of whom presented the napkin to the prince as he sat down with graceful ceremony.

With the superb self-mastery which won for him his name, the prince banished on this occasion, the eve of a crucial turning-point in his life, every trace of anxiety and every shade of disturbance, and led the conversation with the grace and charm for which he was throughout his life distinguished.

XIV

THE GREAT REBEL

" A ND you have already written a final letter to the king ? "

It was a young cavalier clad in light armor, a man of slender, spirited figure, with fair hair, flashing blue eyes and clear-cut features, who spoke thus to the prince on the following morning. They sat together in the cabinet of Orange in the castle at Breda.

"Yes, Louis. The duel is begun. My letter went by special post from Antwerp two days since."

The prince spoke freely and without restraint, for the young soldier, who listened with kindling and responsive face, was Count Louis of Nassau, his best-beloved younger brother, just arrived with letters and dispatches from Germany.

"I told his majesty," continued the prince, " that to take the new oath was for me impossible, and that I had therefore no choice but to withdraw from his active service, while I should always remain his loyal servant in all which I believed could rightly promote his cause."

" Bold words and fearless, but, as you say, final."

" Most surely. They constitute me, from his majesty's point of view, a rebel."

" And such you are," said Louis, with the accent of solemn but welcome conviction. The day for which he had waited long was come at last.

" And such I am," repeated the prince, rising and pacing the room, his face full of intense mental concentration.

"I have sought for half a dozen years to hold a *via media*," he said slowly, "to bring to some common ground the will of the king and the liberties of the people, to serve the one while protecting the other. But the time is over for such efforts and such hopes. Both king and people have reached the verge of an open and irreconcilable rupture. The conflict is even now on, for Alva has already started on his march. The time for temporizing and middle courses is past. It is war to the knife now, or abject submission to an infernal tyranny."

"The last it cannot be ; but who shall lead this people in their righteous cause, my brother ? Consider their helplessness," and the eyes of Louis were fixed on the strong face of his brother with fervent appeal.

"To lead them against the greatest military power of Europe, without other resource than the land itself can give, is only to throw one's self recklessly into a bottomless abyss, as did the hapless young Marnix of Thoulouse last month," replied the prince. "If the Protestants of France, of Germany, or of England, will join with us, something may yet be done."

"As I live, something shall be done ! " cried the younger brother impulsively, "and that right early. It is for this cause that I am here at this moment with that letter from the landgrave which you have not yet read, and why two hours hence I must be galloping on toward Cleves. I ride and I ride, from camp to court, and from the Calvinists of France to the Lutherans of Germany, if by any means I can win some to our side."

A smile in which was an unmistakable touch of weariness passed over the face of Orange.

"The Calvinists deplore your Lutheran sympathies and the Lutherans give you excellent advice and copious draughts of theology, but they tell you that their consciences forbid their aiding our people

while they persist in following the errors of Calvin.
Is it not so ? Without the Augsburg Confession we
would better die than live. That is the old story.
How well I know it. While our helpless people are
being butchered and burned by the hundred, and
whole towns laid level with the ground, those fellow-Protestants, fellow-Christians, will stand aloof
and argue points of theology, split hairs too fine to
see, instead of coming in hearty brotherhood to
their defense. Ah, my Louis, I may not be an
over-rigid Catholic, but I protest to you these fine
distinctions and endless wars of words between
the various groups of the Protestants make a man
think twice before he leaves the old for the new.
Why can they all not unite in one body ? *Their
differences are not great enough to divide them.*"

"So it seems to us, my brother ; but these con-
victions are honest and deep with those who hold
them and we must have patience."

"Yes, patience without end," said the prince
with strong emphasis ; "and by my faith we shall
have need of all we can muster before we see this
matter through to a close ; but I give you warning,
and through you to all the forces of the Protestant
faith with which you are ever in touch, never, never
shall one feather's weight of my influence go toward
building up a new tyranny in place of the old. A
Protestant despotism is not a whit better than a
Catholic, and if I read aright these endless, petty
bickerings, it might prove even more contemptible.
There is room, my brother, on this broad earth for
the old faith and the new. The one thing for
which there is neither place nor pardon is any con-
straint whatsoever regarding the form in which a
man's conscience leads him to worship God, so long
as it is conformable to good morals. *This I will
maintain,*" and the prince as he quoted the motto
of his house with the emphasis of unalterable resolution, showed for the moment that iron will whose

shape was oftenest disguised beneath the courteous grace of his demeanor.

Louis looked with wonder and even with consternation at his brother, for these words were such as no other man of his time had spoken. Both Catholics and Protestants held coercion and repression of the opposite form of faith as their lawful prerogative and even as their sacred right and duty.

"You go far, sir," he said gently; "even the Queen of Navarre, the noblest and the bravest queen in Christendom to-day, while she suffers not persecution in her realm, forbids the idolatrous worship of the mass within its borders, and does so justly, it seems to me."

The prince smiled sadly.

"I trust the Queen of Navarre will live long enough to see her error, Louis," he replied, "but such courage as hers invites an early death. But tell me, have you still that letter which she sent to you by the printer of Middelburg from some convent, if I remember, near Meaux ? "

"Nay, for safety's sake I destroy all letters of such nature speedily. I can tell you, sir, however, the matter it contained."

"It dealt, if I remember, with the Bayonne conference, and was written during that same summer, well-nigh two years since, when you were at Spa?"

"Yes. It gave me that pregnant saying of the Duke of Alva to the queen-mother, overheard by Prince Henri, 'better one salmon than ten thousand frogs.' It may be well to recall that in these days."

The prince bent his head gravely and looked with musing intentness into the face of Louis.

"Ah, if it were but in my power rightly to read that word to Egmont!" he exclaimed presently with emphasis.

"Egmont!" cried Louis of Nassau impatiently.

"He is impossible! He takes to Spanish honey as if it were a very nectar. Have you seen him of late, sir?"

"I have seen him, alas, to the best of my belief for the last time. We met a week ago at Willebroek, met and parted. Nothing can shake his confidence, not so much, I think, in the king, of whose perfidy he has had full many a proof, but in himself, in his star, in his brilliant and conquering career. Can such a favorite of fortune, the hero of St. Quentin and of Gravelines, the idol of the army, good Catholic and royalist to the core, can such a man be made seriously to feel his monarch's displeasure? He scorns the suggestion. On the bitter jealousy of Alva at his military success he will not reflect."

"And Horn?"

"Horn stands with Egmont, also Mansfeld and all the leaders. I remain to-day strangely alone, for I only among the regent's councillors have refused to take the oath."

"But this being so you surely cannot now remain here?"

"My life is already, in Philip's sight, forfeit; that is a foregone issue, and Alva's creed as given at Bayonne has long been familiar to me. But were there no menace to life or liberty, think you, Louis, I would stay on the spot to take my commands from Alva henceforth? Sooner would I engage to serve the devil himself! He at least can play the part of a gentleman on occasion."

The prince spoke with unwonted and imperious passion in which perhaps was mingled secret disappointment of his own cherished ambition to succeed to the governor-generalship of the country.

After a moment of silence, Louis rejoined earnestly: "You are far too powerful, my lord, for this action regarding the oath to be passed over. That is clear. Moreover, you have a personal

enemy not less malignant and determined than
Alva himself—Granvelle. He has the ear of Philip,
and is behind Alva and his army. Four years ago
he warned the king that you were a dangerous
man, having unbounded influence with the people,
and given to keeping your own counsel, while Egmont, he said, was harmless, being vacillating, in-
credibly vain, and open to flattery."

"Was that, in sooth, his judgment ?" asked Orange, with manifest interest. "The cardinal did
Egmont scant justice."

"And you have ever done him more than justice, my lord————"

At this word Louis was interrupted by a light
knocking on the door of the cabinet, and at the
summons of the prince a page appeared, saying
with great deference :

"Monseigneur, will it be your pleasure to see the
young Tontorf of Middelburg at the time appointed?
He has waited now for an hour, and will go and return later if such is your preference."

"Marry, I had clean forgot the lad!" said the
prince rising.

"Tontorf !" exclaimed Louis. "And from Middelburg ? I know the youth well, by name. He
has trained troops for me in Walcheren these two
years past. I have work for him, and a captain's
commission will be his ere long if he is of the mettle I think."

"Would you choose to see him now ?" asked
the prince. "The time is short."

"Short, indeed, but nevertheless have him in. I
have many questions to ask concerning Zeeland,
and if the fellow has his father's intelligence, he,
may be exceeding useful."

"As you please," said Orange ; then turning to
the page : "Send in the young man, but bid the
groom saddle two horses at once for Count Louis
and myself."

K

Then, as the page withdrew, he remarked with a smile to his brother :

"We will have one last gallop together, sir, through the dear old park. Who knows when you and I may meet again in Breda ? "

A shadow clouded the animated face of Louis for an instant. Did some voice whisper within him, *Never?*

Then entered the room Norbert Tontorf, his tall, well-knit figure set off to advantage by a slashed doublet and hose of hunter's green, his shapely head uncovered, his alert grace enhanced by the mingled bashfulness and boldness which the moment aroused in him.

The Nassaus received his obeisance graciously, and Louis exclaimed with frank comradery :

"Now tell me, young sir, are you the son of my good friend of Middelburg, Nikolaas Tontorf ? "

"I am, my lord," was the reply.

"Nay, then shake hands and let us be friends," cried the impetuous Louis; "for if the son be like the father there is not in all Zeeland a sturdier patriot nor a more courageous." Then turning to his brother, Louis added :

"Mijnheer Tontorf, my lord, has traveled up and down through Flanders and through France in one disguise and another, distributing Bibles and hymnals of his own printing, carrying letters and dispatches between the Huguenot leaders and their brethren in the Low Countries, and proving himself in all ways a discreet, fearless, and patriotic gentleman. I count it a rare pleasure to meet his son, of whose service I have spoken but now, and to make him known to you, sir."

The prince took Norbert by the hand and looked for a moment in his face, while the youth, with reverent yet fearless gaze, met that searching glance which had power to pierce through the outer mask and divine the hearts of men.

"You are welcome to Breda, Norbert Tontorf,"
said the prince, as if satisfied with what he read.
"I would gladly hear of you much concerning our
compatriots in Zeeland, but at present time fails us
for conference. You bring me a letter?"

Norbert, with a low bow, placed in the hand of
the prince the petition of his father and was about
to withdraw, but Count Louis detained him with a
question.

"Tontorf, I have a word for your ear," he said;
"you are already in training for a soldier. Would
you like to enter the service of my brother and myself presently? There will be work on hand for
every loyal Dutchman ere long."

Norbert's face flushed high.

"Nothing could be better to my mind than to
serve the house of Nassau, and, with that, the
cause of our country. Command me, sir, if I seem
to you deserving of such honor."

"Why not ride with me even now, to-day, back
to Germany?" cried Louis. "There is need
enough of young, active fellows of leal heart like
you to carry dispatches hither and yon. Later
there will be sterner business in plenty."

Norbert's heart bounded with the eager desire to
follow the dashing and enthusiastic nobleman on
the spur of the moment, but the thought of the two-
fold nature of the errand on which he was bound
constrained him.

"With all my heart would I join you at once,
my lord," he replied with embarrassment, "but I
am at this time on my way to Antwerp, sent thither
by my parents with my young sister. She has a
grievous malady of the eyes, and we are forced to
consult a famous physician of Antwerp, one Hoekstra. I cannot leave the little maid, I fear, until I
have discharged this duty. May I still hope that
you will receive my service when this is accomplished?"

148

"Of a surety," said Louis. "Come when you are ready and I will enroll you among the men of my escort."

The prince, who had been carefully perusing the letter of Nikolaas Tontorf, now laid it down and said with musing seriousness :

"You may tell your father, my young sir, that I have read his appeal with deepest sympathy. I am honored by the confidence which such men as he evince toward me. The extremity of our country lies heavily on my heart, and I believe that the time for resistance will come. To act over-soon and without resources will be to lose all and gain nothing. This much he and all who look to me may believe—when the time comes for action I shall act. So much for your father. For yourself, I like your face and the vigor of your manhood and your youth. I can use you. If you are foot-loose next week, next month, or at any future time, seek me out in Dillenburg. If I am not there, this jonker," and he threw his arm affectionately over Louis' shoulder, "is like to be, or some Nassau of us, and we are all one. Farewell," and with the last word the prince and Louis preceded Norbert from the cabinet.

When the latter reached the courtyard he saw the brothers as they mounted the prancing thoroughbreds which had been awaiting them and galloped off through an arched gateway into the vast reaches of the green park beyond, which with its abundant game, was one of the famous features of Breda Castle.

As he crossed the bridge over the castle moat Norbert encountered a personage with whose appearance he was already familiar, as he had passed the previous night at the house of Mijnheer Van Marle, Norbert's uncle, having come from Antwerp in the train of the prince. This man, whose age was something more than thirty years, wore the rich but sober attire of a Flemish alderman. He was of florid complexion, with a handsome face and huge, curling, reddish moustachios, and he bore himself with easy confidence and conscious importance.

"Ha, my young friend," he cried, on seeing Norbert, "have you prospered with your mission? It is my turn now to have speech of his highness. Know you yet if that is true, which rumor says, that the family is about breaking up to start for Germany?"

"I have no information, Mijnheer Rubens, on that matter," said Norbert, somewhat briefly, having already learned that it was best not to discuss the affairs of his betters, and he hurried down into the town, while the councillor [1] from Antwerp went on his way into the castle.

Crossing the wide *Rasteel plein* Norbert now passed under the shadow of the Groote Kerk, with its noble Gothic tower, already hoary with age. Within, in the dim shadows, were the imposing monuments of the Nassaus, the famous forerunners of the two men whose princely favor had been now so signally shown to him. Norbert had often stood with awe and veneration to gaze at the majestic war-lords, whose statues surrounded the tomb of old Engelbert II., and more than all at the imposing face and figure of Cæsar. At this moment, in the passion of devotion with which William of Nassau had inspired him, he said to himself, glancing through the open portal of the great church:

"A greater than Cæsar is here!"

Mijnheer Van Marle, to whose hospitable home Norbert now hastened, was a barrister of some standing in Breda. His wife, a younger sister of Nikolaas Tontorf, resembled the Middelburg printer in the thoughtful repose of her countenance. She was of gentle and matronly presence and little Jac-

---

[1] Father of the famous painter, Peter Paul Rubens.

queline found the comfort she needed in her sufferings, in her motherly care.

"And which of these *grands seigneurs* found you
the finer gentleman?" asked Vrouw Van Marle,
when Norbert had rehearsed his interview with the
Prince of Orange and the Count of Nassau.

"Either one is a man one could follow right
gladly," said Norbert thoughtfully. "Count Louis
sets you on fire with those clear, flashing blue eyes,
and that joyous, gallant ardor of his, but Prince
William is on a greater plan. You feel in him
the master of men, the majesty of authority and
power."

"Were you not afraid of him then, Norbert?"
asked little Jacqueline.

"Oh, yes, afraid as I could be, for I knew that
he read me through to the last thought and intent
of my heart. And then he is the order of man
whose displeasure methinks would be terrible, but
whose favor would be worth dying to win. It was
the proudest moment I ever knew, little sister, when
he asked me to join his service. Oh, I am his! I
belong to him with every drop of blood in my
body, and am eager now to go forth to do battle
for my prince, my land, and my lady!"

Norbert in his young enthusiasm had gone far
beyond his wonted reserve in this outburst and his
color deepened as Vrouw Van Marle said playfully:

"May we be so bold as to ask who is the
lady?"

"I know," said little Jacqueline, laying her head
down on Norbert's shoulder, "do I not, brother? It
is the white abbess, a lovely, hapless princess
away off in France somewhere, whom Norbert
vowed to rescue from her enemies if ever the chance
should come to him. He even wears her device,
the three *fleurs-de-lis* royal on a field azure which I
embroidered on a scarf of white silk for him before
my eyes became so painful. My father alone has

seen her, but we all would gladly serve her if we could and Norbert most of all."

"How very pretty and romantic ! I shall hope to hear that our young knight prospers when he fares forth on such an errand, and that he may not be forced to wait overlong."

"Perhaps you will have to serve the Princess of Orange now, dear brother," said Jacqueline. "Is she worthy of so noble a lord ? "

There was no reply, but presently Vrouw Van Marle said musingly:

"Pity is it that madame the princess seems not to feel for the prince aught of the devotion which he awakens in all others."

Norbert glanced up quickly. His curiosity regarding the enigmatical personality of Anne of Saxony was all the more keenly aroused since he had met the prince.

"How chances it that the princess is so strangely perverse ? " he asked.

"An enormous vanity," replied his aunt, "is at the bottom of much of her waywardness —— " but at that moment a door was opened, and Master Rubens entered the room.

"Ah, you have come just in time, mijnheer," said Vrouw Van Marle ; "we are about sitting down for our noonday meal."

The Antwerp councillor expressed his hearty satisfaction in the fact, and as the little company gathered about the bountiful table, he exclaimed, with palpable complacence :

"Master Norbert, I know not how it fared with you at the castle, but for me I have got that which I came for."

"Then you had the good fortune to see his highness? " asked Norbert, concealing a slight surprise.

"Nay, you are wrong there, my lad. I saw not my lord, but I had the good luck to see my lady, who is, it mayhap, easier of access. His highness is too much the *grand seigneur* to suit a man of my kidney. Now the princess is a frank, free-hearted lady, and though she be the great elector's daughter, has a good word for a man, even if he be but a plain citizen."

" And the princess was able to bestow what you came for, mijnheer ? " asked Vrouw Van Marle.

" Now you are all a little curious, I dare say, good people, as to what brought me hither just now, since I have no pretext of business with my friend Van Marle," began Rubens, looking about him with patronizing familiarity. " Between old acquaintances and fellow-Protestants like ourselves, what need of concealment ? Be it known then, that since the image-breaking in the Church of Our Lady and other Antwerp churches, suspicion has fallen upon our aldermen and magistrates of having been at least not over-zealous in restraining the mob. It has come to my knowledge that my name stands on a black-list which in due time will find its way into the hands of the new governor, Alva.

" This being so, it behooves Jan Rubens to seek some new haven where he may perchance employ his legal abilities to earn an honest living and provide for wife and child in peace and quietness, out of reach of the long arms of the duke. What could be more reasonable than for this same Antwerp councillor," and Rubens touched his capacious chest with a gesture of satisfaction in his own sagacity, " to attach himself in some sort to the fortunes of monseigneur, the prince, who is himself about departing from Spanish soil, where in truth his head would remain but few weeks longer on his shoulders!

" Very well ; my lord being off in the park with his brother, I made bold to crave audience of my lady, and to tell her frankly of my errand. She encouraged me to follow their court and establish myself as a retainer of the house of Orange when they are settled."

"Did madame, the princess, tell you where the family was to be established?" asked Mijnheer Van Marle, who had listened to the narration of Rubens with a somewhat sardonic smile.

"After a time in Cologne. But they are to go for a few months, her highness told me, on a visit to the ancestral castle at Dillenburg. She went so far as to confide in me that country life among so many brothers and sisters-in-law would be little to her liking and she should return to Cologne at the earliest time she could compass. I shall be there awaiting her," added the councillor with a flattered and unctuous smile, "ready to throw myself and my humble devotion at her feet." With this, and a little flourish, Rubens rose from the table.

"Mijnheer Van Marle," he said, "my errand in Breda is done. I see no reason now for lingering longer. Will you send a *knecht* down to the *Gooden Leeuw* and order my groom to get the horses ready to start at once?"

"Is it not somewhat late in the day to begin the journey to Antwerp?" asked his host.

"And the sky is dark and lowering" added Vrouw Van Marle.

"My aunt," cried Norbert, with sudden resolution, "like Master Rubens my errand in Breda is done. What should hinder me, if he is willing, to avail myself of his escort, to proceed on my journey with Jacqueline. The cloudy sky suits her weak vision better than sunshine. Going now we will save taxing you for escort, and we shall be even to-night at our journey's end."

Little could be said against a project so manifestly judicious, and Master Rubens welcoming the companionship of the young Tontorfs with careless good-will, the three shortly set out on stout horses, accompanied by the groom of the councillor, to ride the thirty miles of level road which stretched between Breda and the good city of Antwerp.

XV

IN THE HOUSE OF STRANGERS

"THERE, little sister, it is even here on this very spot that his grace, the Prince of Orange, stood hardly a month ago with the arquebuses pointed at his breast, and held at bay by his own steady courage the howling mob which broke loose after the bloody fight of Osterwell. If I could but have been there then to see him!"

So spoke Norbert Tontorf to his sister Jacqueline as they rode down the famous Place de Meir in the city of Antwerp late that same evening. They were seeking the house of a certain engraver, by name Bouterwek, with whom their father had directed them to take lodging. The rain was falling in torrents, the April evening was chill, and darkness was deepening through the city. Jacqueline making no response to her brother's exclamation, the young man turned to glance at her face and exclaimed:

"What, Jacqueline, are those salty drops that are falling down thy cheeks? What ails thee, little one? Art tired beyond thy strength? Listen to those chimes! Is not their sound most musical?" and Norbert looked up at the lofty spire of the great cathedral which dominated the city, as it had done for centuries and should do for centuries to come.

"I do not care to hear them," cried Jacqueline piteously. "I would far rather hear the chimes of Lange Jan. Oh, Norbert, I want my mother, I want to go back to Middelburg. I hate this great, gloomy city. The people look at us with wicked looks, and these strange streets frighten me."

They had turned now into the labyrinth of narrow, crooked streets, which intervenes southward
between the cathedral and the river. Above them
the tall, dark houses seemed to lean across the narrow spaces as if to touch each other, foul smells
rose from the gutters, bold-faced women fleered at
them from the windows, the few passers-by eyed
them with sullen, even hostile, curiosity, and the
rain beat pitilessly upon their unprotected heads.

Norbert stopped his horse and asked a cobbler
who stood in his greasy leather apron, bare-armed
before his shop, if he would direct him to the Rue
d'Augustin.

For answer the man looked up at an open window above the shop, from which a red-faced woman
leaned, and called:

"Beshrew me, but the young master is seeking
a refuge from the rain in the Rue d'Augustin!"
upon which the woman burst out into coarse, derisive laughter, which terrified Jacqueline indescrib-
ably. With sundry nods and smiles the stout cobbler now took Norbert's horse by the bridle and led
him on a few paces to a corner where the street
was intersected by another, gloomier and more un-
savory than the first.

"Follow that, my fine fellow," he said pointing
east, "until you come to a small alley leading
south. That will take you, with a few twists and
turns, safely to that same Rue d'Augustin which
you desire," and with that he retreated to his
shop.

"Norbert," cried Jacqueline, trembling and unable to restrain her tears, "there must be something wrong. My father would never have sent us
to such a place as this bids fair to be. Do not let
us go farther."

"Where should we go then, Jacqueline?" asked
Norbert cheerfully, keeping straight forward.

"Mijnheer Rubens should have remained with us,

and not left us as he did at Oude-God. Oh, if only I had not been hungry and tired and forced you to halt ! " the child lamented.

" He was somewhat overhasty to reach his own comfortable home before dark, I will allow," said Norbert; "but he meant well enough. He gave me endless directions, thou knowest, for finding the Rue d'Augustin properly, but somehow in this medley of strange streets I have lost the clue. Cheer up, little one, we shall presently find Mijnheer Bouterwek, and there will be an end to all this *fâcherie*."

In a few moments, having threaded a most forbidding and tortuous alley, they did indeed turn into a wider street, and one of better aspect, which proved to be the Rue d'Augustin.

They rode slowly, for darkness had now fallen and it was only by a small torch which he had lighted that aught could be discerned save the outline of the tall beetling housefronts. Norbert searched these closely, as they passed, for the small sign he sought. With an exclamation of satisfaction he cried presently :

" Here we are at last ! Now dry thy tears, Jacqueline, and end thy fears. See, ' Gerard Bouterwek, engraver,' " and as he plied the great knocker Norbert held his torch up to a large, polished shield of brass, which bore this name, surrounded with fine chasing, showing symbols of the owner's craft.

" But why is the house so dark ? " asked Jacqueline.

In fact the windows of the house front were all alike closely barred, and not a ray of light penetrated from within. A silence oppressive and sinister followed Norbert's knocking ; no person passed, no voice or sound reached the place which seemed now to the strained perceptions of the young Middelburgers strangely deserted.

Again Norbert knocked with sharp strokes, which sent echoes sounding down the length of the street, but produced no other result. The house of Master Bouterwek remained dark and silent as before.

"Norbert, what will become of us? Where can we go? The people must be gone away altogether."

"One would think they would have left at least a servant," muttered Norbert, his hand again on the knocker.

At the first sound of his renewed knocking a shutter in the house opposite was pushed cautiously open, a faint light shone out, and a harsh voice called:

"*Mort Dieu,* you there! Can't you go to perdition fast enough without seeking entrance yonder?"

"What mean you, sir?" asked Norbert, hastily crossing the street and looking up at the window.

"By Saint Ildefonso! my good fellow, can you not see by your torch the God's mark on the doorpost?"

Norbert involuntarily made a gesture of dismay as he now for the first time perceived the fatal token.

"Two of the family of Master Bouterwek died of the plague last week, and the printer himself is at the last gasp even now. If you are wise you will cease your pounding on that door and seek shelter otherwise," and with this the man drew back from the window and was about to close the shutter.

Jacqueline gave a faint cry, and her white face and evident exhaustion impelled Norbert to immediate action. Without further pause for consideration he called to the man above:

"My good friend, tarry a bit, an' it please you. My young sister is too weary to go farther in this darkness and pelting rain. We are strangers in

Antwerp and without escort. The city is full of reckless prowlers and we cannot safely search out such lodging as befits us. Can you not grant us your hospitality for this one night ? "

An unpromising and unintelligible muttering was the only reply, but Norbert saw that the man who now left the window had not carried out his first intention of closing the shutter.

" Be not downcast, Jacqueline," he said cheerily, " the fellow is churlish, to be sure, but he is plainly not the master ; and see, it is no mean house, but I should judge the residence of some personage of quality who would scarce refuse so reasonable a request," and Norbert lifting his torch let its light flicker over the carved façade before them.

But Jacqueline was in too great an extremity to take heed of such matters, and she made no reply to Norbert's stout-hearted encouragement, but sat now with her head drooping even to her horse's mane. The slow moments passed painfully, but suddenly the sound of slipping bolts and turning keys in the house door close beside her called Jacqueline's aching eyes down from the window on which they had been fastened. The man with whom they had been speaking now appeared in the doorway, the lamplight in the hall beyond sharply outlining his figure.. Norbert perceived that he was a man of twenty-five, or thereabouts, of harsh and angular frame, shabbily dressed, and yet obviously above the rank of a servant.

" Are we to enter ? " asked Norbert, for the man did not speak nor relax in any degree his sour and sullen aspect.

To this question he replied only by a curt nod and a motion of his hand.

Norbert turned and lifted Jacqueline down from her saddle and she stood for a moment on the swimming pavement so dizzy and her limbs so stiffened and aching that to move forward seemed impossible.

A servant now appeared who took their horses and led them off to a neighboring stable, Norbert having removed the saddle-bags containing their few personal belongings. Laden with those and supporting Jacqueline's faltering steps, he led her into the house, whose dubious hospitality was at least better than the dark and dangerous streets.

Following their silent guide they now crossed a faintly lighted court, in which Norbert descried bales of merchandise, indicating the occupation of the owner of the house. From the gloomy precincts of this court they stepped immediately into a large, well-lighted room, luxuriously furnished in a style wholly unfamilar to the young Zeelanders.

Leaving them to stand in the center of this apartment in their dripping garments and still without an unneeded word, their guide now disappeared into an inner room, the door of which he carefully closed.

Again the interval of waiting seemed interminable, and their surroundings began to assume a dreamlike and fantastic aspect, when at the end of the long room a silken curtain was lightly lifted and a young woman entering approached them with soft, gliding steps.

More than ever was Norbert possessed of the sensation of being in a dream as he watched the approach of this person, who was of singular and striking beauty and dressed with extravagant richness and with a brilliancy and boldness of color which bordered on the grotesque.

"Now by Saint Eulalia of Madrid!" cried this lady, in a soft, silvery voice, through which an under-current of derisive laughter seemed to vibrate, "what have we here? Saints save us, but who are you, poor dripping pilgrims? and what wind blew you hither?"

She now came up to the two as they stood in dazzled bewilderment, and lifting Jacqueline's chin

in her taper fingers studied her face for a moment,
remarking: "You must e'en go to a surgeon for
those eyes of yours, my pretty child."

Then turning with startling suddenness to Norbert, she gave him a swift, sharp tap on the ear
which brought all the blood in his body to his head
and for a moment completed his bedazzlement.

The young lady watched the effect of this little
admonition with peals of light, musical laughter,
and as Norbert rallied his wits, she cried:

"Off with your bonnet, sir! Do they not teach
you Dutch jonkheers to uncover in the presence of
ladies?"

Hastily Norbert removed his soaked and now
shapeless cap and bowed low to his monitor, with
the words:

"Your pardon, madame! I was so bewildered by
the beauty of all about me after the desolate gloom
without, that I forgot myself entirely."

"Yes, I will pardon you, since you excuse yourself so gallantly, and since, by our Lady, you look
so infinitely more agreeable without that wretched
cap."

The door now reopened and their guide appearing led Norbert and Jacqueline into the inner room,
the young lady throwing them light kisses and following their departure with gay trills of laughter.

The room which they now entered was small,
but so brilliant were its walls, hung with crimson
Spanish leather, illumined by numerous waxlights
held in branching and gilded sconces, that even
after the brightness of the apartment which Norbert and Jacqueline had just left, it burned like the
heart of a rose with throbbing color.

A table stood in the middle of the room strewn
with papers, near which on the floor a small brazier
held a red fire of coals. Some strange foreign pas-
tilles strewn upon the coals filled the room with
heavily fragrant fumes. A long, carved cupboard

of old ebony held a dense array of curious flasks, crucibles, and jars of chemicals. The door stood open into a small laboratory beyond.

In the center of the room, beside the table, a man was seated, whom Norbert at once perceived was the master of the house, and to whom he now presented himself with respectful and apologetic greeting.

This man was wrapped in a long, loose robe of black velvet, which opened at the breast disclosing wrought linen of unusual fineness. His face was long and the cheeks sallow and sunken, the eyes singularly keen and glittering under the pent-house roof of the heavy projecting brows. Long, black hair hung to the shoulder from a pointed black velvet cap, delicate lace fell over the bony, nervous fingers, and a black beard, waving and flecked with gray reached to the girdle, which was loosely tied at the waist.

Fixing his eyes upon Norbert's face with avid keenness the Spaniard, for such the young Zeelander now with little pleasure recognized the master of the house to be, spoke in a voice of singularly melodious quality.

"My clerk tells me, young sir, that you seem minded to force an entrance to my house to-night by your importunity. The times are ill, and a prudent man would fain know of what strain may be strangers whom he harbors. What have you to say for yourself ? "

Despite the peculiar melody of the voice and the conciliatory smile with which the Spanish merchant said these words, the cold suspicion expressed in them acted upon Norbert with harshly repellent effect.

"I am Norbert Tontorf," he replied proudly, "son of Nikolaas Tontorf, an honorable citizen and master-printer of Middelburg, whose name should not be all unknown even in Antwerp. I have come

L

hither to bring my young sister to the care of a physician, Doctor Hoekstra. My father directed us to lodge in the house of Master Bouterwek, who is his good friend, if he be yet alive, but I am told by your clerk that he is in extremity at this very hour. The city councillor, Jan Rubens, gave us his escort hither as far as Oude-God, where I tarried for rest and food for my sister, and hence we arrived in Antwerp alone and strangers. We ask, monsieur, nothing at your hands but that for which we are able to pay, and in the morning we will gladly depart to seek such lodging as your good city can doubtless furnish to those who enter it neither as vagabonds nor beggars."

The boyish independence, wounded pride, and sturdy boldness of Norbert's speech and of his bearing appeared to awaken a species of not unsympathetic amusement on the part of the master of the house, while something in his statement noticeably quickened his interest in the youth. He nodded several times, and the curiously fascinating irony of his smile went far to disarm Norbert of his rising anger.

"Excellent, my young friend," he said, fixing his piercing eyes on Norbert's face, "well and gallantly spoken. The high repute of your father's house is in fact well known to me. Antwerp itself and the great Plantin find in Middelburg and its master printer a worthy rivalry. If I am rightly informed, your father's establishment has of late been increased by several new presses. This augurs well, Master Norbert, for the prosperity of your father's business," and the merchant smiled with stately courtesy.

"Our business has indeed grown rapidly of late," returned Norbert in a matter of fact tone, but with characteristic reticence he followed the Spaniard's lead no further.

"Sent forth on such an errand," proceeded the

merchant graciously, "and from such a house, it
were needless to inquire whether the son and
daughter of Mijnheer Tontorf are amply equipped
for the costs of their residence in a strange city."

He paused slightly and Norbert bowed a silent
assent, at the same time drawing from his pocket
several gold pieces which he advanced as if to lay
upon the table.

The Spaniard made a gesture of protest, although
his eyes scanned the coins shrewdly for an instant,
and he said with dignity :

" Put up your gold, Master Tontorf. I need no
further guarantee. In truth, I am about to propose
that you seek no further on the morrow for an
abiding-place. My house, though small and poor
in comparison with that of your father, is nevertheless hospitable——"

As the Spanish merchant thus spoke he was
interrupted by a low cry from Jacqueline. Turning
quickly, Norbert was but just in time to catch her
as she sank fainting on the floor. His own head
was growing dizzy and his vision dim. The fumes
which filled the apartment with their languorous
fragrance, the brilliancy of color, the enervating
warmth, produced an overpowering influence even
upon his hardy vigor.

The Spaniard rose, his tall figure erect in its long
black robe, his sharp glance fixed upon the pros-
trate child. A silver bell stood on his table, which
he rang, and then crossing the room to the open
shelves, he returned with a small vial just as the
door opened, and the lady whom they had previously seen appeared.

" Here is work for you, Señora Valerie," he said
quickly.

" Ah, poor little one ! " she cried pitifully, and
she drew the drooping head upon her knee with a
gentleness which brought a grateful moisture to
Norbert's eyes.

Seeing Jacqueline evidently reviving, he turned to the Spaniard and said :

"We are like to be glad, it seems, monsieur, to accept your hospitality for some days to come, and at least for to-night it is most urgently needed."

"Of a surety," replied his host, with grave cordiality, "and now, without more ado, we will put this little maid to bed," and he led the way up a flight of stairs, Norbert and the lady whom he had addressed as Señora Valerie supporting Jacqueline between them.

Above they were led down a dim corridor and ushered into a small room at the back of the house, from which opened another scarcely larger than a closet and without a window, both, however, being simply but sufficiently furnished as sleeping rooms.

A servant who had been hastily summoned now brought several flasks of medicine and cordials, which he placed upon a table, together with food and wine. While Norbert and Jacqueline partook of the latter their host and Señora Valerie spent a moment in serious, low-voiced consultation outside the door. The instant, however, that Jacqueline turned wearily from the scarcely tasted food the lady was at her side.

Norbert retreated to his narrow sleeping-closet, while Señora Valerie, with deft and gentle hands, disrobed the shivering child and made her ready for the night. In brief time she sank into a restless, feverish slumber, over which Valerie watched for a little space. Then gently pushing open Norbert's door, she whispered :

"Go you now to rest. It is easy to see that you are yourself dead tired and must sleep. Your sister will sleep now. My room is hard by and I will watch over her until morning. She is in good hands. If Señor Anastro your host were something cold in his reception, you will find him but the warmer in his hospitality since he knows your true degree."

The gentleness of these words was so far removed from the wild gayety of Señora Valerie's
former manner that Norbert almost doubted if it
were indeed the same person.

"Thank you, señora, with all my heart," he
whispered back. "Rest would indeed be welcome," he added with evident misgiving.

Something touched his breast lightly. It was the
hand of Valerie. A soft musical laugh came with
the words :

"There, kiss my hand in token that you forgive
my welcome which was, in sooth, over-sharp, and
fear not to trust a lady who thus does you grace."

Norbert touched the delicate hand with his lips,
then the door closed softly between them. In the
darkness he groped his way to the narrow pallet,
threw himself upon it, and knew no more until
morning.

Valerie returned noiselessly to Jacqueline's bedside. The child slept, albeit with rough and troubled breathing. Valerie's hand now unfastened her
nightdress at the throat and after a moment of dex-
terous manipulation and the aid of a small lancet-
shaped knife which severed a ribbon, she appeared
to obtain something for which she sought.

In another instant she stood outside the door,
which she closed and locked, and then laid a small
book bound in white vellum in the hand of Señor
Anastro, who stood waiting.

"There," she said laughing softly, "I had not
far to seek for a token. No rosary did I find, nor
crucifix, nor *Agnus Dei*. Still if this is a missal——"
and she paused, her head drooping on Anastro's
shoulder, while they scanned the tiny book together
with intense eagerness by the light of his candle.
It proved to be the four Gospels finely printed and
bound.

"By Geronimo !" breathed rather than spoke the
Spaniard. "It is no missal! My scent was right! I

knew I had heard a whisper concerning that Middelburger. His affinity, moreover, with our ill-starred neighbor opposite did but deepen the complexion of my doubt."

"Yes, but know you even now," whispered Valerie, "that the Middelburger himself printed this little book? What is the sign or imprint?"

Anastro turned to the title-page and pointed with his lean brown forefinger to the device of the cross enclosed by the circle or crown, with a *fleur-de-lis* in the center.

"Is that sufficient? Is that proof?" asked Valerie, smoothing the soft fur of the Spaniard's robe with her light, jeweled fingers, and watching his face with undisguised eagerness.

He shook his head, his glittering eyes searching greedily, but in vain, through the leaves of the book for further sign or token.

"Nay, my Valerie," he said then, "thou hast done well, but better yet must be. Restore the little book; then seek in thy woman's wit for some shift whereby the child shall give thee the knowledge we seek and give it ere daybreak. But let her suspect nothing, else all will be in vain."

Within Jacqueline's chamber Valerie carefully replaced the little book on the child's breast, fastening the ribbon, then listened at the inner door and satisfying herself from his breathing that Norbert slept soundly, she turned the key in the lock. This done she lighted a candle, and with quick, sure motions poured out into a small basin portions of the oil, rose water, and other simple lotions which were standing ready on the table. Kneeling then by the bed she proceeded with her slender, flexible fingers to rub the compound thoroughly into the throat and chest of Jacqueline.

In a few moments, as she expected, the young girl opened her eyes and murmured a confused, half-articulate question.

"A shame to waken thee, dear child," said Valerie in a cordial, cheering voice, "but I needs must rub this *fricace* into thy throat to soothe thy breathing. I fear thou hast taken a strong chill and fever may follow. Keep awake, little one, yet a moment, that I may also administer the cordial that the kind Señor Anastro hath sent thee."

Jacqueline awoke at this and rubbed her eyes open when suddenly Valerie appearing to discover the little book for the first time and lifting it in her hand, exclaimed :

"Oh, what have I found ! Jacqueline, surely this is the very word of God. Is it possible that thou art so happy as to own this wonderful book for which I have longed for many years, but in vain?" And pressing her lips passionately upon the cover the Señora to all appearance was lost in a transport of mingled joy and longing.

Jacqueline stared, half-dazed for a little space, dimly remembering the many injunctions to secrecy regarding this book which she had received at home, but feeling them in this case to be wholly out of place.

Presently Valerie lifted her head.

"Jacqueline," she whispered, dashing away the tears which were supposed to fill her eyes, with a frank, artless gesture, "no one knows my heart. I do not dare to let them. If I could but own a book like this I believe I could live a different life and die happy ! Canst thou not tell me where thine was procured ? Couldst thou aid me to obtain one like it ? What is money ? I would pay any price !" and her large eyes, glowing fervently, were fixed upon the innocent face of the girl.

"With all my heart, dear lady, I will help you to get a book like mine," said Jacqueline, full of sympathy for the stranger lady's religious devotion, "nor shall it cost you even one stiver. It is a secret, but to you I can tell it ; my own dear father prints

Bibles and hymnals at our printery in Middelburg, although just where and when nobody knows. But this is one that he printed, and when I return I will ask him to send you a far better one than this, large and well bound, for your own, and Helma, that is my sister, shall illuminate the title-page for it."

Valerie kissed the unsuspecting girl with a rapturous joy quite unfeigned by reason of her genuine exultation in the success of her little experiment. She admonished the child earnestly, however, to absolute silence, as she dared not let any living soul know her secret desire.

" Now take this cordial, and go fast to sleep, good, dear little girl. We shall grow very fond of each other since we have this great secret together. Good-night," and Valerie extinguished the light and noiselessly rejoined Anastro in the corridor outside.

Passing to the end farthest from Jacqueline's door, Valerie rehearsed with much spirit the scene which had just taken place and every word spoken by the daughter of Nikolaas Tontorf. Anastro listened with closest attention and signified his satisfaction by a still smile and slow approving nods.

" Thou knowest the reward, Valerie, if this pestilent printer be brought to justice ? " he asked with significant emphasis, when her tale was told.

" Nay, Anastro, I know it is worth an effort, but of the exact conditions I am ignorant."

" One-tenth of the substance of the man's possessions in such a case is pledged by the crown to the one giving unmistakable proof of his infracture of the edicts. This man's violation, gross and flagrant, is now absolutely confirmed ; and my part, *our* part, my peerless friend, cannot fail to be recognized and duly rewarded. The man is rich, that I have heard ere this, and what the lad let drop just now below made me doubly sure. It was a lucky wind that blew them in hither to-night. To

win the favor of God and Our Lady and repair my
fortunes at one stroke is not a bad night's work!
And thy skillful furtherance, my Valerie, shall not
be forgotten. Thou shalt lack no longer those
jewels which will so well become thy beauty, and
which I have hitherto so unwillingly denied thee.
Good-night. It is necessary to make all haste in
this matter, for this same Tontorf has come under
suspicion from other eyes than mine, and I may
yet be too late.''

Gaspar d'Anastro returned to the burning red
light of his private cabinet, and bent for hours over
his writing table.

At daybreak his clerk and trusted confidant,
Venero, departed from the house in the Rue d'Augustin with a sealed letter addressed to the secretary of her highness the Duchess of Parma, regent
in the Netherlands of his Catholic and Christian
Majesty Philip II., King of Spain. At an inn in a
neighboring street Venero called for a horse and
was soon on his way to the city of Brussels.

XVI

A SCRAP OF PAPER

"BUT what an' if you have been here with us more than a month, Master Norbert, have you not, even so, ample cause for content?" asked Señora Valerie of Norbert on a morning in early June. "Says not Doctor Hoekstra daily that our dear Jacqueline's eyes mend apace?"

The lady was watering her flowers, cactus and oleander and orange trees, in the small garden enclosed by high walls at the rear of the residence of Anastro, in the Rue d'Augustin, while Norbert paced the narrow walk impatiently with knitted brows.

"Nay, dear lady, pardon me if I seem ungracious," he cried with sudden boldness, "but in truth I am not content, and I will for once speak plainly. Doubtless Doctor Hoekstra is skillful and Jacqueline's cure goes forward as rapidly as may be, although she is still, as at first, shut up with bandaged eyes in that dark, stifling room," and with the words Norbert glanced up at the closed fenestral of Jacqueline's chamber, "and, as it seems to me, she grows ever paler and weaker. I note the doctor tarries daily for conference with Señor Anastro and it disquiets me somewhat. Can you inform me if they are keeping from me aught concerning my sister's condition."

Norbert faced Valerie, who was slowly walking by his side, with deep anxiety plainly written on his face.

She smiled a soothing, playful smile as she replied:

170

"That can I, fond, faithful Norbert, with your grim northern fears and your grave anxieties. Can you never learn to trust your friends and be at ease with them ? Doctor Hoekstra has told me plainly that Jacqueline was surprising him by her rapid recovery, but it is a case which must take patience for many weeks to come. He and Señor Anastro are old friends and enjoy a moment now and then of social interchange which bodes no ill, believe me, to your sister. Is it so hard, then, Norbert, to be patient ? Are you not made one of us ? We have become so fond of you it is grievous to feel that you are still bursting with impatience to leave us," with which words Valerie shook her head with charming pensiveness.

Norbert's face grew gentler, for he was by no means insensible to the señora's bewitching ways.

"I could even bear the long inaction, señora," he said soberly, "eager as I am to be free to join the gentleman who, as I have told you, has granted me the honor of calling me to his service, but how can I or how could any man patiently endure the life I live in Antwerp ? I am little better than a prisoner, and that you yourself know perfectly. Every step is guarded, every motion watched. I can never leave this house without procuring the key from Señor Anastro, who is thus cognizant of all my movements and who never permits me to stir abroad unless accompanied by one of his servants. I like it not, and, by my faith, I will not much longer submit to such needless and humiliating surveillance ! "

Valerie saw in the indignant eyes of the young man that he had in fact reached the climax of resistance to the limitations persistently set upon him by Anastro, which she had foreseen was inevitable sooner or later.

"Norbert," she said softly and with a serious gentleness which moved the young man far more than her gayer words, " shall I tell you the veritable reason for the surveillance, as you call it, in which you are held ? "

" I know the reason Señor Anastro gives me," he replied, " that the city is still in such tumult that it is dangerous for a stranger to go unattended ; but surely my safety is my own affair rather than his. I am not afraid of any one I have seen in Antwerp yet," he added with a touch of youthful bravado.

Valerie bent her head and concealed a curiously cold smile which passed over her face.

" That reason is true," she continued in the same quiet tone, " but it is not all of the truth. It has been rumored of you, Norbert, in Antwerp, that this nameless nobleman whose service you have told me you are about to enter is none other than the Great Absentee, the Prince of Orange himself, and that your real purpose in Antwerp is to levy troops in the name of the prince to share full soon in a general uprising. Now Señor Anastro, knowing all this and knowing the imminent peril which these rumors have brought to threaten you, stands firmly, even in spite of your own resistance, as your friend and guardian."

" And yet," said Norbert to himself, " he is a Spaniard and a Catholic. It is passing strange."

Perhaps the thought left its trace in his frank face, for Valerie continued :

" Señor Anastro, while himself a good Catholic, is not of the bigoted strain, which can see no good in them of the New Religion, for such we divine you to be, my friend. Antwerp is full of plots and counterplots. Catholics and Protestants alike betray each other, and there are few who can be trusted. It is against the dangers which surround you that your noble host, with his knowledge of the Antwerp mob, is seeking to protect you. And," she added almost tenderly, " although you may not dream it, even I, weak as I am, have used all my power to aid you, Norbert."

Norbert murmured a somewhat formal acknowledgment, being indeed less impressed with the magnaminity of his hosts than with the surprising nature of Valerie's disclosure as to the suspicions concerning himself.

"Are all Hollanders cold and impassive like you?" asked the señora, who had expected more effusiveness and whose face showed a shade of pique at Norbert's evident absorption.

The young man smiled and said: "I fear you find me cold indeed, madame, and unresponsive."

"Perchance your heart is warmer than your words," suggested Valerie with a glance of coquettish challenge.

"Nay, by my troth, madame, I think not," answered Norbert stoutly, courteously, but not the less palpably indifferent to the lady's somewhat obvious approaches. "These times are ill-suited to gallantries, and were it not so I have no heart for them. I myself am under a vow to the service of a lady in a distant land, not as lover, look you, but as servant; but it is a service which commands my whole heart."

"Ah, is it so?" cried Valerie concealing a very pungent sense of mortified vanity. "Tell me something of this foreign lady. She is most beautiful, I'll wager, at least in the eyes of her bold knight," and she laughed mockingly.

"I have never seen her, madame," said Norbert; "but none the less my sword and my service belong to her if ever she should condescend to command them. I pray you excuse me now. These morning hours pass wearily to my sister," and with a respectful salutation Norbert hastened and entered the house, leaving Valerie alone among her blossoming oleanders with an unpleasant light in her eyes and a slight flush on her cheeks.

Although too inexperienced and unsuspicious to entertain special migivings as to the position of the señora in the house of the Spanish merchant, Norbert had responded but coldly to the advances which she was prompted by instinctive coquetry as well as by other considerations to make toward him. He realized at every moment acutely that he was placed in a position of peculiar peril in which he must never for one moment relax his vigilance.

For Anastro himself Norbert had grown to entertain a species of respect which was yet deeply tinged with doubt. His manner of serious and even lofty dignity and of unvarying kindness toward himself was well calculated to allay suspicion. And yet Norbert did not trust his host.

The ostensible occupation of the Spaniard was that of importing drugs and spices and in those commodities he drove a fair business in the small shop on the Rue d'Augustin. In this he was assisted by his confidential clerk, Venero, and by several servants. Norbert's quick perceptions, however, grasped the fact very soon that apart from his regular avocation, Anastro conducted a variety of lines less reputable, that he dabbled in money lending and usury, in a dubious sort of medical practice, and that his evenings were spent in the small laboratory, which opened from the Red Room, in experiments which Norbert vaguely fancied to be of doubtful beneficence.

While the house was luxuriously appointed, its master courteous and affable, the señora charming, the doctor attentive and apparently successful, the servants deferential, there was one inmate of the family whose sour and sullen disfavor toward Norbert never showed change or softening. This was the man whose initial, surly reception of them in the storm and darkness Norbert could not easily forget, Venero, the trusted and confidential clerk of the merchant.

Norbert had experienced a distinct relief in not finding this man upon the scene the morning after their arrival. From Señor Anastro he had received tidings of the death of his father's friend, Master Bouterwek, in the house over the way. He had found himself forced by Jacqueline's condition and the imperative orders of Doctor Hoekstra to abandon any idea of seeking another lodging as he would fain have done among people of like faith and purpose with his own family. He remained therefore on terms of guarded watchfulness in the house of a man by race and religion hostile, although in disposition, as it appeared, peculiarly friendly to himself and his sister.

Venero had returned after a day's absence, but only to depart again, and at no time since Norbert had become a member of the family of Anastro had the cashier, as he was usually styled, been present for more than a few days at a time. His various short journeys were explained by the merchant as being taken on urgent business relative to a large purchase of indigo.

When Norbert reached Jacqueline's chamber he found that Doctor Hoekstra had just left after assuring her that she was doing well, but must by no means leave her bed nor remove the bandages from her eyes. She complained of a weary sense of weakness, and suddenly sitting up in bed she exclaimed in a whisper to her brother:

" Norbert, I believe that if I could get out in the free air and once have all I want to eat I should now be as well as ever ! You cannot think how hungry I am, and they never let me have any food stronger than these little blanc-manges and custards. I long for a good hearty meal, and if I could have it I believe I could leave this hateful room and this wretched town and go home to my dear mother."

Norbert looked at her for a moment without replying, a sudden and startling thought for the first

time stirring to life. He had closed the door on entering, and now holding it with his hand to guard
against intrusion, he whispered :

" Jacqueline, has it ever entered thy mind that
this long bandaging of thy eyes might be needless ?
Hast thou tested them at all since the doctor oper-
ated on the lids ? "

" No, the doctor has strictly forbidden me to do
so."

" Never mind what Doctor Hoekstra has forbidden. I have a notion he will spin out his visits as
long as he gets a good gold crown for each, and
mayhap there is little left him now but to keep
thee from growing strong and to keep us both in
the dark. Take off that bandage, little sister, and
let me have a look at thy eyes."

Jacqueline obeyed. After earnest inspection and
a series of simple tests they were both satisfied that
the eyes were indeed weak, but that the serious
trouble was at an end.

" It is even possible, Jacqueline, that they would
grow strong faster now were they left unbound.
This hot, heavy bandage to my mind does but increase the fever and weakness in them. However,
put it back now, lest Valerie notice its removal, but
instead of lying here growing steadily weaker, take
the time when we are all at dinner to walk about
the room and exercise thy limbs. If possible I will
procure thee some stronger food at noon. The
fashion of thy treatment takes on a new and suspicious color to my thought, and I have much to
consider, for I greatly misdoubt that we are no
longer guests in this house, but blinded and deluded
prisoners."

As he entered the room below at dinner time,
Norbert found the family increased since the morning by the arrival of two persons. Venero, the
cashier, who had been absent now for several days,
had returned to the Rue d'Augustin within the hour,

and a young Dominican monk, a frequent visitor, known in the house only as "the *padre*," sat down with himself, Valerie, and their host at the table.

Norbert found his eyes involuntarily drawn again and again to Venero, whose appearance, ill-favored at best, had never impressed him as so repulsive as at this hour. His face showed itself as haggard and jaded to a degree ; his shabby doublet was weather-stained and soiled ; his roughened hair and glassy eyes seemed to indicate that he had not slept for many nights.

To Norbert's greeting he replied only by a sullen nod of his head, not even lifting his eyes. Norbert, however, who had in the last hour received a new arousal of purpose and was not minded to be easily daunted, asked after a few moments :

"And where has the indigo business taken you this time, Master Venero ? "

The cashier glowered at him for a moment without a word. A slight, hardly perceptible motion of Anastro's hand, however, seemed to admonish him to reply and he accordingly said harshly :

" Only as far as Mechlin this time," and therewith lapsed again into morose silence.

Norbert felt throughout the meal an unwonted and inexplicable sense of oppression which he strove to shake off, as well as to conceal, by forcing himself to careless talkativeness. He noted swift glances of unknown significance now and again between the master of the house and Valerie, and it seemed to him that a strangely sinister expression lurked in the glittering eyes of Anastro whenever they rested upon himself. The *padre* was watchful, given to bland smiles, but unwontedly silent.

The more Norbert's vague suspicion was aroused, and the more ill at ease he became, the more careless and confident grew his demeanor. As they all rose from the table he declared that he had eaten

M

so heartily that he must take a little exercise in the garden, and accordingly singing a gay little song he passed through the narrow hall which led between the kitchen and offices to the garden door.

At the entrance to the kitchen, which was open, he stopped and looked in. The cook's scullion, a miserable urchin known only as Juan in the household, was cleaning knives at a low bench. The cook herself, a stout Fleming with white cap and apron, stood bare-armed before the fireplace preparing a stew of meat and vegetables for the servants' dinner. Norbert had ingratiated himself with this woman, a good-natured body, and stepping in now and crossing the kitchen to where she stood, he said low, but in broad Flemish dialect:

"Look you, Kristel, why not give a poor fellow whose appetite is never still, a chunk of that cold mutton on the table yonder? That's a good mopsy! By four of the clock I shall be as hungry as a wild boar, and marry but that would relish!"

"Well, then, jonkheer, you must stir the mess here for me," the cook answered in her thick, husky voice, laughing and stepping to the table.

"Cock sure will I that," replied Norbert heartily, taking the great iron spoon from her hand. As he did so his eye caught sight of a small bunch of paper crushed and soiled, at the edge of the hearth among the ashes. Something in the character of it gave him a strange thrill of surprise and recognition. Bending he picked up the paper, asking carelessly:

"See, Kristel, who threw this ball of paper in the ashes? Is it worth aught, think you?"

"Nay, Master Tontorf," said Kristel hoarsely; "it is not worth half a maravedi, else would not Master Venero have thrown it there as he did but now. Trust him for that. There, put that in your pocket, my fine cavalier, and remember poor old Kristel when you eat it," and therewith she placed in his hands a thick wedge of the cold mutton.

"Trust me for that," whispered Norbert and accompanied the words by a hearty smack on the hard, red cheek of the good woman, at which the boy Juan grinned broadly. Then crowding meat and paper both into an inner pocket, he made haste to reach the garden in time to avoid being found in the kitchen by Valerie, who almost immediately appeared, coming out to gather a few roses, so she said.

An hour later, having sustained his part in a prolonged conversation with the señora, Norbert took refuge upstairs, first giving Jacqueline the mutton to satisfy her ravenous hunger and then withdrawing to his own cell-like room.

Here he lighted a candle and at last opened the crushed and dusty paper which he had snatched from the ashes of the kitchen fireplace. As he smoothed it out on his knee and recognized its familiar aspect, Norbert's heart beat fiercely with wonder, doubt, and dread. What could it signify? The paper, which was a small, printed sheet announcing a new edition of the writings of Murmellius by the house of Tontorf, in Middelburg, was the fac-simile of a hundred which Norbert well remembered lying in a pile on the shelves of his father's salesroom. How had it come into the hands of Venero on his expedition to Mechlin? Some chance might have brought it about, and yet Norbert was seized with ominous foreboding. The paper he found contained a few crumbs of cake, dry and stale, and also a small label which had at first escaped his notice. Holding this up to the light of the candle, Norbert read the printed name of a Middelburg baker, whose shop in the Lange Delft was nearly opposite his father's house.

Instantly the truth flashed upon his mind beyond the reach of further question. Venero had been in Middelburg, not in Mechlin—what were lies to a varlet like him? He had been not only in Middelburg, but had been in the Lange Delft, had purchased food at the shop of their neighbor, had also visited the printery of his father, and had there casually or by intention obtained the printed sheet used later to wrap his food. All very plain, but what then ? Norbert asked himself. Why should these facts, which seemed clearly enough indicated, cause him such strong alarm and agitation ? Why should not Venero visit Middelburg and the Lange Delft and his father's house ?

A moment's thought convinced Norbert that in the sinister secrecy of the expedition, in the concealment of it by sullen silence and falsehood, there lay ample reason for apprehension, reason not easily to be argued away. Had his errand to Middelburg been one of an honorable and ordinary character, why had Venero not informed him, Norbert, that he had been thither ? Why had he not made himself the bearer of letters or messages to him and Jacqueline from their father's house ?

With his mouth hard set, but with resolute quietude of manner, Norbert now re-entered Jacqueline's room, the ill-boding papers hidden in the pocket of his doublet. He found his sister sitting up in bed, her eyes unbandaged, looking almost as bright and vigorous as before her illness.

" Little sister," he whispered, sitting down on the bed's edge and taking her hand, " think over all the days since we came to this house and see if thou canst recall any time when by any means thou mayest have allowed Señora Valerie or Doctor Hoekstra to suppose that our father conducted the secret business we know of at the printery, or that our place was used for the meetings of the congregation of the *Fleur-de-lis* ? ''

Jacqueline's eyes dilated with sudden alarm, for the very quietness of her brother's manner suggested a strong effort of self-control.

"Oh, Norbert," she whispered, "I did—the night we came here, when Valerie found my little book here on my bosom and asked me concerning it because she so sadly desires to have one herself, —I did, yes I did tell her that father printed this one and that I would send her one better and larger when we go home. Was that wrong? In the morning I felt afraid and in doubt about it, and although she has often since tried to talk with me about what father does and all, I never, never have spoken again, nor mentioned the meetings of the *Fleur-de-lis*. Oh, Norbert, why dost thou look so?" and Jacqueline, thoroughly terrified, burst into tears.

White to the lips, but with strong self-command, Norbert constrained his voice to gentleness, and replied :

"Do not cry, Jacqueline. We must act now and keep our heads cool. I am satisfied that some devilish treachery is on foot concerning my father, and that we must leave here this very night, if possible, and get to Middelburg in time to give him warning. Thou must be brave and strong and steady and help me as thou canst. Where are thy clothes?" and Norbert drew out from a chest the saddlebags in which Jacqueline had brought a change of raiment to Antwerp. Chest and bags were alike empty, nor was there to be found in the room a single article of apparel belonging to the young girl.

"The señora has looked out for that," said Norbert under his breath. "She has played her part well throughout, but she has not wholly blocked us even so," and he went into his own room and quickly brought back the green doublet and hosen which he had worn on the journey to Antwerp, and which, as they were stained by rain and travel, he had laid aside.

"There, Jacqueline," he said, smiling in spite of

the stern oppression on his heart, "we will see what a soncy lad thou wilt make. Stand a moment! See, thou art not two inches less than I, and thy half-long locks would not be amiss for either man or maid. So! Now hide these things well under the bedclothes. Lie upon them to keep them from Valerie's sharp vision. Tie the bandage again upon thy eyes, and for the rest, hold thyself ready when the time comes to move. It may not be to-night. In sooth I know not how we shall ever be able to make our way from this house, since the liberty to do so will by no means be given us, and the request on our part would but add to our perils. How about this door?" and Norbert touched the latch of the one opening upon the corridor.

"It is always locked on the outside at night," replied Jacqueline, "but no key is left to be seen by day."

"Valerie doubtless keeps the key," said Norbert, reflecting anxiously. The obstacles encompassing their departure from the house, whose hospitality they had so ignorantly sought, seemed at the moment insurmountable, but the dogged courage of the young Zeelander rose with the difficulties.

With buoyant step he ran down the staircase, dallied for a moment with Valerie in the parlor, then saying that he had a mind for a stroll along the river since the day was so fine, he repaired to the shop where he found Anastro. His request for the key of the house door was promptly complied with. Anastro himself opened the door, after having summoned the man who was usually appointed as escort to the young Middelburger, and thus accompanied, Norbert was soon strolling on the bank of the Scheldt, where the dense forest of masts gave token of the enormous trade of the city.

Loitering along, Norbert presently recognized a small vessel whose skipper he knew, a vessel which plied between Antwerp and Middelburg with fish and oil. The skipper himself, with his hands thrust deep into his breeches pockets, was lounging on the deck of his boat. With a sudden impulse and access of boldness, Norbert stopped, his companion stopping also, and shouted a greeting to the sailor.

The man responded with a cheery holloa and an expression of surprise at seeing Norbert so far from home.

"When do you set sail for Middelburg?" called Norbert.

"To-night with sundown, if I get my cargo in time, else with daylight in the morning," was the shouted answer. "Better come with us, jonkheer. We'll land you in Middelburg in twenty-four hours if this wind holds. You'll scarce find a better boat nor a faster."

"Thanks, Master Reuser," said Norbert gayly, "I know your boat well and gladly would I sail with you; but not on this voyage. A week or two from now it may be thought of. I'll promise to look up your boat then if she is in harbor."

The skipper made a flourish of his hands in acknowledgment, and Norbert and his escort passed on.

For a moment the temptation to give the fellow the slip and board the Middelburg craft had been overstrong. His heart had leaped wildly at the thought of thus speedily and unhindered reaching his father and giving him the warning which he felt to be so urgently required. The thought of leaving little Jacqueline, however, in her lonely prison, for as such Norbert now fully recognized the house of Anastro, sufficed to calm his sudden impulse. Moreover, a glance at the fellow by his side had shown him a swift motion of his hand to the short sword which hung at his belt, and he concluded, with a strong revulsion of feeling, that the man had received orders from his master to forcibly prevent any move toward escape on his part.

As they walked along the river a sense of bitter and vengeful wrath mounted hotly to Norbert's brain. He saw himself tricked, trapped, deceived, betrayed, and held fast in the toils of the Spaniard, whose artifice and craft had so easily gotten the better of his youth and inexperience. On and on with rapid strides he walked through the narrow streets and under the dark shadows of the houses, the agent of Anastro ever dogging his steps, the tempest of rage ever mounting within him. Then unawares, for Norbert had paid no heed to the direction he took, they came out under the soaring spire of the great cathedral whose chimes rang out just then in joyous benediction over his head.

With their thrilling peal a softer feeling came into Norbert's heart and subdued his fierce anger. The memory of holy thoughts and sacred words of love and forgiveness stirred within him, and with it his mind grew clear and steady, and with all the power of faith of which he was possessed he cast himself upon the Divine love and protection.

XVII

THE NIGHT WORK OF SEÑOR ANASTRO

THE evening had passed. The chimes of the cathedral, distant but heard distinctly in the Rue d'Augustin, had rung out the hour of midnight when Norbert, cautiously pushing open the fenestral of his sister's chamber, leaned out, looking down into the shadowed garden.

Jacqueline, fully dressed in the garments with which he had supplied her, but covered in the bed-clothes to her chin, had fallen into a light slumber, as Norbert could see by the faint moon rays which qualified the darkness of the room. He had tried the door and had found it, as he expected, securely locked on the outer side. His own closet possessed no window and no other door save that which communicated with the chamber of Jacqueline.

Norbert was studying quietly, but with a loudly-throbbing heart, what means might be within his grasp for immediate escape from this ill-omened house, means such as were, thus far, hard to discover.

For himself he had a brace of pistols at his belt and a sharp dagger within his doublet. Around his waist, inside his shirt, he wore a money belt which was still fairly well filled, despite the heavy drain of the doctor's and Anastro's charges. Such were his personal resources, to which might be added a lithe body, a stout heart, and a clear head. Jacqueline, he was sure, could be counted on for courage, for obedience, and for silence, but what would all these resources avail if no means were to be found to put them to the touch ?

The chamber was in the second story of the house. Looking down, Norbert took keen note of the ledges of the windows of the offices immediately below him. They projected slightly. To let himself down by the aid of them into the garden would be difficult, but not impossible for him, but for Jacqueline ?—there was the rub. And, once down, to scale the high, blank walls of the garden would be hardly less difficult. But what other method offered itself as even remotely possible ?

With a sudden impulse and an audacious belief that if he could get down by this means he could also return, Norbert, having closed the door of his own room, swung himself lightly out of the window, and by hard and breathless scrambling with hands and feet, ending in a severe but not serious fall, found himself a minute later on the garden walk not far from the kitchen door.

To his keen surprise this door stood open. The night was breathless and sultry, the air heavy with thunder from clouds which, hanging low, intercepted the moon's rays ever and anon.

With the daring bred of the desperation of the hour, Norbert stole noiselessly into the kitchen, which was wholly dark, save for a single ray of red light which pierced it from the farthest corner. As his eyes became accustomed to the gloom Norbert, gazing with intense eagerness around him, discerned a narrow flight of stairs, hardly more than a ladder, indeed, which he at once concluded gave access to the servants' sleeping apartments. These, he knew, extended beyond his own quarters, and were connected with the main corridor of the second story by a dark, winding passage, the outlet of which he had often noticed, near Jacqueline's door. This was a discovery worth making, if dubious, for Norbert had been forced by his own experience to wholly abandon the hope of accomplishing Jacqueline's descent by the window. The question of his own return by that same path was causing him poignant anxiety, but for the present he determined to investigate a little farther in the direction of that red light, which he was confident proceeded from the laboratory of Anastro, the more since from time to time he heard low voices coming from the same direction.

Groping his way with utmost caution, he soon found that the cook's store-room intervened between the kitchen and the source of the light toward which he was working. The store-room gained, he discovered that the light streamed through a small aperture in the wall, arranged evidently to connect the laboratory with the kitchen for the convenience of the master of the house.

Stooping low, Norbert was able to look through this narrow opening and command a small portion of the laboratory. The door of it stood open into the Red Room, and it was from this apartment that the light and the murmur of voices had penetrated into the kitchen, the intervening laboratory being unlighted.

A faint, sickening odor pervaded the place, and despite the heat Norbert descried in the Red Room a brazier in which a deep bed of coals was burning. Over this brazier stood Anastro in his long black gown, holding in one hand a small porcelain box from which he took something between his thumb and finger, something which he slowly and carefully sprinkled upon the live coals. This done, he lifted to his nostrils a large sponge and withdrew out of sight. And now a cloud of steam arose proceeding from the brazier and the air became charged with the strange odors perceptible before in a slight degree.

A light laugh startled Norbert. He had not dreamed that Valerie was present, nor could he see her now, but her voice though muffled was unmistakable.

"Holy Virgin, señor!" she exclaimed, "will you put an end to us all first? I pray you, excuse me. I congratulate you on your success. Another moment and I should offer in my own person full proof of it."

Norbert heard a door softly open and close and supposed Anastro now to be alone. Dizzy himself, with the mysterious fumes which now filled even his hiding-place, he leaned against the wall, his breath coming hard and fast, and a strange dimness clouding his vision. A sense of vague, bewildering beauty, of nameless, impossible delight surged through his brain. He felt his limbs sinking beneath him in a delicious languor which he cared not to resist. Voices seemed to ring in his ears, mingled with the cathedral chimes and a great onrushing tide as of many waters. Far away in some incalculable distance a voice like that of Anastro seemed saying : " Come, now, it is all over." Then a sound, as of a door closing.

"It would suffice to kill a hundred men."

Who was it that spoke? Surely that was the voice of Venero, harsh and menacing. The suggestion startled Norbert back to his senses and, as the fumes slowly escaped from the narrow closet and the air cleared, he rallied his intelligence and listened again as for his life.

"Yes. There can be no mistake this time. My part, Venero, is fulfilled. All depends now upon you."

"Were it not better to make short work, and deal with both? Two heretics less were better than one."

"Nay, nay," was the impatient answer, and something followed unintelligible to Norbert's ears as both men now apparently had turned to leave the room.

Still for another second Norbert waited with straining ears and starting eyes.

" Over this brazier stood Anastro in his long black gown."

He saw Anastro as he passed again across the field of his vision, rubbing his hands slowly together, his face full of grave reflection, not agitated, not flushed nor excited.

Then again the door was opened.

"Well, Venero, what now?" was Anastro's question.

"I returned, señor, only to say, that having accomplished the errand on which, please remember, it is you who send me——"

"On which I send you, Venero, and for which the *padre* has fully absolved you, pray remember," and a touch of scorn could be detected in Anastro's voice.

"Having done your bidding, if it please you, I will not return hither but get me forthwith to bed. I am weary beyond reason and my head will burst if I cannot soon sleep."

"*Mort Dieu!* what care I what you do when you have done your work," muttered Anastro, and again the door closed.

In three bounds Norbert was up the steep kitchen stairs and at the top of them found himself in a long low room extending over the kitchen in which he dimly discerned several beds. Surely there must be access from this room into the passage whose outlet he had so often seen! But to find it in this darkness, to find it without stumbling and waking one of the servants! Was it not to attempt the impossible?

Falling on his hands and knees Norbert felt his way along the floor until he came to the wall, which he followed, groping every inch of the way for the sign of a door. The seconds seemed like hours, the close darkness seemed to enswathe him like a mantle and clog his motions, and the sense that with every second Venero was approaching the chamber where Jacqueline lay in her innocent unconsciousness almost maddened him. Then sud-

denly he felt a break in the smooth surface of the
wall and knew it for the frame of a door. Thanks
be to heaven, the door was open! In a flash he
had gained the dark passage and creeping stealthily
along its winding wall in another instant he had
reached a point whence he could command a view
of the door of Jacqueline's chamber, dimly lighted
by the lamp in the corridor.

It was closed. Absolute stillness was upon the
place. Was he too late? Where was Venero?
Had he, Norbert, been moments, hours, or only
seconds in reaching the spot? Norbert's brain
reeled with the uncertainty, but even then soft
footsteps could be heard approaching, and he distinctly heard in the hush of the midnight the door
of Valerie's room close.

It flashed through Norbert's quickened perception
then that Venero had been delayed by the need of
securing the key, which was doubtless in the keeping of Valerie, and he thanked God and braced
himself tensely in the dark shadow where he stood
for what should follow.

A sudden coolness and calm came to him as it
does to many men in moments of crisis. As if it
were quite a matter of course, he saw Venero approach the door, holding in one hand the brazier of
glowing coals, in the other the key. He saw him
unlock the door and softly set it wide open, then
turn and take from his doublet the porcelain box
which he had noted just now in the hands of Anastro.
He saw how, with a swift but careful hand, he scattered the powder with which the box was filled
upon the coals; again the fumes rose slowly about
him and Norbert saw no more, but he followed
hard after, with one swift, noiseless bound, the
form of the cashier almost lost now in the en-
shrouding mist proceeding from the brazier.

As he entered the chamber, Venero was in the
act of opening the inner door, and, with a frenzied

sense of exultant release, Norbert perceived that it was he, not Jacqueline, who was to have been the victim.

In the darkness Norbert stood motionless, while with stealthy swiftness the Spaniard, stretching his arm to its length, placed the burning, steaming brazier inside the threshold, nothing doubting that Norbert was quietly sleeping within. Even as he did so a swift, stinging blow, as from a hammer, struck him behind the ear, knocking him instantly senseless, and, without a sound, he fell in a miserable heap to the floor.

"Rise instantly, Jacqueline, and be ready to follow me," said Norbert, and the young girl sprang from her bed, awake and ready on the instant, watching with speechless amazement as her brother tied a towel tightly around the gaping mouth and limp, hanging head of Venero, pinioned his arms to his sides with his own belt, and then opening the closet door, dragged or rather flung him on the bed.

For one instant then Norbert stood irresolute, but, in the school in which he had been taught, revenge had been forbidden.

Snatching the ewer from Jacqueline's room, he poured its contents upon the brazier, extinguishing its fire ; then he closed the door, locked it, and dropped the key into his pocket.

Struggling fiercely against the benumbing power of the noxious vapors with which the room, despite the open window, was filled, Norbert, holding Jacqueline hard by her hand, forced himself to pause at the door and listen a second. The stillness of the corridor was unbroken. They must dare all to win or lose within the moments next to follow.

A few seconds sufficed to close and lock the outer door, the key of which Norbert also pocketed, and then, still undiscovered, brother and sister, hand in hand, panting and dizzy, but still undaunted, fled down the darkness of the narrow passage to the door by which Norbert had hardly five minutes before emerged from the servants' room.

"Drop on thy knees and keep close to me," whispered Norbert, as he himself set Jacqueline the example. Suddenly he stopped, for against the dim, gray square of a window the outline of a head was lifted. Juan Jaureguy, the cook's scullion, half-awakened, sat up in bed for an instant, murmured a few drowsy, meaningless words, and dropped again upon his pillow. More stealthily than before the two crept on again through the long room. The stairs were reached at last, and in another moment they stood in the dark kitchen below.

The red light still filtered through from the pantry door, but the place was still and the outer door yet open. Light-footed as creatures of the field or forest, the two sprang through into the garden and in another moment were safely hidden among the clustering oleanders lining the high wall. Hardly had they reached this point of vantage when they saw a faint light moving to and fro in the kitchen, and with wildly beating hearts they beheld the tall, gaunt figure of Anastro, a candle in his hand, framed in by the kitchen door. Slowly he descended the shallow steps, advanced a few paces into the path, then turning, gazed fixedly upward at the open fenestral of Jacqueline's chamber, from which thin wreaths of steamy vapor still floated.

Norbert pressed his sister's hand with a tense grasp.

"Do not tremble," he breathed in her ear; "he has heard nothing."

Apparently satisfied with the results of his examination, since the exhalations told that Venero had done his errand, and the open window gave guarantee that Jacqueline, whose presence might still serve his diabolical purpose, would remain unharmed, the Spaniard returned to the kitchen. They heard the noise made by the rude bar with which the door was made fast, saw the tiny light diminish, and then all was dark, and the hush of the garden remained unbroken.

"God helping us," whispered Norbert, "we have four or five hours now in our favor. The next thing for us to do is to take this wall. What may await us in yonder inn, who can tell?" and he looked up at the house whose upper stories rose dark beyond the wall.

"We can do it, and nothing we can ever meet can be so bad as those Spanish people," whispered Jacqueline firmly.

A new spirit and courage had taken possession of the young girl, stimulated by the crucial dangers through which they had already passed and yet more by the joy of at last being free.

Springing upon an oleander tub, Norbert gave a mighty leap and grasped the upper edge of the wall, which was not less than ten feet high. With the agility of youth and much practice in such feats he had soon swung himself to the top, but instantly fell flat upon his face, measuring his length upon the stones.

"There are people over here," he whispered cautiously; "wait a bit."

The moments passed in almost unendurable suspense. The moonlight which filled the garden showed Jacqueline Norbert's figure still flattened and motionless above her head. Then she saw him slowly lift one finger to the sky. She looked up. A black cloud of enormous bulk was sweeping upward. Jacqueline saw and her confidence was, renewed. Five minutes passed and then, the moon swallowed up in the black folds of the mantling cloud and its light extinguished, Norbert moved again.

He scrambled to his knees and stretched his hands

down to Jacqueline, who, holding them fast in hers, was quickly though painfully, with many scratches and bruises, drawn up to his side.

Before them, in the house whose rear court they were about to enter, they could now see lights streaming from the lower windows, doors set wide open, and could hear a confused sound of many voices of men.

Leaping to the ground, Norbert held up his arms, Jacqueline sprang from the wall into them, and they now stood together and reconnoitered the situation.

"I have taken pains," whispered Norbert, "to observe this house. It faces on a street which leads something directly down to the river, and we must pass through the house to reach the street. There is no other way. It is an inn, but one of a somewhat doubtful character, I have been told. Closed and silent it is through the day much of the time, as I have myself noticed. The goodman, however, seems to do a thriving business at night. I have my own suspicion that it is a resort of Gueux.[1] In any case, Jacqueline, our only hope now is to swagger it through. Be bluff and bold. Do not shrink from thy part, but chance it cheerily; use thy wits and we shall win through. Now, forward!"

In another moment, with an air of careless confidence, the two had entered the rear door of the brightly lighted public room of the inn, their entrance scarce observed among the many coming and going. The host, however, Norbert noticed, followed them steadily with his eye from his place behind two great kegs of ale. The room was well filled with gentlemen drinking and dicing, the air redolent of the fumes of wine and spirits and filled with noisy revelry.

---

[1] The Beggars or Revolutionary party in the Netherlands.

Norbert lounged easily down the room, followed by Jacqueline, who held her head gayly, thrust her hands deep in her pockets, and even whistled a blithe little tune as she looked fearlessly about her.

"Holloa, jonkheer!" cried a cavalier, glancing up from his game of venter point as they passed, "has Brederode come, know you?"

"Nay, messire," replied Norbert, doffing his cap, "but I heard outside that he was on his way hither. I will e'en look down the street and see if he be not in sight. He should be ere this," and he moved toward the door, one eye uneasily keeping watch of the landlord.

"Do, if you will, jonkheer," replied the other, carelessly returning to his flagon of Rhenish and his game. "The Great Beggar is late to-night. We have waited on his motions a full hour already."

Norbert and Jacqueline now quickly gained the door of the inn room, which opened upon a narrow entry, giving exit to the street.

As the door swung to behind them they saw standing at the street door, which he held open with one hand, a man of burly and coarse figure, richly dressed, with long, curling locks, a striking face, features bold and handsome, but purple and coarsened by debauchery. In his right hand he held the reins of his horse, which Norbert could dimly discern standing just beyond him in the dark and narrow street.

"Body o' me, lad, come hither and hold my horse!" cried this notable personage imperatively, adding a bewildering string of oaths. "Here have I stood now a full minute, pounding on this door and never a varlet to answer my summons. I was promised here a good hour since, but such a coil as I have had to hinder me, and when at last I could start, not a devil of a servant was to be found!"

Norbert had already taken the reins from the

hand of the Seigneur de Brederode, for in the cavalier before him he instantly recognized the notorious
leader of the Beggars, the wild, reckless descendant
of the sovereign counts of Holland. That he had
been during the preceding months ceaselessly engaged in the enterprise of secretly enrolling troops
for an attack upon the Spanish troops in the town
of Walcheren was well known to Norbert. His
presence in this obscure Antwerp inn to meet such
a company was wholly in character.

"Can you stand for me here an hour or two, my
lad ? " asked Brederode, as he pushed open the
inner door, too impatient for long parley ; "Beggars
pay in gold sometimes, you know," he added with
a careless laugh.

"Gladly, gladly, my lord," returned Norbert
with hearty emphasis ; "and you can pay in silver,
or pay not at all, as you please. It were little to
do for the cause," he added in a lower voice.

"Right, youngster, right," answered Brederode,
and paused, albeit impatiently. "I see you're
made of the right stuff. Have you enrolled with
any of my men ? You're of fighting age, and that
young brother of yours is old enough, methinks, to
wear a sword."

"I have entered the service of the prince," said
Norbert, sinking his voice to a whisper, "and shall
soon be on my way to Germany."

"Hah, sits the wind in that quarter ? " cried the
great seigneur ; "take my loving greeting then to
the Nassaus, but bide not over long in Germany.
Bid them hurry back. There will be wild work
here ere long," and with the words the door closed
upon his burly figure.

Norbert and Jacqueline now stepped into the
street, closing the inn door behind them. The
reins of Brederode's horse, a spirited, blooded creature, were over Norbert's arm. In silence and deep
thought he stood for a moment.

"Jacqueline," he said at last, "there is but one way for us, much as I mislike it. My lord of Brederode must wait a week or two for his horse. Mount," and therewith he held out his hand and Jacqueline mounted at once, then Norbert leaped into the saddle and touching the animal a light flick of the reins, they dashed down toward the river.

"Is it not wicked, Norbert?" whispered Jacqueline, terrified at this procedure.

"Very," replied Norbert, too much absorbed in the immediate solution of the problem of their instant departure from Antwerp to canvass the moral aspects of the step he had felt forced to take.

Without hesitation they directed their course to the Scheldt and to the ship of Master Reuser. Dismounting, Norbert left Jacqueline to hold the horse, and, dropping over the edge of the rude wharf to the deck of the vessel, he hailed the watch with a curt command to knock up the skipper on the instant.

Stupid and drowsy, Master Reuser presently stumbled up the hatchway, his sharp surprise at seeing Norbert, however, making him instantly wide awake.

In a brief, whispered colloquy the young man now offered the ship's master a sum of money so large as to completely dazzle the worthy man if he would up sail and start down the river without a moment's delay, taking as passengers, so far as Hoedenskerke, himself, his young cousin, and his horse.

The slowness of the phlegmatic sailor in reaching a decision produced perhaps the most painful crisis of the night's experiences to Norbert. At every sound he felt the approach of a pursuer, and his eyes stared painfully into the darkness to discern Jacqueline still waiting, still in safety.

"But, my young sir," said Master Reuser at last, "what an' if we do drop down the river a league or so? We can make no progress till the tide turn, for this wind is hardly enough to fill a flag. We could but anchor under Osterwell and wait for day."

"That is all I ask," cried Norbert eagerly. "You admit that your cargo, though late in coming, is now complete. You hear my offer, my good friend. You know my father's son would not ask you to go on a fool's errand. What I ask is '*under the cross.*' What say you?"

Norbert believed that the sailor was at heart a Beggar, and he determined to risk this last appeal, well as he knew the danger.

The captain turned quickly on his heel.

"Pipe up the men," he said, turning to the man on the watch. "Tell them to make small noise about it, but get her under weigh quicker than ever they did before."

Then turning to Norbert, who was already climbing back to the wharf, he said softly:

"I conceive you, sir. Your haste is for *the cause*, either to save life or country. That is enough. You can command me."

Jacqueline and the good steed of the Baron of Brederode were soon safely conveyed to the deck of the vessel, and, to Norbert's indescribable relief, they found themselves in half an hour slowly slipping down the river.

Anchoring a few leagues down stream beneath the walls of the small village of Osterwell, where, but three months before, the patriots under young Marnix had met such a bloody death, they were ready to take early advantage of the turning tide.

With the first dawn of day, under a fair and favoring breeze, they set sail for the village of Hoedenskerke, whence the horse of the Seigneur de Brederode and a ferry across from Beveland to their own island of Walcheren would bring them in a few hours to Middelburg.

XVIII

IN THE KING'S NAME

THEY had left their horse outside the city gates to be stabled for the night and sent back to the lord of Brederode in the morning.

Under the stars of the sweet June night they stood, Norbert and Jacqueline, at the carved portico of the house in the Lange Delft. At last they were at home. The house was dark, however, and strangely still, as still as the house plague-visited at whose door they had knocked in vain two months since in Antwerp.

"Norbert," said Jacqueline, with a strange tremor in her voice, "what is that fastened across the door? Look! It is a chain."

Yes, a chain fastened by a padlock, a padlock sealed and stamped with the king's arms, the cognizance of Philip, by the grace of God king of Spain and the Netherlands.

Norbert's heart gave one mighty leap and then stood still. For an instant they stared at one another as if paralyzed. Then taking Jacqueline's wrist in a grasp which was like that of a vice, Norbert hurried out from the portico and around the street corner, down the dark alley to the vaulted entrance to the courtyard.

In a house across the narrow way a casement window was pushed open then and a light curtain blew out in the wind of the summer night.

They had reached the inner gate of wrought iron now with its gilded crest of the Tontorfs. Through its grating they could look into the moonlit courtyard, most familiar, most dear, and yet wearing now a cold, unresponding emptiness. The long low buildings with their ivied walls and their many windows, darkly mysterious, seemed to stare at them as if they were strangers. Nowhere was welcome, no light burned for them, no eye watched.

Norbert passed his hand across the iron gate and felt a chain. On the chain was a padlock, and on the padlock the seal of the majesty of Spain.

Then there was a step behind them and Hendrika, the faithful servant, stood in the deep shadow of the vaulted entrance and wept.

"Come," she said. "I have watched for you. Come. You must not be seen here," and she led them across the dark lane and into the open door of a house of the humbler sort. Upstairs they followed her to a garret room without a window. Here Hendrika gave them seats and set down her flickering candle on a broken stool.

Then they saw that her eyes were well-nigh washed away in tears and her poor face deeply furrowed, changed to that of an aged and woe-worn woman.

"Children, dear young master, precious little Juffrouw Jacqueline, I cannot talk about it. It is more than can be borne," and she burst into bitter weeping. "All are gone, all, all!"

"Gone where?" Norbert spoke at last. He was as if paralyzed. Were they too late? Had the bitter struggle they had made availed naught?

"To God, dear young master," and Hendrika sobbed wildly. "Saints in heaven are they now, my master, my mistress, my angel, little lady Helma!"

"Hendrika," said Norbert steadily, "you must be quiet and tell me if it is surely too late for me to strike a blow for them yet." The thing was monstrous, incredible! He refused to believe it. Such things were doubtless of daily occurrence in the stricken country, but not to them, his own, his dearest, noblest, best beloved. Such a doom could not have come thus swiftly, thus awfully!

"Too late," wailed Hendrika; "oh yes, too late. Pastor Droust and Mijnheer Heldring went after them to the Hague and would fain have interposed, but it was all in vain. The warrant was served by the servants of the regent herself. The complaint had been lodged they say in due form with the authorities in Brussels."

"By whom was the complaint made?"

"No one knows!"

"When did it happen?"

"Four days ago we were routed out of bed at daybreak and searched and examined as to our religion and our loyalty. The master and Mevrouw Tontorf and the dear Juffrouw Helma and the bookkeeper were the only ones taken into custody. Oh, but the wretches went everywhere searching for Bibles and such like tokens, but not one could they find. They were securely hid, even from our own people."

"Was there among these officials a man who spoke with a Spanish accent; a man of dark brow and evil, lowering glance; a man clad in a brown doublet, much stained and worn?" asked Norbert with stifled voice.

"Oh, yes!" cried Hendrika. "He was the worst, the most pitiless and bitter of all. He had an evil eye and most determined was he to find some trace of printed heresy."

"Go on," said Norbert. His arms were around Jacqueline's waist, her head had sunk upon his shoulder.

"I cannot, dear young master, I cannot! It is too terrible! Others will tell you of their glorious death, for so it was, in full faith and constancy. To have a father and mother who wear the martyr crown is not that greater glory, dear master Norbert, than if they wore a kingly one?"

"Hendrika," said Norbert, rising with the calmness of despair and untwining Jacqueline's arms from his neck. "Care you for the child. You see she is fainting. I must visit the pastor and know all that he can tell me."

"Go to Mijnheer Heldring, the cloth syndic. He was ever your father's friend, and he also went to the Hague and showed himself loyal and courageous. He can tell you all," interposed Hendrika.

"Rather will I go to Pastor Droust," said Norbert. "He went with them also, you say."

"Yes, Master Norbert; the poor man was with them to the very end. But go not to him—not now," and Hendrika began to sob and wring her hands.

"Wherefore should I not ? "

"The sight of it, the shock of it," moaned Hendrika, "have crazed him. He is wild and wandering in his speech, and has neither slept nor eaten since that dreadful day. 'Doom and darkness! Doom and darkness!' he cries incessantly. It is better that you should not see him."

For a moment Norbert stood as if stupefied and then staggered out into the night, determined, if it took his own life or reason, to know the story to its last dregs of agony.

Until daybreak he sat with the kindly syndic, Heldring, the faithful friend of Nikolaas Tontorf, who had accompanied the doomed family to the Hague.

All that Heldring could say but confirmed Hendrika's story and filled out with heartrending details the awful outline which she had given. From the scene of martyrdom, it was but too true, the faithful pastor and devoted friend of the Tontorf family had returned with heart broken and reason shattered.

As for details, the complaint had been duly

lodged and credibly certified by citizens of names unknown of Antwerp that Nikolaas Tontorf printed and distributed Bibles and hymnals at his establishment at Middelburg, where he also permitted gatherings of malcontents and heretics and harbored and succored such persons. On this complaint the printer and his family had been arrested and conveyed to the Hague. Neither the master nor his wife nor daughter could or would deny the charges, which were furiously pressed by one Venero, who had been sent as witness by the regent from Brussels. The trial had taken place immediately upon their arrival at the Hague. They had all four been lodged for the night in the Gevangenpoort, where they had spent the night in singing hymns, repeating portions of Scripture, and in prayer, praying most of all for the beloved absent children.

At daybreak they had been led to the scaffold erected in the Binnenhof, and, with majestic fortitude and unfailing, fearless faith, had faced and tasted death.

"No one who looked upon them," said Mijnheer Heldring, "could pity them, but rather envy them that they witnessed so good a confession and met a death in which they seemed to find no sting. If you could but have seen the look on your father's face! He saw what others saw not. His last words were, 'Master, I come.' As for Helma, her face was like the face of a bride going out to meet her husband—serene, high, and of a seraphic sweetness. Your mother alone wept, but it was not for herself, nor even for those who tasted martyrdom by her side."

"I know," said Norbert softly. "It was for us."

XIX

"AS A WOODCOCK TO MINE OWN SPRINGE"

A T five o'clock in the morning, in the house in the Rue d'Augustin, Señor Anastro was stirring.

Too restless, too eager to know the results of his experiment to await the appearance of Venero, who was not likely to present himself for an hour or two longer, the Spaniard soon proceeded to the chamber of the cashier.

Opening the door cautiously, Anastro looked into the room only to find it empty and the bed undisturbed.

For a moment the Spaniard stood irresolute, wholly unable to explain to himself this surprising turn of affairs. Then, with swift steps, he hastened to Jacqueline's door, which he found locked, as he expected, and the key gone.

Valerie's room was next visited, but here a new surprise awaited the master of the house. Venero had not brought back the key to her. In fact, she told Anastro that she had requested that he should not disturb her again that night. The less she knew about the proceedings the better it suited her.

The present whereabouts of the cashier now became a matter of intense nervous anxiety to Anastro. That he had not left the house the close-barred outer doors and windows seemed to give full proof.

"Where is he?" Anastro hissed between his teeth, standing with cadaverous face and haggard eyes in the middle of the Red Room in the gray

204

early light. "What has been going on here ? " and he bent a malevolent glance of suspicion upon Valerie, who had followed him downstairs, wrapped in a rich purple robe, her hair streaming over her shoulders, her white feet bare.

"You grew a trifle amorous, methinks, over that same yellow-haired Dutch varlet, señora. If there has been treachery here in my own house make sure I shall sift it to the bottom, and that speedily ! "

Valerie faced him without flinching, with a hard little laugh and a slight yawn, whether real or pretended, no one could have guessed. She was born an actor.

"My good friend," she said, "you are something wild in your guessing this morning. I fear you have not slept, or that the fumes of your marvelous discovery have found lodgment in your own brain. The jonkheer was not ill-looking, but a more churlish wight in his attendance upon a lady saw I never. Truly he wearied me too much that I should take his part, the simpleton ! prating of his lady whom he had never seen," and the venomed glance of Valerie's dark eyes satisfied the Spaniard that if her devotion to himself were wavering her spite would yet have kept her true to his interest.

"But the question is," he cried impatiently, "where is Venero at this moment ? "

"Doubless locked into one room or the other of those luckless babes, who may be pardoned if they over-sleep this morning by an hour or two," replied Valerie with a heartless laugh. "It may even be that the very worthy Venero is caught in his own trap."

The idea seized Anastro at once that she was right, that the cashier had locked the outer door upon himself after entering Jacqueline's room, and then, overcome by the fumes of the burning powder, had been rendered powerless to leave the fateful spot.

Selecting two or three tools from a case, Anastro quickly returned to the upper corridor, and in a few minutes had succeeded in forcing the lock of Jacqueline's chamber door.

The morning light and the pure air streamed in through the open fenestral, fast dispelling the noxious odors which still lingered in the dreary little room, but a glance showed the master of the house that the room was empty.

"Surely this becomes mysterious," said the light voice of Valerie behind him. "If yon closet has no tale to tell, we may confess ourselves outwitted."

Without a word, but with face livid now with poisonous fury, Anastro, finding the inner door likewise locked and the key gone, again applied his tools. The door soon sprang open under his pressure, disclosing the cold, flooded brazier and the figure of Venero, gagged, bound, and insensible on the narrow pallet.

With trembling hands, hard, eager, loveless, Anastro tore off the bandages and laid his ear upon the man's heart. Valerie read in his look as he lifted his head that there was yet life remaining.

She turned back to Jacqueline's room and brought therefrom certain flasks, which she handed to Anastro.

"He will live," she said carelessly, disgust plainly written on her face as she glanced at the ghastly object on the bed. "Knaves of his kind die hard. Besides that poor, pious fool who bound him destroyed his own weapons—see!" and she pointed to the black, swimming brazier, shaking her head and adding with low laughter :

"Fools! Fools!"

Anastro looked but did not speak.

"Beshrew me, Señor Anastro," Valerie continued, "but I had hardly thought you could have been so merrily outwitted by those children! In good sooth they seem to have been shrewder than you. My dear little Jacqueline must have ruffled it bravely in the streets of Antwerp in her nightgown ! Pardon me if I do not offer my services in nursing our excellent Venero back to life. I am so confident, you see, of his recovery, but his appearance at the moment is most shocking," and with that Valerie made good her retreat to her own room.

During the hours which followed, Doctor Hoekstra, hastily summoned, succeeded in rousing the benumbed brain of Venero, and promised at least partial recovery in time. Anastro, keenly mortified but not seriously embarrassed by the escape of his victims, swiftly ferreted out the means and ways of their departure. The servants confessed that on account of the sultry heat of the night the door of their chamber which gave entrance upon the inner passage, had, against the master's orders been left open. This door, which he had supposed securely barred on the inner side, might have given exit. The boy Juan remembered vaguely that something had disturbed him in his sleep, although what he could not tell.

"Ah, well," reflected the merchant, restored to his wonted grave and philosophical calmness ; "it matters but little at most, unless the Brussels people call my claim in question. In that event I would gladly have had the child Jacqueline ready as a witness ; for if put to the torture we could doubtless have drawn the whole story from her, and she would have been palpably a witness of my procuring. The brother was wholly superfluous and withal dangerous and would better have been quietly and painlessly slipped out of the way. He may yet make us trouble, though I hardly think it."

But a threat of trouble came a day or two later from an unexpected quarter.

Anastro, sitting in his shop, was studying with

greedy satisfaction the documents newly arrived from Brussels, conveying full transference of his share in the confiscated estates of Nikolaas Tontorf. He looked up to note the entrance of a man of powerful, massive figure, flushed face, and fiery eyes, who with threatening air stepped straight to him and in whom he recognized with keen alarm the dreaded, albeit derided, lord of Brederode.

In his hand the great seigneur held a slip of paper.

"Hear this!" he cried with startling abruptness, "you black-hearted plotter," and he read in a roaring, declamatory tone:

"'Pardon the unwilling kidnapping of your good horse. It comes herewith back to you—with money for its hire. It was taken only because our case was for life or death and perchance to save many lives better than ours. Beware of the merchant Anastro. He is the foul fiend incarnate.'

"Do you know, sir," thundered Brederode, "who scratched those lines on that scrap of paper?"

"I can guess," said Anastro, grown yellow and with wild, wandering glances.

"You can guess, and so can I," and Brederode coming yet nearer by a step, took the long beard of the Spaniard in his mighty hand, around which he sharply twisted it and continued to emphasize what he said with merciless jerks and shakes of the merchant's head.

"Look you, you mammering coward, you sneaking informer, you poisonous reptile, you foul murderer! Antwerp knows to-day of your damnable deeds and is ready to visit them on your head. You, gloating over the booty you rob from the men whom your infamous treachery betrays to their death; you, true subject of your king; you, fit only for the pad-midden, where I fain would fling you! Hear me—get out of Antwerp ere the sun set or I will put a bullet through that devil's brain of you, or soil my blade with your heart's blood!" And almost foaming at the mouth, the great Beggar gave the Spaniard a final mighty and paralyzing shake and threw him half across the shop.

This done, he strode out of the place, with clenched teeth, clanking sword, and face flushed with furious anger.

An hour later he left Antwerp for Embden never to return. Dying within the year the Seigneur de Brederode had not the cause which would have come to him with the coming years, bitterly to repent that blade or bullet had not in that hour extinguished the life of Anastro.

That night found the house in the Rue d'Augustin deserted. Whither its master and inmates had fled few cared to ask. Some said that Paris was their destination, being a refuge well suited to those who chose for a time to be forgotten.

XX

BURG—FRIED

IT was the close of an August day. Over the richly wooded Nassau country, far to the east of the Rhine, diversified with range upon range of purple hills, outposts of the Taunus Mountains, the sun was shedding his last gorgeous rays.

Following the course of a shallow, sparkling river, the River Dill, a high-road threaded a verdant valley and furnished an approach to the red-roofed village of Dillenburg, clinging around the base of a precipitous hill.

Towering far above this rugged height, into whose rocky surface it seemed to have been impregnably rooted, rose the lofty and lonely feudal castle of Nassau-Dillenburg.

The setting sun illuminated the battlements of the vast, imposing pile, softening the surface of the rough and hoary stone and giving a strangely solemn beauty to the massive façade with its numberless towers, gateways, barbicans, and outworks.

The stillness of the great and almost unbroken wilderness lay upon the landscape, upon the sea of billowing hills stretching to the dim horizon, upon the rich green of oaks and beeches clustering close about the quiet village, upon the valley piercing its way westward between the hills, with the flashing river touched now with the golden radiance of sunset. The whole scene seemed, however, subordinate to the castle which in its stern grandeur appeared as much a primitive part of the landscape as did the rocky height on which it was built or the dim peaks of the Taunus Mountains on the horizon.

A dash of hoofs on the rough paving of the narrow village street brought the Dillenburg children to their cottage doors only to see a young man upon a dark bay horse, unattended, spurring up the steep ascent to the castle, whose walls frowned formidably hard above the roofs of the timbered houses.

This rider, who now proceeded more slowly between the solid walls of masonry which guarded the approach to the castle, was Norbert Tontorf.

Two months had passed since, in the agony of their maddening grief, he and Jacqueline had forsaken by night the city of Middelburg, so dear in its associations to them, the sealed and darkened home no longer theirs, and had wandered on their heart-broken way to Breda. With them had come the Pastor Droust, still piteously crazed, but harmless and sacred to Norbert for his devotion to their father.

Norbert, at first fierce with the thirst to visit such punishment as was meet upon Anastro and his despicable tools, found himself baffled by the knowledge which soon reached him that the guilty trio had disappeared absolutely from Antwerp. A price was set upon his own head, for the Spaniard had had time to cause the issue of a warrant against the son of Nikolaas Tontorf by the authorities of the regent, before he fled the town. Condemned therefore to keep in hiding, reduced to poverty by the confiscation of his father's estates, and to submission for a time at least to a life of utter inaction in the friendly shelter of the home of the Van Marles, Norbert sank into a listless, hopeless apathy from which nothing availed to arouse him.

Then, with the first days of August came the tidings to Breda that the Duke of Alva with his army, hasty and terrible, had accomplished the march through Burgundy unhindered, and in twelve days had entered Lorraine. Another fortnight of such marching could bring them to the Flemish borders. Like an alarum this tidings struck the Protestants of Holland. Some it paralyzed. Some it aroused to flee for their lives, and day after day a stream of out-wanderers flowed steadily on by every road leading into Germany or France, and by every ship departing for England.

The family of the Van Marles were among the emigrants and Heidelberg, with its devout and great-hearted Protestant elector, Friedrich der Fromm, was their haven of refuge.

A day's preparation sufficed, for few household goods could be carried with the exiles, and so with aching hearts the little cavalcade on the third day of August started up the Rhine on its long journey.

At Cologne the unhappy Pastor Droust, who had accompanied them so far, disappeared from their company and they saw him no more.

Arrived in Heidelberg the refugees found themselves in an atmosphere of calm and safety which made amends for the sacrifice of the home they had left, shadowed as it was with dread and danger.

Through the kind offices of friends, Vrouw Van Marle was appointed to a post of usefulness and honor in the economy of the great castle. The heartbroken child, Jacqueline, whose crushing sorrow commended her to the tender sympathy of the noble electress herself, found at last a place of peace and consolation, and so it came about that on that late August day Norbert Tontorf was set free to start out and win his spurs in the cause of his prince, his land, and his lady.

With manly courage he shook off the languor which a grief over-great had laid upon him, and with his heart strengthened by new resolve he fared forth on his way to Dillenburg. He was no longer the light-hearted ardent youth of six months ago, impulsive and buoyant. The awful baptism of blood through which he had passed had set its seal forever on his heart. He was a man now, of a purpose sterner and more determined, devoted with a mighty passion to the salvation of his oppressed people, a passion in which love and hate, scorn and sorrow were welded together.

With less of romantic enthusiasm, therefore, than he would once have felt in like circumstances, but with a deeper and more unconquerable devotion, Norbert, now at his journey's end, made his way up to the isolated chateau which had been the birthplace and was now for a time the place of refuge of the Prince of Orange.

The young Zeelander found the courtyard of the castle, which he entered by a noble stone gate emblazoned with the Nassau arms, filled with a merry company of young noblemen, with their grooms and attendants. A magnificent buck had just been brought in as the result of the day's hunt in the forest and the young counts of Nassau, Adolf and Henry, were presiding over the inspection of its points.

Norbert was amazed at the impregnable strength of the castle, which was also a fortress, and at its vast extent as seen now from within. Ample for the accommodation of a thousand persons he judged it, and no longer did he wonder that the prince with his retinue of over a hundred and fifty persons could find hospitable entertainment here.

Before one of the castle doors Norbert soon caught sight of the Princess Marie of Orange, standing whip in hand in her graceful hunting habit, a charming girlish figure. He had seen her several times in the early spring riding through the streets of her father's own city of Breda.

A bluff gentleman, with the aspect of a country squire, a man of somewhat immobile face and a figure of massive proportions, now came from the interior of the castle and stood looking down at Marie with a fond, fatherly glance.

Seeing him the young girl moved to his side with an affectionate exclamation :

" *Ach, lieber Onkel !* " and nestled her small hand in the large cordial clasp of his.

Norbert as he watched these two thus evidently drawn together by close and tender sympathy despite the disparity in their years, concluded that Marie's *lieber Onkel* was Count John, next in age to the Prince of Orange and the present lord of Nassau-Dillenburg.

Count John bore the unmistakable Nassau physiognomy, albeit Norbert found him almost stolid and commonplace in comparison with his illustrious brothers, William and Louis. Nevertheless he perceived, even in this casual observation, a certain sturdy strength and rugged constancy which might be hardly less important in a time of crisis than the penetrating intellect and commanding power of the one and the blithe audacity and high spirit of the other.

The Princess Marie caught sight ere long of Norbert and after a moment's scrutiny she beckoned him to her side.

"I have seen you before. I have seen you in dear old Breda. What, if you please, is your name ? "

"Norbert Tontorf, your highness."

A swift change came over the face of Marie, and she murmured a few gentle words of sympathy for his loss, of which the news had reached Dillenburg.

" Do you wish to go at once to my father, Master Tontorf ? " she asked kindly.

" If it please your highness," said Norbert in a low, toneless voice, his face grown gray and stern on the instant.

Count John called a page and bade him accompany Norbert to the antechamber of the prince. He gave the young Zeelander a hearty welcome to Dillenburg, and Norbert felt with quick gratitude the free-hearted hospitality of the house and its head.

Passing through a lofty and ancient hall, decked with the trophies of the chase, with stone floor rush-strewn and roof upheld by mighty rafters, Norbert was led on to a distant part of the castle known as the Diedrichs·bau, which was set apart for the accommodation of the most distinguished son of the house with his family and retinue.

Entering a meagrely furnished apartment, dimly lighted now by such evening gleams as filtered through the narrow windows, which were scarce more than slits in the huge depth of the wall, the page, indicating a closed door at the far end of the room, remarked :

"His excellency is at present engaged at the evening meal with the princess. When he comes into this room, and that will haply be ere long, you can easily present yourself to him if I am not here."

Smiling a little, Norbert sat down near one of the windows through which he could catch a glimpse of the enchanting valley of the Dill. Plainly etiquette at the Nassau-Dillenburg castle was something relaxed from the ceremonious character which belonged to the court of the prince in his own castle. Moreover, the bare though noble simplicity of his present surroundings suggested a striking contrast to the luxurious magnificence of Nassau-Breda.

Norbert's attention, however, was soon forcibly attracted from this casual consideration by a series of shrill and angry exclamations in the adjoining room, distinctly audible, although a heavy oaken door was closed between.

The voice he recognized as that of Anne of Saxony.

"I will go to Cologne! I am going! You cannot stop me! I will die rather than stay in this place !"

Cries like these, interspersed with passionate pro-
fanity and incoherent raving, jarred upon Norbert's
ears painfully ; with them were mingled two other
voices ; that of the prince himself, quiet and gentle,
and that of a woman.

Unwilling to listen to the shameful and distress-
ing tokens of what was plainly a furious outbreak
of the stormy temper of the princess, Norbert rose
and paced the floor, seeking to withdraw his attention from the lamentable sounds. Suddenly, after
a loud series of violent but unintelligible protests,
there struck upon his ears the noise of shivering
glass and the crash of metal thrown upon the stone
floor. In another moment the door upon which his
eyes were involuntarily fixed, opened into a brightly
lighted dining hall, and he caught a glimpse of the
prince himself as he bowed from the room a grave
and stately dame who, as the door closed after her,
passed rapidly down the antechamber and departed,
not having observed Norbert's presence in her evident agitation.

The young man, however, had taken note of the
dignity of her person, the grace of her bearing, her
plain black velvet gown, the keys hanging from her
girdle by their silver chains, the wide, transparent
ruff and simple widow's cap of sheer white muslin.
He believed that he had seen the noble dowager,
Juliana of Stolberg, mother of the Nassaus, and
chatelaine of the castle.

A long half-hour ensued, in which Norbert, despite
his own will, could not but hear a prolonged sound
of low sobbing and the steady, soothing tones of
the prince himself. Doors opened and closed ; steps
could be heard going to and fro in the room ; these
sounds ceased also, and then at last the prince himself entered the antechamber.

His countenance was careworn, his dress dark
and plain, his step hurried. Around his left wrist
he had carelessly wound a white linen napkin, ap-

parently snatched in haste from the table. A dark
stain of spilled wine discolored a corner which hung
from the wrist, but as Norbert stepped hastily forward his eye caught, on the wrapping of the wrist
itself, a more vivid and a slowly increasing stain.

On seeing Norbert, the prince, with his rare self-
mastery, instantly banished every token of his own
anxiety and preoccupation, and received the young
Zeelander with gentle cordiality and sympathy.

The first interchange over, he insisted on leading
Norbert into his own dining hall, and calling for
fresh food and wine, entertained him with substantial hospitality.

All tokens of the accident had been removed, the
crash of which Norbert had so plainly heard, and
the painful consequence of which he could not fail
to see. The room was worthily although not luxuriously furnished, and the meal of which Norbert
now partook was served on the prince's own gold
and silver plate, brought from Breda, with the magnificence of which Norbert was mightily impressed.

As Norbert ate with sound and hearty hunger,
the prince asked questions which he answered, as
far as he was able.

Yes, he had seen the Elector Friedrich at Heidelberg, and had brought affectionate greetings from
him to the Nassau household, and above all, to his
excellency.

Heidelberg court was full of the new excitement
among the Huguenots of France, which had followed
the march of Alva through the borders, the raising of
royalist troops, and the secret which had leaked out
that the king and queen mother were engaged in a
treacherous correspondence with Alva which could
only threaten the betrayal of the peace of Amboise,
so sorely strained already.

The famous saying of the queen-mother, already
bruited abroad, that it was the privilege of French
monarchs *never to make a perpetual edict*, had

sounded the note of warning and stirred the Huguenots to secret preparations for a second civil war.

"Yes," said the prince, as Norbert rehearsed
these important matters, "the war is inevitable
and cannot long be averted. No doubt Coligny is
in communication with the elector. Saw you
tokens in Heidelberg or elsewhere in the Pfalz, of
a muster of troops ? "

"Assuredly, my lord. Heidelberg was full of
soldiers, both foot and horse, and his highness the
elector's son, John Casimir, is continually enrolling fresh ones. All are fierce to be off for France
and effect a junction somewhere in Lorraine with
Coligny. Nevertheless, I misdoubt their moving
very soon."

"Why so ? "

"The court seems to be full of an influence
against the Huguenots and their cause."

A hasty exclamation escaped the prince.

"Bochetel has been at work, then, at Heidelberg
also, he or Lansac," he said, "and has found the
ear of the elector. I suppose it is the same story
he has used to bring the landgrave and the other
princes over to the royalist side."

The prince paused, biting his lip and looking
before him in fixed thought.

"I know not, your highness," said Norbert.
"The elector said I might tell you that there were
some reasons to fear that if a second civil war were
begun in France it would not be for the cause of
religion but as a political and treasonable revolution, to gain the throne for the Prince of Condé.
'I have no desire,' his highness said further, 'to
aid in an unholy war of treasonable ambition, and
I may yet advise my son to disband his troops and
make no further levy.'"

The prince rose and paced the room in close
thought for some minutes. At length he stood still
before Norbert and said with grave emphasis :

"Tontorf, you may not see yet what you will see as you live deeper into this time of ours, that the cause of the Huguenots in France is the cause of the Gueux in the Low Countries, the cause of Protestants everywhere. If one suffer, all suffer. There will be a long struggle, fought out now on one field and now on the other, but the cause is one. A wider question is at stake and a deeper than many see—not a question merely between the Mass and the Bible, but a question of the freedom of the human spirit for all time to come.

"In these quiet months here in my old home I have had the leisure which aforetime failed me to study and reflect. Two tremendous forces have come into mortal clash in our time—the newly awakened spirit of liberty and the mighty and ancient spirit of tyranny. The latter undeniably has its seat and stronghold in the Roman system, with its kingcraft and priestcraft and its established control over the motions of men's souls. To it I can no longer adhere. My place is in the other camp. I am ready now to take my part openly in the struggle, whether its stage be France or Flanders or elsewhere, albeit the cause of the Netherlands must always lie closest to my heart.

"Matters grow urgent," continued the prince. "Alva has already reached Brussels and letters from Rome and from Spain which have been intercepted show that the great powers are all girding themselves for a swift, concerted movement to stamp out freedom and toleration.

"These poisonous slanders against Condé and Coligny are but the subtle weapons with which Catharine de Medici seeks to rob the Huguenot party of the help of their brethren in Germany. A messenger must come from Coligny and Condé themselves to the elector inviting him to search out the truth of these charges. I would fain communicate with Coligny as soon as may be, for time presses. Would you be ready to make the journey into France for me at short notice ? "

"Ready, my lord, with all my heart," said Norbert promptly.

"Very good. We must wait a little for my brother, Count Louis, for this is work for him also. He should be here ere long. He is hard at work now in Friesland seeking to rouse the people to arms, but they are slow to move. And now you must have chance to rest. How far have you ridden to-day ? "

"From Giessen, your highness."

"You have a right, then, to be weary and you will find Dillenburg as good a place for rest as all Germany could give you. Have you observed the stillness ? "

With these words the prince led Norbert out from the antechamber to a long balcony overlooking the approach to the castle. The forest lay black and murmurous in the hush of the night, with the great dome of the sky studded with the splendid August stars bending over. The air was fresh and laden with the aromatic breath of the firs and balsams. Nowhere was sound or motion to break the profound silence. Then the plaintive call of the night raven issued from the forest, and a warm wind swayed the lofty treetops below the castle wall.

"What peace ! " said Norbert under his breath involuntarily.

"Peace here, Tontorf," said the prince quietly ; "peace to-day, but to-morrow, I tell you, not peace but a sword."

XXI

NEWS FROM BRABANT

TWO weeks had passed.

It was a late hour of the September night.

Norbert Tontorf, leaning over the parapet of the terrace before the Diedrichs-bau, looked down upon the sleeping village of Dillenburg below the castle.

The peace of this valley, above all at night, possessed an exhaustless power to soothe and heal his aching heart. Behind him, within the castle, late as was the hour, lights were moving to and fro, but for the time they were unheeded by Norbert.

For, as he stood and drank in the purity and peace of the silent hills, stretching dark to the horizon, there had risen afresh before his mind the thought of that lovely princess whose device he still wore and whose unseen presence had ruled his fancy and held his devotion by mysterious chains through these silent years. Far, far beyond this valley, he mused, lay the convent where she lived her life in still seclusion, beyond the Rhine, beyond the border, in the unknown west. What might have befallen her in the years since his father had visited Jouarre ? The times were full of fresh peril, her enemies were powerful, her friends scattered. Who could tell if she had even now the protection which he himself so ardently longed to give her ? Who could tell if she yet lived ? Should it yet be given him to put his sword and service at her feet ?

His reverie was interrupted.

Steps approached, coming from the castle. Norbert turned to see a man in a long, black cassock,

with white lawn bands, crossing the terrace to his
side, a man of serious and reverend mien.   It was
Herr Nicholas Zell, a Lutheran clergyman, who had
been for some weeks in attendance on the prince.

"This air is most refreshing," he exclaimed.
"I can breathe freely now.   All our fears are over.
A son is born to his highness!"

Norbert made an exclamation of pleasure and
Zell continued in a low voice of quiet satisfaction :

"Yes, a lusty young prince, to be named presently after the deceased father of the princess, the
Saxon elector, Maurice."

"This is good news," returned Norbert warmly.
"And is the mother at rest ?"

"A pointed question, young sir," said Zell
smiling thoughtfully ; "yes, for once the wild and
foaming torrent is stilled.   The great tide of mother-
hood and the exhaustion of her travail have sufficed
at this hour to silence the tumult of the princess'
strange spirit."

"You have seen her ?"

"I have just come from her bedside.   The
Countess Dowager and the Lady Elizabeth have
cared for her with tenderest devotion, despite the
harsh and contemptuous treatment she has ever
accorded them.   No queen could have had gentler
nursing.   It might seem that even 'the great elector's daughter,' as she is wont to call herself, might
be satisfied, and cease for a time at least her clamor
to return to Breda."

"When she was in Breda," said Norbert, "it
was well known that the princess never ceased to
rail against the land and the people, but now it
seems she is fain to return to them."

"The life here at Dillenburg is too dull and too
simple for her highness," said Zell.   "If Breda
is impossible she has wearied the prince night and
day to permit her to go to Cologne and set up her
own household.   She fancies herself holding a

little court there and playing the queen among the many Netherlandish refugees—ruling without a rival."

Both Zell and Norbert smiled involuntarily at this characteristic wish of the fantastic Anne of Saxony.

"How the prince bears with her stubbornness and her violence is beyond my wit to discern!" exclaimed Norbert, after a pause.

"His patience is most marvelous. I doubt me sometimes that he is too patient, for more than once his very life or that of others has been in jeopardy. Harsher measures might perchance the sooner bring the lady to her senses. His highness can be stern, however, when pressed too hard. I have seen the princess in a towering passion, ready to dash to pieces everything she could lay hands on, when she has quailed before his mere look and become meek and penitent as a chidden child."

"What is that?" cried Norbert suddenly, leaning over the parapet to listen. A sound of horses' hoofs became more and more distinctly heard through the silence of the night on the village street below them.

"It must be Count Louis!" cried Norbert with rising excitement, as a small body of horsemen came into view in the moonlight, threading their way up the steep, rocky approach.

"He has come at last, and he will bring news from the Netherlands!"

As Norbert said these words he added to himself silently :

"And now at last we can start on the mission to France and to Coligny, and that means Châtillon, and on the road to Châtillon who knows but we may pass the Abbey of Jouarre?"

In another moment Norbert and the clergyman had joined a small but eager crowd in the main hall of the castle gathered around Count Louis, whose appearance was hailed with rapturous delight by the Dillenburg household.

Chief among the group stood the prince, his arm around his mother, whose sweet old face showed in its tremulous smile the strain which the night had brought her.

Having received the affectionate congratulations of Louis on the birth of his son, the prince cried :

" And now, my brother, you came straight from Brabant, I take it. Tell us, then, in a word, what is passing there. I will content myself to wait till morning for private conference."

Louis instantly lost the bright enthusiasm with which he had discussed the advent of the prince's son, and his face grew stern.

" The first news and the worst news," he said, " is the arrest of Egmont and Horn by Alva. Most foully and treacherously were they trapped by the duke into a conference over plans for a new citadel at Antwerp, and while thus engaged, in his own house, Alva surrounded them with soldiers and put them under guard."

" When was this ? " asked the prince, who had changed color at this swift fulfillment of his worst fears.

" Five days since. All Flanders rings with the horrible scandal of so treacherous an outrage on two Knights of the Fleece. The people everywhere, gentle and simple, are in a kind of frenzy of indignation."

" Oh, Egmont, Egmont ! " murmured the prince, under his breath. " If you would but have been warned by me ! From a prison of Alva's making the only door will be the scaffold."

" Ah, my lord," cried Louis, with passionate fire, "we can but down on our knees and thank God, fasting, that your hasty departure prevented Alva's devilish plot in your own case. It is freely said among the Spanish gentlemen who surround the duke, 'After all, Alva has caught nothing. The *Silent One* is not in the net.'"

The prince made no reply. A letter from his secret agent in Madrid, Vandenesse, the private secretary of Philip, had long ere this brought him a copy of Alva's secret instructions, one clause of which bade the new governor-general "*First and foremost, to seize the prince and bring him to execution within twenty-four hours.*"

"You can have no other tidings as dark as this, my brother ? " the prince asked, the shadow of deep, suppressed emotion on his face.

"I know not if the second theme which divides men's minds in Flanders with this treachery may not bid fair full soon to be a thousand-fold more disastrous. Alva has now at the very outset of his rule established a new tribunal for the Netherlands, which takes the place of every other court of justice in the land. He calls it the Council of Troubles. The people call it the Council of Blood. The duke is himself the head of it, and its powers are absolute. Its penalties are, briefly, death and confiscation of property."

"The latter will supply Alva with his sinews of war," commented the prince, "the former will be a truly Spanish method of quelling revolt. A river of blood flowing through the Netherlands, a river of gold flowing into Spain ! Alas for my poor land ! "

"There is no doubt, my lord, that your own estates will soon be swallowed up by the governor. The castle at Breda is already filled with Spanish troops, and they swarm everywhere in the town."

The prince fixed a startled look upon the count.

"They are making short work, surely," he said, "but better landless than headless ! Come, the mother looks sadly weary. We have heard of many troubles, but we must not forget that to-night a son is born to this house. God grant that Maurice of Nassau may live to do it honor ! "

P

"*Hoch soll er leben! Er lebe hoch!*" cried all the company in deep and full accord.

Then in turn the prince and his brothers, John, Louis, Adolf, and Henry, with chivalrous and reverent devotion, kissed the cheek of their stately mother, who looked with proud eyes at her five gallant sons, and so closed the midnight family conclave.

But for the prince there was no sleep that night. Egmont, the gallant hero, whom he had loved with all the generous ardor of his young years, had been trapped to ignominious and fatal imprisonment by the abhorrent craft of the Spaniard! With the hard-wrung tears of his stern and outraged manhood, the prince consecrated himself anew in that vigil to the deliverance of his land from a tyranny which seemed inspired by devils rather than men.

XXII

THREE FLEURS–DE–LIS ROYAL

THE mind of Louis of Nassau was as strong and supple as his body and both might be likened to tempered steel.

From stirring up the fisherfolk of North Friesland with bold and hardy comradery, from fighting all day and sleeping in his saddle, he would turn to the most brilliant court festivities or to the most delicate negotiation of statecraft with a Catharine de Medici, and prove himself in each line master.

Buoyant and ever ready for action, he waited but a day at the castle before he announced himself ready to set out with Norbert on the long journey to the Huguenot leaders in France.

In the early September morning, therefore, while the dew was yet on the grass and the mists hung white on the hills around the castle, the two young men, Norbert now dignified by a captain's commission at the hands of the prince, both well-mounted and full of the eagerness of fresh adventure, galloped down the Dill Valley. They were riding forth on the prince's errand, bound for France and for Châtillon-sur-Loing, the home of Coligny, eighty miles due south of Paris.

Threading in succession the valleys of the Dill and Lahn, crossing the Rhine at Oberlalustein, following the Moselle to the imperial city of Trèves and crossing the border at Sedan, it was the evening of the twenty-sixth of September when, at nightfall, the two young men came within sound of the Cathedral bells of Rheims.

"Now, at last," said Count Louis as they rode

into the courtyard of the *Bonsecours*, "we shall find a friend with whom we can speak freely and throw aside our disguise."

"And who is our friend, my lord?" asked Norbert; "for truly this city, with its ancient cathedral, with yonder magnifical palace of the great Guise archbishop, and all its proud show of the ancient religion at every turn, seems the least promising town for us which we have entered."

"You say truly," replied Louis; "we are in the very stronghold of the Lorraines and may be under the watchful eyes of the great cardinal's servants when we least expect it. Neverthless, Huguenoterie has a foothold even in Rheims, as I shall presently show you."

Having put up their horses at the *Bonsecours* and partaken of the evening meal for which they were well inclined, the count and Norbert left the inn, and crossing the great place before the archbishop's palace, they made their way through narrow streets, with which Louis seemed to be perfectly familiar, to the Rue de Tambour and knocked at the door of a high, timbered house of quaint, attractive aspect.

To the servant who responded to their knocking Louis put the question whether he could see Maître Chaudon, and added in a low voice a few words which Norbert did not understand. They were at once ushered into a spacious room where beside a table covered with books sat a venerable man with white hair falling almost to his shoulders.

He rose and greeted Count Louis with marked cordiality and respect, and seemed fully cognizant of Norbert's parentage.

"The name Tontorf," he said quietly, "must be sacred among Protestants of every nation."

Maître Chaudon, Norbert soon learned, was the pastor of the secret congregation of the Huguenots of Rheims. A somewhat stern and taciturn man Norbert found him, but one to be fully trusted.

A long conference followed, in which Count Louis discussed with the old minister the uprising of the Huguenot party.

"It is coming," said Maître Chaudon ; " it is even now hard upon us. I can feel the ground tremble beneath my feet with the tramp of armed men, and yet on the surface all is quiet. The Admiral Coligny is quietly gathering his vintage at his home in Châtillon. Condé has, indeed, left the court in anger and disgust at the insolence of Anjou and the barefaced breaking of her pledged promise to him by the queen-mother. Where he is, however, is not known, nor will be, methinks, until he is ready to strike."

" Where is the court ? " asked Louis.

" At the castle of Monceaux, in La Brie."

Norbert's interest quickened at the name. Was not the Abbey of Jouarre in La Brie ?

" Know you what place has been chosen for a rendezvous ? "

Maître Chaudon looked keenly into the face of Count Louis, who smiled slightly at the old man's caution.

" You are safe," he said gently, and glanced significantly at Norbert.

" The brother of the Silent Prince and the son of the Printer of Middelburg can surely be trusted," responded the pastor as if satisfied. " Rozoy-en-Brie will be the place, and the time is now not distant."

Louis was thinking. To Norbert it often seemed that he could watch the very movements of his swift and eager mind in the mobile, changing face. With a flash of sudden perception he exclaimed :

" Condé is somewhere in La Brie ! He could not be elsewhere ; and Coligny will not much longer linger among his vines. We must reach them ere they are swept beyond our reach in this rising storm. Come, Tontorf, let us hasten back to the *Bonsecours*, sleep what we must and be ready to hasten

on at daybreak. If it is possible we must reach
Meaux to-morrow night.''

"An extravagant hope, fair sir," remarked the
Huguenot. "If you come by Chateau-Thierry you
will do well."

"Haply I am over sanguine, monsieur," said the
count, "but our business has haste. And so, good-
night."

"Stay yet a moment, Sir Count," said Maître
Chaudon; "it may be that I am over cautious, and
that it would better serve our cause that so tried a

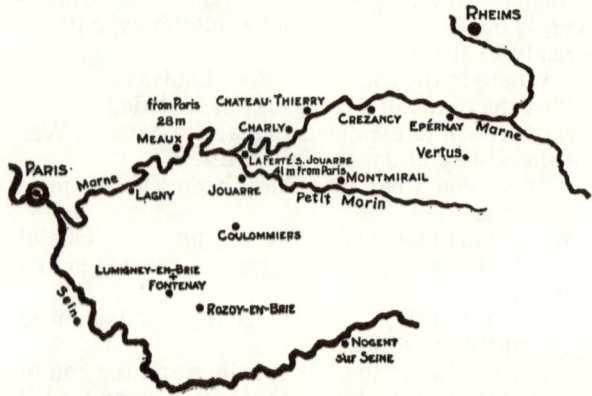

champion of it as Louis of Nassau should be entrusted with our whole counsel.

"There is a plot on foot," he continued, lowering
his voice to a whisper, "of doubtful good, to my
thinking. It seems justified, however, by the continued massing of the Swiss regiments, which can
only mean that the royal party, led by the Guises,
is preparing for a sudden *coup* against our people.

"The prime object of the undertaking, which is
wild and hazardous, indeed, is to rid Charles of the
baneful influence of our neighbor here in Rheims,
the archbishop, the great Guise cardinal. The

means to be employed are to seize the persons of the cardinal, the king, and the queen-mother, and then to present a petition, humble and respectful, but imperative, to the king for the removal of the cardinal and the dispersion of the Swiss mercenaries."

"If the plot succeeds," said Louis, who had listened with eager attention to this surprising narrative, "it will be a *coup d'état*. If it fails, it will be high treason. Condé is playing for high stakes. I see him in this rather than the admiral. Is Monceaux to be the scene of the attempt?"

"Meaux, more likely, as the court will hardly fail to leave their hunting and dancing for a day or so to celebrate the feast of St. Michael, at the cathedral ; but this will be determined by events as they befall."

"The feast of St. Michael!" cried Norbert, "that is but three days hence."

"The twenty-ninth," said Chaudon, quickly.

"Then is our need of haste even greater than I supposed," said Louis. "Let us, if we may, seek our interview with Condé and Coligny ere they are too deeply involved in the consequences of this most amazing attempt."

Again they bade the Huguenot good-night and returned to the *Bonsecours*.

As they galloped at daybreak the following morning, down the green Marne Valley in the direction of Crezançy, between the rich vineyards, hanging full of grapes, still coated with their azure bloom and of a delicious fragrance, the count said laughingly to Norbert :

"Have an eye to the vintage, Roubichon! Do not forget the object of your expedition to Champagne and the great interests of the brothers Certain. What think you, will the yield be large?" and Louis looked with a well-feigned connoisseur's eye over the vineclad hills.

Their expedition was ostensibly made on busi·
ness for the fictitious firm of George and Lambert
Certain, the prince being the chief and Count Louis
the junior partner. Norbert, the confidential agent,
was to bear the name of Roubichon.

"You ride, Master Lambert Certain, all too much
like a lord, and too little like a wine merchant,"
quoth Norbert. "The tradesfolk's air sits not ob·
viously upon you."

"Neither does it upon you, sir," retorted the
count blithely; "can you not abate by a shade
that soldiery bearing, that gallant and knightly air?
And have a care, good Roubichon, of that silken
scarf which I note you wear within your doublet!
Pray tell me, an' you will, what is its device which
mine eye can never quite decipher?"

Norbert blushed and hesitated for a moment.

"Fear not to own that you have espoused the
cause and wear the colors of some fair lady, my
friend," said Louis, in his frank fashion; "and
yet speak not unless you are fain rather of speech
than silence. I am not over curious in other men's
matters, and yet, soothfast, I do love a lover."

"Nay, my lord, no lover am I," said Norbert, by
no means sorry to speak of a subject so near his
heart; "no lover, but a servant pledged, all unknown and silently, to a lady whom I have never
seen."

"Nay now, man," cried Louis, "this grows interesting. Is there more that may be told? Is this
lady of the Religion?"

"I know not, but deem it scarce possible," replied Norbert, and after a pause he continued:

"All that I know of her to whose service I would
gladly devote myself, so far as I may while serving
my lord, was learned full two years since. To-
day I know not in truth even that she lives."

"But if she lives she is fair, safe to say; some
modest maid of Middelburg, mayhap, of Breda?"

"Nay, my lord. Not of Middelburg, nor of Breda, not of Holland nor of all Flanders, nor yet of Germany. Neither is the lady, as you might think, the modest maid whom any man, least of all, a man like me, penniless and homeless, might hope to wed. This is no love affair," and again Norbert's cheeks grew ruddy; "the lady is of princely rank, as well as of rare loveliness. Furthermore, she is under the vows of the Benedictine order. There is one sole thing that could call an unknown burgher's son and soldier of fortune like me to her side."

"And that is ? Say on. I am eager to hear."

" And that is, that the lady has been, and may be now, in a place of danger, may be defenseless, may need a common fellow who loves not his life overmuch to stand for her guardiance or to strike a blow for her defense."

Louis of Nassau looked into Norbert's melancholy and yet ardent face with earnest response.

" The lady is of princely rank," he said musingly, as they walked their horses up a long hill where the sun beat down fiercely upon their heads ; " she is, as it may chance, in a place of peril ; she is a Benedictine nun of great beauty and loveliness, dwelling not in the Netherlands nor in Germany. Well then, Norbert Tontorf, I am ready to hazard a guess that this same peerless *dévote* lives in France ! "

Norbert nodded without speaking, and Louis glanced shrewdly into his face.

" Are we now, as we make our way into La Brie, approaching the abode of this same lady ? "

" We are, my lord."

Louis drummed with his finger-tips on his saddlebow for a moment, looking aside at Norbert's scarf, an end of which had fallen outside his doublet, in the breast of which he carried it.

" Does the lady bear for her crest three *fleurs-de-lis* royal on a field azure ? " he asked gayly.

"With a *bâton péri* added, monsieur."

"Is the lady known, haply, to some who have had the privilege of seeing her, as ' the White Abbess of Jouarre ' ? "

"I have heard so."

"Beshrew me, then, if the lady — beautiful, princely, yet defenseless, and, it may be, in peril —be not daughter of the Duc de Montpensier, Mademoiselle Charlotte de Bourbon !" and Louis' face reflected the almost devout enthusiasm of Norbert's.

"Monsieur has heard of the lady—haply knows her ? "

"Much, indeed, have I heard of this lady through her cousin, her majesty of Navarre, and the story of her life has ever touched my heart profoundly. Tontorf, she is all that you believe her to be in herself. That she is in peril I do not know. I trust that in this you may be wrong. But it will go hard with us if we seek not out that same Abbey of Jouarre, which lies between Meaux and this Rozoyen-Brie, and offer not ourselves and our swords for the lady's service if so be there is need of them."

With these last words Louis extended his hand and took that of Norbert with a strong, expressive grasp.

"I like you, Norbert Tontorf," he said, as they put their horses to the gallop at the top of the hill, where a level stretch of country lay before them. "I have always felt my soul drawn to yours in the manliness of your sorrow, your self-command, and your patriotic devotion. But now I am knit to you by another bond, for in this troubadour-like pledging of your service to an unknown lady, invisible and remote, but sacrosanct to you, like the vision of an angel, you have shown me your inner nature, high and chivalrous, and I love you for it. Hereafter the bond between us two is strengthened."

Touched too deeply to reply, Norbert received the words of the gallant count, himself as pure a virgin knight as Sir Galahad, religiously, as if they bestowed a priestly benediction. In silence they rode on together.

XXIII

"THE AFFAIR AT MEAUX"

"WHAT river mouth is that?" asked Louis of Nassau, pointing to the southern shore of the Marne, where, between long lines of verdure, a smaller stream poured its waters into the deep river, its shallow rapids tossing brightly in the morning sun.

"The Petit-Morin, monsieur," replied the boatman.

"And what is that little town?" inquired the count, indicating a cluster of houses at the river's mouth, with three fine stone bridges and a quaint old mill built on a shoal in the middle of the stream. In the distance, on a green hill, rose the towers of a stately abbey.

"La Ferté-sous-Jouarre, monsieur."

Louis and Norbert exchanged a hurried glance.

They sat, the one in the stern, the other in the bow of a small boat which they had hired at Charly. The pastor, Chaudon, had been right, and Count Louis had been disappointed in his hope of reaching Meaux on the preceding night. Lodging at Charly and leaving their exhausted horses behind, early in the morning they had started down the Marne, hiring two boatmen to row them as far as Meaux, where fresh horses could easily be obtained.

Hardly had Louis had time to frame the question which sprang to his lips, when, as they rounded the bank which rose to the east of the mouth of the little affluent, the boatman exclaimed:

"*Voilà!* There comes at the moment the barge of the ladies of Jouarre!"

236

As he spoke a white-canopied craft, covered with crimson cloth whose gold fringes nearly touched the water, shot out into the Marne, strongly propelled by four sturdy oarsmen, and, steering eastward, preceded their own boat in the direction of Meaux.

From a slender staff at the bow a small white pennon was flying.

At a signal from Louis their boatmen bent more vigorously to the oars, and they soon approached the little craft, so nearly as to discern the device on this flying pennon.

Both young men bent eagerly forward with kindling faces. Louis spoke.

" Three *fleurs-de-lis* royal," he said, " on a field azure ! Yes, the *bâton péri* also," and, much marveling, he glanced at Norbert.

The young Zeelander maintained his characteristic silence. His lips were firmly closed, no excitement or impulsive fervor broke in words from them, but in his eyes was a new light, high and eager.

They were now nearly abreast of the boat. In the bow sat three blackrobed nuns of the Benedictine order. Next were the rowers' seats. The stern was concealed from their eyes by the curtains which fell from the canopy.

Suddenly from the right bank of the river a wherry came into view filled with armed men, and a shot from an arquebus struck the water just athwart the bows of the graceful canopied craft.

The stout fellows who filled the rowers' benches dropped their oars and seized their short swords, while Count Louis swiftly guided his own boat to a point where it lay between the other two.

Again a shot skipped across the river's surface followed quickly by a third. Louis and Norbert had both drawn their pistols and stood in their boat ready to repel the attacking party.

They could see plainly now, with a joyous thrill of wonder, that behind the curtains in the stern, beside another black-robed Benedictine, sat a lady in the habit of *supérieure*, but clad wholly in white.

The wherry had now approached midstream, and as it came within speaking distance a tall man in the dress of a Huguenot officer waved a white handkerchief as he stood in the prow and called :

" Where are you bound, and who are you ? "

Instantly the white abbess in the stern rose and stood her full height, and in a voice not loud, but so clear that every syllable could be distinctly heard, replied :

" We are sisters from the Abbey of Jouarre, bound for Meaux to the festival of Saint Michael. Who are you who fire upon defenseless women ? "

When Charlotte de Bourbon rose in her place the nun who had been seated at her right had sprung to her feet as if to interpose her own body between her lady and the soldiers.

Norbert, who at first could see only the pure face and queenly form of the lady of his dreams, marveled even in that fleeting moment at the flashing eyes and fearless spirit of the young *religieuse* in contrast with her companions, whose faces were blanched with terror at this alarming onset.

The captain of the little company had turned and spoken with one of his men.

" But you fly the lilies of France on your banner ! " he called again, and a ring of menace could be distinctly noted in his voice.

Count Louis and Norbert made ready to fire. The Abbess of Jouarre although she had not turned toward them seemed to see their intent. With a motion of her hand she forbade it.

" We fly the lilies of France," she answered, " because the Abbess of Jouarre is of the house of Bourbon. We are on a peaceful and a pious errand. Suffer us to proceed on our way." With

this word she gave a signal to the oarsmen, who instantly bent again to their rowing and the boat
shot swiftly onward, the ladies waving their thanks
to Louis and Norbert, who covered their retreat
with their own stout little shallop.

Seeing that the soldiers in the wherry and their
leader were still irresolute whether to follow the
boat from Jouarre, the count, having approached by
a few strokes, cried imperiously :

"Why do you make war on nuns, monsieur ?
Surely this was a bad blunder !" and in a lower
tone he murmured the secret countersign of the
Huguenots, received from Mâitre Chandon, carelessly adding his own name. Instantly the threatening manner of the leader changed and he saluted
Louis of Nassau with profound respect.

"We were on the watch, to be sure, monseigneur," he said, "for larger game, and at first flash
thought we had it. But I am not sure that this
ought to have slipped through."

"Wait for your larger game, my friend," said
Louis carelessly, " and forbear to attack women on
their way to church, whatever flag they fly. Row
on," he added to the boatmen, and they were soon
following in the wake of the boat from Jouarre as
it glided now between the houses and gardens of
the city of Meaux.

From the distance they watched the boat as it
was made fast at the watergate of the episcopal
palace garden, and saw the four black figures follow the one in white into the enclosure of the
palace and disappear.

Shortly after they themselves were landed farther
down the river. Having paid and discharged their
oarsmen they followed the moving crowd which
filled the streets of the little city flocking to the
cathedral of St. Etienne, where the ceremonies
preceding the great feast of St. Michael were about
to be celebrated.

As they entered the nave, pushed forward by the throng, some one touched Louis of Nassau on the shoulder. Turning quickly he saw close behind him two gentlemen, plainly dressed but of self-possessed and noble bearing, the elder of whom, a man of not less than fifty years, with a finely cut face, said in a low voice :

"Well met, monsieur. I will wait your convenience.

"D'Averly !" was the exclamation of the count under his breath. "What could be better timed !" and he saluted both gentlemen with gracious courtesy.

"Know you where Condé is ? " Norbert heard his whispered question and caught the reply :

"He should be here anon or his quarry will escape him." But there was neither time nor chance for further speech, for the organ and trumpets were thundering forth their music and up the nave swept the great procession of chanting priests and acolytes, monks and nuns, bearing lighted candles, and attending the effigy of the saint, borne aloft beneath a baldachin and preceded and followed by gorgeous banners. Last of all, in full pontificals, walked the Lord Bishop of Meaux.

Norbert's eyes scarcely noted the details of the brilliant concourse, for they were fixed upon the ranks of nuns of various orders, black and white and gray, who paced onward with downcast eyes and slow steps. He stood beside Louis in the front row of the crowd, where both could scan the ranks for the figure of the white abbess.

A touch of Louis' hand upon his arm gave warning of her approach. Yes, she was there, and upon her fair young head rested the slender golden circlet; from her shoulders swept snowy, ermine-mantled drapery ; her white hands clasped the crucifix upon her breast, her eyes were lifted with a steadfast, forward gaze, and upon her face was the radiant repose of an undefiled and noble spirit. Both young cavaliers felt their pulses leap with the ardor of devotion with which a presence so pure, so lofty, so removed from out their reach, inspired them. But already the vision was fading, the lady had passed. Behind her, bearing the sweep of her long train came two black-robed figures, both slender and *gracieuse*, with faces fair and young framed in by the white, conventual bands. Surely she who walked nearest, as she reached them, raised the dark lashes which swept the soft bloom of her cheek, and beneath them broke forth a lustrous gleam of recognition. It seemed to Norbert, moreover, that that bloom deepened to a richer hue as she caught his eager gaze resting upon her. He knew her for the young nun who had stood by the side of her *supérieure* in the boat in their recent encounter. Then the long lashes drooped again to the demure propriety of the monastic habit and the procession had swept on, leaving Norbert with all his blood tingling in his veins, he knew not why.

An hour later, at the close of the celebration, as he and his companions were trying to force their way out of the crowded cathedral, the brothers d'Averly having closely attended Count Louis since their first encounter, Norbert felt a slip of paper thrust into his hand. Turning hastily, he searched in vain among the throng which hemmed him in on every side for sight of the personage who had thus approached him. He could see no one who showed the slightest interest in himself nor the shadow of a desire to communicate with him.

Holding the paper concealed in his hand, he read with amazement the few words which were written upon it with evident haste :

" *The lady whose colors you wear awaits you at the foot of the palace garden.*"

Norbert's heart beat high with startled excitement. Was the exalted, inaccessible Abbess of

Jouarre indeed about to favor him with the long-desired interview and afford him the opportunity to lay his sword and service at her feet? So great an honor seemed impossible, and yet—her attendant, the young *religieuse*, whose youth and beauty and high spirit suited so ill the severity of her garb and the austerity of her vocation, surely she had given but now a token of recognition which might foreshow even such favor as this.

Norbert, who had for several moments lost sight of his comrades and who now found himself pressed onward to the outer portal of the cathedral, looked anxiously about him for a sight of Count Louis, but in vain. He and the gentlemen who had joined him had wholly vanished, and to seek them out in the throng was plainly useless.

What was to be done?

The note in Norbert's hand gave him his answer. " *The lady* . . . *awaits you.*" This present tense was imperative. A gentleman could not fail to respond swiftly and promptly to such a summons.

Meaux was but a small city. He remembered the name of the street—the Rue d'Acier—in which dwelt the d'Averly brothers, the Sieurs de Minay, for his father had lodged with these well-known Huguenot gentlemen two years ago, after his visit to the Abbey of Jouarre, and had laid much stress on their gracious hospitality. He could find his lord later. He must seek his lady now.

Passing through the palace garden, Norbert soon reached the margin of the river, where a fringe of willows overhung the bank and a flower-bordered alley stretched far into dim, green shadows.

No one was in sight. At the left and not far removed from where he stood rose the high palace wall. In it, at the end of the alley, was a heavy iron gate, before which paced a double guard of soldiers. Men and women in gala attire were sauntering through the pleasant paths of the garden, but none seemed inclined to turn their steps his way.

Then, suddenly, coming he hardly knew from which direction, there was a light footfall and the figure of a woman, slight and graceful, wrapped closely in a long, black mantilla which covered her head and fell nearly to her feet, approached him.

It was not the Abbess of Jouarre. This Norbert knew on the instant and felt at once also the wild presumption of dreaming that she could have proposed meeting him thus. But there was her attendant, the dark-eyed Benedictine; surely it was not impossible that she might have come as a messenger in place of her mistress!

With deepest deference, Norbert made his obeisance before the lady, catching between the folds of her mantilla the flash of a pair of bright, dark eyes.

Two swift steps brought her close before him, and he heard with quick amazement and dismay a low, rippling laugh, in which he caught the familiar echo of a voice he had hoped never to hear again.

"Valerie!" he cried under his breath.

"You will wear my colors now, at least, you key-cold varlet!" she whispered, and quick as a flash she darted into his breast a thrust of a small dagger which she had held concealed in her drapery.

The coat of chain mail which Norbert wore under his doublet turned aside the dagger, so that it drew no blood.

"You are out of practice, señora," he said contemptuously. And as he spoke he struck her wrist a sudden flick which shook the dagger from her grasp. It shot upward and then fell on the grassy path at her feet.

"*Au secours! au secours!*" cried Valerie at the top of her voice, springing back. "Hither to me! Hither! A spy, a spy!"

With these cries, shrill and alarming, ringing

through the quiet precincts of the garden, a crowd gathered about them, but foremost of all, and before he could turn or seek escape from the place, the guard from the palace gate was upon him.

"Seize him, seize him!" cried Valerie passionately. "He is a Huguenot spy. I know him. He recognized me as I walked quietly on the river's bank, and feared I would betray him. See," and she held up the dagger, "he sought my very life to save himself from discovery. He came from Condé, and he is in the plot against his majesty."

Throwing back these artful words, Valerie slipped into the crowd and disappeared from Norbert's sight not only for the time but forever. Her later history he never knew. That of her infamous Spanish accomplices became but too well known to him in the following years.

Resistance being obviously useless, Norbert submitted to the guard, who now hurried him to the water-tower of the bishop's palace and thrust him into a small, cell-like chamber.

"It matters not," said his captors curtly, in answer to his remonstrance, "whether the jade spoke truth or not. If she lied, it will do thee no harm, young master, to partake for a day or two of the bishop's hospitality. If she told truth, the best place for thee is the bottom of the river, which thou mayest shortly find. The uproar about the court and the plot against their majesties forbid that we should leave at large gentlemen who may chance to be in the Little Man's employ."

With this terse explanation, Norbert saw the door of his prison closed upon him. As the slow hours dragged on he strode up and down his narrow cell, hot with rage at his own fond, credulous folly, which had suffered him to walk thus open-eyed into Valerie's snare. A hundred questions rose to which he could find no answer.

Whence came Valerie and how had she found

him out ?   Why was she at Meaux ?   What would
Count Louis think of his inexplicable desertion ?
If he escaped alive from this trap would the prince
cease to honor him with his confidence, since he
had shown himself thus easily betrayed ?   Upon
such food for thought did Norbert feed that day.

Evening was well advanced when the door of his
prison was cautiously opened, and a stout fellow,
armed and wary, bearing a trencher of coarse food,
presented himself.

Convinced that the court had actually reached
Meaux despite the watchfulness of the Huguenots,
and was even now in hiding in this same episcopal
palace, Norbert, concealing his real desperation,
said in a tone of easy confidence as he took the food :

"Hold there a moment, my friend !   Know you
what fools those soldiers were to shut up here the
fellow who has risked his life to break the Huguenot lines, and who comes to bring tidings of the
Swiss from up the river at Chateau-Thierry to their
majesties ? "

"How is that ? " asked the servant, staring
blankly.

Norbert repeated the words.

"Here am I," he continued, "no spy, but a true
man, coming on a mission of high importance from
the Palatine Elector to the court of France, fighting on my way to rescue a princess of the blood
from the Huguenots as she attempted to reach
Meaux, and then, on the brazen slander of a Spanish
wanton, I am thrown into this dungeon ere yet I
can discharge my errand or have speech of her
majesty the queen-mother.   I demand to be taken
at once into the presence of her majesty ! "

With these words spoken with convincing authority Norbert confronted the perplexed servant.

"Do you know that lady whose word sent you
here ? " he asked, after a pause, blinking dubiously.

"To my infinite regret," said Norbert coolly,

"I have seen that person several times in Antwerp. What devil's business brings her to Meaux, do you know?"

"Devil's business, by St. Michael!" said the serv-ant, laughing silently. "She purports to be *modiste à la Royne-Mère*, and to come hither from Paris in attendance on the court. It is easy to guess, mon-sieur, that she has other business, as you seem to have already learned to your sorrow. *Au revoir* for the present. I can do no less than present your de-mand to the major-domo."

With this the man departed, but to Norbert's sur-prise and speechless relief, he returned in a brief half-hour, and bade him follow him to the central portion of the palace.

The hour was late, but the halls and passages were full of excited, hurrying retainers and gentle-men. Every entrance was carefully guarded, Nor-bert noted, by detachments of the Swiss soldiery, the personal bodyguard of the queen-mother.

At a rear entrance a little group of men were hur-riedly attending a prelate of tall and imposing figure, wrapped closely in a long mantle, who was about to make a hasty exit.

"The cardinal himself!" whispered Norbert's attendant. "He dare not wait longer, you see. He knows full well the Huguenots would show him no mercy."

Reflecting with some emotion that he had seen the arch-enemy of Protestantism in France, Charles de Guise, Cardinal Lorraine, Norbert now followed his guide up a fine staircase to a portal closely guarded by four Swiss of gigantic stature.

Here the major-domo, whose appearance showed great agitation and anxiety, met Norbert with the abrupt question:

"Your name, monsieur?"

"Roubichon."

"Your errand?"

"I come from the court of Heidelberg, with important information for her majesty. On my way hither I have had opportunity to observe the movements of the Swiss soldiery, also of the Huguenots. I can give the court advices which may be of service."

Norbert's firm and serious countenance, his grave, confident speech, and the grace of his bearing seemed to carry conviction with them. The one thing which the court frantically desired at that hour was knowledge of the whereabouts of the Swiss.

In another moment Norbert found himself in a brightly lighted room, magnificent in its appointments, but full of confusion and the marks of hasty preparation for departure. Dazzled by the moving groups of great ladies and gentlemen, among whom he discerned the Lord Bishop of Meaux and other dignitaries of the procession which he had witnessed in the cathedral, Norbert followed the major-domo into an inner apartment, where a lady in a black velvet robe and pointed white cap was walking the floor in uncontrollable excitement. A youth in rich costume of velvet and miniver, with pallid face and nervous restlessness, was standing by a window through which he cautiously peered from time to time into the street below. Knowing that he was now indeed in the Presence, Norbert dropped upon his knee, but without waiting for aught of ceremony Catharine de Medici, whose usually impassive face wore at this time the stamp of fierce terror and ire, exclaimed harshly :

"Tell me quickly, young sir, what you have to tell. I care not so much for the tidings you bring from Germany. That can wait till this present danger is overpast. I learn that you have come down the river to-day and have broken through the Huguenot lines. Where were the laggard Swiss when you passed them and why do they not move forward rapidly ? Is it not understood that the court is in imminent peril from this shameless conspiracy of Louis Bourbon ? "

"Your majesty," said Norbert, looking with a calmness with which he was himself amazed into the darkened and bitter countenance of Catharine, "to the best of my belief the advance guard of the Swiss must by this time be as near us as La Ferté-sous-Jouarre."

"Say you so ? " cried Catharine. "Listen, monsieur," and she turned to the young king, who had been furtively watching Norbert with cold and restless eyes.

"I hear, madame," he said shortly. "It were better that they were at Meaux. Upon what do you build your belief ? " he asked, glancing at Norbert with sullen *hauteur*.

"As I passed Château-Thierry, sire, they were mustering rapidly, at Cheszy I saw a large detachment, and Charly was full of them;" thus Norbert sought to expand to its utmost the small knowledge in his possession, feeling himself subject to keen suspicion on the part of the king. Catharine's agitation was so great as to rob her for the moment of her wonted penetration.

"We knew as much as that before," said the king, whose incredulity appeared to be increasing. "What is it we hear, young man, regarding your attempt to rescue some member of our family on the way to Meaux this morning ? The court reached Meaux last night."

Norbert's cheeks flushed scarlet. To be guilty of boasting of such small service as he had attempted in behalf of the Abbess of Jouarre seemed a craven trick. He hesitated and stood confused, conscious that the eyes of both Charles and Catharine rested upon him with awakening suspicion.

"It was but the slightest service, your majesty. I shame me much to mention it," he murmured.

"The name of the lady, sir, if you please," said Catharine sharply.

"Her grace, Mademoiselle de Bourbon, lady *supérieure* of Jouarre."

Norbert spoke the words low and as if he feared to profane the name by thus using it in his own defense.

"Bid Mademoiselle de Bourbon come hither," said Catharine, promptly turning to one of the ladies who attended her.

A light step, the rustle of a silken train, and the inner doorway of the room framed in the actual presence of the fair maiden-abbess, the vision of whom, as painted for him by his father, Nikolaas Tontorf, Norbert had so long borne in his imagination.

Before she spoke, seeing him thus standing, Charlotte de Bourbon smiled, and her eyes smiled a sweet, slow recognition before her lips, and, seeing her thus, Norbert felt as if he were in a dream and wished that the dream might never know waking.

But when she spoke in answer to the queen-mother a sharp pang shot through his heart that it was she who, after all, must needs come to his guardiance, not he to hers.

"Oh, yes, your majesty," he heard her say quite simply, "this young gentleman and another with him, although I know neither their name nor nation, adventured their own lives in true knightly fashion for us on our way to Meaux this morning. Glad am I that I now may speak our heartfelt gratitude. The banks of the river were patroled, your majesty, by Huguenot soldiers waiting to intercept and seize your persons should you approach the city by the river, not knowing that you were already safely here. They mistook us for your majesties and fired upon us."

"And from this danger you were rescued by this

bold young gallant, whose name even I do not now remember ! " cried Catharine. " It was well done, young man, and you have earned your release from duress in advance."

" Madame," exclaimed the king, coming to her side, " let us take another time for the exchange of compliments. The street below is swarming with Swiss. They are here at last."

Instantly the room became a scene of the liveliest commotion as Catharine, Charles, and their attendants prepared to avail themselves of their longed-for escort and make good their escape in the direction of Paris, knowing not how far they would be able to proceed without encountering the forces of Condé.

Norbert stood apart, in no wise disturbed as to what should follow, but deeply interested in watching the Abbess of Jouarre. One after another the four nuns of her company had entered the room and they now formed a group around her, a group forgotten and overlooked it seemed in the hasty excitement of the moment.

" We are ready now, your majesty ! " It was the Lord Bishop of Meaux himself who made the announcement.

Catharine de Medici wrapped closely in a long black cloak swept through the room followed by a trembling crowd of her ladies. Her eyes rested on Charlotte de Bourbon standing quiet and undismayed among her nuns.

" *Voilà, ma chère petite cousine !* " she exclaimed. " What a shame to leave you thus unprotected ! But alas, what can I do ? Five women more on this wild midnight flight might cost us all our lives. By my faith you are safer here ! "

" Your majesty, do not waste a moment more," said Charlotte with gentle urgency. " Hasten, hasten, every second counts ! Have we not a protector here, and one whose courage is already proven ? " she cried, and smiled celestially upon Norbert.

" Truly, what a mercy ! " cried the queen already at the door ; "I charge you, sir," she called back, " as you are a leal gentleman, to defend Mademoiselle and see that she and her maidens reach their convent in peace and safety. *Au revoir !* "

With which she was gone and with her the whole frightened company of courtiers and dames, and the bodyguard of Swiss in attendance.

XXIV

SUNRISE ON THE ROAD

" **D**EATH to the traitor ! Tear the tiger limb
from limb ! *A bas le Cardinal !* "

Through a frenzied, raging mob, the
canaille of Meaux, surging about the bishop's
palace, and filling the air with cries like these,
Norbert, with the aid of their own stout serving-
men, conveyed the ladies of Jouarre.

Mademoiselle de Bourbon had hastily caught up
an ecclesiastical mantle left behind by the bishop,
and had wrapped it closely about her to conceal
the gleaming white of her dress, and without a
moment's delay they had fled from the palace.

Wild with excitement at the plot of the Huguenot party to seize the persons of the king and queen-
mother in their own quiet city, the inhabitants of
Meaux had been yet further infuriated by a report
of an infamous counter-plot on the part of the
powerful and unpopular Guise cardinal. The scum
of the city rose to the surface, and regardless of
party or religion the mob rushed to the residence
of the bishop, armed with weapons of the motliest
sort, their purpose to lay hold of the cardinal if,
as was suspected, he were still there in hiding, and
then to sack the palace, now left unguarded.

Guided to the residence of the Sieurs de Minay
in the Rue d'Acier by one of the men from the convent, Norbert was overjoyed as they approached
the house to see in the moonlight, pacing the pavement before it, the figure of a gentleman, wrapped
closely in a long military mantle below which could
be seen the point of his sword.

252

" Count Louis ! " he called in a low voice.

The street, which was at a distance from the palace, was almost deserted.

The count moved to Norbert's side and saluted Mademoiselle and her ladies with graceful courtesy.

" This is better than we dared hope ! " he exclaimed. " The d'Averly brothers are searching the palace for your highness even now, but will soon return. We knew that you were there earlier in the day and that you were not of their majesty's company when they left Meaux."

" And how has it fared with your lordship meanwhile ? " asked Norbert. " I trust you lost no time by my disappearance."

" Nay, man," laughed Louis, who was as cool and debonair as if this were a masquerade, " we doubted not you would come to light in good time. We hastened on to Lagny to secure speech with the Prince of Condé ere it was too late."

" Are the Huguenot forces then at Lagny, monsieur ? " asked Charlotte, with eager interest. " Then the royal party will be intercepted."

" Doubtless, your highness; but I think not for long. The Swiss have gathered in overpowering numbers. Condé has but five hundred gentlemen with him. The plan is foredoomed to failure. But what I would say is, Condé, learning of your presence, madame, in Meaux, feared you might be in danger. He therefore put half a dozen of his men wholly at my disposal for your protection, and they are now awaiting your orders."

" This was most thoughtful of my cousin of Condé," returned Mademoiselle. " Let us lose no time then, monsieur, in setting out on our homeward way."

Count Louis at once conducted Mademoiselle and her ladies into the house, where they received hospitable refreshment, and an hour later, their number reinforced by the d'Averly brothers and the escort of Condé, the strangely assorted company set out on horseback from the excited little city on their night ride to Jouarre.

The size of the party protected it from molestation or attack, and at four o'clock in the morning they had reached La Ferté-sous-Jouarre, where fresh horses were awaiting them.

"Are you not very weary, madame ?" asked Count Louis, as he lifted Charlotte de Bourbon to her saddle at the door of the low stone inn where they had made their rendezvous.

"Not weary in the least, my lord," she replied composedly. "It is a rare chance for me to have an early morning ride, and I assure you I mean to enjoy it mightily."

Louis gayly applauded the buoyancy of her spirit, and with new courage the company set out on the last stage of their journey.

It was sunrise when they approached the little hamlet of Jouarre on its green slope, and could see the Petit-Morin gliding under the morning mists through the fair abbey meadows.

But what was that which darkened the road in the distance as far as the eye could see ?

Count Louis bade the cavalcade halt, and stood in his stirrups to scan the prospect. A hurried conference with the Sieur de Minay confirmed his own belief. The sun's first rays fell upon white banners and serried ranks of men-at-arms.

"There is nothing to fear, madame," cried Louis with good heart. "Yonder march the Huguenot forces, which Admiral Coligny himself is bringing up to join Condé at Lagny, as was expected."

Jeanne de Mousson, as they again rode forward, but at a slower gait, remarked shyly to Norbert, who rode at her side :

"You are to have your wish, monsieur. You are to see the Admiral of France, the greatest Protestant leader in Europe, they tell me !"

"I believe one is rising to-day who may prove himself yet greater than the noble Coligny," Norbert made earnest answer. "I would that you could see monsigneur the prince."

"You speak of *the* prince, Captain Roubichon, as if there were no other princes," said Jeanne, laughing blithely. "Whom mean you?"

"There is but one prince for me, mademoiselle," said Norbert sturdily, "the brother of the Count of Nassau, William of Orange."

"Say you, then, that he is a finer gentleman than the count? That I think can scarcely be! Surely he is the very beau ideal of a young knight; courtly, brave, and chivalrous," and the dark eyes of the young *religieuse* brightened with undisguised admiration.

"Is he not?" cried Norbert eagerly. "I could follow him to the earth's ends, and so would every man who knows him. To his own family, the beautiful old mother at Dillenburg, and to all the brothers and sisters, Count Louis is like the Angel Gabriel. He comes and goes, swift and sudden, on his ceaseless quest, and they watch for his coming, and mourn when he departs, as if he were the very light of day."

"What mean you by his ceaseless quest?" asked Jeanne.

"The quest for aid for my own poor land," returned Norbert, in a more serious tone. "Ah, mademoiselle, you know little, here in your quiet life, of the agonies which are desolating the Low Countries under the rule of the Spanish king and his deputy, Alva."

"I have heard of the terrible bloodshed," replied Jeanne; "and even among us of the Catholic faith in France the name of Alva is execrated. Small wonder, seems it to me, that a new uprising of them of the Religion should follow, since it has become known that the queen-mother invites him to enter

France and employ here the same methods with which he is stamping out heresy in the Nether- lands."

"If they did not rise they would be less than men!" cried Norbert impetuously. "But let us not stain the radiance of this fair morning with such thoughts of gloom and dread."

"Tell me, rather," said Jeanne, "how you can say all that you have of that gentleman," and she nodded her head toward Count Louis, who was riding in advance of Norbert, "and still say that there is a yet nobler Protestant prince."

Norbert was silent for a moment. Then with a smile he said:

"Perhaps you will better conceive my meaning if I say that the count is the Mercury of our Olym- pus, but the prince is great Jove himself."

Jeanne de Mousson shook her head with a smile, roguish and demure.

"You are quite beyond my depth, fair sir. I have heard, indeed, that our own convent was in far-away ages a shrine of that same divinity, for Jouarre is but a corruption of *Jovis ara*. But we nuns are not encouraged to search into the stories of those heathen personages. Our lady makes sure that we all have our thoughts employed on higher things."

Norbert glanced into the face of the piquant Béarnaise, in whom he could with difficulty discern the monastic character, and replied:

"I suppose life in the Abbey of Jouarre is one long succession of prayers and penance."

"Nay, Captain Roubichon," was the earnest re- sponse, "not so. Such was it, indeed, with much tithing of our revenues added, in the earlier time, when we had Madame de Long-Vic and Madame Cécile Crue over us, but all that has been changed since Mademoiselle has come into power."

"She has changed, then, the convent life?"

"That has she; and the greater is the marvel since her years are even now but twenty. We are taught to seek less our own perfection and the enrichment of our own abbey than to save and succor all the poor and unfortunate around us. Our lady is a very angel of light through all this part of La Brie. You might hear her name blessed in every lowliest hut, for no need escapes her. If we did not prevent her she would give away all that she possesses, for she thinks never of herself."

"Her highness is of a most charming presence," said Norbert, who had found the reality even beyond his romantic dream.

"Is she not?" cried Jeanne de Mousson. "Her spirit seems to fill our convent in every corner like the blessed sun. When there is trouble, we find her ever of a steady courage. When all is bright, she shames not to be frankly gay, and thinks a laugh and a song no sin. Look at her now! Saw you ever so sweet a saint and so captivating a creature? As I live by bread, at this moment I could e'en wish she were not a *religieuse*, and may I be forgiven for saying it!"

The little cortége, now nearly abreast of the gate of Jouarre Abbey, had halted, awaiting the Sieur de Minay, who had galloped forward to hold parley with the leaders of the approaching Huguenot force.

Charlotte de Bourbon had dismounted before the portal of her own stately domain and stood speaking to Count Louis.

"By my faith I could swear my lord echoes that wish!" murmured Norbert, under his breath.

In another moment three gentlemen, handsomely mounted, and accompanied by the Sieur de Minay, galloped up to the little group and dismounting engaged for a moment in conversation apart with Count Louis. At a distance stood the halted regiments, and sang as they stood in strong unison one of the thrilling hymns of the Huguenot army.

R

"Coligny," murmured Jeanne de Mousson to Norbert. "Ah, but he is, after all, every inch a soldier!"

Norbert looked, with breathless interest and deep veneration, at the central figure in the small but illustrious assemblage, the gray-haired veteran of serious and gentle face and of imposing, albeit quiet dignity. With him were the Chevalier de la Noue, a spirited, soldierly figure, and a younger nobleman of peculiarly winning aspect and patrician grace of person, the lord of Teligny, brother-in-law to La Noue.

These distinguished gentlemen greeted the Count of Nassau with hearty and unaffected cordiality as a friend and brother-at-arms, but without waiting for more words of explanation than were demanded by the unique situation, the count led the admiral across to where she stood and presented him to Charlotte de Bourbon.

The level rays of the new-risen sun illuminated the face and figure of the young abbess as she stood beside her horse, both set against the background of the dim gray convent wall, the glistening folds of her white robe sweeping the dewy grass about her feet, while hanging loosely from her shoulders swept the heavy folds of the long bishop's mantle. The nun's hood and wimple, by their demure severity, accentuated the soft, girlish contour of her face, while whatever of monastic gravity might at other times subdue its brightness had vanished in the stirring and eager emotion of the moment. The delicate bloom of her cheeks deepened as she received the stately greeting of the admiral, her blue eyes were full of the light of high and thrilling excitement, and upon her whole aspect rested the morning dew and freshness of her maidenhood.

"Will my lord and the gentlemen with him do such honor to the humble convent of Jouarre as

to take breakfast within its walls ? " she said, in
her clear tones, half-bashful, half-imperious, and
smiled with unconscious, delicate flattery into the
face of the grave old warrior.

"Very gladly would we thus take honor to ourselves, your highness," replied Coligny, bowing profoundly with a look of admiration at once fatherly
and knightly; "but we might by thus doing bring
some scathe to the fair abbess of this same convent. Were it well that it should go abroad that
soldiers of the Religion had broken bread within
your walls, Mademoiselle ? "

"At Jouarre, my lord," Charlotte made answer,
"you will find yourselves on neutral ground. According to our rule and order, no one who requires
our hospitality can be turned away. To-day we
will gladly give your lordship such entertainment
as suits our simple estate, and to-morrow we will
as gladly, if need be, give the same to my lord of
Montmorency."

"Wisely and worthily spoken, Mademoiselle,"
said Coligny gravely, "and on such terms we will
gladly avail ourselves of your favor."

Command was quickly given to the regiments,
which remained halted on the highway, that an
hour would now be taken for breakfast, and followed by her own company, augmented by the
admiral, La Noue, and Teligny, Charlotte de Bourbon entered the abbey gates.

But if the young chevaliers had for a moment
dreamed that the hospitality of Jouarre was to be
administered to them in person by its fair and
princely *supérieure* they quickly found their mistake.

Having attended them with all good grace and
courtesy to the noble guest house at the right of
the convent court, where she entrusted them to
the care of the guest-master, Charlotte parted with
them on its threshold. But ere she withdrew to
her own hall the lady beckoned the Count of Nas-

sau and Norbert to her side and thanked them for
their devoted service and the rescue of herself and
her demoiselles from the perils of the night and of
the previous day.

"Your highness," said Louis, looking with frank
devotion into the shining eyes of the lady, "this
young soldier is Roubichon only to his foes, but to
his friends Captain Tontorf, son of the printer of
Middelburg, not unknown to you, I believe. He has
in silence and secret held himself consecrate, may
I make bold to say, to your service now these two
years past, and by my faith I believe he came to
France less to do the bidding of my brother of
Orange than to seek such chance as might betide
to lay his sword and his service at the feet of Mademoiselle de Bourbon."

Charlotte held out her hand with swift, grateful
impulse to the young Zeelander, who dropped on his
knee as he touched it reverently with his lips.

"Is it possible that you are the son of Maître
Tontorf," she said, "the trusted friend of Madame
Jeanne d'Albret, the fearless messenger who saved
us from the espionage of our enemies ? He it was
who brought me the book which has led me to the
feet of my Lord and Saviour. Of his noble martyr-
death my cousin has informed me. Deeply have I
deplored it and devoutly in my heart have I honored
the memory of so good and so brave a Christian."

"The son is worthy of the father, Mademoiselle,"
Count Louis said gently ; "and if I were permitted
to speak for myself I should say that for both of us
alike there is no deeper desire than that you should
command us to any service it may ever be in our
power to render."

In the innermost heart of him Norbert felt the
generous condescension of Louis in this union of
their names. Not less keenly did he perceive the
touch of an emotion far exceeding his wonted
courtly gallantry with which these words were

spoken. No trace of jealousy, however, clouded the mind of the young soldier. The Abbess of Jouarre remained to him, in fact, as she had ever been in fancy, exalted far beyond earthly passion, save that of pure knightly devotion.

Despite her monastic inexperience the lady was not oblivious to the profound and scarcely disguised homage of the count.

With changing color, drooping eyelids, and as if hastening to cut short an interview which she feared to continue, she murmured a few words of gratitude and farewell, swept a low courtesy, and hastened to cross the green courtyard to her own hall.

The seven gentlemen who shortly surrounded the great round table in the hall of the guest house and partook of the daintily furnished and liberal fare which the convent provided, spent the hour in weighty and earnest conference. The relations of the Elector Palatine to the Huguenot uprising, the errand on which Count Louis and Norbert had come to France, received the first consideration. Later they discussed the prospects of the Protestant cause at large, and to the urgent struggle in the Netherlands to which, as the admiral and his lieutenants heard with deepest satisfaction, the Prince of Orange stood ready to commit himself.

" And now," cried the valorous La Noue as, the brief hour ended, they were about to rise from the table, " let us clasp hands together as we stand around this board and drink a health long and deep to our gracious and noble hostess. Life, health, and joy to the White Abbess of Jouarre ! *Vive la très illustre dame, Mademoiselle Charlotte de Bourbon!*" At these words all sprang to their feet.

" Gentlemen," exclaimed Louis of Nassau with kindling eyes, " a moment yet ere you drink the pledge of the Chevalier de la Noue ! The lady whom we pledge is surrounded by peculiar perils, perils of which I may not speak, but which cannot

fail in this fierce and turbulent time to wait upon
one who is at once the daughter of the Prince de
Montpensier and the close friend of her majesty of
Navarre. This venerable abbey in whose protection we are now secure is set in the path of
gathering armies and hard by the seat of the war
now already on, this very day openly declared—
the second civil war of France. Shall we who
have seen her and who revere the grace and exalted
goodness of the Lady of Jouarre, enjoy her bounty
and fare forth our several ways leaving her unprotected, exposed to dangers from within and from
without ? ''

A response of ardent protest passed from man to
man, and a pledge of knightly guardiance of the
lady was added to the toast.

Accordingly when the illustrious company presently broke up, each man to follow his own perilous and eager course, a small bodyguard of soldiers
was left at the abbey for the protection of its mistress, under command of François d'Averly, the
elder of the Sieurs de Minay.

As Count Louis and Captain Tontorf, setting out
alone on their long return journey to Germany,
reached a turn in the road which must presently
conceal from their view the hoary pile of the old
Abbey of Jouarre, the count exclaimed with a
humorous and yet rueful smile as he looked backward :

'' Happy d'Averly ! Would I could change places
with him ! ''

XXV

THE CHAMPION APPEARS

L EAVES from the note-book of the Demoiselle de Mousson :

Jouarre, 2 October, 1567: I walked with my lady in the garden after prime this morning, and we spoke of the strange events of the two days past.

We know that the court reached Paris unharmed, meeting in sooth sore dangers on the way. The king himself fought at the head of his own body-guard and but narrowly escaped the soldiers of Condé. My lady lets me speak as I will, which in truth is full freely, of the bold rescue of ourselves on the day before Michaelmas, of that long dark night when we,. peaceful nuns of Jouarre, rode between ranks of armed men, and were escorted by unknown cavaliers through those strange hours till dawning. Truly war works sudden *bouleverse-ment*. Marvel was it that wild and ill-assorting our condition as was the whole adventure, we yet could feel ourselves as little robbed of our dignity and re-spect as had we been at service in our own chapel. Such was the noble courtesy and reverence which encompassed us. Surely these foreigners are most chivalrous and regardful gentlemen.

Jouarre, 10 October, 1567: I had even in my se-cret heart wondered if my lady might find it hard to forget the good graces and adoring glances of the very worshipful Count Louis of Nassau, for I think not, save my lord of Teligny, has she ever chanced to meet a young knight of that strain. She is unwontedly silent and thoughtful. The rather doubtless have I held this fancy that I have striven in vain myself, even when I was at my devotions, to bar wholly from my sense the figure of the young captain from Holland who rode by my side from La Ferté, and who surely is as goodly a man as the count himself, and a full half head taller, and of as keen a wit.

But to-day my lady showed me that it was not on the Count of Nassau she was musing, since his unfeigned devotion, I fancy now, she found a thought too open, but rather of that which had made the substance of their talk together as they rode hither side by side. This was, in brief, that the Catholic Prince of Orange, brother of the young count, and a most puissant and noble lord, as had been long ago made known to Mademoiselle by Madame Jeanne d'Albret, has within short time given over the ancient religion. I hardly know why this fact, which indeed must have its influence upon all the world to-day, should have so great a place in my lady's meditation, unless it be that she is fain herself to take the self-same step.

And yet, how can she? It is my belief that if she were to declare herself of the new religion, the Duc, her father, would gladly take her life with his own hand, to such a pitch of fury has his zeal risen since the late troubles. The Huguenots call him "the Savage Butcher," and I have noted that my lady turns pale when tidings come of the part he plays in this terrible contest. But for all this, she has long converse with the Sieur de Minay, who bears himself toward her right fatherly, and who is a most devout, god-fearing man. Moreover, she reads the book brought her by Maître Tontorf continually, and spends many hours daily in prayer, wherein she uses no rosary nor missal, and no name of saint or Virgin. I know not what is before us, but for myself, I would in my own heart that I could even to-morrow quit this convent and declare myself what I am in truth, albeit no person save my lady dreams it, a Huguenot.

Jouarre, 3 November, 1567: To-day, as we sat within the hall, the rain falling in torrents, and the clouds so heavy that we were forced to sit close within the niche of the window to gain aught of light for our tapestry work, while we so sat, Jeannette only with us, my lady said, with her arch smile :

"I noted, Jeanne, that you had much converse with the young Middelburger, Captain Tontorf, as we journeyed from La Ferté, two weeks since. I have been minded, having your spiritual good to care for and oversee, to inquire as to the substance of your talking."

Like the silly thing I am, the blood rushed to my cheeks, and not for my life could I then have lifted mine eyes from the canvas and met my lady's look.

"I mind not now so particularly, Mademoiselle," I made haste to answer ; "one can scarce keep such trifling things in mind so long."

May I be forgiven, since do my best to have it otherwise, not one word which that same Roubi-chon-Tontorf spoke have I been able to forget ! So then, making haste to salve my conscience, I added thereto :

"We spoke, if I remember, among other things, of his grace, the Prince of Orange, brother to the Count of Nassau, for it seems that to him this same young officer has a devotion which one might call religious. It is really naught less than that."

My lady made upon this no reply ; but I felt that she wished me to pursue the subject further.

"To the thinking of this Dutch gentleman," I proceeded, "in comparison the Admiral of France is not so grand a hero, the Count of Nassau so gallant a gentleman, nor any prince to be found besides him worthy the name. 'There is but one prince for me !' so he said downright stoutly."

"It is even so that his brother discourses," returned my lady quite soberly. "The Protestants of the Low Countries are fortunate to have at last won so great a champion." And with that she became silent.

I can see clearly how slight a hold, after all, the dashing and generous count has taken upon my lady's thoughts. She passes him whom she has seen and is fain to dwell on an unseen figure, sterner, graver, yet more majestic, which he himself drew for her.

What can the Prince of Orange be in actual presence since the bare mention of him on the lips of his friends can so control the pure and virgin heart of such a one as my lady ?

Jouarre, 12 November, 1567: There has been a great battle outside the walls of Paris at St. Denis. The wounded of the besieging army of Condé have even been brought as far as Jouarre, and we have a new charge of nursing.

The constable, my lord of Montmorency, alas, is dead, killed by one Stewart, from private malice.

Both sides claim victory, but both have grievous losses. Fifty towns have now declared for the new religion, notably La Rochelle. I would that one poor demoiselle might follow suit.

Men speak freely, we are told by the Sieur de Minay, who, with his little band of soldiers, keeps safe watch over us, of the dire and black treason of the Cardinal de Lorraine. He has, it is now clear, in very deed attempted to betray the crown of France to Philip of Spain as having a claim thereto through his wife, Isabella of Valois. I could almost wish he had fallen into the hands of the populace of Meaux last Michaelmas. The whole land is in tumult. Nowhere is safety, and the very foundations tremble. It is a marvel to all that the queen mother still suffers the cardinal to have voice in her counsels.

Jouarre, January, 1568: Word has reached us that the son of the Elector Palatine, John Casimir, has at last entered Lorraine with the promised German *reiters*, and that the Huguenots, with the admiral and Condé, have met them. This proves that the mission of the Count of Nassau and Captain Tontorf last September was not in vain, for which even neutral nuns like ourselves may rejoice in our secret hearts.

Jouarre, March, 1568: We have had a visit from the Chevalier de la Noue, who has brought us the welcome news that the war, so fierce and bitter, although so brief, is at an end, an edict of peace having been signed at Longjumeau on the twenty-third. La Noue calls it a limping and rickety and wicked little peace, and prophesies that it will not last long and bodes dubious good to the Huguenots. Coligny, who was very loth to take up arms, and who had little relish for " the affair of Meaux," which the king and the queen-mother still bitterly resent, is more loth now to lay them down. The Royalists, he says, have too often been proved guilty of bad faith that they should be trusted now with no security. However, Condé is as eager now for peace as he was erstwhile for war, and has prevailed.

La Noue had also news for us from Brussels, where the Prince of Orange has been in January summoned by the Duke of Alva to appear before the Council of Troubles *in three fortnights,* as chief author and promoter of rebellion in the Low Countries. He was accused of being at the root of every movement against the Spanish government. If he refuse to appear, he is condemned to perpetual banishment and his vast estates are confiscated. Count Louis is also summoned with others to come before this terrible tribunal on the charge of conspiracy.

I asked the chevalier if the Prince of Orange would obey the summons, at which he laughed heartily, and asked me if men were wont to walk into a den of ravening wolves with their eyes open. My lady spake not at all, but listened with wondrous attentiveness, and La Noue, continuing, told that the prince has thrown the summons back right boldly in Alva's face and claims his right as a Magnate of the empire to be judged by the emperor, the electors, and other chiefs.

"The prince has, indeed," concluded the chevalier, "thrown down the gauntlet of war to the death, for although he claims that it is not the king who has proceeded against himself, but men who ill-serve his majesty, he says boldly that he is, *for frivolous and false accusations, contrary to all right law and usage, not only despoiled of his property, but insulted in his honor and robbed of his child, both dearer than life.*"

This child, La Noue made known to us to be a mere lad, the eldest son of the prince, who has been abducted from the college of Savoy at Louvain, and taken away to Spain.

"What will come of such bold action as this?" asked Mademoiselle.

"War, your highness," was La Noue's answer, "a war of which I can already see the beginning but cannot see the end. None the less it was a brave man's deed."

"It is, however, a terrible thing," said my lady, "to take upon one's self the responsibility of such a war."

"That indeed is it, madame," La Noue said very gravely; "but the responsibility is not upon the Prince of Orange, but upon the Holy Office which a month since *condemned all the inhabitants of the Netherlands to death as heretics*, save a few persons especially named."

" Oh, monsieur," cried my lady, " that is almost beyond belief ! "

" Nevertheless it is true. The Prince of Orange, believe me, is not moving over-hastily. Such is not his habit."

" What can be the results to the prince himself of such a war ? " asked Mademoiselle.

" If it succeed his renown will be most glorious, for he will have broken the greatest military power and the most intolerable tyranny in Christendom. If he fail he will be the loneliest man in Europe. But one thing can be assured : no defeat, no discouragement, no disaster will ever quench his spirit nor break his purpose. Death only will be the end. He possesses a power of silent endurance and a most unconquerable persistency of spirit when once he is aroused. Furthermore, there is not in any court of Europe a more masterly diplomatist. I dare to prophesy that as long as William of Nassau lives the Netherlands will never yield to the tyranny of Spain. It is my own desire, when once peace is established firmly in France, to go to the Netherlands and place myself and as many men as I can gather at the prince's disposal. There is no man living, after Coligny, under whom I would liever fight, and never on the face of the earth was there a juster or a holier cause."

My lady did not speak, but she had no need to. Her eyes spake for her.

Jouarre, August, 1568: From letters of Captain Tontorf to the Sieur de Minay we know something of the sorrowful course of affairs thus far in the Netherlands. In May, in certain watery pastures near a monastery called Heiliger-Lee, was fought

the first battle, audacious and over-early, but brilliant and successful. Count Louis led the patriot
forces with such boldness and wild valor that the
Spaniards were utterly routed. But his young
brother, Adolf of Nassau, was left dead on the field.

In his fury Alva then marched in person into
Groningen at the head of a strong and disciplined
army, having taken the precaution ere he left
Brussels to put to death eighteen prisoners of distinction, among them Count Lamoral of Egmont
and Count Horn, to the horror of all the world. He
met the " rebels " under Count Louis in Friesland,
drove them by superior numbers into a kind of
cul-de-sac formed by the river Ems, and there, after
brave but futile resistance, the count serving his
cannon with his own hand, he massacred the entire
army in his most bloody and ruthless manner.
Count Louis escaped with Captain Tontorf only by
swimming the Ems naked and fleeing for his life
back to Germany.

" It was," wrote Captain Tontorf, " most grievous and heart-breaking tidings which we had to
carry to the household at Dillenburg Castle. The
first Nassau to shed his blood for the cause had
fallen at Heiliger-Lee, fighting in the front of battle,
the brave and modest Count Adolf. Heavily fell
the blow upon his true-hearted mother, the Countess
Juliana, and upon the noble band of brothers and
sisters. To this was added for the prince, the mocking glory of a barren victory and the gloom of a
crushing and most bloody defeat. The hearts of
those who might otherwise have helped us are now
chilled and the difficulties of levying fresh troops
mightily increased. But, albeit the rash opening
of the campaign in Groningen by Count Louis was
against the will and judgment of the prince, he
uttered no reproach. ' *With God's help I have determined to push ahead* ' was his calm comment on
the whole deplorable issue.

"On that very day," went on the letter, "in which the prince wrote those words, July 31, he made a declaration to all Europe, and especially to the Netherlands, which is so calm and full a setting forth of his position as he now enters the lists to do battle with the most powerful monarch in the world that I shall send you herewith a copy of it. It may be, the ladies of Jouarre will also find interest in the reading."

Here follows this proclamation, which, beyond doubt, the ladies of Jouarre have read with eager interest, their hearts thrilled by its steadfast, serene courage and amazed by its marvelous mingling of sternness with conciliation.

My lady says it is a masterpiece of diplomacy as well as of boldness, and points out that the prince makes war against the king's government in the king's name, for to the manifesto he had affixed his motto: *"Pro lege, grege, rege,"* for law, people, and king.

"*We, by the grace of God Prince of Orange, salute all faithful subjects of His Majesty: To few people is it unknown that the Spaniards have for a long time sought to govern the land according to their pleasure. Abusing His Majesty's goodness, they have persuaded him to decree the introduction of the Inquisition into the Netherlands. They well understand that in case the Netherlanders could be made to tolerate its exercise they would lose all protection to their liberty. . . We had hoped that His Majesty, taking the matter to heart, would have spared his hereditary provinces from such utter ruin. We have found our hopes futile. We are unable, by reason of our loyal service to His Majesty and of our true compassion for the faithful lieges, to look with tranquillity any longer at such murders, robberies, outrages, and agony. We are, moreover, certain that His Majesty has been badly informed upon Netherland matters. We*

take up arms, therefore, to oppose the violent tyr-
anny of the Spaniards, by the help of the merciful
God, who is the enemy of all bloodthirstiness. Cheer-
fully inclined to wager our life and all our worldly
wealth on the cause, we have now, God be thanked,
an excellent army of cavalry, infantry, and artillery,
raised all at our own expense. We summon all loyal
subjects of the Netherlands to come and help us.
Let them take to heart the uttermost need of the coun-
try, the danger of perpetual slavery for themselves and
their children, and of the entire overthrow of evan-
gelical religion. Only when Alva's bloodthirstiness
shall have been at last overpowered can the provinces
hope to recover their pure administration of justice and
a prosperous condition for their commonwealth."

Together and in secret we read the whole letter
of Captain Tontorf, which was writ from Dillenburg Castle ; the proclamation we read more than
once, and my lady, whose eyes were dim, said so
low that I scarce caught the words, "May I live to
see one day the man who had the heart to write
those words ! "

Jouarre, October, 1568: Truly the times wax
worse and worse and these days are of the darkest.
In Flanders the great army of the Prince of
Orange, which he had sold his plate and jewels to
levy and equip, has been utterly scattered by the
tactics of Alva, the easier an achievement since
they were but mercenary soldiers fighting for pay
and plunder. Never once would Alva give battle
to the prince, but wore his army out with hanging
upon their skirts, destroying all their means for
obtaining food, harassing them with matchless and
wily cunning, forcing them to change their en-
campment twenty-nine times in as many days,
until at last, as the crafty duke foresaw, the troops
became maddened and mutinous. The prince is

even now re-crossing the Meuse, as we hear by my
lord of Teligny, who hath been more than once of
late at Jouarre on his way to or from the court,
with which he has had much conference. With
what feelings must the prince return from a campaign so valiantly undertaken! Bitterest of all
must it be, says Teligny, that the Netherland folk
themselves stirred not hand nor voice to meet the
prince at his coming. Not one town or city opened
its gates to him, even to within a few leagues of
Brussels itself, where he has been ever the idol of
the people. The people are stupefied, it needs must
be, by the barbarous cruelties of Alva, until every
last drop of hope and courage is frozen within them.

I should think all hope for the Netherlands gone
were it not for what the Chevalier de la Noue declared to my lady concerning the unconquerable
nature of the Prince of Orange. Surely he is
sharply tested now, for his great army is wasted
with no gain and his ill success has turned his
warmest friends cold, except among the poor and
oppressed. Where can he now turn? Dukes,
electors, and princes fall away from him like water.
Well did La Noue prophesy that if he failed the
prince would be the loneliest man in Europe.

So much for the cause in Flanders. I say *the
cause*, for although it must not be dreamed here in
Jouarre, there is no longer disguise nor concealment
between my lady and Jeannette and myself. Our
cause is the cause of the Religion.

For France the case is even worse, if worse can
be. Coligny and the Prince of Orange have entered not long since into a mutual compact and
more than ever we realize that the cause is one.

Alas, we are ourselves plunged again in civil
war, for the peace of Longjumeau has proved indeed but a "wicked and rickety little peace," seeing that in these six short months ten thousand
Huguenots have been treacherously murdered.

s

Hardly can war be worse, as the Prince of Condé declared to the queen-mother. He has implored her to dismiss from her counsels the Cardinal of Lorraine, the infamous plotter against both crown and people. The Emperor Maximilian has well said that "all the wars and all the dissensions that are to-day rife among Christians, have originated from two cardinals, Granvelle and Lorraine."

The Guisards now have their own way at court, and the first great deed with which they sought to usher in their rule was nothing less than a desperate attempt to seize the persons of Coligny, Condé, and the Queen of Navarre, last month. All three barely escaped, fleeing to La Rochelle, now the Huguenot refuge.

Only war could follow an event like this, and war is now upon us.

Our own private matters have suffered shock with all the rest. Since my lady has little by little, under the teaching of the Sieur de Minay and other influences, come into full sympathy with the Huguenot cause, she finds it ever more difficult to fulfill the office of *supérieure* with whole heart and conscience. The Queen of Navarre learning of her altered mind, a short while since, offered Mademoiselle and her two Jeannes a haven and a home in Béarn could she go so far as to break wholly with the Catholic faith. I think not that my lady fully intended to put this generous purpose to the test, since Monseigneur de Montpensier might have made terrible reprisals upon her majesty. Nevertheless, we had some consideration of disguises and of remaining, by the aid of the queen, for months in strictest hiding in the Pyrenees. All this is now at an end since Madame d'Albret has herself become a wanderer.

The three great spirits of Huguenoterie, whom Alva's and Philip's and the Guises' evil wills have so fiercely desired to destroy, are for a little time

all together within the protecting walls of La Rochelle. It is said that Madame d'Albret, by the
vigor and penetration of her intelligence, never so
nobly displayed as now, animates all the councils
of war, and is the very soul of the Huguenot body.

The Chevalier de la Noue and young Teligny are
high in command. The flower of the nobility is
flocking to Condé's army. There has been a general call to arms.

XXVI

A DEAD MAN

ON a dismal February evening, on the road leading into the city of Cologne from the south, through stinging sleet and searching wind there rode two men.

The elder of these, a man of thirty-five years, wore a padded worsted doublet, wide grogram trousers, and over all a long and well-worn surtout. Upon his head was a broad-brimmed hat drawn over the forehead and concealing the face. His companion was young and soldierly, and dressed in an equally plain and nondescript fashion.

Shortly after entering the city gate the two men parted, evidently by agreement. The younger turned his horse's head in the direction of the Domhof, and using his spurs was soon out of sight. The elder, following for a space the street by which he had entered the city, presently turned aside into a narrower one and drew rein before a low-roofed inn of the humbler sort, above the door of which hung the sign, *Zum Hirsch*, surmounted by a rude wooden figure of a stag, painted red.

Giving his horse to an hostler who came out from the stables, the gentleman entered the inn in a manner calculated to attract as little attention as might be and asked for the landlord.

The host of the *Hirsch* soon appeared, a heavily built man with coarse, mottled face and bushy eyebrows, under which looked out a pair of very shrewd and calculating greenish-gray eyes.

"Can I have a room, mein Herr?" asked the stranger civilly.

276

"For the night ? "

" Perhaps not for the night. I have yet to hear
from my clerk whether he has found accommodation elsewhere. I should like a private room, however, at once."

"Oh, yes ; oh, yes," said the landlord, rubbing
his hands with great show of cordiality, but
glancing sharply under the broad and drooping hat
brim at the stranger's face. " A room, oh, *gewiss,*
a room. That is easy. And what is the gentleman's name ? "

" George Certain."

" And the calling of mein Herr ? Our regulations
are of necessity so strict in these wild times."

" Wine merchant from Rüdesheim, traveling on
business with my confidential man."

" Whose name is——? "

" Roubichon."

" Thanks, mein Herr," and the host bowed obse-
quiously. " You will pardon if I seem over-inquis-
itive. I am obliged at the present time to take
these precautions even with the most exalted Herr-
schaften."

The stranger cut short the man's protests, being
apparently in some haste to reach the retirement
of his room. He was now conducted up a steep
flight of stairs, at the top of which the door was
thrown open into a low, gloomy, garret-like apartment directly under the rafters, with a single window overlooking the courtyard where heaps of
manure were melting into the sodden snow and a
foul, dank steam was rising.

The stranger looked about the fast-darkening
room for a single instant with a measuring glance.
It contained two narrow beds, as many chairs, a
light-stand, and a plain deal table. He stepped to
this table and tested it with a movement of his
hand to see if it stood firm.

"Yes," he said, " I can write on this. The

room is well enough. Thank you, mein Herr.
Send me hither presently, if you please, such meat
and drink as you may have in readiness, and two
or three candles.

While he spoke the stranger was taking from a
deep pocket of his coat a traveler's ink-horn, several quills, and a thick leather letter-case, which he
laid on the table.

The host who saw himself dismissed had noted
the extreme beauty and fineness of the hands of
his guest, and as he left the room to do his bidding
he said to himself:

"A marvelous fine gentleman for a wine merchant, for all his shabby dress and his small require-
ments. There is something more to this than appears. Men of that ilk frequent not hostelries of
this quality unless they have reasons for keeping
out of sight. We shall keep our eyes upon you,
fair sir, and perchance come nearer to discerning
your title and degree than will be welcome to you."

Meanwhile the younger man had galloped as fast
as his tired horse could go through the Domhof and
on down the Hochstrasse, alighting before a large
house of comfortable but by no means pretentious
description. A general air of neglect and indifferent oversight pervaded the whole establishment,
and it was with some little difficulty that the young
man succeeded in calling up a lackey to take his
horse and another to conduct him to the house
steward.

To the last functionary, a Netherlander named
Hauff, he made the statement that he was Tontorf, a secretary of his highness the Prince of
Orange, and desired to speak with the wife of that
gentleman immediately upon pressing and private
business.

The steward looked at Tontorf for a moment
with scarcely veiled insolence.

"Her highness is somewhat indisposed this evening and has remained in her room. You might come in the morning, Master Tontorf."

Norbert bit his lip but restrained his temper.

"My master's business can hardly wait," he said briefly. "You will, I am sure, do me the favor of announcing me to her highness."

"You can follow the page upstairs, if you please," the steward responded, calling a lad in shabby livery, who had been peering at Norbert from a door throughout the interview.

"Here, Hans, run up in advance of this gentleman and see if her highness has a mind to receive him."

Norbert followed the lad up the main staircase of the house which belonged to John Molen, the prince's treasurer, and through a wide hall to an open door. Here Norbert stood, forced to overhear the dialogue which ensued between the page and the Princess of Orange, whose discordant voice he recognized with peculiar disrelish. A moment later he was bidden into her presence.

Anne of Saxony was reclining on a broad divan in a confused medley of bright-colored draperies and cushions in the midst of a luxuriously appointed but untidy bedchamber. A table held a handsome service for a supper for two persons. A lamp burned on an escritoire beside the divan and a fire blazed on the hearth.

Norbert saw at a glance that the princess had changed markedly since her departure from Dillenburg. She had grown very fat, and the gross and sensual character of her face was highly augmented; but her eyes were still of burning brightness and her manner no less imperative than ever.

"Oh, it is you, sir," she said abruptly, not moving from her easy attitude. "I remember you perfectly. I saw you last at the château of the Nassaus. What have you come here for?"

"To bring a message from his excellency, madame. Can I have the honor to speak with you in private ? "

"We are alone," said Anne of Saxony care-lessly. "You can close the door behind you, an' you will."

Having done so Norbert stepped back to his position near the divan, and said in a low voice :

"The prince, madame, is even now in Cologne. Needless is it to say that his presence must not be known. He has sent me hither while he awaits my return in a common inn where he may hope to avoid recognition, to inquire whether your house-hold at the moment is such that it will not embar-rass your highness nor imperil himself if he come here for twenty-four hours. He most earnestly de-sires that he may have speech with you before he sets out for France."

The countenance of the princess had grown steadily harder and more bitterly repellent as Norbert went on.

"For what does he desire speech with me ? " she cried excitedly. "I can guess. He wishes to persuade me to go back to his relations in that bar-barous prison of Dillenburg. No, he need not come here for that, Master Tontorf. You can tell him as well as I and with less bitterness, that I will never, never as long as I live, go back into that wretched wilderness," and she proceeded to rave against the miseries and distresses of life where in the whole Westerwald there was not even a barber-surgeon to be found ! where she could not even get a glass of wine often when she wished it ! and where there was no one whom she found in the least amusing to break the tedium of the long, wearisome days !

"What do the Nassau ladies do ? " she cried. "Sit and look out of window to watch for their lords and run to meet them like dogs at their coming ! Or else they trot about the castle with their eternal *bürgerliche hausfrau* cares, and visit the dark, dirty cottages of that horrid little village, and for the rest let themselves be preached to and prayed at night and morning till I should think they would die of piety ! And because I, the daughter of the great Maurice of Saxony, accustomed to the state and magnificence of the court of Dresden, could not condescend to do as they did, they would leave me to sit alone often a day at a time till I thought my head would break of ennui. And now it will be worse than ever, since they are in mourning for Adolf. He was a pretty junker, the best of the lot. I wish it had been Louis, since one must fall at Heiliger-Lee. Him I never could abide ! "

"Madame," said Norbert quietly, when at last the princess paused for breath, "I think it is not altogether in the matter of your return to Dillenburg that the prince desired to confer with you. He is, as you must be well informed, immersed in difficulties, and needs such comfort and friendly interest as a man may look for from his wife."

"Let him not come to me for comfort ! " exclaimed Anne, straightening up with sudden vigor, her face flushing high ; " nor if it is money that he is after ! Not a stiver have I save what certain good friends from Antwerp advance me. Have I not suffered my plate to be sold to aid him in this good-for-nothing Beggar war ? Did I not warn him from the first how it would end ? But he only turned a deaf ear to me and now he is nicely caught in the net ! Of course he is in difficulties, but they are of his own seeking ! I have enough of my own."

At that moment a heavy curtain at the opposite end of the room was lifted and in stepped a personage of portly figure, wrapped in a long dressing gown of crimson velvet, edged with fur, a man with a full florid face and wide moustachios, a man whom Norbert instantly recognized with unspeakable amazement, as the Antwerp councillor, Jan Rubens, who had emigrated two years before to Cologne.

He had entered the room without knock or warning, in fashion most intimate and familiar, and had
advanced a step or two before he appeared to discover that it was not some member of her household whom the princess was rating. Catching the
eyes of Norbert fixed upon his face, the recognition
became mutual, and in awkward confusion Rubens
was about withdrawing hastily when the lady called,
quite unabashed :

"Do not go, my friend. I was even on the point
of sending for you. You have seen Master Tontorf,
as you have told me, long ago in Breda. Is it not
so ? *Eh bien*, he is now clerk or something to the
prince, and I wish you to show him the letter you
are writing for my attorney, Betz, to present at
Vienna."

With these words Anne of Saxony stepped to the
desk near at hand. As she spoke she looked across
the room at Rubens with a broadly flattering glance.

"Come," she added, with brutal mockery, "it
must surely please monsieur to know that I have
so goodly an advocate in his absence to care for my
interests."

The sudden change from the heartless coldness of
her manner while speaking of her husband to her
undisguised blandishment of the Antwerp refugee
aroused in Norbert a sudden whirlwind of anger,
and a wild desire to draw his pistol and shoot the
guilty pair on the spot, for that guilty they were
no smallest doubt remained in his mind.

Rubens, meantime, restored to his wonted com-
placency, nodded patronizingly to Norbert and advanced to the desk, over which he and the lady
now leaned together, whispering and smiling with
an infuriating air of confidential understanding.

"This is the letter, my good Tontorf," Rubens
began as he turned from the desk and faced Norbert, holding a newly written and yet unfolded
letter in his hand.

"It is addressed," he continued pompously, "to his Imperial Majesty, the Emperor Maximilian. It is written in the name and person and by the desire and demand of this most worshipful lady, the Princess of Orange, but composed and framed by her humble and unworthy servant, Jan Rubens." And with the words, which he rolled forth unctuously, he made a deep bow to the princess, who responded by a languishing smile which made Norbert's blood tingle with disgust.

"Whereas," Rubens read on, "my quondam husband, the Prince of Orange, Lord of Breda, etc., etc., has refused obedience to the summons of his liege lord, his majesty of Spain, through the Duke of Alva, and in consequence of the proclamation now in force against him, he has suffered civil death, in the eyes of the Netherland law he is a dead man ; *ergo*, on Netherland soil, I, his former spouse and consort, am now a widow ; *ergo*, the Netherlands estates, of which the aforesaid Prince of Orange, now deceased, was possessed, belong ——"

Rubens read no further.

A blow, swift and sudden, with the flat of a short sword had torn the paper in twain and tossed it on the ground, and a sharper blow of the same sort on the head of the councillor sent him abjectly reeling, though uninjured, to the floor.

Norbert turned then to the lady, who stood in rigid and speechless consternation at his temerity.

"Madame," he said sternly, his sword clenched hard in his hand, his mouth set, "you have done most foul and cowardly injury to the noblest gentleman and the faithfulest husband whom it has ever been my lot to look upon. He whom you despise as dead is living, and his name will live through coming ages. But you, who have shown yourself unworthy to share his great name, incapable of perceiving his great nature, will, ere long, trust me, find yourself dead in the eye of the law, and dead past resurrection.''

With these words, Norbert strode from the room and down the staircase.

In the halls below he encountered Hauff the house-steward.

"Tell that scoundrel, Rubens, up there, if you will," he said coolly, unheeding the piercing shrieks which now resounded from above, "that I would be glad to fight him, if he is not afraid to fight, when next I am in Cologne. Nothing would please me better than to throw his carcass in the Rhine to make food for the fishes. Remember, if you please."

With which words he called for his horse and galloped out again into the miserable stormy night back through the streets of Cologne to the *Gasthaus zum Hirsch*.

As he entered the low inn-room with its sanded floor and sordid comfortlessness, Norbert found it occupied by a half-dozen Hessian soldiers of the roughest sort. Ill pleased at this fact, he was scarcely better suited when he found himself confronted almost as he crossed the threshold, by a tall, haggard shape, a man of emaciated face and sunken, wandering eyes, in whom he recognized at once his father's old friend, the Middelburg pastor, Droust.

Norbert knew that the unfortunate man still lingered in Cologne, homeless, but harmless in his lunacy, but it had been far from his expectation to meet him. However, recognition being unavoidable, he returned Droust's emphatic greeting with as little circumstance as might be, and was about to cross the room to the low counter where the landlord stood, watchful-eyed, among his stoups and tankards, and to inquire of him whether the merchant, George Certain, from Rüdesheim, had lodging in his house, when he found the hand of Droust laid hard upon his shoulder.

His manner, which had not at first been noticeable, had changed with the marvelous swiftness of
insanity. Lowering his voice and speaking in an
awestruck whisper, which was, however, to be
heard throughout the room, he said :

"*Know you who is there ?*"

With these words he pointed upward to the low
murky ceiling not over a foot above his head.

Norbert felt his hair rise with sudden dread.
He would have shaken the man's hand from his
shoulder, but feared to arouse him to a more perilous violence.

The soldiers in the room, who had not appeared
to notice Norbert on his entrance, now looked up
from their beer mugs and stared at the speaker with
coarse, jeering wonder.

Still pointing upward and striking into a singular,
chanted wail of mournful solemnity, Droust now
cried :

"O thou Hope of Israel,
Thou Saviour thereof in time of trouble,
Why shouldest thou be as a stranger in the land?
As a wayfaring man who turns aside to tarry for a night?
Why shouldest thou be as a man astonied?
As a mighty man that cannot save ! "

Startled for a moment by the wild pathos of
these words and the passionate intensity with which
they were pronounced, Norbert now rallied himself
to check any further outburst, and had broken away
and approached the door, feigning to be afraid of
the man, when Droust cried at the highest pitch of
his voice, trembling with fierce upbraiding : " O,
ye of Nederland, answer ! Cravens and cowards,
make reply !

"Wherefore when I came was there no man?
When I called was there none to answer? "

Look upon him whose heart his countrymen have
broken ! "

Then sinking his voice again to a whisper and addressing Norbert with curious, childish exultation, he added:

"The *prince* is here. Could a man who had once seen him forget?"

At this word the soldiers, who had been gaping wide-eyed upon the scene, sprang as with one consent to their feet, and with fierce and hostile glances advanced toward Norbert, the foremost among them, exclaiming:

"What is all this, young man? This madman, it seems, knows more than any of us! Who is in this house? If you know, make answer!"

"How should I know?" exclaimed Norbert, with bluff impatience; "have I not just come in, my good friends? As for yon arm-gaunt lunatic's raving, an' so you be such gulls as to pay heed to it, I will bid you good even and seek my bed if mine host can direct me to one up yonder. Sleep were better than such idle chaffer."

As he spoke Norbert had little by little made his way to the door. Lowering looks and muttered curses and calls of "Nassau! Nassau!" had met his speech. His intent was, if matters became more threatening, to make a bold dash up the stairs, warn the prince, whose room in that small house he could not fail to find, and stand guard while in some way he should make good his escape.

But already he saw that such action would be impossible. The soldiers, who were of the hired Hessian troops of the army which the prince had but two weeks since disbanded at Strasburg, half-paid in spite of his desperate sacrifice and efforts, were already surrounding him, hands on swords, their swarthy faces aflame with fierce suspicion. Droust had sunk back into his corner in a miserable collapse of uncomprehending bewilderment. The host stared, impassive and neutral, from his place.

"You come not off so easy with your cheap

talk, master," cried the men. "Bide you here! Fools and madmen speak sometimes truer than other men. If William of Nassau is in this house we shall see him, he shall not escape us!"

"Look at our shoes!" cried their spokesman, pointing to his ill-shod feet; "look at these rags," and he displayed his tattered doublet. "We fight for pay and no pay have we got. Neither food nor drink nor shelter has his excellency provided us this month past. And now we hear he is off to France, to their lordships at La Rochelle, while we poor devils drop in our tracks of cold and hunger!"

"Has the Prince of Orange wherewith to pay you, my friend? I have heard that he is himself impoverished," returned Norbert, seeking now only to stem the tide and unable to foresee the issue of this most unlucky encounter.

"We'll have it out of him!" cried a big blonde giant with hollow cheeks and a coarse bristling moustache who had stood in the background staring at Norbert under fiercely knit brows.

"But he has sold his plate, sold his jewels, sold his horses, harness, his very tent!" cried Norbert, whose passion was now rising hotly and who could no longer sustain his futile show of indifference. "His Netherlands estates are all confiscate. He has done his uttermost!"

"He has his castle of Dillenburg yet, however," growled the man savagely; "we will make holiday and ride over the hills, a dozen or two of us, and see what he may have tucked away there."

"It may hap," said the leader, with a coarse laugh, "that we find enough to fill our pouches for a day or more. It's worth the ride. But we'll see who is hid here in the house first—heh, my men?"

At this moment the host of the *Hirsch*, who had stood on the edge of the angry group and to whom Norbert thought to appeal in the defense of the prince, interposed with the remark:

" There is in good sooth, my masters, a gentleman who sits writing at this moment in the room
above us who seeks to pass for a wine merchant
from Rüdesheim. It may be that such is his person and degree, but beshrew me if ever until this
night I have met wine merchants whose letters, as
they lie on the table, bear the seal of Spain and
of the emperor ! "

A wild uproar greeted this statement and Norbert noted with deepest dread the harsh implacable
determination on every face. More than once, in
the months just passed, he had seen the life of the
prince in imminent danger from the mutinous mercenaries, had even seen his sword shot from his
side in such an outbreak.

How many of these ferocious brutes could he
dispatch before they would dispatch him ? was all
the question which now seemed left him. To die
fighting for the prince had no terrors, but to make
that death availing, this alone was left.

A hand was laid then on Norbert's shoulder.
Turning he saw the prince himself at his side. The
gray surtout and broad-brimmed hat had been removed and he stood with bared head, the striking
nobility of his face now fully displayed.

For an instant, while the soldiers for awe of him
fell back, their wild and murderous clamor dying
down to a sullen muttering, the prince stood in
silence looking at them with fearless repose of bearing and yet with a light of proud and regal command in his dark eyes :

" I heard my name called," he said then quietly ;
"you are men, if I mistake not, who have been
with us in our campaign in Flanders."

" That we are," cried the foremost Hessian
threateningly. "We have seen service with your
excellency, but we have not seen our wages yet.
Look at our condition," and he displayed his deplorable habiliments.

Norbert kept his hand on his pistol and his eye on the savage blonde fellow who stood against the wall and whose look was ominously ugly as it rested upon the face of the prince.

" My men, your plight is hard enough," returned the prince with freehearted earnestness ; "if it were in my power to relieve your necessities most gladly would I do it. But I am, as you now see me, stripped down to the barest needs. I have scarce two horses left or a second doublet to my back, a roof over my head or a gulden in my wallet. What I have had has been shared with my soldiers, and what I shall have in months to come shall be likewise. Can I do more ? "

Stubborn murmurs, "We want our wages," still arose.

" You might take my life," said the prince, noting their savage temper "but a dead man pays no debts. I am not loth to die, and I stand defenseless before you ; and yet a stab in the dark is little to my liking. The Nassaus are not cowards, but we would fain die in the field, fighting for faith and freedom. The boy Adolf left dead in the bloody marshes of Heiliger-Lee was the first of us to fall, but he will not be the last. But as long as I have life I shall labor to discharge my just debts to my men. If I had aught it should be yours this very night. But what have I left ? "

The blonde fellow in the background growled between his teeth :

" We will go to Dillenburg and see ! "

"You might go to Dillenburg," returned the prince with a vibration of passion in his voice which he was unable wholly to control, "and what would you find there ? A heartbroken, aged mother, weeping for her dead son, and praying that those remaining may be spared to her ; a company of faithful wives and sisters and little children ; a house stripped bare of all but necessities for the

T

sake of the cause for which we have fought together. No, my men, go not to Dillenburg. Go
rather with me to France, as a thousand of your
fellow-soldiers are pledged to do, and bear arms for
the same good cause on French soil. Count Louis
is already there. We shall come back to the conflict at home when the time is ripe. The Huguenots are not so poor as we Gueux. You will get
your pay fighting there. If I return alive I pledge
you now, herewith, on my honor as man and prince,
my body itself, which you can hold alive or dead for
ransom if I cannot by other means pay you the last
penny I owe you!"

The men looked in open-mouthed wonder at each
other and were silent. No man had ever known
the Prince of Orange to break a pledge. The security was unfamiliar, but it might be sufficient.
And this French campaign was perhaps the next
best thing to turn to. Even their brutal selfishness
was touched for the moment, moreover, by the
fearless confidence of the prince and by the steady
·patience with which he met their demands.

He was quick to see the advantage he had gained.

"My men," he cried, "I am tired. I have
ridden far to-day and have farther to ride to-
morrow. Ride with me, as many of you as are
ready for the fight in France; but I would be glad
now to rest. If you want me you can find me,
although where I am to lodge, in faith, I know not
yet. Tontorf, how is that?" he added, turning
quickly, for a sudden, eager question was brighten-
ing his eye. "Have we other haven for the night
than this house, whose master methinks might
have proved friendlier to a somewhat weary way-
farer?"

"Nay, my lord, alas, we have nowhere else to
go," said Norbert under his breath.

A swift change passed over the face of the prince.
The grim finality and bitterness of Norbert's words

and tone gave the outline of a picture whose colors he could but too easily imagine. For a moment the sense of homelessness and desolation pierced his heart and entered deep into his soul. Slowly and with an effort he spoke again.

"I am going up to the room yonder now, where I shall sleep for a few hours." Then with swift command he cried heartily : "How many of you, then, will meet me here at six in the morning and ride with me to Trèves ?"

After a moment, in which they exchanged glances, every man held up his hand, the big blonde alone surly and reluctant still.

The prince bade them shake hands upon it, and, with a courteous good-night, withdrew. Norbert followed him up the dark staircase and they entered the dismal chamber together.

The prince made no comment on the encounter with the soldiers which he apparently dismissed at once from his mind as of small importance, nor did the least apprehension of further danger from their hostility seem to remain in his mind.

"Have you any word, any message for me, Tontorf, from my wife ?" he asked as he threw himself upon his narrow bed.

"None, my lord," was Norbert's brief answer. More he could not say for very ruth.

There was silence for many minutes, then the prince spoke again.

"The first dispatch I opened to-night was a copy of a letter to Alva from Cardinal Granvelle."

"Yes, your excellency."

"He says '*Orange is a dead man.*' Tontorf, we shall have to convince the cardinal that he is mistaken."

"Yes, your excellency."

In another quarter of an hour the prince slept.

At daybreak, as Norbert stood guard at the chamber door a tall figure stole down the narrow passage in silence to his side, a figure which he presently discerned to be that of the preacher Droust as it stood motionless before him.

"Here," he said, holding out a small and dirty canvas bag containing gold and silver, "this is for *him*. I have no more need of it. I can see now what I saw not last night below there. I know what I have done. But for God's mercy my hands might have been covered with blood—*his* blood!" And a groan of agony broke from his trembling lips.

Norbert sought to soothe his anguish of remorse, but straightening himself suddenly, Droust whispered sternly under his breath:

"Why did you not put your pistol to my head and fire when I spoke the first word? You nad saved my doing it now. Farewell."

So saying, the broken-hearted and shattered man turned on his heel and disappeared.

XXVII

THE ROMANY WOMAN

L EAVES from the note-book of the Demoiselle
  de Mousson.

Jouarre, March, 1569:

> " *Le Prince de Condé*
> *Il a été tué;*
> *Mais Monsieur l'Amiral*
> *Est encore a cheval.*"

This rough verse a soldier went singing down
the road into the village as my lady and I were
taking our way back to the abbey. We had been
training the village girls, who are preparing for
their Lady Day *fête*. Spring is in the air, and we
had found violets and anemones at the wood's edge.
The breath of peace seemed to blow in the soft
wind and to stir in the buds and to speak in the gay
little chirp of a robin. There was a thrill of the
joy of it in my lady's voice, and it stirred in my
heart, for war seemed a thing incredible, and room
yet in our fair France for hope and gladness.

Then the soldier went singing and swinging down
the road, and our hearts stood still, and the dear
light seemed stained, and all the world grew gray.

My lady bade me stop the man, who wore the
king's colors, and call him to her.

"What is this you sing?" she asked, her face
grown white.

"God's truth," he said, and stared at her, but
with reverence, as all men will, for that high look
in her face and the gentle authority she bears.
" *Le Petit Homme est mort!* "

" Did he die in battle ?" asked my lady.

" Madame, there has been hard fighting on the Charente, near Jarnac. The enemy were out-flanked. Condé had an arm crushed, and a kick from the horse of La Rochefoucauld broke his thigh. But he dashed upon one of our battalions, eight hundred strong, his banner flying, at the head of but three hundred gentlemen. He cried, ' Nobles of France, mark in what plight Louis de Bourbon enters the battle for Christ and Fatherland ! ' "

" A gallant charge ! " I cried, unable to forbear.

" Madame," said the man, " the Prince of Condé was a soldier. His worst foe cannot say otherwise, but he was the great enemy of the Mass. His horse was killed under him and he was surrounded. Montesquiou dispatched him with a pistol shot. The body was thrown across an ass and so carried to Jarnac."

" I would they had thrown his banner over him," said my lady. " Dost thou remember, Jeanne, the motto of the Prince of Condé, ' Sweet the peril for Christ and country ' ? "

With that her voice broke and the tears came in a sudden shower.

" It was a great victory," said the soldier stolidly ; " the enemy lost hundreds and many officers were slain or taken prisoner."

" Coligny ? " asked Mademoiselle.

" He escaped and led the retreat back to Cognac, but we captured the Chevalier de la Noue, which was a lucky stroke. Better yet would it have been could we have seized that yellow-haired rover from Germany. He fought like the devil himself and yet with a smile on his face as if he were at a dance."

" The Count of Nassau ! " I exclaimed.

" That is the man," said the soldier. " His brother, the Prince of Orange, they say, is on the march now into France with reinforcements from

Germany for the enemy. Those Dutchmen would better stick to their country and leave us French-men to fight our own battles. Madame, I bid you good-day," and with this the soldier swung on his way to Jouarre singing his dreadful little song.

Jouarre, September, 1569: Jeannette Vassetz hath a pleurisy. She is not in serious case, but this same pleurisy will give the story of I know not how many lives a different turn and issue.

For the Prince of Orange, crossing France in dis-guise from Chatellerault to Montbéliard on an urgent mission from Coligny to the German princes, halted at Montargis and sent a secret messenger ostensibly with news from Angers, but in reality to offer safe-conduct to my lady into Germany if she were mindful to leave Jouarre at such short notice.

The messenger, disguised as a gray friar, was none other than Captain Tontorf, and my lady gave him private audience, the rather that he brought a word from the Queen of Navarre strongly advising her to avail herself of this means of escape.

"Your friends are in no small concern, madame, for your safety," proceeded this same soldier-friar earnestly.

"And why, good Tontorf?" asked my lady. "Methinks nowhere is human safety to-day, and yet everywhere is the divine protection."

"Hitherto, madame, it has been the belief of your friends that whatever threatened you, your friends were powerful to be your shield. To-day we are no longer confident. The army has had terrible reverses and is hard pressed. The forces of Coligny rest for the moment, thinned and ex-hausted at La Faye. The royalists, under the Duc d'Anjou and the Prince Dauphin, Madame's brother, are so near us as Moncontour in great force, fresh and well appointed. There will be bloody work ere long."

"Is my father in command of monseigneur's vanguard?"

"Even so. Mademoiselle has heard of the contemplated marriage of the Duc de Montpensier?"

My lady started violently.

"To whom?" she whispered.

"To Catherine of Lorraine, daughter of François of Guise."

My lady hereupon became greatly agitated.

The Lady Catherine is but eighteen and of a most wanton character, with a name even now notorious for her rancorous spite against Huguenoterie, even beyond what one might expect of the niece of the Cardinal de Lorraine, "the Tiger of France."

Was it possible that at fifty-five the husband of that noble lady, Jacqueline de Long-Vic, could form a union with such a creature?

"Monsieur," said my lady sternly, "are you sure that what you say is true?"

"Madame, there is unhappily no further doubt on the subject. The alliance has been negotiated by the bishop of Angers, Jean Ruzé, and the marriage is expected to take place shortly in that city."

This was indeed news from Angers. I could see how my lady put to use all her will and control, so crowding down her outraged feelings, as she now said quietly to Tontorf:

"This being so, monsieur, I can the better understand the concern of my friends. I am indeed doubly alone in the world if such is my father's choice. Tell me, then, what is in the mind of Madame d'Albret?"

"Your highness, as you know, it is no longer possible for her majesty, who shares the dangers and fortunes of the army since she has put her young son at the head of it, to offer you a safe retreat. It is her belief that nowhere in France can such be found for the daughter of so bitter a Romanist and so powerful a prince and soldier as your father."

"Whither could we go?" asked Mademoiselle, trembling not a little.

"The Prince of Orange has with him forty mounted companions, true blades every one. He engages to convey Madame l'Abbesse and two of her ladies safely over the border, and to any court in Germany she may name. He makes bold to assure her warm welcome and strong protection at the hands of the Elector Palatine."

"The Prince of Orange," said my lady slowly, "has met with reverses, as we hear, himself. But he has a heart for the needs of others, it seems, even strangers."

"Madame," replied Tontorf, and his voice betrayed strong feeling, "I have seen my lord when he lived in royal splendor, the most magnificent grandee of the Netherlands, and I thought him then the greatest man I had ever seen. But now I have seen him when, like our blessed Redeemer, he had not where to lay his head, when he was hunted, poor, threatened, rejected, and counted as dead even by the woman who is called his wife, and in such extremity I have found him far, far greater, such is his constancy, his courage, his fortitude. Forgive me if I speak over-boldly, but my lord has been greatly misjudged, and there are few now to raise their voices on his behalf."

"You do well to speak, Captain Tontorf," said my lady gravely. There were tears in her eyes, but there rested on her face that new light of lofty yet humble homage with which the mention of the prince ever inspires her. "Sure such a man can yet win victory out of defeat, and by God's grace he will. It touches me deeply that amid his own private anxieties and upon his urgent mission the prince should thus turn aside and suffer delay in my behalf. Have you considered by what means so bold a venture could be contrived, for to me it is full sudden?"

"Yes, your highness, we have presumed to frame the plan that you and two of your ladies should on this very morning, even within an hour or two, set out on an alleged mission to the convent of Sainte Foy, at Coulommiers. There I will meet you with the small guard which now awaits my return. By sharp riding we can reach Montargis by noon to-morrow. His excellency awaits our coming. The rest follows."

I could see that my lady was greatly moved. She gave her hand to Tontorf without a word, and he touched it as if she had been the Holy Virgin to whom he had just sworn himself.

"Oh, my lady," I burst forth, unable longer to control myself, for all my pulses were running wild in my longing to be free, "do not stop to think! You will hesitate and the chance will be lost! Say yes, I beg of you, and take me with you!"

Vain, selfish words! I saw it in a moment.

My lady had flushed high, and for a moment I believe she was indeed ready to follow my poor counsel. The tender care of the Queen of Navarre, perhaps yet more the determined effort of the prince, her own indignant protest against the insult to her mother's memory by this marriage of the Duc, and the fresh dangers which would now be brought to threaten her own life and liberty by the close alliance with the Guises, for a moment combined to a mighty force.

"Jeanne," she said slowly, "at this moment I feel my duty here ended. The vows of my childhood I have long held to be null and void. My father has chosen to sever the ties which bound me to him and which might have availed to hold me here in obedience to his will. I am free. Never again perchance will such noble guardiance be proffered me."

"Then, dear lady," urged Tontorf, "say quickly you will go. One word is all, and I am off."

There was the silence of a moment, and then :

"I cannot," said my lady simply, paling suddenly, her hands falling languidly apart. "Go, my friend. Give my deepest gratitude to his grace of Orange, but say it is impossible."

"Why, why, my lady?" I begged.

"Have we both forgotten our poor little Jeannette on her sick bed? Jeanne, have you forgotten too, that old promise we children made in Our Lady's Arbor: 'Together we stay, together we go'? You would not break that pledge, dear Jeanne?"

"No, my lady," I said, and my head drooped low, for the great, mad, joyous hope with which all my body was thrilling died then. "No, my lady, we will keep our pledge."

In few words Mademoiselle showed our case to Tontorf. He chafed hotly for a little, and yet saw that other decision could not be.

"Your highness, there is no more to be said," he said under his breath. "Be of good courage. Heaven has such as you in holy keeping. Your friends, be sure, will never cease to watch over you while life and liberty are theirs."

And with that he was gone, strangely, mysteriously as he had come.

Then said my lady, lifting a finger of warning :

"Jeanne de Mousson, if you should ever let this be known to the good little Vassetz I will have such a penance given you as will take all your life to accomplish," and so, smiling, she brushed a few tears from her eyelashes and betook herself straightway to the infirmary.

Jouarre, June, 1570: My lady talked with me long and seriously to-day and I had a glimpse into the deep life of her spirit.

The conflict of the two great forms of religion has become doubly severe for her by reason of her

office as abbess of this house. She can no longer
find satisfaction in the Mass, in confession, and in
the invocation of the blessed Virgin and the saints.
The power of the immediate, simple approach to
God and our Saviour which Protestantism offers,
appeals to her mightily. And yet she sees much
that is noble and true in the ancient faith and seeks
with fervent will to overcome the discord between
the two. She longs for freedom to follow her inner
light and leading fully, but since freedom may not
be, she seeks in humility and patience to walk in
her appointed path.

Jouarre, 10 August, 1570: Great rejoicing throughout France to-day, for, thanks to the good offices
and skillful conduct of the negotiations of Messieurs
Teligny and La Noue at St. Germain-en-Laye, a
new and favorable edict of peace has been declared,
and the land at last is to have rest. This has been
the fiercest civil war that France has ever known,
and the whole land lies bleeding.

The terms of the peace, as might be expected,
leave much yet to desire for the Huguenots, but
the king formally and in good set terms recognizes
as faithful relations and servants the Queen of
Navarre, the Prince Henri her son, and the late
Prince of Condé and his son; their followers as
loyal subjects; and by name, as good neighbors
and friends, the Prince of Orange and his brother,
Count Louis of Nassau.

Jouarre, January, 1571: We have been for a time
without a confessor in residence, the good priest
of La Ferté serving our needs most cheerfully. But
now a chaplain has been sent us, sent we are confident from the Cardinal de Lorraine himself, at
the instance of his niece, Madame de Montpensier,
who has lately visited our convent.

Truly her visit boded us little good. Her insolence, as also her suspicion of my lady's Catholicity, were scarce veiled by her very indifferent courtesy. To me, for some cause, she manifested a peculiar aversion. On her departure, having learned through Sister Marie Beauclerc that Mademoiselle absents herself from confession, and even from Mass as far as may be, she forebore not to speak in palpably threatening terms.

"Monseigneur le Duc, *ma chére*," she said with a cruel sneer, "will, in his fatherly tenderness, watch over you something more carefully henceforward. In truth you have been sadly neglected, and I shall so admonish the excellent Ruzé, whom we hold Mademoiselle's spiritual father still."

Shortly after there appeared upon the scene this young and fiery Benedictine monk, whom we call Père Brodier. This is the first effect upon us of the marriage of Mademoiselle's father.

Père Brodier has taken up his abode with us, my lady consenting perforce since he came direct from the Bishop of Meaux, and she has no reason to urge against him.

The sight of the man chills me, and he is everywhere I go. He has cold, measuring eyes, sharp as a ferret's withal, and a soft, low voice, which angers me every time I hear it. With him set to watch over us, Jouarre becomes intolerable.

This much is certain. We can no longer receive the Sieur de Minay as hitherto, and enjoy his pious and learned instruction, and no longer do we even venture to receive his letters nor those of the Count of Nassau nor of Madame d'Albret, all of whom are warned. We know ourselves now to be keenly watched. The cardinal, sulking in his tent there at Rheims, in his bitter rage against the peace has now turned his eye upon us, and close in his counsels are his niece, Madame de Montpensier, with her strangely wanton cruelty, her husband, my lady's father, and the Bishop of Angers.

Oh, to flee away from their dark and hateful shadow! Yet whither can we flee? We were forced to reject our one opportunity. My lady's serene patience and steadfast cheerfulness are a marvel. I think she keeps ever before her mind one noble exemplar.

Jouarre, 3 August, 1571: Six weary and anxious months have passed; but to-day, at last, a ray of hope has pierced our convent wall, and truly by a means most unexpected. This morning there strayed into the abbey courtyard in the burning sunshine a Romany beggar woman, with her swarthy face, a motley kerchief tied on her blue-black hair, a bright-eyed marmot of a baby on her arm, a lute hung by a riband from her shoulder, and a gay little song to sing to us. Many of the sisters gathered about to hear her, and from the door of the Sainte Chapelle Père Brodier stepped out into the shadow of the portal and stood looking on coldly at our levity.

As she sang I noted the woman's eyes turned oftenest to my face, and when her song broke off she smiled broadly, showing her white teeth, and cried:

"Ah, but the young lady is too pretty for a nun! Let me tell your fortune, mademoiselle," and quite to my dismay she therewith incontinently seized my hand, held it fast in hers, lifting it close to her face. I struggled to be free, noting the malicious smile on the face of Sister Marie Beauclerc, who would like full well to see me convicted of vanity and indecorum, and conscious as well of the eyes of Père Brodier. Laughing blithely and quite undisturbed the woman cried shrilly:

"Ah, what is this I read? First of all, your name is plainly written on your hand—the Demoiselle de Mousson," and she eyed me sharply.

My face turned red, and indeed I found most

amazing this seeming *clairvoyance*, which in truth was no clairvoyance at all, and a murmur of curiosity and surprise ran around.

Little minded to furnish so doubtful amusement for an idle hour I frowned, and with a strong effort snatched my hand from the woman's brown fingers.

"Fie on you, mademoiselle," she cried shrilly, as springing away into the center of the group, and touching the strings of her lute, she broke out into another song.

But in my hand I found she had, quite unseen, left a small, close roll of paper. I tossed the woman a coin, but feigning offended dignity and displeasure, hastened from the court and sought the refectory, which I found deserted. There I made haste to unroll the tiny note. On one side of the paper was scrawled faintly the characters, much faded by contact with the woman's palm :

To the Lady of Jovis ara.

On the other side were the words :

" *The court is at Lumigney. Hasten thither for good reason.* N.*"

Much excited I sought my lady, noting in the way that the Romany woman was slowly departing from the court. Blurred and dim as was the writing, we recognized it on the instant to be that of the gallant Count of Nassau. We knew already that the king and queen-mother were at their castle near Fontenay-en-Brie for a week of hunting. On the moment our decision was made.

Throughout the day, the incident of the Romany woman quite forgot by all save ourselves, my lady has spoken freely of her desire, if the weather be not too warm, to do her devoir in a visit to the queen-mother, whom she had not seen since the "affair of Meaux," she being now so near us as

Fontenay. She has discussed the project freely with Sister Marie Beauclerc, who is strangely like Cécile Crue, and whose opinion she feigned to desire as to the time required for the ride to Fontenay. Sister Marie warmly approves the excursion.

So then at four in the afternoon, which is but an hour hence, with Jeannette Vassetz and four of our men for escort, we shall set forth for Fontenay, wondering much what shall there befall us.

Lumigney-en-Brie, 4 August, 1571: Blessings on the black-eyed Romany woman! She did us the goodliest service and most deftly too she did it!

We found ourselves abundantly welcomed on our arrival at this castle late last evening by Queen Catharine, who professed to have been hurt that her dear little Bourbon *cousine* had not sooner ridden over to pay her compliments. The king in his dull, languid fashion was most gracious also to my lady, but far more to us at the moment than royal favor was it to find at the castle and on the friendliest footing with their majesties, and watching eagerly for our coming, the Count of Nassau and our good friends the Chevalier de la Noue and de Teligny.

My lady, who had brought with her a court dress of white satin embroidered with silver and pearls, attended the queen-mother at a banquet in the castle hall at a late hour last evening, looking a very queen herself in her fair and stately beauty, with but her white nun's wimple and the ring on her forefinger to mark her as *religieuse*, and these methinks, with her gentle loftiness do but render her the more enchanting. The Princess Marguerite is in attendance on her mother. She is dazzlingly beautiful, but hers is the beauty of the court lady—artificial, heartless, and haughty. Never did Mademoiselle in her grave, pure repose look lovelier than by her side.

We hear a hint that, to seal this present peace beyond chance of rupture, a marriage between the Princess Marguerite and the son of the Queen of Navarre, my old playmate Prince Henri, is contemplated.

It was midnight when I was called to my lady's room, and I found her flushed with gladness, her eyes full of light. She held a letter in her hand.

"Jeanne, my Jeanne!" she cried, her voice low but thrilling with eagerness, "I have good news to bring thee. Our friends are working in our behalf. So much is certain. There is hope for our speedy release. I have had but five minutes with Teligny alone, and less with the Count of Nassau, but we shall meet at the hunt to-morrow."

"And was it really Count Louis who sent the Romany woman to Jouarre?" I asked.

"Of a surety. He is most delighted over the success of his little enterprise, which in sooth was a somewhat doubtful one. Look, Jeanne, what Teligny has brought me—this letter from the Queen of Navarre, whom he left but a few days since at La Rochelle. Let us read it together."

So our heads were soon bent over the sheet.

"*Ma cousine,*" wrote Her Majesty, "*I have received your letter and am infinitely sorry that I am unable to serve you as I desire. I pray you not to doubt my affection, which can never fail toward you. Your affair is of such importance that it would take only a small blunder to spoil everything. Since the bearer promises me bien surêment to convey my letter to your hands, I will now say plainly that we find no better expedient for you than for you to go to Madame de 'Bouillon, your sister (in Sedan), and thence to Germany, . . later to return to my own country and to me. This is what I infinitely desire in order to show you my affection and that you are to me as my own daughter, for if this plan shall succeed I shall be*

U

able to bear toward you the office of mother in all that which concerns your dignity and happiness (votre grandeur et contentment).

" *It is necessary, ma cousine, that the plan shall be carried out with utmost wisdom and secrecy. I beg you, by means of Monsieur de Teligny, who can be relied upon to bring me your letters, to tell me what you would desire me to do in proof of my love.*

" *In this assurance I pray God, ma cousine, that he will abundantly grant you of his holy grace.*

" *Your good cousin and perpetual friend,*

JEHANNE." [1]

My lady kissed the letter over and over with her eyes brimming with tears.

" This gives us much to think of, little friend," she said, looking then into my face. " This is no light nor easy step for us to take. How is it ? Art thou ready to hazard all, leaving the plan to be worked out for us by Madame d'Albret and our other good friends ? Art thou strong enough, Jeanne, to bear all the dangers, all the poverty, the calumny and ill-report that our flight from Jouarre will surely bring upon us ? Think now before it is too late to draw back."

" Mademoiselle, I am ready," I said without hesitation ; " and I know that Jeannette is also."

Surely naught can be harder to endure than the espionage and menace and religious bondage which we now suffer.

Lumigney-en-Brie, 5 August, 1571: This morning I alone of our little party accompanied my lady to the hunt, to which she rode with her majesty the queen-mother, but only so far as to a lodge in the heart of the forest of Fontenay, where breakfast was served.

---

[1] Letter of the Queen of Navarre to Mademoiselle de Bourbon from La Rochelle, July 28, 1571.

The Count of Nassau rode beside us through the green woodland path. Methinks the war has but knit the firmer the supple grace of his body and quickened his buoyant energy. An indescribable lustre is in his eyes whenever they chance to rest upon my lady. La Noue generously tells us that, although a foreigner in France, the count has become the hero of the Huguenot army, and, had Coligny not recovered from his illness a year ago, he would without doubt have been called to lead the forces. Queen Catharine is, it would appear, enamored of the count's presence, and keeps him continually at her side, giving him the place at her right hand at the table.

The Chevalier de la Noue himself shows more than does Count Louis the ravages and rigors of the war. He is worn gaunt from his many months' imprisonment, and has a clumsy and wearisome device of iron to replace the arm that was shot off at Fontenay a year ago, and which has given him the sobriquet of *Bras de fer*. But he bears himself, as ever, with right soldierly spirit, and all three of these gentlemen stand at the moment high in the royal favor.

That they are here for a great State purpose it needs not to say. But my lady tells me that she learns that this rather mysterious conference is held at the instance of his grace of Orange and in his name and in behalf of the Netherlands.

The prince has noted the change in the temper and disposition of the court, and with his masterly diplomacy seeks to make swift use of it to gain their majesties wholly over to the cause of his people, which is hopeless without foreign aid.

Four powerful motives may contribute to the end the prince so ardently seeks, as the Count of Nassau has told my lady :

First, the king is jealous of the warlike reputation of his brother, d'Anjou, and wishes the distinction of military success for himself; in fine, would like to embark on a new campaign wholly of his own choosing.

Second, to ensure the success of such an under-taking he must engage the brilliant leadership of Coligny, who has now in this last war abundantly proved himself the greatest military genius in France. This would bring the court and the Hugue-not leaders into close relations.

Third, Charles has conceived a deep distrust of Philip of Spain since knowing of the treacherous plotting of the Cardinal de Lorraine with Alva, while Queen Catharine is greatly embittered by the current report that her daughter, consort of Philip, met her death by reason of poison adminis-tered by him. Charles sees Spain growing too powerful, furthermore, and he is not adverse to putting a check upon its aggressions by opposing the progress of Alva in the Netherlands.

Fourth, an alliance is now actively projected between the king's brother, Monsieur the Duc d'Anjou and Queen Elizabeth of England. This, if it should go through, would bring into harmony England, the Protestant princes of Germany, the patriots of the Netherlands under the Nassaus, and France, a magnificent combination, and one which my lady says appeals powerfully to the ambition of Charles. Apparently the queen-mother favors it also. If only she could be trusted to do to-mor-row what she promises to-day! If only one could read behind that smooth, ivory mask! If only she were either Catholic or Protestant! She remem-bers me well, and pretends to rail against the Queen of Navarre who has, she says, spoiled such a pretty maid of honor for her to make a poor, pining nun, whose beauty is all thrown away on a lot of dull old women.

I like her less than ever, but I confess she treats my lady most affectionately and has given her in token of her kindness a large mirror of rock crystal, framed in gold, set with two diamonds and six rubies, the reverse being of lapis lazuli curiously engraved, a right royal gift. And now to return to our morning in the forest of Fontenay.

We came out upon the terrace of the hunting lodge, breakfast over, and my lady strolled slowly down a green alley between the tall beeches with my lord de Teligny in earnest converse. He was most eager to seize this moment to lay before her the details of his plan for her departure from Jouarre. He wishes all to be now laid in readiness even to the final signals by which we shall act, since we cannot hope again to meet face to face and we dare not trust aught concerning our plans to letters. Teligny and Count Louis engage to confer ere their return to La Rochelle with the Sieur de Minay, at Meaux, through whose kindly offices my lady will seek to sell her property of Saint Christ, thus securing funds for our long and perilous journey into Germany.

I had myself strayed down from the terrace where so much royalty oppressed me and had found a nook where a small shrine was screened and half enclosed by a clustering jessamine thick with blossoms, when I heard a light step and there stood in the pathway before me the Romany woman. She was gazing with a strange fixed look in her eyes down the path where I could myself see in the long golden green vista the charming figure of my lady with my lord de Teligny walking beside her, his head bent toward her, her eyes lifted to his face.

I do not know whether the woman observed me or not in my little nook. She appeared to take note only of those two figures. Something in her face gave me a mysterious thrill of dread. *She saw what I did not see.*

I held my breath for now she lifted her lute and

touched the strings with slow languorous fingers, and with a plaintive voice, from which all the joyance had fled and with eyes still fixed upon those two she sang a strange little chanson, so strange that I cannot forget it. It was on this wise:

What though she wear the veil?
Full soon her vows shall fail,
   Fail not her grace.
Sharp speeds for him life's close.
Myrtle for her and rose—
   Yet, death apace!

Both whom they love shall wed.
Death haunt the bridal-bed,—
   Fetch-lights burn ever!
Mark how the lady's knight
Knight's lady then shall plight!
Death shall their hands unite,
   Death quickly sever!

While she sang the last few words the Romany woman turned her eyes slowly and fixed them upon me, then without a word looked again at the two forms far down in the flickering shade. Was it a fancy, a delusion, a dream?—what was it? As I too looked fixedly at the twain I saw on either side another figure—dim, shadowy, wraith-like—by my lady there seemed to walk a knight in armor, by my lord de Teligny the shape of a woman, wringing her hands.

For a moment then I saw nothing, for all grew black around me. When I opened my eyes the Romany woman was nowhere in sight, but vanished in the woods like some wild thing, and my lady was there and was saying:

"Jeanne, my girl, I have spied you here in your hiding-place. Why do you stare so with great, frightened eyes, and why is your face so pale? Have you been dreaming? Waken then and give joy to my lord de Teligny. He has told me as we

"Was it a fancy, a delusion, a dream?—what was it?"

Page 310

came hither that he is about to marry the lovely Demoiselle de Coligny, daughter of the admiral.''

As she spoke my lady looked like a creature of life and joy, and upon the face of my lord was a proud though gentle gladness, and all his mien instinct with youthful vigor. No shadow of death could I see on either face.

What meant that mysterious, ill-omened song ? Would God I had never heard it ! And yet it was but the random rhyming of a wandering Romany wench. I will think of it no more.

XXVIII

SEVEN DUTCH BULBS

ON the first Friday in February, being the fourth day of the month, Mass being just over, the Abbess of Jouarre was met in the calefactory by one who said that the gardener's man Harlay, from Meaux, was waiting in the cloister with tulip bulbs which he had brought her.

It was one of those February days when spring bids fair to come before her time, when pools of water on the pavements reflect a sky blue as summer, and there is soft relenting in the air, and a greening of the willow branches by the river.

Charlotte de Bourbon hastened to the cloister as if the tulip bulbs were very welcome, with their speaking of spring, and with her came a little bevy of nuns, and others were strolling under the gray arches enjoying the balm of the air.

There on the worn stone pavement stood the gardener's man from Meaux, a quaint, bent little varlet, in leathern breeches and a dingy doublet, scraping and bowing and touching his forelock to Mademoiselle.

She greeted him graciously by name, as he had been on many an errand to Jouarre from his master, and Sister Marie Beauclerc thought afterward that she could remember an unwonted excitement in her manner, and that her hands trembled slightly as she received the bulbs.

"Here they are, madame, come all the way from Holland," the man said, taking them one by one from his inner doublet. "I have kept them warm and good. They will blossom in the spring."

"How many have you brought me, Harlay?"
asked Mademoiselle.

"Seven only, madame," and he counted them
out into her hand—"*une, deux, trois, quatre, cinq,
six, sept—voilà!* That is all my master had this
time, but they are rare ones."

"You are sure he sent seven?"

"Yes, I was to say that he would not mix them
to send your highness any of inferior kind. He is
most desirous that these may please madame la
princesse."

"Very gladly will I take these, tell your master," was Mademoiselle's reply; "and *I will pay the
price.* Will you tell him that this is my word?"

"That will I, your reverence."

"Remember!"

Mademoiselle then returned to the calefactory
with the sisters, all most anxious to examine the
little colorless bulbs, so much like onions, which
could produce such brilliant and queenly blossoms,
and none seemed more interested than the abbess
herself.

On the way to the refectory an hour later for dinner, in a dark corner of the stone passage, she met
Jeanne de Mousson, who had but then returned
from an errand to Jouarre.

"The bulbs have come," said Charlotte quite
carelessly. "*Seven,* Jeanne."

The bright color of the Béarnaise maiden grew
deeper and her dark eyes flashed.

"Monday, then, is to be the day!" she said
softly. "What did you say, Mademoiselle?"

"I said, '*I will pay the price.*'"

Jeanne de Mousson put out her hand in the darkness and gave that of her mistress an ardent pressure.

"If you had said, *the price is too high,* my lady,
you would have broken——"

"No matter, Jeanne," interrupted Mademoiselle,

hastening on to the refectory; "the price is certainly high, but when we see the blossoms I am sure we shall not regret it. Have you found those glasses yet for the bulbs, Radegonde ? " for the old nun had joined them now.

"Yes, my lady, and I have set them in the sunshine."

"When they bloom, sister——" but with the word the lady broke off, leaving Radegonde much perplexed at the wistful smile on her lips.

This was on Friday, which was the fourth of February in the year of grace 1572.

On Monday morning, at an early hour, being the seventh, the Princess de Bourbon, with the demoiselles de Mousson and Vassetz, prepared to start from Jouarre on a long anticipated visit to the cousin of her highness, the abbess of the monastery of the Paraclete, at Nogent-sur-Seine, the ancient shrine of Héloise. With them as escort from the abbey went five men : Loys Lambinot, who had been longest in the convent ; Petit, Parent, Leroy, and Conches. The visit was of uncertain duration. It might be for two weeks, it might be for even longer. Mademoiselle de Bourbon was devotedly attached to Madeline de Long-Vic, abbess of the Paraclete, and it had now been a year since they had met.

Very early that same morning, in the hours before she set forth, at the close of the sunrise service of lauds, the young abbess lingered, kneeling in the Sainte Chapelle when all others had left it.

In her white conventual robe, fastened with a silken cord at her waist, her white veil falling all about her, the lady knelt long on the steps of the choir in the hush and dimness of the place. The first rays of the sun even then began to touch the stained windows into radiance and to cast their gleams of color through the gloom.

As she knelt, Charlotte de Bourbon bent her

head even to the stones of the choir steps and pressed them with her lips. Then there was a light step and Jeanne de Mousson came to her side. She rose, then held out her hand to Jeanne and whispered low, her lips trembling and tears on her lashes:

"I am ready, little friend. It must suffice. But, oh, Jeanne! it is the last time, and, after all, it has been the only home I have ever known. If I only dared weep!"

"You must not, dear lady, indeed," whispered Jeanne anxiously. "Tears would betray everything. Père Brodier is even now coming back into the choir."

Charlotte grew calm at the sight of the priest, whose footfalls were so light that he had nearly reached them quite unheard.

With a word of greeting the two now passed out by the south transept door, but as Charlotte left the Sainte Chapelle she laid her white hand in a lingering caress on the cold, rough stones of its wall.

"Adieu," she breathed so low that only the walls heard her.

Then in her room, with old Radegonde to wait upon her, the Abbess of Jouarre laid aside her white robe and veil for the black traveling habit of her order and the long blue cloak, ermine lined and ermine hooded, which expressed her degree and rank.

Radegonde, as she served her lady, noted that she trembled, and was of a strange pallor.

"Dearest lady, are you not well?" she cried, anxiously.

"Well? Oh, yes, quite well, Radegonde. Kiss me. Again. Hold me close, as you did when I was a child. I love you so."

Amazed at her emotion, the old nun pleaded to know its cause.

"It might be," said her lady, "that I should fall into danger on this journey, and not come back to you. The land is full of bands of marauders and wild soldiers who know not how to turn to the pursuits of peace. Who can tell what might befall even on the way to the Paraclete? One must think of such things. Kiss me once more. How dear and true you are, Radegonde. Pray for me always. Farewell, dear old friend."

So she ran down the stairway from her hall, casting a glance as she left it at the old Abbess of Jouarre above the fireplace, and Radegonde noted the tremulous, anxious smile that went with the glance. There in the court below were her two Jeannes in their long black nun's cloaks, waiting her coming.

From the path down to the offices beyond the hall of the abbess came the sound of hoofs on the softened earth, for the mild weather held yet, and up rode the little company of horsemen, and those who came before led each a small, stout-limbed jennet.

All the nuns had gathered at the gate and with them stood Père Brodier. To him Mademoiselle said sedately:

"Guard well the flock while I am gone; and Sister Marie Beauclerc, kindly open all letters which come to the Abbess of Jouarre in my absence. I empower you to act in this matter, knowing you will be faithful."

So gently was this spoken that even the old nun herself failed to see the touch of gentle irony which underlay the lady's words. Far less did she dream that there was nothing more now for Charlotte de Bourbon to fear from the spies of her entourage.

Then Mademoiselle kissed all her nuns kindly, with tender words of blessing, for all were dear to her and she so beloved by them that this short absence seemed to them an affliction. Her bearing was firm now and full of spirit, no tears dimming her eyes, but rather were they overbright and a high color burned in her cheeks.

As the little procession passed out at length through the gray abbey gateway in the morning sun, the aged porter dropped on his knees murmuring his blessing, and old Radegonde, watching with weary eyes, caught the last fond look which her adored lady turned to cast behind her.

And so they galloped on to Montmirail, near thirty miles eastward, the first stage of the journey to the Abbey du Paraclete, at Nogent, but also the first stage of a far different journey.

At the Auberge de St. Omer in Montmirail, Mademoiselle and her ladies dismounted and entered a private dining room. The landlady of the inn, overcome with delight at the honor of serving the Abbess of Jouarre, had hardly hastened from the room to prepare a meal worthy of her great visitors when François and Georges d'Averly, the Sieurs de Minay, quietly entered and the door was shut.

Both of these gentlemen bore the air of highest satisfaction mingled with eager solicitude for the welfare of Mademoiselle.

"Thus far all goes well," said François, the elder, Mademoiselle's devout instructor in the Bible and the new faith. "Our Dutch bulbs blossomed fully and in due time. Did the signal give you space to prepare for your departure?"

"Quite enough, monsieur," said the lady. "I confess I had had many doubts of the value of so fantastic a signal, but nothing could have been simpler nor safer. Poor Harlay's complete ignorance of his own mission, and of the significance of the number of his bulbs, ensured success."

"But you have waited and watched for those same Dutch bulbs, few or many, month after month. Better speed we could not make, but I fear it has seemed long?"

"Long, indeed, and yet now, all too short," said Mademoiselle with a deep sigh. "I had not thought it had been so hard."

"We had been looking, monsieur," said Jeannette Vassetz, whose wonted demureness was suddenly transformed into vivacity by the sense of adventure, "for twenty bulbs to come, or even thirty, as each month advanced, and feared a slip in so large a number, and then confusion and all going amiss. But when Harlay said with such *empressement* that his master could send but seven, we felt no further misgiving."

A lively but brief discussion of the simple cipher employed followed.

"All your friends are deeply concerned for the success of this present venture," said the Sieur de Minay presently. "Captain Tontorf, who will still be known as Roubichon, if you please, awaits us outside the east gate with five picked German *reiters* whom the Count of Nassau has sent you from La Rochelle, from his own immediate followers. This packet is from Madame d'Albret," and he put a letter into the lady's hand. "The Chevalier de la Noue and Count Louis send you their most devoted wishes and sincere regrets that it is impossible for them to leave La Rochelle at this juncture. Teligny and his bride wish you good speed and joy. Coligny is at court urging forward the two great reconciling movements, the marriage of the Princess Marguerite with Prince Henri of Navarre and the war in Flanders. The latter project gives the Count of Nassau much of delicate State business at this time, and the other gentlemen must needs ride back and forth from the Queen of Navarre to the queen-mother continually in the furtherance of the former."

"Is Madame d'Albret more favorable to this marriage for her son than at first?" asked Charlotte quickly.

"She is yielding, Teligny writes me, to the arguments of Coligny, albeit ever with a strange, invincible sadness and reluctance. The admiral assures her it will be 'the seal of friendship with the king' and thus make for a sure and stable peace, and Charles himself declares, '*I shall give Margot to my good cousin Henri of Bourbon, since by this means I shall marry not only them but the two religions.*'"

"That sounds most hopeful and reasonable," said Charlotte thoughtfully. "How goes forward the other scheme, for the war in Flanders?"

"The discussion of it is conducted with utmost secrecy but Count Louis is convinced of the sincerity and resolution of Charles in the matter. It is safe to trust him to put these promptly to the test, we may be sure. Yes, dear Mademoiselle, the future of our holy cause seems bright with promise. Truly, it is my ardent hope and belief that there will soon be such mutual confidence that you may even return from Heidelberg in all honor and comfort to grace this Navarrese marriage."

Charlotte, thinking of the bitter wrath which her flight from Jouarre would stir in the mind of her father, shook her head sadly, but Jeanne de Mousson clapped her hands softly with a low laugh of irrepressible delight.

"To dance at the marriage of my old playmate, Prince Henri, and the Princess Margot—ah that would be a very miracle of joy!" and she snatched the hand of Jeannette Vassetz, who in her quiet way was no less full of excitement, crying, "Oh, Jeannette, Jeannette! truly we are to be free!"

The Sieur de Minay, strict Calvinist as he was, looked with some surprise at the maiden whose Gascon blood was aglow with a gay audacity in strange contrast with her severe and sombre garb and the seriousness of their situation, and Charlotte made haste to ask:

"And how do you plan to overcome the next difficulties in our way, monsieur?"

"The most serious one just before us is the management of your own escort, Mademoiselle. To send them back to Jouarre is plainly impossible, and moreover, we need every man of them. When we leave Montmirail it will no longer be possible to sustain the appearance of journeying to Nogent, as we must strike at once into the Epernay road. The men must, therefore, be at least in part made acquainted with our real destination. Can you trust them?"

"I think so, I believe so," said Charlotte with some anxiety; "at least I could choose none better."

Dinner being over and the short February afternoon well advanced, the whole company again mounted, galloped down the street of the ancient and sleepy little town, and passed through the east gate.

Here, after a short half-mile, at the point where the road to Epernay diverges from that to the south, they came in sight of Tontorf and his five well-mounted *reiters*, armed with halberds which glittered in the winter sunshine.

Tontorf rode back to meet and salute the company and pay his respects to Mademoiselle and her ladies. After a few moments of discussion, the Sieur de Minay, turning to Loys Lambinot and the men who had ridden with him from Jouarre, said:

"My men, her highness, owing to certain advices which we have brought her, finds it wise to delay yet a little her visit to the Paraclete. Our attendance being offered her for a little time she thinks it better to avail herself of so goodly an escort and the fine weather and proceed on her way to Sedan, the residence of Madame la Comtesse de Bouillon, her sister. You will have a longer distance to traverse, but the return to Jouarre will be no later than was purposed. Forward, then, all together. We must sleep in Vertus to-night."

Then speaking low to Mademoiselle he added :

"Rheims to-morrow night, Sedan and safety in two days more, if it please God."

"Rheims," murmured Charlotte ; "is it impossible to avoid that city ? There sits the Cardinal de Lorraine, like a spider in his web. Dear Monsieur d'Averly, I fear me greatly to go thither ; it is to march straight into the clutches of the enemy."

"Is your person known to the cardinal or to those of his household ? "

"Not to himself, but to his niece, the wife of my father, who is not, however, likely to be in Rheims."

"I beg you, dear madame,"—it was Tontorf, riding on the other side of the lady, who spoke,— "do not let this alarm you. We will enter Rheims after nightfall and leave at daybreak. There need be no cause for alarm."

This hopeful prophecy seemed justified by events. The company was apparently united and well organized, no man murmuring at the longer journey nor showing suspicion regarding the sudden change of plan. The champaign country was safely traversed, the Marne crossed at Epernay and, toward dusk of the second day, the famous old city of Rheims, in its wide, arid plain, was reached.

In a decent but obscure inn just within the city wall, and at a safe remove from the palace of the great Guise cardinal, accommodation was found for Mademoiselle and her company. When she retired to her room Charlotte went to the window, and looked out upon the sleeping, moonlit city, above₄ which rose the airy twin towers of the great cathedral.

As she looked, the joyous thrilling clang and clamor of *le gros Bourdon* filled the air with its thundering vibrations.

v

"Jeannette," she said, stepping back involuntarily from the window, "we may be able to escape the cardinal's eyes, but not his voice. Do you know the legend on that bell? Monsieur Tontorf told me an hour since:

"*'I am Charlotte, so named by Monseigneur the most illustrious Charles Cardinal of Lorraine, Archbishop and Duke of Rheims, first Peer of France, and the most illustrious Lady Renée of Lorraine, Abbess of Saint Peter of the said Rheims, his sister. Pierre Deschamps, native of Rheims, made me.'*"

"I could e'en wish," cried Jeanne de Mousson, looking up at the cathedral towers, "that the said Pierre Deschamps had given you a less uproarious clapper, that so we might have better chance to sleep!"

"How think you, dearest Mademoiselle," asked Jeannette Vassetz anxiously, when silence fell, "shall we really sleep in Sedan at the castle of Mademoiselle's sister on Thursday night with no more fear and dread?"

"I believe it, *ma petite,*" was her lady's cheerful answer. "O Françoise!" she cried with a sudden outburst of joy, "shall I in very truth look in your dear face again so soon? When once we are safely out of Rheims even such grace will seem possible!"

When the morning came it brought a chill and dismal rain. The ladies, however, mounted with good courage and the little cavalcade was speedily set in motion, when to the discomfiture and alarm of all, it was discovered that Loys Lambinot was missing.

XXIX

MY LADY'S CLOAK

A HURRIED council of war was held just outside the eastern gate of Rheims.

Sharp misgiving smote Norbert as he now for the first time recalled a dim memory of the name of Lambinot as that of the treacherous servant from Jouarre encountered by his father, Nikolaas Tontorf, years before.

A stern inquiry among the men from Jouarre showed them honestly ignorant of Lambinot's whereabouts and unaware of any treachery in his intention.

Suspicious circumstances were, however, produced by Parent, who stated that when they were dining in the room of the inn, late the previous night, Lambinot had laid him a wager that the Abbess of Jouarre would never return to the convent. He had asked Parent then if he had observed that Mademoiselle had not dismounted to worship at the sacrosanct image of Our Lady nailed to the famous oak tree, as they came through the forest between Epernay and Rheims.

Parent had paid his own devotions and had not thought it his business to mind what his betters did. No wonder Mademoiselle did not choose to kneel in the mud.

Lambinot had then further confided to him that from one of the German *reiters* he had learned that they at least were bound for Heidelberg, not merely Sedan. Whether her ladyship would proceed beyond Sedan was unknown to them, and none of their concern.

323

At this, so Parent deposed, he had become impatient and told Lambinot that he was the worse for the wine he had taken. What on earth could possess Mademoiselle to go to Heidelberg? She was more likely to go to Jerusalem. The gossip was too wild to be interesting and he had therewith betaken himself to bed in the stable loft, and had supposed Lambinot had done the same. In the morning he failed to appear, and his horse was likewise missing. His cloak, however, he had left behind him. This being a part of his livery as a retainer of the Abbey of Jouarre and bearing its blazon, Norbert himself, for prudential reasons, assumed in place of his own, borrowing the hat of Parent, to whom he gave in exchange a small furred cap.

"I will wear your livery to-day, Mademoiselle," he said gallantly, "the better to defend you."

They were riding slowly eastward, the towers and walls of Rheims looming large through the fog and rain behind them.

" Then do you apprehend some danger from this desertion of Lambinot, captain ? " asked the Sieur de Minay.

" I apprehend that the fellow has started to give the alarm of Mademoiselle's departure from Jouarre," replied Norbert, "either to the Duc, her father, in Auvergne, or to the Cardinal de Lorraine in Rheims, hoping for reward."

Startled looks greeted this brief statement.

" The latter is far the more probable," said Georges d'Averly. " Lambinot could hardly dream of going to Auvergne. He would have no means at his disposal for such a journey."

" I cannot believe that Lambinot would go himself to the Cardinal de Lorraine," said Mademoiselle. " He would not have the courage nor the audacity. In any case, messieurs, we are safer outside than inside the walls of Rheims. Let us gallop forward and make up for lost time. It is too late to go back ! ''

" Courage ! Bravo ! '' cried Tontorf. "*Allons !* "

Through the morning hours they rode steadily onward through the pelting rain.

"I am not afraid of Lambinot nor any of his kind," said Jeanne to Norbert, who rode at noon beside her. "Surely he would not dare attack us."

" There are those abroad who would," was the reply.

"But we have still eleven good men and true to defend us," said Jeanne ; "and I can use a pistol myself on a pinch. That I learned to do long since in my girlhood in the mountains of Béarn."

"We will give you one to wear in your belt, mademoiselle," said Norbert, and therewith handed her a small pistol of his own. The girl fastened it into her belt with a bright, spirited smile and nod which set Norbert's heart beating much more irregularly than had the defection of Lambinot.

"A nun carrying pistols in her belt!" she exclaimed under her breath. "Praise be to the saints I can soon have done with these stiff and tiresome swathings and the perpetual black gown. I was never meant for a nun, good Captain Roubichon, and I believe I shall be far more pious out of the convent than in it."

"You have not liked the life ? " asked Norbert gravely, riding a little closer to her side.

"I have been happy in a way because I loved my lady so dearly. But Madame d'Albret—you have seen her ? "

"Yes, seen her when she stood before the army after Jarnac and offered the soldiers her son and Condé's. I shall never forget the sight of her that day."

"She must have been magnificent."

"The men cheered her until it seemed as if they

would split the very heavens. She put new life and courage into the whole army.''

"She puts new life into every one, and so she has into me. She was my dear godmother, and I was almost Protestant ere ever I went to Jouarre, but a wild, romping, light-hearted child, caring little for religion at best. I took the vows only because I must and because Mademoiselle was forced to and I could not forsake her,'' and Jeanne recounted to Norbert the circumstances of Charlotte's childhood.

"Mademoiselle's courage and spirit are a marvel after so oppressed and sorrowful a childhood,'' said Norbert thoughtfully. "Ah, Mademoiselle de Mousson, if my little sister, my poor Jacqueline, could but win something of her buoyancy and power to throw behind her the memories of the past!''

"Jacqueline, is she the little sister of whom *monsieur le capitaine* has told me? the sister who was with you in the house of that murderous Anastro, in Antwerp?''

"The same. She and I alone are left of all our family. I believe there was never a happier household than ours. The old home in Middelburg is the one spot on earth that I love, and there are times when, strong man and rough soldier though I am, I could weep for longing to hear once more the chimes of our old minster tower, Lange Jan.''

"What has become of the house of monsieur?''

"It belongs to Spain, for Middelburg, I shame to say, still adheres to the government. I hear it is used at present as headquarters for the officers of the Spanish garrison of Walcheren. If I could win it back and once more call it mine, mademoiselle, I could die happy.''

"You love it, then, so much! But tell me more of the young sister, Jacqueline.''

"Since that dreadful night when we found the iron chains and the seal of Spain upon our own door," said Norbert, with stern sadness, "and learned of the fate of those we loved and honored most on earth, the child has never smiled."

"*Pauvre enfant!*"

"She is now a tall and comely maiden. She has grown up with our aunt in the household of the elector at Heidelberg, my aunt being in personal attendance on the present electress. Her excellency is a Dutch lady, the widow of our famous Heer of Brederode. The first electress died soon after Jacqueline went to Heidelberg."

"What if we should see your sister some day!"

"You will surely see her if you are at the court of Heidelberg."

"Madame d'Albret, in her letter to my lady, strongly urges our going thither shortly. She thinks there can be no safety even in Sedan."

"There is no safety here, so much is sure!"

Norbert, who had been riding with the demoiselle de Mousson near the rear of the little procession, had cast his eye ever and anon at a spot of red in the distance behind them.

This spot, as he now saw, halting and rising in his stirrups to reconnoitre, began to define itself as a company of horsemen, distinguished by the red cloaks of royalist soldiers.

The country to the east of Rheims was swarming with bands of wild marauders, disbanded soldiers living by blood and plunder. They had passed several such groups during the morning without molestation. There was something, however, in the bearing of the men now rapidly approaching which awakened Norbert's suspicion.

They were now not more than a mile from Machault. At Norbert's order they all put spurs to their horses and broke into a gallop.

Instantly a bullet from an arquebus whizzed past them, near enough for danger, a sufficient warning.

Quick as thought, her lips set firmly, a light

flashing in her eyes, Jeanne de Mousson was at the side of her lady.

"Quick," she cried, "dearest lady—I want your cloak. I need it. Quick, I beg of you!"

Confused and mistaking her meaning Charlotte paused to unfasten the long ermine-lined mantle from her shoulders. Jeanne grasped it eagerly, and Mademoiselle found the plain black nun's garment of her devoted attendant thrown around her own person.

"*Voilà*, Mademoiselle!" cried the girl, drawing the deep-furred hood over her head. "Is it not becoming?"

The Sieur de Minay, who instantly detected the purpose of this maneuver, and who had felt uneasy at the mark of rank and identity furnished by the princely garment, made an exclamation of approval. But there was not an instant for further preparation. The band of nine men, one of whom they now knew for Lambinot, by the familiar black and white livery of Jouarre, were within close range. Their hostile intent was but too manifest.

Norbert sent the women forward and formed his little company of *reiters* and servants in a double line of defense. With savage and reckless boldness the attacking party charged them, shouting, "A Guise! A Guise!" while the others responded to the cry, "A Bourbon! A Bourbon!"

There was a sharp and desperate encounter, and falling back, Norbert saw to his dismay that two of his *reiters* lay wounded or worse upon the ground, their horses galloping madly into the woods which lined the road on either side.

Two of the Red Cloaks had also fallen, however, and the party, somewhat daunted, seemed to pause, irresolute.

Norbert gave the order to retreat and they were soon in full flight, as he had no desire to risk a second engagement of such peril for Mademoiselle

and her maidens. On they rode, Norbert and the
Sieur de Minay holding the rear, facing backward
in their saddles, pistols in hand. There was no time
to reload their heavier arms. The Red Cloaks had
recovered and were now thundering down the road
behind them. Escape still appeared possible, for
they were the better mounted, when the horse of
Jeanne de Mousson becoming unmanageable, Norbert spurred to her side, and grasped him by the
bridle. Then a shot, fired with deliberate aim,
struck the animal behind the shoulder, and with a
convulsive shudder he fell, Jeanne falling with him,
but with almost inconceivable agility springing from
her saddle and thus avoiding injury.

The Sieur de Minay halted. "Forward!" cried
Norbert at the top of his voice. "Forward, as fast
as you can. We will overtake you!" At this order
the little company rode off at full speed down the
road to Machault.

The words were scarcely out of Norbert's mouth
before the foremost of the pursuing party were
upon them.

Norbert had leaped from his saddle and planted
himself squarely in front of Jeanne, who had
wrapped her face closely in her hood.

He noted that an order was given to cease firing.
The purpose of the attack was plainly not to kill
but to kidnap. Fixing his eye upon Lambinot,
easily distinguished by his black livery, Norbert
waited until he came within pistol shot, and sent a
bullet through his breast. The treacherous varlet
fell dead on the instant.

"What odds?" cried the leader of the band
coolly, and on the instant Norbert recognized him
as the savage blonde Hessian whom he had once before encountered in the *Gasthaus zum Hirsch* in Cologne. "So much the more for the rest of us. The
lady! The lady!"

Norbert, who now wore an abundant beard, had

no fear of being recognized by the Hessian, who
had evidently deserted from the prince and turned
freebooter. Seeing himself overpowered he had
held up his handkerchief in token of surrender, and
in another moment his hands were bound to his
sides, his weapons taken from him, and he was
mounted on the horse of the dead Lambinot.

"We have gained our point ! We have the lady !
Not a bad little skirmish !" were the fragments of
talk which he overheard among the men whom he
saw, to his relief, were not retainers of the great
cardinal, as they had heretofore supposed, but a
lawless band of freebooters who had doubtless followed Lambinot in hope of a generous reward for
intercepting the flight of the Abbess of Jouarre.
Hardly less welcome was the discovery that owing
to her borrowed cloak Jeanne was safe to pass for
Mademoiselle, there being no one left to know to
the contrary. Mademoiselle, then, they might hope,
would proceed on her way to Sedan without further
scathe.

Norbert's own stern, imperative admonition to
the men to treat the Princess de Bourbon with the
courtesy befitting her rank was scarcely needed.
Plainly the big Hessian, who was called Hugo, was
confused by the loss of Lambinot, who was the
moving spirit of the party, and somewhat overawed
by the magnitude of the consequences of their wild
onslaught, and of the danger to themselves if the
princess suffered at their hands. Jeanne de Mousson was accordingly cared for with rude but respectful deference, and all mounting, they turned back
to Rheims at a rapid pace. The high and dauntless
spirit of the Gascon girl and the genius of her mer-
curial temperament were signally shown in the ease
with which she assumed the rôle of the "high and
puissant" Lady of Jouarre. That Norbert was to
bear the part of steward of the abbey had been
fixed between them in one whispered word.

It was nightfall when they came in sight of the city gates. Norbert had decided to use his rôle of the servant of Mademoiselle to its full value. He succeeded in achieving a rough familiarity with Hugo himself by speaking to him in German, and they rode on side by side in the rear of Jeanne and the others of the band.

The cathedral towers, soaring up into the mists, admonished him that his time was short, for he perceived the purpose of Hugo, once arrived in Rheims, to conduct the Abbess of Jouarre immediately to the presence of the Cardinal de Lorraine and claim the reward vouched for by Lambinot.

Assuming a certain bold and braggadocio air, calculated to impress the very limited intelligence of the big Hessian, he said : "It was a scurvy trick of Lambinot, rest his soul, not to take me into the secret of this affair. I would have been fast for it. But he wanted the prize for himself, the platter-faced varlet! I knew a hundred-fold more of her plans," and he made a gesture of his thumb toward Jeanne, "than ever Lambinot dreamed of. If he had let me in I could have managed the thing for you without so much as a pistol shot, and without danger of running your heads under the axe's edge for kidnapping a princess of the blood."

Hugo, in his blundering, thick-witted fashion, was now beginning to perceive the need of a trifle more finesse than he was possessed of to carry the undertaking through to success.

"Is there danger of such business ? " he asked, uneasily.

"By my halidom, man, I should think a blind mole could see the fix you're in now ! Here you have on your hands the daughter of the proudest peer in France, the Duc de Bourbon-Montpensier, whose person you have seized by force and violence, without the first shred of proof that she was bound on any other errand than she professed—a

visit to her sister, in Sedan. Who is going to vouch
for you with the cardinal if he should give you an
audience, which is far from probable ? "

Hugo scratched his head, much puzzled.

"By Saint Blasius, I am in a trap !" he stammered. "If I could talk their miserable gabble it
might go better. It was a knock-down to lose
Lambinot. We knew nothing of the matter save
that there was booty in it."

"If you will share with me," said Norbert, lowering his voice to a confidential whisper, "I will do
the business with the cardinal for you. I could
give him proof positive that Mademoiselle was running away that nobody else could. I've had
chances at many a letter, and I've used them too.
I can fix it with his eminence, and we can hand
the lady over and divide up. Of course I'll be contented with less, as I wasn't in at the first."

Hugo at once seized this proposition as his last
and only hope and, having entered the city, they
rode straight to the palace of the dreaded cardinal,
the powerful and hated "Tiger of France." That
Lambinot had in no way himself communicated
with the cardinal, and that his highness had never
seen Mademoiselle, Norbert was fortunately assured.

The heart of Jeanne de Mousson, brave heart as
it was, throbbed violently as she presently found
herself passing through the brilliant corridors of the
magnificent house, with Norbert in his Jouarre livery, on one side, and the tall ruffianly Hessian freebooter scowling fiercely and gnawing his moustache, on the other. The rest of the rough band
had been left behind at the outer gate of the palace
to await the event.

Overawed by grandeur such as he had never
before witnessed, at the smooth, contemptuous indifference of the servants to whom he sought in
vain in his broken French to make known their

errand, Hugo quickly gave over the conduct of this interview into the hands of Norbert.

"This is your affair, do your best," he cried sullenly; "but if I see you trying to turn things or play me false I'll put a bullet through your head as quick as if you were a rabbit."

Without the slightest doubt of the sincerity of this declaration, Norbert now boldly took the initiative. Addressing a page courteously he stated briefly that her highness the Princess Charlotte de Bourbon-Montpensier, Abbess of Jouarre, humbly but urgently requested immediate audience of his eminence, being in severe straits. The page received this request with great respect, and as a consequence, the three ill-assorted companions found themselves in short order admitted to the ante-chamber of Charles de Lorraine.

As he followed her into the apartment Norbert had an instant in which to whisper in Jeanne's ear:

"*You, Abbess of Jouarre, on your way to Sedan to visit your sister, have been foully abducted by this miscreant for ransom; protest your indignation, claim protection!*"

Jeanne put her hand into the bosom of her dress. Yes, it was there! She had taken into her keeping that morning a small bag of her lady's jewels. Among them was the abbatial ring which Mademoiselle had taken from her finger as soon as she left Jouarre. Jeanne slipped it quickly upon her own forefinger. Then a door was thrown open, and lifting her eyes she saw before her a prelate of imposing figure and singularly handsome face, clothed from throat to feet in a cassock of brilliant scarlet silk, and bearing on his head a berettina of the same color, and around his neck a thick gold chain from which depended a large and exquisite crucifix.

Jeanne, the two men kneeling at a distance behind her, dropped trembling but self-possessed upon her knee and kissed the hand of the great cardinal, craving his blessing. The rich ermine mantle falling around her delicate, *gracieuse* figure, the rigid conventual garb, the striking distinction and beauty of her person, and the sweetness of her voice disarmed any suspicion on the part of the prelate, and he pronounced a brief blessing, eying Norbert and Hugo with cold suspicion.

"I beg your eminence to intervene and save your daughter in Christ, me, Charlotte de Bourbon, Abbess of Jouarre, from yonder ruffian," she whispered imploringly. "Will you graciously call my steward hither and let him recount our horrible adventure? In truth, holy father, I am too exhausted for much speaking."

With these words and an air of extreme weariness and agitation Jeanne de Mousson rose and by a nod the cardinal beckoned Norbert forward, at the same time touching a jeweled bell on his table and giving a command in an inaudible voice to an attendant.

"Your lady speaks, sir steward, of a horrible adventure. What is it? Say on."

Speaking very low and very rapidly in French, not one word of Norbert's was intelligible to Hugo, who as he stood grew more and more bedazzled with the sense that he was out of his proper element and knew not what unexpected outcome this adventure would yet take. He saw himself, however, completely in Norbert's hands.

"Monseigneur," said Norbert, "my lady, the exalted and most noble Princess of Bourbon, Abbess of Jouarre," and he bowed profoundly to Jeanne, who folded her hands calmly before her, the official ring full in view, looking as she lifted her charming head with languid grace, every inch a princess, "was on her way to visit her illustrious sister, Madame the Duchesse de Bouillon, in Sedan, taking with her a sufficient escort, and certain of her

household, such as myself. One of our number,
an unspeakable scoundrel and traitor, named Lambinot, deserted our company this morning, having
conceived the infamous plot of betraying her highness into the hands of a band of border freebooters. Of these, the man you see yonder is the
head. The rest are now waiting at the palace
gate. Their purpose is to hold my lady for ransom ; and of this, Lambinot looked to swallow up
the lion's share.

"In the affray which followed the attack of these
ruffians we both lost men, and on their side Lambinot himself fell. We were, however, worsted,
and her highness was captured as you see, upon
which the residue of our escort put spurs to their
horses and escaped. I defended my lady to the
utmost of my power, my lord, believe me, but I
was overpowered," and Norbert's voice trembled
with apparent fear lest his faithfulness as a servant
might be called in question.

"Yes, yes, my good fellow," said the cardinal
with careless condescension, "the amazing thing
is, how you got yonder villainous-looking knave in
hither. In sooth I greatly mislike his looks."

The cardinal's characteristic timorousness made
him vastly uneasy as he kept his eyes on Hugo's
dark and threatening face.

"I cajoled his ignorance, monseigneur, into believing that your eminence would willingly pay
him a ransom on the spot for the recovery of the
stepdaughter of Madame de Montpensier, your
niece."

"Ah, that was adroit of you, my friend."

Without stepping nearer the cardinal raised his
voice, and addressing Hugo asked with a slight
smile, and speaking in German :

"Was it you, my man, who made this capture ? "

Hugo nodded emphatically and his eyes shone
gaunt and avidious.

"Yes, I, my lord."

"Who is this lady?" and the cardinal indicated Jeanne with a sweep of his white and jeweled hand. "Were you aware of her title and rank?"

"Yes, yes, my lord. The Princess of Bourbon, the Abbess of Jouarre."

The cardinal shrugged his shoulders.

"Self-convicted," he murmured, and again touched the bell, this time very lightly.

On the stroke six halberdiers entered the room by a door behind Hugo, and before he knew of their presence he was overpowered, bound, and dragged from the room.

"Bah," said the cardinal. "I breathe freer! He was a man by his countenance who would murder you any day for his dinner. Moreover, he smelt vilely of the stables. Madame, I congratulate you on escaping from such company."

With color and vivacity and confidence returning, Jeanne expressed her gratitude for her deliverance in a manner which the cardinal, who was a keen judge and admirer of feminine charms, found singularly captivating. He was furthermore extremely glad to have a chance for personal acquaintance with the distinguished and possibly heretical Abbess of Jouarre, whom he had fancied as of a very different strain.

"You are over young, and I might add over pretty, Mademoiselle, to make a proper abbess," he said with impressive gallantry; "and truth to tell, we hear that you are not so rigid in your rule as might be. How about these rumors which reach us that the daughter of my good friend, Montpensier, gives place to heretics and harbors and listens to the enemies of Holy Church? Now we have you, my charming child, at our mercy, we must e'en apply the questions which comport with sound discipline," and the prelate bent upon Jeanne a look curiously mingled of caressing flattery and stern suspicion.

"Ah, but monseigneur," said the girl, with naïve and bewitching coquetry, "I fear me much that I am too young for so great a charge ; and then pity us poor sisters—think of us, with armies all about us, war on every side ! What can we do ? We have no one to defend us. One day we must feed Huguenots and the next our own friends, or be at the mercy of both. Pardon our little delinquencies this time. We promise to give no cause for your reproof in the future, oh never, never again ! "

The shy, beseeching glance under Jeanne's long lashes with which these words were spoken, had its full effect upon the amorous cardinal. It would come not amiss, he reflected, in the tedium of his present retirement here at Rheims to have this charming spiritual ward for a while as a guest of his house. His niece, her stepmother, was even now present on a visit, and would furnish all due chaper-onage. He would keep the dainty little abbess as a kind of *prisonnière sur parole* until he was assured of her Catholicity, and a few hours spent daily in the light of such glances would be a welcome recre-ation.

His cold yet passionate eyes, the lids drawn nar-rowly, now scanned the face and figure of the young Benedictine with an eagerness which he was too arrogant to seek to disguise. Startled by something which caught his glance, he exclaimed :

"But what is this ? Madame l'Abbesse carries a pistol at her belt ! " and he pointed his forefinger at the weapon with which Jeanne had been fur-nished by Norbert.

"In truth, your eminence, in the wild encounter through which we have just passed I had need enough for arms," she murmured in some con-fusion.

"What should a maiden like you, bred in a con-vent from her cradle, know of the use of arms ? " rejoined the cardinal incredulously. "You could

w

not hit a man though he stood an arm's length before you. That is no toy for you, Mademoiselle," and with these words he quietly drew the pistol with his own hand from her belt and laid it on the table at his side, his eyes resting upon hers the while.

The blood mounted scarlet, then, to Jeanne's cheeks and her eyes flashed fire, for in both glance and action lurked a subtle significance which she could not miss.

"I could at least make shift to aim it at my own breast, monseigneur, if need were," she said coldly and with a fearless hauteur which thrilled the heart of Tontorf as he stood mute and aghast perforce with a very passion of sympathetic admiration, despite the danger which her daring might involve.

Charles de Lorraine, however, plainly found his new protégée but the more piquant for her defiance. A smile, soothing yet implacable, played around his handsome mouth, a smile which frightened Jeanne de Mousson far more than a frown would have done.

"Very good; Mademoiselle has courage," he said carelessly, but the note of command was unmistakable as he continued : "happily, however, such conjunctures are now overpast. We shall have time presently to admonish the fair Abbess of Jouarre for her lack of prudence in this dangerous journey, as also to search somewhat narrowly any weakness of faith such as has been alleged against her. You will remain under our roof for a season and I shall expect you to promise me," he added graciously, "when you are again at Jouarre, Mademoiselle, to follow in all respects the teaching of— what is his name ? that abbé I sent to Meaux for you the other day ? "

"Père Brodier," said Jeanne. "Ah, monseigneur, we like him not so very well. Have you not a more agreeable confessor for us ? "

The cardinal laughed.

"Ha, ha! Brodier is rather a dull fellow, I admit. Perhaps we will look into the matter. And now, Mademoiselle is tired with these untoward adventures. Are you aware that Madame de Montpensier is here?"

Jeanne's color fled. Was recognition, after all, inevitable.

"No, monseigneur. Is it so?"

"She is at present in the extreme wing of the palace, occupied by my sister, the *supérieure* of St. Peter's. How if I send you at once thither? The ladies will be careful that you have all fitting attendance and comfort."

"Thanks, monseigneur. May my steward accompany me?"

"Surely, surely, my daughter."

Dismissing her with an almost affectionate benediction, the cardinal now summoned an attendant to whom he gave direction to conduct the Princess de Bourbon to the presence of her stepmother, Catherine of Lorraine. Jeanne, with Norbert, followed the servant from the room and down a flight of stairs to the ground floor of the palace.

To both of them it seemed that the most ominous crisis of their adventure was now just before them. The first sight of the Duchesse de Montpensier, who had been recently herself at Jouarre, would betray the whole situation, and, worst of all, might yet involve most serious consequences to Jeanne's beloved lady. As they went on Norbert's eyes turned swiftly from side to side, on the alert for a means of yet evading this most to be dreaded encounter.

At the main approach to the palace the band of men was still waiting for them. Escape must be by a different entrance if at all.

They had entered now a long, dimly lighted corridor, having a row of low casement windows opening upon a garden or inner court, dark and deserted.

This might offer one last, desperate chance. As they passed these casements, Norbert exclaimed :

" Your highness, your ring ! Do you remember, you removed it to show its design to monseigneur ? You left it, I fear, behind you."

Quick as lightning in her perceptions, and quicker now than ever, since every sense was stimulated by terror, Jeanne, swiftly removing her ring which she concealed in her left hand, held up her right, exclaiming :

" You are right. It is gone. I have either lost it, or left it behind."

They had stopped now. Turning to the attendant, Jeanne, in her sweetest manner and with her most winning smile, said :

" Ah, my good friend, will you be so kind as to return and seek my ring, my large ring of office ? But if you fail, by no means disturb his eminence in the matter. We will meanwhile move slowly forward."

With no faintest suspicion, the servant darted back to do her bidding.

The instant he turned the corner of the corridor Norbert had forced a casement open and they were in the open air, the casement softly closing behind them.

A moment later he and Jeanne de Mousson, having fled through the dark garden and emerged without challenge of the guard from it by an open gateway, found themselves alone and free in the streets of Rheims, *le gros Bourdon* thundering over their heads the hour of seven.

XXX

SHORT WOOING

" YES, I can help you, and I will to the extent of my power; but you must obey me absolutely in one particular or I can do nothing."

Thus spoke Maître Chaudon, the Huguenot pastor of Rheims, to Jeanne de Mousson and Norbert, standing before him in his own study one half-hour later. They had reached this place of refuge in safety by Norbert's lucky memory of the house in the Rue de Tambour, which he had visited with Louis of Nassau. Their story was already told, their imminent peril manifest.

" And what is that condition, monsieur ? " asked Norbert, cheered by the strong promise of aid in the Huguenot's first words, but something chilled by the sternness and severity of those which followed.

" Is there any impediment on the part of either of you to marriage ? "

With unspeakable amazement they both replied in the negative.

" As I supposed. That is very well. I will provide you with a change of garments, with horses and with a shelter outside the gates of Rheims for the night, in fine, with all possible means of escape, on the one condition that your marriage take place here and now, within the next fifteen minutes."

From both young faces the color fled, and then rushed back in deep mantling blushes. Jeanne trembled violently while Norbert drew back, confused by so startling a proposition, and yet seeing the wisdom of it as Maître Chaudon now said more gently :

341

"With all confidence in the honor and virtue of you both I yet cannot in justice to your own good name and the fair fame of that noble lady whom Mademoiselle de Mousson represents, give my sanction to your wandering *à deux* around the country in this wild fashion except you go as man and wife."

Norbert hesitated no longer. Offering his hand to Jeanne he led her into an alcove at a slight distance and said in a low voice:

"Mademoiselle, every moments counts. The pastor is right, I believe, on my honor, but it must be short wooing. I offer you my heart and hand, an' you will have me, to serve you in all faith and fidelity while I live."

Then Jeanne lifted her eyes and looked straightway into his and said with a cold though gentle little smile:

"Sir, I will, if I may, take the protection of your name this night, and will hold myself in so far your chosen and lawful wife that no other can ever claim my heart. But I too must make a condition."

"Mademoiselle has but to name it," said Norbert bowing with ceremonious courtesy.

"My love and duty belong first of all to my lady. Will you promise me that until she bids you so to do you will never claim me as your wife nor bear yourself toward me as a husband?" and her eyes fell and her voice faltered for all her high spirit.

"I promise on my honor as a soldier and a Christian," said Norbert solemnly.

Then Jeanne laid her hand in his and the look in his face of purpose high and pure sent the blood bounding through her veins with mysterious joy.

The daughter of Maître Chaudon, who had been in the room throughout this brief interview, now 'led Jeanne into an adjoining apartment and assisted her to lay aside the coif and wimple and all other articles of conventual costume. Around her shoulders she tied a white lace scarf over the plain black robe and thus attired, with a pale, serious face, Jeanne presented herself again before Maître Chaudon.

Fixing his eyes upon her the pastor said : " Do you, Jeanne de Mousson, solemnly declare that you have now of your own free will and with true religious conviction laid aside your habit and your vows as a nun of the Order of St. Benedict ? "

" I do."

Maître Chaudon then pronounced the irrevocable words which made of these two man and wife, and the wedding being brief as the wooing, Jeanne was presently again given into the hands of Maître Chaudon's daughter. For the next matter in hand was to furnish the pair with adequate disguise and so hasten their departure within the hour from the city where could be no safety for them when once the Cardinal de Lorraine awoke to find himself outwitted, which might be soon or late.

So, a half-hour later the bride and bridegroom met again and neither knew the other at first glance. The nun had disappeared forever, and in her place now appeared a peasant lad, for Jeanne's hair had been cut straight and square across her forehead and below her ears. Upon her head sat jauntily a small green cap. She wore a well-worn leather jerkin and wide fustian breeches, coarse knit stockings and wooden sabots, and looked to admiration, with a basket of tools on her shoulder, the vinedresser's boy for whom she was to pass. Norbert was similarly arrayed, but his beard was shaven, his face stained to a dull brown hue, and his body bent well forward under the weight of a much larger basket, from which protruded picks and shovels.

Maître Chaudon faced the two and his countenance relaxed its gravity.

"I have married many a pair," he said, "gentle
and simple, but this is without doubt the motleyest
bridal party that ever left my door. The Cardinal
de Lorraine would hardly recognize the Abbess of
Jouarre in this gentle knave. Listen to me now.
You will have no difficulty in making your way out
of the city by the gate for foot passengers if you
start at once. Do not go to the east, but take the
north gate and proceed on the road to Guignicourt
for a mile. Turn then to the right where the stone
crucifix stands at a parting of the ways and follow
the path until you come at the vineyard's edge to a
small hut of the vine-dressers, which you will find
empty. Here you must keep yourselves in hiding
until dawn, when two horses will be brought you
by two of our own trusty Huguenots. Ride, then,
as fast as you may to Rethel. There you will find
a considerable band of the troops that came into
France with John Casimir. They are about leaving for the Palatinate and if you present this letter
to their leader, a true and worthy officer, he will
give you safe-conduct speedily to Sedan."

"Then shall we surely be in time to warn my
lady not to linger in Sedan?" asked Jeanne.
"In truth I am greatly fearful lest her safety may
be threatened when once the cardinal finds that
there has been a trick."

"It will take the cardinal a day or two, madame,"
said Maître Chaudon, "to unravel this very com-
plicated web which you have woven for him. I
have no doubt you will reach Sedan in good season to hasten your lady's journey to Heidelberg.
Doubtless there should be no delay in this.

"Now farewell. In the basket of Madame Tontorf," at which Jeanne grew rosy red, "there is a
thick, warm blanket, food, and wine. Be of good
courage and may God speed you on your strange
wedding journey."

A moment later Jeanne and Norbert were on the

street, and bending under their burdens, which were, however, in reality of little weight, they plodded on to the northern gate of Rheims.

There was no evidence of the excitement or confusion of an alarm or search in the streets through which they passed and they ventured to infer that the companions of Hugo had scattered in disgust, and that the cardinal was still unaware of the ruse of which he had been made the victim.

Passing the gate without notice the pair were soon swinging at a good pace along the hard white wintry road, bleak fields and woods lying cold on either side under the pale starlight, the silence of night reigning all about them.

Then when they reached the wayside hut, drear and dark and deserted, Norbert entered first, and finding all safe made shift to pile a little straw in a corner and calling Jeanne, said gently, as she stood in the doorway of the poor place :

" Dear lady, it grieves me that I can do no better than to offer you such cold comfort. Wrap you well in the blanket which your basket holds and sleep if you can while I without hold guard with God and all good angels till dawning. Good-night," and with this he closed the door and all through the hours till morning, armed and alert, he paced the frozen field before that forlorn cabin, and yet he found the hours not too long.

Then in the morning, through the chill and gloom of the daybreak came two mounted men who stopped not to parley, but dismounting before the hut gave over their horses to Norbert and turned swiftly back on foot the way they came. The sound of hoofs brought Jeanne to the door, and Norbert thought, for all her quaint, disfiguring disguise, he had never seen her eyes clearer nor her smile so softly bright. He lifted her to her saddle, and her little hand rested on his shoulder a thought longer than was needful and she said ruefully :

"Monsieur has not slept. It was too bad."

"A man does not sleep, madame," said Norbert leaping into his saddle and trotting after her out from the field into the high road, "when he has to guard his most precious treasure."

This made the demoiselle very thoughtful for some minutes, but when she spoke it was to say timidly:

"I think it is a bad practice for Monsieur Roubichon to address me as 'madame,' since we wish to keep our secret most carefully."

"Very well," said Norbert, smiling over at her, "but I must beg you to remember that I am no Frenchman and we can now drop the Roubichon. Remember that every drop of blood in my body is Dutch, and my name, such as it is, is yours."

All day they rode onward, but the wearier the way the blither grew Jeanne's spirits. A certain undercurrent of reserve and hauteur kept Norbert ever at a safe distance, but over this played an arch and irresistible coquetry as natural to the girl as its song to a bird. Snatches of song, gay laughter and merry nonsense brightened the anxious hours and the bleak rigor of the day.

> "Tell me, tell me, am I fair?"

Jeanne sang the old Champenoise virelay with ripples of musical laughter:

> "Does my mirror show me true?
> Sweet of face and *cropped* of hair,
> Tell me—is that so to you?
> Tell me, tell me, am I fair?"

With the challenge came a glance of arch and mocking merriment from under the dark, short elf-locks which set Norbert himself to laughing in spite of his grave anxiety for their perilous journey. But no sooner had she succeeded in bringing him thus to suit her mood than the Gascon maiden with one

of her swift and irresistible transitions fell to singing another strophe with gentle, pensive appeal :

> " If my lover gentle prove,
>   Knightly, brave, and true to love,
> Slave and servant will I be,
>   Tell me, tell me, am I true?"

Half angered with himself that this unclaimed bride
of his could thus play upon him and control his
emotions, with a pair of eyes and an old, old song,
Norbert found the tears nevertheless springing to his
own eyes in response to the demure sweetness of
the shyly lifted lids and the pathetic wistfulness of
the beautiful mouth.

"What are you, mademoiselle?" he cried stormily, "elf or sprite or Christian maiden? In sooth,
for a plain Dutchman like myself you are a riddle."

"Maître Chaudon said I was Madame Tontorf,"
said Jeanne with a pensive little shake of her head.

"He had some reason so to say, I believe," said
Norbert quickly.

"Ah no, *monsieur le capitaine*, no, no! Maître
Chaudon is a very good man, but he told a very
great falsehood. Not Madame Tontorf, never that
until my lady of her own free will shall bid me be.
Remember your promise."

In silence they rode on toward Rethel.

XXXI

AWAKE AT LAST

THE year 1572 in its dawning brought everywhere a mysterious quickening to the hearts
of men. Passionate pulsations of the new
and larger hope of liberty beat and surged through
whole nations.

In that spring the castle of Dillenburg in the
lonely Westerwald became for a time the nerve-
center of the Protestant movement in Europe.

With superb rebound William of Nassau had
emerged from the oblivion into which he had been
forced by political and military defeat and by the
disgrace of his wife's dishonor. Again his profound
capacity for great combinations and bold yet states-
manlike measures was at work.

The great immediate purpose to which all his
energies were now directed was the alliance of the
French with the Netherlands patriots for the war
with Spain. Coligny and Count Louis together had
pressed the project forward and everything now
pointed to swift success.

In his remote fastness the prince sent couriers
incessantly flying over all Europe, communicated
daily with kings and queens, levied troops, issued
letters of marque to the rude navy known as Beggars of the Sea, and sent his messengers into every
corner of the Netherlands to gather funds with
which to inaugurate a new war of independence.

On an early April morning the prince entered the
small room overlooking the wooded hills to the
northwest of the castle, which was for the time
being his cabinet. Brunynck, his secretary, sat

waiting with a pile of letters and dispatches heaped high on the table before him.

Before the prince could take his seat there was a volley of light knocks on the door and in poured the pretty troop of his motherless and worse than motherless children, the golden-haired five-year-old Maurice leading the line. All had their hands full of blossoms of the yellow gorse, with white and rosy hawthorn, and were full of sweet affectionate joyance as they gave their father morning greeting.

The prince received the little embassy with tenderest fatherliness, and with that peculiar yearning wistfulness often seen in men who have to fill the place of both father and mother.

Leaving their treasures of gorse and hawthorn to light up the gloomy little cabinet the children followed the beckoning hand of the gentle elder sister, Marie, and as they closed the door the prince, without haste but without waste of a second's time turned to his secretary.

" *Wohlan!* Brunynck, what is first ? "

" A courier from the Elector of Saxony, your highness, has brought this letter and awaits your reply."

The prince swiftly scanned the letter handed him. His face grew stern, and the traces of the tenderness with which he had just now welcomed his children were lost in the deep lines which remembered agony seemed suddenly to cut afresh in his face.

He laid the letter down and taking his pen wrote a reply which he then handed to Brunynck to copy. The letter said in answer to the proposition contained in that of the elector, uncle and guardian of Anne of Saxony : " Regarding her, who was formerly my wife, it is but just that her relatives shall now assume the care and responsibility for her. You can do with her as you will. *To me she is dead.*"

Down in Beilstein in rage and madness the unhappy Anne of Saxony was even then foaming out
her bitterness and wearing out her wretched life,
while in a cell of the remote Dillenburg dungeon
lay the miserable partner of her guilt, Jan Rubens.
His life by the law of the land was forfeit by his
confessed crime, but the magnanimity of the man
against whom that crime had been committed had
remitted his sentence to imprisonment. To the
world outside the whole affair was wrapped in im-
penetrable silence and mystery.

An hour passed during which the prince had
dictated half a dozen dispatches and written several
letters with that matchless faculty of swift and
facile composition which never forsook him. From
camp or court, from palace or cottage, from hall or
hiding, wherever the fortunes of Orange led him,
flowed forth those numberless letters with which
he led his people, wrought out their deliverance,
out of weakness made them strong, defied their
enemies and put to flight the armies of the aliens.

The handwriting was like the man ;—firm, flexible, sensitive, essentially high-bred, the statesman's, the scholar's hand rather than the soldier's.

Then through the open window from far below
there came a clear loud blast upon a bugle ringing
through the air and echoing and re-echoing from
the castle walls and the steep hills surrounding.

The prince started to his feet.

"That may be a courier from the Netherlands!"
he said, "or it may be from Coligny!"

Hastening down the hill he paused under the
majestic linden tree, half-way down the descent,
for by the sound of his horse's hoofs, the messenger, whoever he might be, was fast approaching.
Another instant and Norbert Tontorf leaped from
his saddle and threw himself upon his knee before
the prince.

"Great news, my lord!" he cried, and again

with irrepressible enthusiasm, as he rose, he put his bugle to his lips and blew a pealing clarion note. Turning to the prince he cried :

"My lord, at last the Netherlands are awake ! They are on fire ! Brill is captured by de Lumey and his men ! Hurrah for the Beggars of the Sea !"

The prince listened to Norbert's impassioned outburst with intense eagerness, but his first response showed anxiety rather than exultation.

"This may imperil our whole enterprise. I fear me greatly the Beggars have cut another of their mad capers which have already brought so much discredit to our cause and against which Coligny has so urgently warned me."

"It may be a mad caper, your highness," said Norbert, undaunted, "but the success of it has awakened our people at last from their sleep. The whole population of Voorn have taken the oath of allegiance to your highness as Stadtholder and all Holland and Zeeland are ready to follow."

"But is this news trustworthy ?" asked the prince quickly ; "how came you by it, since you are on your way hither from France direct ?"

"From a courier, my lord, sent straight from Treslong himself with a message to give by word of mouth, as they dared put nothing in writing. The man had ridden his horse to death and himself near unto it. I met him below in the village and he begged me to convey his message to your highness. You can rely upon it. All the people now ask is that the Prince of Orange will lead them. The tenth penny has struck the slowest hearts and the most selfish to revolt, and I believe the time is ripe for victory."

"Tontorf," said the prince, clasping both the young soldier's hands, while his eyes glistened with quick emotion, "if my people are ready they will not wait in vain ! May God speed the cause and let the oppressed go free !"

With this they turned and walked together to the castle.

There was thanksgiving and praise in the ancient hall of Dillenburg that day, and the whole princely household, from the white-haired lady mother to the tiny Emilia, latest born daughter to the prince, gathered at a joyful feast in the stately banqueting chamber. But no commoner in the land was more simply served than was that noble company, for pewter and common earthenware vessels had long since taken the place on that table of the gold and silver plate, the rare and royal service of earlier days. Shorn of every vestige of outward magnificence for the sake of the holy cause, in the hearts of those patriots the inner glory burned but the brighter.

In the evening Norbert was again alone with the prince, and together they paced the terrace overlooking the village, in the sweet spring air.

"You have brought me great tidings from Netherlands, and a good word from Louis in Blois and from Coligny, but I have yet to hear of your other adventure. How fared it with your expedition from La Brie, Tontorf?"

"Well, my lord."

"I know from the elector that Mademoiselle de Bourbon is safely in Heidelberg. I had supposed that she would remain with her sister in Sedan."

"No, my lord. The Cardinal de Lorraine was over-near her there for safety, and she remained with madame la Duchesse but two days."

"Tell me, if you will, the whole story," said the prince, his quiet manner scarcely veiling a very vivid interest in the subject.

"We had a little encounter with a band of freebooters soon after we left Rheims, and two of us fell into their hands, while the rest, with Mademoiselle, proceeded safely without injury to Sedan, which they reached the second night thereafter, and we a day later, having made a detour by Rethel." As to the personality of his companion in this incident Norbert chose to say nothing unless questioned.

"A band of twenty of Casimir's *reiters*, who came with us from Rethel, gave Mademoiselle her escort from Sedan to the borders of the Palatinate, Mademoiselle sending her servants back to Jouarre."

"Do you know how the tidings of her flight was received there?"

"With deepest grief and consternation, my lord. Far otherwise was it received by her father."

"Ah, surely, you went to Montpensier yourself. The elector wrote me that finding you well qualified for the adjustment of delicate matters he had taken the liberty of retaining you in the interests of Mademoiselle, and of dispatching you almost immediately after your arrival back to France."

"Yes, I remained but a few days in Heidelberg, long enough, however, to see Mademoiselle royally welcomed by the elector and madame, and full of joy in her new religious freedom. The elector treats her as a beloved daughter, and madame can hardly bear to have her out of her sight."

"I have heard that Mademoiselle de Bourbon is a lady of rare charms," said the prince quietly.

"Ah, my lord," cried Norbert, "to those who are within her inner circle the devotion to Mademoiselle becomes a sort of cult. There is about her something that I have never seen in like measure in any other person, and that is the power to lift up those who are cast down and cheer the sorrowful. You know of my poor little sister, and our sorrow."

"Yes, Tontorf; I have thought that the full cruelty of that terrible crime fell more heavily upon her than upon you, since she has had to bear the knowledge that in all innocence she had betrayed those she loved to their death."

"It is true, my lord. The burden of her grief has eaten out all her young life like a canker. No one, not even the electress, fondly as she loves her, has been able to lift up her wounded spirit until she saw Mademoiselle. The first sound of her voice seemed to bring a new light into Jacqueline's eyes, and I believe hope and courage are dawning for her, through the influence of my lady."

"How beautiful !" murmured the prince.

"And such is the saint, the angel almost," cried Norbert passionately, "against whom her father, the Duc de Montpensier rages as against an escaped felon, calling upon all and sundry to '*find her wherever she may be, within or without the kingdom and bring her back, alive or dead, that the injury and dishonor which she has brought upon her father may be atoned for by a punishment and a chastisement so notable that the memory of it may endure perpetually through all time to come.*'"

"Does the Duc so say ?" and the prince's brow knit stormily.

"Such are his words, and such envenomed bitterness as were shown by both him and his wicked little duchesse I have never witnessed."

"Has the elector made formal announcement of the arrival of Mademoiselle at Heidelberg to others."

"Yes, I went also to his majesty, King Charles and to the queen-mother."

"How did they receive the tidings ?"

"With *sang-froid* my lord. The court thinks of little now but the marriage of Princess Marguerite with Prince Henri of Navarre. The king remarked that he had ever thought his cousin de Montpensier a blind mole to cage up in a monastery so lovely a creature as his daughter Charlotte," he added.

The prince was silent for some moments and when he next spoke it was to say with energy :

"And now, Tontorf, for the Netherlands ! All depends upon the swiftness and skill with which

we can carry through our measures. Every town
in Holland and Zeeland of importance must be
secretly visited and a call to action and to arms
placed in the hands of the burgomasters. It will
be a difficult expedition and a dangerous. Are you
ready for it ? ''

" Ready, my lord."

On the fifteenth day of May there stepped from a
small coastwise ship upon the *Rouenische Kade* in the
city of Middelburg, a Breton mariner with bronzed
face, in coarse blue woolen jerkin and knitted cap,
who with hands thrust deep into his breeches pockets strolled idly along the Kade whistling an odd
little tune.

From the Kade the aforesaid mariner entered a
narrow street, looking from side to side with apparent curiosity and coming presently into the great
market place just as the Stadthuis chimes rang out
for seven o'clock. A queer smile crossed the sailor's
face as he looked up at the belfry, and his eyes
wandered from it to the tower of Lange Jan rising
silent from the roofs of the great abbey buildings.
Lounging near the Stadthuis the Breton watched
with apparent indifference the drill of a regiment of
Spanish soldiers in the great square. Several idlers
addressed him in Dutch, but he appeared to understand no language but French and no one could
enter into conversation with him.

When the voice of the great horologe of Lange
Jan smote upon the evening air the stranger turned
his head quickly and walked away in the direction
of the Lange Delft.

It was remarked afterward that the man was
seen hanging about the old Tontorf house, now the
headquarters of the Spanish officers, and some one
reported that they saw tears in his eyes and heard
him mutter to himself incomprehensible words.
Soon after he disappeared, but when the burgomas-

ter and the town council met in assembly the following morning, this same Breton mariner was
ushered into the room and gave into the hands of
the burgomaster a letter and thereafter disappeared
and was not seen again nor could be found in all
Middelburg.

Upon opening this letter it was found to be from
the Prince of Orange with his own sign and seal,
and it exhorted the men of Middelburg not to be
behind their countrymen in the island of Walcheren, but to follow the example of Flushing and
Veere and declare themselves loyal to their out·
raged land and ready for action.

Such an appeal the worthy burgomaster and his
honorable councillors found exceeding troublesome
and dangerous, as involving measures treasonable
to the king of Spain, and as Middelburg was invested with a goodly Spanish garrison, wholly un-
feasible for that present time. Let them of Flushing and Veere declare for the Beggars if they
choose, they of Middelburg depended on Spain for
their prosperity and trade and by Spain they would
stand.

Meanwhile the Breton mariner went on his way
to Flushing, Veere, Enkhuizen, to Alkmaar, Gouda,
Leyden, Dort, and a dozen other places, and wherever he appeared a letter straightway was found
in the hands of burgomaster or alderman, a letter
from the Prince of Orange, and in the letter an
appeal to rise and protect their ancient liberties and
throw off the tyranny of Alva, and, save Middelburg, every town responded.

Then followed a great day, a day which heralded
the freedom of the Netherlands. At Dordrecht the
estates of Holland, Zeeland, Utrecht, and Friesland
assembled and formally recognized the prince as
their lawful stadtholder, and in the cheers that rent
the sky no man cheered louder than that same
Breton mariner.

St. Aldegonde, the patriot poet and ardent friend
of Orange, addressed the estates with impassioned
oratory, rehearsing the outrageous wrongs suffered
under Alva, and prophesying the dawning of a new
day of freedom and release.

Then in loud and thrilling chorus for the first
time was sung the glorious hymn, the *"Wilhelmuslied "* of St. Aldegonde :

> " Take courage, my brave people all !
>   God's grace protects you still ;
> The Lord will never you forsake,
>   Though now ye suffer ill.
> The Lord then pray both night and day,
>   Beseech him faithfully,
> That he will give me aid and power
>   To set my people free."

> " My life and all that is my own
>   I to your cause confide ;
> My brothers, knightly gentlemen,
>   Stand loyal at my side.
> Count Adolf we left lying there
>   In Friesland's woful fray,
> His soul above, in worlds unseen,
>   Waits for the judgment day.

XXXII

WHITER THAN THE WHITEST.

IN the Westwall garden of Heidelberg Castle white lilies were blooming in stately ranks under the shade of the mighty lindens. The June sun pouring over the grim bastion of the Rondel and touching the sun dial at its base showed the day's decline. The woodthrush was fluting in the dense billowing mass of the forest foliage below the castle wall, and the breeze which stirred the treetops came laden with the fragrance of roses.

The scent of the roses brought to Charlotte de Bourbon, who lingered near the castle wall, keen memories of other roses, another garden, and another life in a far land. But though the thought of Jouarre brought the dimness of tears for a moment to hide the valley of the Neckar, stretching westward, green and fair, it could not long cloud the serene joyousness of her spirit.

The Abbess of Jouarre was no more, and in her place moved and lived a radiant maiden, whose simple white gown, without jewels, bespoke her poverty and declared nothing of her rank and consequence. But her firm and spirited bearing and the frank, innocent delight of every look and motion, told of freedom and a heart at ease.

In her hand Mademoiselle held a letter, and turning now from the wall she began slowly to pace the garden path between the lilies, and as she moved on she lifted the letter in her white hand and read again the lines inspired by deepest affection for herself, and undying faithfulness to her interests. It was her "*bien bonne cousine et parfaite amye, Je-*

358

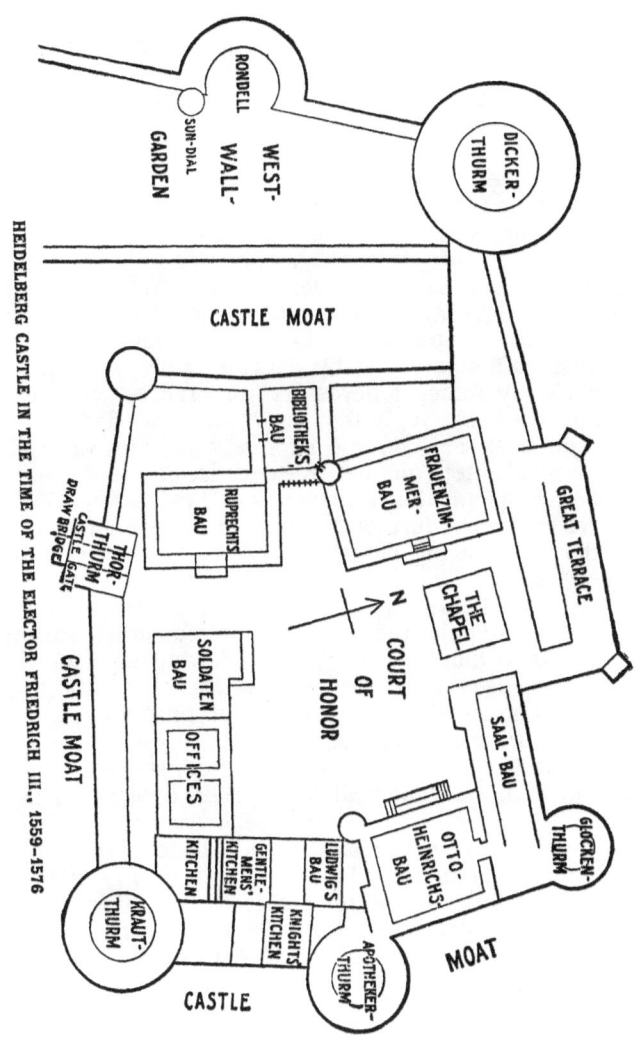

HEIDELBERG CASTLE IN THE TIME OF THE ELECTOR FRIEDRICH III., 1559-1516

hanne," who, in the midst of all the excitement of
the French court and the approaching marriage of
her son to the daughter of Catharine de Medici, still
found time to seek to reconcile the bitter spirit of
the Duc de Montpensier to his child.

With all her tenderness, Jeanne d'Albret could
not conceal from Charlotte the fact of her ill success thus far ; but even this and the knowledge of
her father's persistent, impotent rage could not long
cloud the spirit of the lady. She was free, and her
freedom was safely guarded by her host, the stanch
old elector. A month before he had received the
emissaries of the furious Duc, sent in succession to
demand the person of his daughter and convey her
back, by force, if necessary, to France, with the
imperturbable reply that he would send Mademoiselle back only on the express conditions of her
personal safety and her free exercise of the Protestant religion. Such answer was final. The Duc
desisted from further efforts, and his daughter, although knowing herself fatherless, yet knew herself free. The joy of her newly won freedom
could not be destroyed, the rather that it had given
her the long-desired power to confess herself Protestant, without fear or favor, following unchecked
the impulses of her earnest conviction and entering
in full sympathy into the devout religious life of
the court of Heidelberg.

But Charlotte was not only free, she was unwatched, she who had never been unwatched in
all her young life ; best of all, she was ardently beloved in the household of the Elector Friedrich.
Around her there had formed itself already in the
three months of her residence, a little inner court
of Huguenot refugees from her own dear land, to
whose homesick anxieties and distress she had become a ministering angel, and among whom she
was well-nigh adored for the generosity, the gentleness, and the winning grace of her nature.

And so, as Charlotte de Bourbon let fall the hand which held the letter of her majesty of Navarre and turned to speak to the young girl who was walking a step or two behind her, her blue eyes were clear and sunny as they had been in the days of her childhood. Bending, she broke a lily stem and inhaled the fragrance of the gleaming white chalice.

"Oh, how sweet these lilies are!" she cried. "Ever and everywhere the same! Did you hear the sound of horses' hoofs coming up the hill, Jacqueline?" she asked her companion, a little later, carelessly. "Methinks I heard something a moment since, but now it has ceased."

Jacqueline Tontorf, a tall, slender girl, with heavy masses of brown hair braided about her head, and large brown eyes in which dwelt a brooding thoughtfulness, responded gently in the affirmative.

Then as the eyes of both turned toward the southern entrance of the west wall, they saw approaching them a man of knightly figure and bearing, clad in a light suit of mail with a plumed helmet.

It was the Prince of Orange.

Approaching nearer the prince stayed his steps, with a look of deepest homage, wonder, and reverence.

"Your pardon, gracious lady," he exclaimed. "I find myself mistaken. Catching sight of yourself and your companion as I approached the castle gate I thought I recognized my good friend of other days, the Electress Amalie, and so gave my horse to my groom and made haste forthwith to present myself to her grace. Pardon my mistake and my seeming presumption."

Mademoiselle, who had lost and recovered all her bloom, and much more, while these words were spoken, now said, with a slight tremor in her voice:

"And would I also be in error should I think myself speaking to monseigneur the Prince of Orange?"

The prince had removed his helmet and stood with bared, stately head, his helmet braced against his left side. Approaching the lady now by a few steps he signified a peculiar pleasure in such recognition, bowing profoundly. Then in a voice so low that it was unheard by the maiden, Jacqueline, who had turned back and seemed studying the old dial with deepest interest, he said :

"Your grace, long ago in another garden, in another land, a man who was half a prisoner, and greatly burdened in heart and mind, saw a fair demoiselle, hardly beyond childhood in years. She also was clothed in white and she carried white roses in her hand, as white as your flowers, Mademoiselle, but her face was yet whiter and her eyes tear-dimmed. The man who gazed upon her whom he now knows to be the Princess de Bourbon, and who named her "Sainte Silence," has never forgotten that unknown maiden nor the talisman she gave him that day. Silence, patience, fortitude, such was the message of the rose."

The Prince of Orange in the thirteen years which had passed since he was a hostage at the Palace of Vincennes, had changed from the brilliant, conquering young courtier to a mature and serious manhood. His face was grave, deep lines of thought and care were in his forehead, and traces of gray showed in the brown beard and hair. In place of the sense of joyous and masterful confidence which had characterized the foster-son and favorite of the great emperor in his young years, there now appeared a profound reserve, a searching, even mournful inquiry, a stern, indomitable resoluteness. Yet in far greater measure to-day than in his youth the personality of the prince possessed that imposing and inexplicable quality which, apart from what a man may say or do or appear cries, "Here is a great man."

As he now spoke with a rare and moving gentleness, his dark serious eyes fixed fully upon her face, Charlotte de Bourbon felt that strong influence of the person and presence of the prince in an almost overmastering degree. Her eyes, which had sought to avoid the ardent homage in the looks of the gallant younger Nassau, Count Louis, received and returned the deeper devotion in the eyes of his brother with simple steadfastness, but from head to foot she trembled and something stirred within her heart in poignant, mysterious augury. Unable by reason of her unwonted agitation to reply to his words, Charlotte for answer extended her right hand to the prince and in the hand, unaware, she still held the single lily.

The prince lifted the beautiful hand to his lips, and took the flower quietly into his own hand.

"Thanks are poor, Mademoiselle, for such a gift," he said gravely. "I have told your highness the message of the rose. A day may come when I shall be so bold as to ask you to tell me the message of the lily. May we speedily meet again!" and with a salutation of courtliest deference he turned then and hastened back to the great gate of the castle.

Charlotte walked slowly down the path to Jacqueline, who still stood near the sun dial with her serious, contemplative gaze ranging over the landscape.

"Child," she said softly, "do you know who it is that has come?"

"It is the prince!"

"You have seen him before! seen him doubtless in Breda?"

"Never before, your highness."

"How, then, knew you him? You heard me address him?"

Jacqueline shook her head quietly.

"No, my lady. I knew there was but one man to-day alive who could look like that."

"What is it, Jacqueline, which makes his grace of Orange so unlike other men?" murmured Charlotte.

She was trembling still, touched by a nameless but potent influence which she could not define nor comprehend.

Jacqueline was silent, her eyes full of their strange, melancholy brooding.

"He is no longer the lonely wanderer, outcast, friendless, powerless, as in the time of which your brother has told me," proceeded Charlotte musingly; "he has rallied his forces, compelled his fate, conquered his evil star, and is to-day, so the elector has told me, the central militant figure in the Protestant world."

"Yes, my lady, the tide has turned. His grace is now to return to our dear land with a great army and set my people free."

"Yes, Jacqueline. This I most certainly believe, for is not France also aroused? And with Coligny and the prince joining their forces, success this time seems certain. I feel the sense of power in monseigneur. I feel his steady, conquering courage, and yet—what is it in his face, in his eyes, which gives me this unspeakable pang?"

It was strange. Mademoiselle de Bourbon asked this question of the simple Zeeland maiden with an eagerness which denoted belief in her ability to give her adequate reply.

"Ah, my lady," said the girl, slow tears dropping from her eyes, "it is so plain."

"What is plain, Jacqueline?"

"That my lord is doomed. Do you not see that seal of the martyr on his brow? that shadow of death in his eyes? It was in my father's," and Jacqueline's voice sank to a whisper. "It is a look which, if you once have seen, you never can mistake."

No word or sign responded to this strange utterance, but with face white and awed Mademoiselle turned and hastened from the garden.

That evening the stately Kaiser-Saal in the Otto-Heinrichsbau was the scene of brilliant festivity in honor of the distinguished guest of the elector. At a late hour ten trumpeters in gorgeous livery entering the hall blew a silvery blast announcing that supper was served. The court then proceeded through the eastern entrance of the Kaiser-Saal, and by the long south gallery to the famous Gläserner-Saal in the upper story of the Saalbau.

Here the venerable elector and his wife, the still young and charming Princess Amalie, took their places at the head of the table, the Princess de Bourbon at the right of the grave, fatherly elector, the Prince of Orange at the left of his old friend, the Netherlandish electress. Beside Mademoiselle sat Duke Christoph, the stalwart young son of the elector, and beside the prince, Kunigunde, the rosy-cheeked young daughter.

It had been under the escort of the prince, for whom she had ever entertained a species of enthusiastic hero-worship, that the beautiful widow of his lifelong friend, the famous Heer von Brederode, had, in 1569, visited the court of Heidelberg, and won the heart of its master, then in the second year of his widowhood. Orange was, therefore, the favorite guest of the princely pair, and a spirit of unconstrained good cheer and unclouded mutual confidence reigned supreme.

The prince was at his best. A new influx of power and hope gave lustre to his eyes and added brilliancy to his conversation. Victory and success seemed well within his grasp that night. He knew himself to be among friends enthusiastically devoted to his person and interests, and just before him, inspiring every thought, sat the lovely French princess, in her gracious, girlish beauty, with the serene repose of the cloister still upon her.

To the prince Charlotte de Bourbon was a new type of womanhood. His mother and sisters were noble, pious, and serious-minded women of the sturdy old-German domestic type. Anne of Egmont, the wife whom the Emperor Charles had chosen for him at eighteen, had been an amiable, but colorless and conventional person, who had left no deep impression upon his heart or life. Then had followed his ambitious but ill-fated union with Anne of Saxony, which had resulted in eight years of profound suffering and humiliation. Although borne in proud, uncomplaining silence, the ravages of those years upon the brain and heart of the long-suffering man might never be obliterated.

But the prince, all the more for an experience like this and for his lifelong familiarity with famous court beauties of his time, was quick to respond to the lofty purity, the delicate reserve, the flexible, yet stately grace of the " maiden from afar " of whom so much had already been told him, and in whom with strange emotion he had recognized the " little Sainte Silence " of his long-ago encounter at the court of France.

Uniting in herself in a unique degree the essential beauty of both the ancient faith and the New Religion,—the pure, chastened meekness of the nun, in whose life " obedience, silence, humility " had been the watchword, and the radiant spiritual enthusiasm and divine freedom of the early Protestant cult,—Charlotte de Bourbon produced, at this time in her life, a profound impression upon all who met her.

The court of Heidelberg, under the simple, unostentatious rule of Friedrich der Fromm, was characterized by democratic indifference to titles and rank. On this occasion Mademoiselle's personal following was represented by Jeanne de Mousson and Jeannette Vassetz, the young Jacqueline Tontorf, who had been appointed by the electress to immediate attendance upon Mademoiselle, and the Sieur de Minay, François d'Averly, who remained always with her as her spiritual guide and counsellor. His brother, George d'Averly, had already returned to France.

Although participating but slightly in the conversation, Charlotte listened with kindling and sympathetic response to every word. Much was said of the gallant relief of Mons by Count Louis, which, a month earlier, opened the new campaign in Brabant by a stroke of stratagem so audacious that only its success justified it. Alva could have sworn that Louis was at that very time in the tennis court of Paris. De la Noue, the valiant *Bras de fer*, and the Sieur de Genlis were acting with Louis, but the Spanish, under Don Frederic, son of Alva, had now laid siege to Mons, and the first duty of the prince on the invasion of the Netherlands, which he was about to lead in person, would be to relieve the Huguenot and patriot forces now shut up within the city.

Never had the time been so ripe for success in the cause of freedom for the Netherlands as now. The people were awake at last themselves ; almost every town of importance had declared for the prince save Middelburg, which with its strong Spanish garrison was closely invested by the Beggars. Alva himself was disheartened, sick of butchery and bloodshed, conscious of the waning success of his savage policy, and the universal hatred of himself, and eager to be released.

The prince was at the moment on his way to cross the Rhine at the head of an army of twenty thousand men. To ensure to such a force three months' wages in advance had been indeed a problem, but even of this he was sanguine. He had come to-day from Frankfurt, where he had succeeded in raising a fair sum of money on the last remnants of his own possessions. Charles IX. had recently contributed two hundred thousand crowns, after which who could doubt the seriousness of his purpose in engaging in "the Flemish war"? Money was rolling in bravely from the Protestants of England, although Elizabeth herself, after her wonted fashion, was blowing hot and cold; best of all, Coligny, so high in royal favor as now to be popularly called "King of Paris," would soon join him in person in Hainault.

Despite his natural reserve and his wonted silence regarding his own matters, the high hopes of the prince and the enthusiasm with which he was now again entering the arena to fight for his people could not be suppressed in this presence.

Charlotte de Bourbon saw the light in his eyes, the firm, quiet, yet intense purpose expressed in every line of his face, and yet, ever above and beneath all she saw that strange, brooding shadow, that indescribable, unconscious melancholy.

Was Jacqueline right when she saw in this the mark of doom, the seal of martyrdom set on the man's forehead?

The banquet over, the elector and his guest withdrew for brief private conversation. Having closed the door of his audience room the stern old elector seated himself before a desk and handed the prince a letter.

It was written from Blois early in May and was from Count Louis.

The prince read it through with a swift and startling change of countenance and said:

"May I ask your grace for some explanation? The matter is not clear to me."

"Certainly, I will explain. A certain Ruzé, Bishop of Angers, wrote us early in April, immediately indeed after it became known to the Duc de Montpensier that his daughter had sought our protection, a most infamous letter, impugning the character and motives of the Princess de Bourbon and having

the shameless effrontery to inform us that it was
perfectly understood at the Abbey of Jouarre that
the clandestine departure of its abbess was the outcome of a *liaison* of long standing between her and
Count Louis of Nassau."

The eyes of the prince fairly blazed with fury.

"The Inquisition has many means of torture besides rack and fire," he said under his breath.

"Yes, this was Ruzé's last and deadliest cruelty
to the young Abbess of Jouarre. I sent his letter
back by return messenger with no other word than
that the Elector Palatine declined to receive further
communications from that source."

"And you also informed my brother of the pur-
port of the letter?"

"Precisely, and this is his reply."

Again the prince scanned the letter with strange
intensity of eagerness.

"Did the miserable coward not hide behind his
profession he should answer to me for this base
slander in fair fight," read the letter. "I care little
for the stain upon my own good name. Let it pass.
But in this cruel lie the scoundrel has sought to
defame the whitest-souled and most spotless virgin
whom ever a man worshiped in all reverence from
afar. That I do so reverence the Princess de Bourbon, that I secretly and unknown to her bear in
my heart a pure and honorable passion of devotion
toward her which I have no right in this time of
crisis and uncertainty to declare, I care not to deny.
Such calumny as this craven priest dares to utter
I scorn to contradict. It is beneath contempt. God
grant it may never reach the ears of her highness!"

The prince looked up. "Gallantly spoken, your
grace," he said, "like the gallant junker he is. In
his name let me urge that the foul slander be kept
from Mademoiselle." He spoke earnestly, but
utterance seemed difficult and forced, and his voice
was other than his own.

Y

"You can rely upon me for that," replied the elector, with a grim compression of his lips. "I was ill disposed to give the lad pain, but I thought it right he should have the chance to speak a word for himself. A marvelous fellow that young brother of yours, my lord! It seems none can withstand him. He has won over the court of France, and perchance the court of England. Walsingham writes that he is surely the rarest and goodliest man he has looked upon since leaving England. Burleigh finds his speech irresistible."

"Yes," replied the prince. "Louis succeeds everywhere, but never beyond his desert."

With those quiet words a stone was laid above a new-born hope quickly dead and quickly buried.

XXXIII

DOOM

" JEANNE, my girl, Jeanne, to-night I have the strangest thoughts! You could not understand them. I must not name them," and Charlotte de Bourbon, on her knees in a deep window-niche of her beautiful chamber, in the second story of the Frauenzimmerbau, leaned her cheek aslant on her clasped hands and, turning her head from her faithful friend, looked down into the Court of Honor flooded with moonlight.

It was long past midnight. The lady had exchanged her court apparel for a peignoir of white muslin, but seemed to have no thought of retiring, and it was thus that Jeanne de Mousson had found her, and had seen bright drops gleaming in the moonlight on her cheeks, and so, fearful ever of trouble for her lady, had knelt beside her with arms clasped about her slender body, imploring to know why she wept.

"Are you sure I could not understand, dearest lady?" Jeanne whispered wistfully. "Did I ever fail to understand the sorrows of Mademoiselle, which have been so many, or the joys which of old were so few?"

"But this is different, *ma mie*. This is something wholly new, but whether joy or sorrow I cannot understand myself! It is conflict, confusion, perplexity. Howbeit, it is after all nothing to me."

There was a wise little silence on Jeanne's part. Then Charlotte said slowly:

"Did Captain Tontorf once tell us that his grace of Orange has a wife?"

Of the fact that Captain Tontorf had a wife Mademoiselle still remained in ignorance.

"Yes, my lady, he has made mention of the existence of the Princess Anne of Saxony, but in strange terms."

"I remember. Our dearest Madame d'Albret told me of her also, long since, at Jouarre. It is ever the same. Some mysterious obscurity hangs about the person of that lady. For years now I have not even heard her name."

"This much I know from Captain Tontorf," replied Jeanne, "that she is, or was, a cruel, heartless woman and of a wild and stormy nature, and that the prince has never through all his troubles found in her aught of sympathy or wifely gentleness"

"Oh, Jeanne!"

A little sob broke from Charlotte's lips.

"That he of all men," she murmured, "should miss the common good which is the right of the humblest, and the happiest—he with that look in his eyes that breaks one's heart!"

"How mean you, Mademoiselle?"

"Ah, you do not know what that strange child, Jacqueline, said to me to-day. Jeanne, do you think she has second sight?" Charlotte's blue eyes were lifted with piteous anxiety to her friend's face.

"It may be, dearest lady; I have thought so, but I cannot tell. What did she say?"

"That the prince bears upon his brow the seal of martyrdom, the shadow of doom. She has seen the look in her father's face. She says one could not mistake it."

Each word was spoken with the solemnity of irresistible conviction.

"Jeanne," in another breath, "*I have seen it, now, myself.*"

"Oh, my lady!" Awed and mastered by her mistress' mood, Jeanne could say nothing more.

Charlotte had risen and released herself from the girl's encircling arms ; and now as she stood, tall and white in the moonlight, a strange and lofty inspiration seemed to touch and calm her.

"My friend," she said slowly, "how could a woman, if she had a human heart, miss so glorious a vocation ? How could she throw away such privilege as that of dedicating her life to him, a man so far above his fellows, of warding from him the doom that follows him, even if need were, of dying for him ? To save a nation's leader, and so perchance a nation's faith and freedom, oh, dear Jeanne, what nobler vocation could one seek ? How our cloister hopes pale and shrivel by the side of it ! This were great and high, an inspiration to lift even a weak, unknown woman into the fellowship of the great spirits who are laying down their lives in this awful time for God and men ! "

Before Jeanne could respond a swift change had passed over her lady. From the height of this conception, which had lifted her for the moment above herself, she was swept by a wave of yearning, unspeakable emotion, the ever new, the ever old, and throwing herself into the arms of her friend, she whispered :

"May God forgive me if this be sin, but, oh, Jeanne, what woman would not, if she could, follow the prince to the earth's end if so she might win one look, one smile, one word of such love as souls like his could know, and that won, die gladly, knowing herself the crowned of womankind ——"

Startled by a slight sound at the door Charlotte became silent and turned quickly to see it gently pushed open and Jacqueline Tontorf, in her simple, white robe, enter.

Her eyelids were downcast, but tears flowed fast down her cheeks, and as she walked with slow, groping steps, she wrung her hands with a strange motion, and a low, stifled moan came from her lips.

"She is walking in her sleep," whispered Jeanne. "*Pauvre fille!* She has before."

Charlotte had thrown her arm tenderly about the girl.

"What is it, little one?" she asked gently. "Awake, Jacqueline."

"The gloves, oh, the gloves!" murmured Jacqueline, in a hurried, agonized whisper. "Take them away, quickly, or it is too late. Oh, my lady, too late!"

She had opened her eyes now, and fixed them upon Charlotte's face with a wild, bewildered stare. Meeting the quiet, subduing compassion of her lady's look, she burst into a flood of tears and sank trembling and sobbing upon a low seat.

"You were dreaming, dear Jacqueline," said Charlotte, caressing the maiden's beautiful flowing hair with a steady hand, albeit her heart was trembling within her, "and now you are awake and it is all over."

"Nay, nay, my lady, alas, not all over!" and Jacqueline sprang to her feet, and lifting her finger in token that they should be silent, she stood in an attitude of strained attention.

"Do you not hear?" she asked, after a few seconds had passed, in which each of the others heard only the loud beating of her own heart. "It is the first muttering of a great storm. Soon it will break upon us. O God, have pity."

Then, in the distance and the hush of the night, a far, faint sound, as of hoofs upon the hard high-road below the castle, was vaguely heard, a sound which came nearer and nearer, faster and faster. The hoofbeats were now on the bridge over the moat, they reverberated beneath the great vaulted arch of the Thorthurm, and springing to the window, Charlotte and Jeanne saw a horse and rider gallop into the Court of Honor and draw up before the colonnade of the Soldaten-bau.

"It is a courier from France. His errand must be urgent to bring him at such an hour as this. Look, Jeanne, he wears the livery of my lord de Teligny!" cried Charlotte. "I believe his message is to me," and calling to the guard on duty at the entrance of the Frauenzimmerbau, she bade him summon the rider to come hither.

A moment later Charlotte stood, Jeanne de Mousson beside her, on the moon-flooded pavement of the Court of Honor, and before her the wearied, breathless messenger who had just leaped from his horse.

"What news from France?"

"Ill news, madame," replied the man. "I have letters from the admiral to his excellency, and one from my lord de Teligny to the Princess de Bourbon."

With a word, Charlotte extended her hand and received the letter which the courier drew from a case within his doublet. The superscription was read without difficulty, although the rays of the moon had become intercepted by light clouds. The dawn breeze had awakened and sighed plaintively through the vast arches and cloisters of the great court.

The letter trembled in Charlotte's hands. It brought ill news, it seemed, ill heralded.

"Have you other message?" she asked falteringly, "message by word of mouth?"

"Your highness," said the man, shaking his head, "my lord could not write what all they of the Religion in Paris believe."

"And that is?"

"That her majesty of Navarre met her death from poison in a pair of gloves sent from Monsieur René, the queen-mother's perfumer."

Charlotte looked fixedly at the man for a moment, as if unable to comprehend the import of his words. Then with a gesture of dismissal she re-entered the great portal of the Frauenzimmerbau and, followed by Jeanne de Mousson, walked slowly to her room, where she sank fainting on the bed.

The letter which lay for a time unopened, confirmed the tragic utterance of the courier, in so far as it was concerned with fact rather than with rumor. For Jeanne d'Albret had perished in the prime of her noble and vigorous womanhood, and over the means and manner of her exit from the strange and stormy scenes of her life hung that day, and will ever hang, a dark doubt and mystery.

Moving on the highest plane of action, with a puissant spirit and an unconquerable heart, each new vicissitude of life served to develop a nobler grace and a more commanding courage in the daughter of Marguerite of Valois. Even the foes of her faith were fain to call her one of the greatest spirits of the epoch. Certain is it that no queen of her century was her superior in virile force and political genius, while none was her equal in purity of life and religious devotion.

Such was the queen whom Catharine de Medici "hated with all her cowardly heart." Whether her death were the result of a deliberate plan on the part of Catharine or not, certain is it that in the three short weeks which Jeanne d'Albret most reluctantly spent in Paris at the dissolute Valois court her whole being was poisoned and life embittered by the heartless insincerity, the shameless immorality, and the unconcealed sneering contempt for herself and her religion shown by Catharine and those who surrounded her.

Her death made her son Henri, king of Navarre, and removed an awkward obstacle in the way of the further designs of the queen-mother. His marriage with the Princess Marguerite, which was to have taken place immediately, was now postponed until the seventeenth of August.

In the early morning, which was dim with rain, the slow tolling of the great bell in the Glocken-thurm of Heidelberg Castle announced the reception of the tidings of the death of the Queen of Navarre by the elector.

As the sounds died away Charlotte de Bourbon lifted her white face from the pillow, for sorrow had prostrated her for the time, and seemed listening. She heard another sound.

"Jeanne," she said gently, "look out and tell me what is passing below. I hear the noise of men and horses in motion."

"Yes, dear lady," said Jeanne softly ; "it is the escort of the Prince of Orange. The men are mounted and are waiting now near the great gate."

"Do you see the prince ? "

A faint flush came into the pale cheeks with the words.

"Yes," said Jeanne, "he stands with the elector and madame in the portico of the Otto-Heinrichs-bau. Duke Christoph and Kunigunde are with them. He is taking leave of them."

"I did not think he had left so soon," murmured Charlotte.

"A groom holds his horse just before the steps," proceeded Jeanne. "He is speaking to Madame, but his looks are cast in this direction. Now he is mounting. He turns this way. Ah, my lady, he is like a man who has received a heavy blow. Hardly is your own face paler or more stricken. He is bending low in his saddle, saluting their ex-cellencies. Now he gallops across the court and is close at hand below. Ah, his eyes are lifted. Lis-ten ! " and Jeanne drew back from the window.

The sound of hoofs rang clear from the pavement of the Court of Honor and filled the ears of both the listening maidens for a moment. Swiftly re-ceding the sounds grew duller and more distant and were presently lost.

"Gone without a word," Charlotte murmured faintly. "I may never see his face again."

"Yes, dearest lady," said Jeanne, sitting on the bed's edge and smoothing the brightness of Mademoiselle's hair from her throbbing temples, "but not without a look. I can read the meaning in a brave man's eyes. Trust me, you will see the face of my lord again ; but first there is all the world to lose or win. Sleep now, and be glad that our precious queen sleeps, no more to suffer sin and sorrow."

The prince rode slowly in the mist and rain down the steep and slippery declivity into the town of Heidelberg and out through the gates down the valley Rhinewards.

A heavy oppression was on his heart, for he was leaving without word or sign to her whose radiant loveliness and innocent joy he knew to be clouded now with sudden grievous sorrow. He could have tarried yet a few hours, could have seen perhaps and spoken with the Lady Charlotte and told her the grief which his heart held for her in this loss of her " perfect friend " and second mother, for whom, as the elector phrased it, she " so marvelously grieved," but he did not trust himself so to do.

Could he look again into those blue eyes, whether clear as he had seen them or dimmed by tears of poignant sorrow and keep his own secret ? And that secret must be kept at all hazards since his brother's heart had been so unexpectedly revealed to him. What then ? No sacrifice could be overgreat for Louis, the loyal, generous brother who would have died for him with a smile on his lips any day, as he well knew.

Let it pass with other hopes! Only to have looked into the pure face and pure heart of the Bourbon maiden was a consecration. And what of

this mysterious death of her majesty of Navarre ?
What did it portend to his own good cause, the
cause of freedom and of the faith ?   Over-timely
was it for the Catholic party, and if the dark rumor
were true concerning the manner of the queen's
death, what was the pledged word of Charles and
Catharine de Medici worth in his own behalf ?   A
dark riddle and no answer came that day as the
prince rode on his way to join his troops and lead
them forward into the Netherlands.

The summer, however, did not pass without an
answer, an answer terrible, appalling, and in a sense
final, to all the larger hopes of Christendom forever.

Having crossed the Rhine early in July, captured
Roermond and advanced victoriously through Brabant, his garrisons received and his authority
accepted by the towns through which he passed, the
prince hastened on toward Mons to raise the siege
and release Count Louis and his gallant Huguenot
companions within the beleaguered city.

On August eleventh, a week before the Paris
wedding, he writes to his brother John at Dillenburg :

"*I must not fail to tell you that to-day I had letters
from the admiral (Coligny) informing me that . . .
he was levying twelve thousand arquebusiers and three
thousand horse, intending to come himself, something
that I hope will be a great aid to us.   The admiral
advises me not to enter lightly into an engagement
with the enemy, until by the grace of God we can join
our forces. . . We may see how miraculously God de-
fends our people and makes us hope that, in spite of
the malice of our enemies, he will bring our cause to a
good and happy end, to the advancement of his glory
and the deliverance of so many Christians from unjust
oppression.*"

The letter of Coligny, alluded to by the prince,
was written with the full sanction and approval of

Charles IX., with whom he was apparently high in favor.

But hardly had Coligny thus written, when it became apparent that the weak and fitful king had already grown cold toward the Flemish project. His mother's influence was at work, for the time was nearly ripe for Catharine de Medici to show her hand.

The ineffaceable blot on the pages of history which the next fortnight was to bring was not, however, the work of one woman of wicked will alone. The undying shame of it must rest also upon the duplicity, the double-dealing, the cowardly shiftiness of another woman, the Protestant Queen of England.

While all the forces of Protestantism at that crisis, and even the wavering and selfish Catharine, were looking to Elizabeth for her powerful aid in the struggle against Spain, dark rumors went abroad that the Queen of England was in reality holding a treacherous correspondence with Alva himself, with the intent of seizing the Zeeland city of Flushing, now in the hands of the patriots, and betraying it into the hands of Spain.

Such rumors as these reaching Catharine de Medici, drove her into a panic. She found herself forced by her own and her son's pledges, to embark, apparently single-handed, on the dangerous enterprise of a war with Spain. England was playing her false. All the Catholic powers would be arrayed against her, and even the Protestant German princes, aside from the Elector Palatine, being subject to the emperor, whose daughter Philip of Spain had now married, had already withdrawn from the Prince of Orange.

Thus cornered, Catharine saw one speedy, bold, and yet effective means of release. This means she employed, harking back to the bloody councils of Alva at Bayonne, in 1565.

While Louis of Nassau was patiently awaiting release in the city of Mons, and his brother was advancing as rapidly as his ill-disciplined and ill-paid army would permit, eagerly awaiting the coming of Coligny and his force, there fell upon them both, upon the hosts of Protestantism, upon all Europe, the "sledge-hammer blow" of the butchery of St. Bartholomew, under which all Christendom reeled and staggered.

Coligny would never lead an army against the dark tyranny of Spain. His body, stabbed through the breast, was thrown from an upper window of the house where he lodged into the Rue de Berthesy, and for three days that body was dragged through the streets by the canaille of Paris. The head of the noble old Christian warrior, severed from the trunk, was sent to the Cardinal de Lorraine, who chanced to be in Rome. Among the first to fall was the noble lord de Teligny, whose fair young wife, Louise de Coligny, bride of but a year, thus saw her father and her husband perish in a single night. Again and again, it is said, those sent to murder the chivalrous young nobleman, "overcome by compassion for his youth and manly beauty, or by respect for his graceful manners and extraordinary learning," departed, laying no hand upon him. A shot from an arquebus, fired from the street by a guard, struck him down, however, but too speedily.

Among the bloodiest and most insatiable of the assassins was the Duc de Montpensier, and no court lady reveled in the carnival of blood with the wild abandon of his young wife, Catherine de Lorraine.

With full effect the unparalleled crime of St. Bartholomew's Eve, in which all the Huguenot leaders were foully murdered, fell upon the campaign of the Nassaus in the Netherlands.

"*It has pleased God,*" wrote the prince, "*to take*

away every hope which we could have founded upon man; the king (Charles IX.) *has published that the massacre was by his orders, and has forbidden all his subjects, upon pain of death, to assist me; he has, moreover, sent succour to Alva. Had it not been for this, we had been masters of the duke, and should have made him capitulate at our pleasure."*

The troops of the prince, finding him unsupported and unable to pay them promptly, mutinied and threatened to betray him into the hands of Alva.

Unsuccessful in his attempt to relieve Mons, where Louis lay confined with fever, the prince was forced to flee for his life, after the rout at Hermigny. Louis, heart-broken at the event of St. Bartholomew, in which scores of his friends perished, was released by Alva after the fall of Mons, for even the Duke's harsh spirit was not proof against the singular charm of the count. He suffered him to be carried back to Dillenburg on a litter, and his fond mother nursed him back to life.

The prince, meanwhile, retreated to Zwolle, the capital of Overyssel, whence he wrote to his brother John, October eighteenth: *"I have determined to go over to Holland and Zeeland to maintain their interests, so far as may be possible, purposing there to make my sepulchre."*

The prophecy was of literal fulfillment. Never again did the prince go beyond the borders of the Netherlands. His lot was cast with the land of his adoption from that day until the bitter end. He had seen again a powerful army, raised by incredible sacrifice and personal labor, collapse almost without a blow; the great combination with the court of France, in which he had trusted, and which had been built up by years of negotiation, had been shattered in a single night of treason and horror. Again his powerful friends fell away, and insult and reproach fell thick and fast upon his head.

Never in the darkest night of his humiliation, in

the year 1568, had the prince known the depth below the depth of defeat and disappointment which
his soul now sounded. He had been a profoundly
ambitious man, not unlawfully or wholly selfishly
ambitious, but still cherishing ardent hope and desire to carry out in a brilliant maturity the promise
of his brilliant youth.

But, as heretofore, the prince had been ever
greatest when his fortunes were at their lowest,
so in this extremity the true grandeur of the man
shone forth.

Stripped finally and forever of the last trappings
of worldly splendor, he who had been the cousin of
emperors and the comrade of kings, felt at last the
great primitive bond of humanity, the sense of the
equality of all men before God, and with cheerful courage and with what one who observed him
names "an incredible sweetness," he made common cause from this time onward with the simple
burghers of Delft and of Dordrecht and the other
towns.

Alone on this his narrow isthmus, the "historic
strip of swamp" to which his horizon was now for
the time bounded, the prince girded himself for
"single combat with the great Spanish monarchy,"
not for a moment deceived as to the terrible odds
against which he must fight.   With unfaltering devotion he set himself to the defense of the towns
of Holland and Zeeland from the onward march of
the now victorious Alva.

"*If he prove too strong for us,*" he cries in an impassioned letter to the King of Spain, "*we will rather
die an honorable death and leave a praiseworthy fame,
than bend our necks and reduce our dear Fatherland
to such slavery.   Herein are all our cities pledged to
each other to stand every siege, to dare to the utmost,
to endure every possible misery, yea, rather to set fire to
all our homes and be consumed into ashes together,
than ever submit to the decrees of this cruel tyrant.*"

Small wonder that the people to whose cause he thus gave himself "worshiped the prince as if he were their Messiah!"

He who had once seen great things for himself saw them now no more ; but his vision, purified in anguish and humiliation, had become clearer and he endured henceforth as seeing the invisible.

XXXIV

ROUBICHON ONCE MORE

IT was 1574, the second year of the War of the
Towns. The Duke of Alva had departed from
the Provinces forever, deploring bitterly that
he had not gained the approbation of his king while
he had incurred the malevolence and hatred of
every individual in the country. Don Luis de Re-
quesens, who had succeeded the bloody duke, found
upon his arrival that his most pressing duty was the
relief of the besieged city of Middelburg, which alone
in the island of Walcheren was still held by Mondragon for the King of Spain. For this purpose
seventy-five Spanish ships were collected at Bergen
op Zoom under command of Julian Romero, while
a smaller fleet was assembled at Antwerp under
d'Avila. Both fleets were provisioned for the starv-
ing garrison in Middelburg, and their duty was to
effect a junction of forces as speedily as possible.

The early twilight of a January day was settling
over the besieged city. In the old Tontorf mansion
in the Lange Delft light already shone from the
windows of the great oak-wainscoted room, once
known by its owners as the "Gossaert-Saal."

The portrait of the Master of the Rolls, Adolf
Hardinck, once the glory of the place, had disappeared, having been destroyed by the Spaniards,
and with it the other portraits, the finely carved
cabinets, the plate and crystal which adorned the
room. The massive table, however, which still
held the central space, was the one at which Nikolaas Tontorf, nine years ago sat with wife and
children around him : and in the place of the master-

printer, yes in his very chair, sat the Spanish veteran Mondragon, who stoutly defended the city
against the besieging Beggar forces that surrounded
it by land and sea.

A great fire roared up Nikolaas Tontorf's hospitable chimney giving an aspect of cheer to the otherwise dreary room which, littered with officers' ac-
coutrements, pieces of armor, pistols, arquebuses,
and piles of dispatches, had little left of the stately
beauty, the shining cleanliness, and exquisite order
which belonged to it in the lifetime of Wendelmutha Tontorf.

Mondragon, a careworn, grizzled warrior, of countenance severe and fiery glance, looked up from
the letter he was writing with a rapid hand and
mouth hard set. A young officer, whose uniform
hung loosely on his lean shrunken frame and whose
famished eyes looked out mournfully from their
bony sockets had entered the room.

"What is it, captain?" Mondragon asked, impatient of interruption.

" Your pardon, your excellency, but a sailor has
made his way through the enemy's lines," replied
the younger man.

" Whence comes he ? "

" According to his story, from the fleet of General
d'Avila."

" Hah ! is it so ? " exclaimed Mondragon, starting
to his feet. "Is it then confirmed that the ships
seen off Flushing are Spanish ? "

"Yes, your excellency. We have received signals which we believe unmistakable."

The old warrior's face brightened. " Call the
fellow in instantly, Trenchart ! " he cried.

In another moment there stood before the Spanish general a tall, sinewy sailor in Spanish uniform,
gaunt-eyed and brown indeed as a Spaniard, with
cheeks as hollow as Trenchart's and heavy brown
beard and moustachios.

"Your name, sir ? " demanded Mondragon, fixing his fiery eyes full upon the stranger.

"Roubichon, excellency."

"You come from the fleet of d'Avila ? "

The reply was a brief, respectful bow.

"At your service, excellency."

"What are your credentials ? "

"Nothing save the dangers I have faced to come hither. I was dared to do it by my shipmates, and believed his excellency would honor my effort with his confidence, and permit me to serve him."

Looking sternly at the speaker, something in the sturdy manliness of his bearing seemed to satisfy the veteran. With a sound between a growl and a greeting he proceeded with his questions.

"How many ships do you number ? "

"Five and twenty."

"That is well. We had counted but a score. With what purpose do they lie off Flushing ? "

"To learn how much longer your garrison can stand the siege."

Mondragon laughed shortly.

"Tell your master that he can perhaps reckon for himself. The death rate among my men from starvation is twenty a day."

"I will tell my master."

"In the month since Christmas a thousand souls have perished within these walls. Our daily fare is linseed husks with an occasional *ragout* of mice or dog-flesh. Tell your master I invite him to keep the feast of St. Blasius with me. I can perhaps make shift to dine him on a young kitten or a well-fed rat if it suits his stomach."

Roubichon did not reply at once. His eyes had strayed momentarily from the face of the old general and in that one instant had swept the room with a glance of devouring eagerness. With a curious thickness in his utterance he said :

"My master, the Señor d'Avila, fearing that you

must be in extremity says that if he cannot effect a union with the fleet of Romero in a few days he would beg to advise that you capitulate."

The old man's face grew grim.

"Where is Romero? know you?"

"Nay, excellency, that is what above all things my master desires most to know. If they can meet, a bold blow can be struck, and will be speedily. Of that he begs you to rest assured."

"Meanwhile, what can d'Avila do for us? Has he strength enough to force passage through the Beggar fleet?"

"Nay, excellency. What are five and twenty ships when it comes to meeting those devils?"

"True," said Mondragon, nodding thoughtfully. After a moment's reflection he spoke again.

"Well, my brave fellow," he said, "it is at least something to know that our fellow-soldiers have a heart to come to our defense. Your coming is welcome, and also timely, since I was about dispatching this letter," and he pointed to the sheet on the table beside him, "and dreaded to send one of my poor famished fellows on so perilous an errand as to take it through the enemy's lines."

"I can take it to my master in brief time, señor, and will do it gladly."

"How will you make your way through the lines?"

"As I came; swimming where there is water, running where there is land, fighting where there is need of it."

A sombre smile relaxed the features of the soldier.

"Well answered," he said grimly. Turning then to Trenchart, who had stood in silence at the closed door throughout the interview, he said:

"Send in some of our famine fare for this brave fellow, captain," and as Trenchart left the room, he added:

"We have an old Dutch woman who seems to

belong to the house to cook for our staff. She can make a very fair mess of a haunch of dog or cat on occasion. We will share what we have with you, sir. Pray be seated."

A moment later Trenchart re-entered the room closely followed by a tidy old woman in white cap and apron, bearing a tray of food.

In the wrinkled visage of this woman Norbert Tontorf at once, with a wild throb of his heart, recognized Hendrika, the old family servant of his father's house.

In another instant he grew calm for well he knew that in his present self the faithful soul could never recognize the blithe, blonde, ruddy-cheeked Dutch lad, once her pride and darling.

Without even looking at him, moving with a curious mechanical submissiveness, Hendrika placed the food before him, and was about to withdraw when Mondragon signalled to her to wait.

"Will you have wine or spirits, my man?" he asked with gruff kindliness. "I have still something left of my private store."

"Neither, thank you, excellency."

Norbert's back was turned toward Hendrika. She could not see his face, and all the more for that reason the sound of his voice broke on her ears with startling effect.

Clasping her hands together in a wild gesture of amazed recognition, she darted forward, fixed her eyes on his averted face and then, seeing in it for all its ruggedness some witness to his identity which only a loving heart could have found, and forgetting all else in her joy she threw herself on her knees before him, crying out:

"Oh, Master Norbert, it is yourself, come back again to your old home and poor old Hendrika after all these weary years!"

Looking up at the old general with the familiarity of her senile weakness, she added with tears:

"I have held him on my bosom, your excellency, when he was but a babe, in this very room!"

Norbert, white through his sunburned skin, rose and lifted the poor woman gently to her feet.

Mondragon had risen also.

"What means this, sir?" he asked sternly. "A son of this house is no Spaniard, nor even a Glipper. So much I know. Trenchart, call up your men. Methinks our good Hendrika has unmasked a spy."

Trenchart left the room on the instant.

"Pardon me, your excellency, but a moment," said Norbert quietly. "Hendrika," turning to the trembling and bewildered creature, "we will meet again; but now this gentleman and I have matters of importance to discuss."

Taking her hand then, while Mondragon gazed in mute amazement, he led her gently to the door, and having dismissed her with a smile, turned and faced the Spanish general.

"Excellency, I am your prisoner," he said then.

Marveling much at his composure and the firmness of his bearing, Mondragon exclaimed:

"By our Lady, then, who is our prisoner, who wears a Spanish uniform, bears a French name, and seems to have been born a Dutchman?"

"Your excellency," Norbert said, almost as if relieved to speak at last in his true character, "I was born indeed, in this very house, and grew up at this very fireside," and he pointed to the still glowing chimney. "From this house my father, my mother, and my young sister were led to cruel death at the hands of traitors, and this, which was aforetime the happiest home in all Zeeland, was lost to me forever. If I have come back here to die I can at least say that there is no spot on earth where I would sooner die," and he folded his arms across his breast, and with mouth firm set and steadfast look faced the Spanish general.

"Small doubt about your dying," said Mondragon grimly. "We give but short shrift to spies, my man, however cleverly they play their parts."

At a signal from Trenchart several soldiers at once entered the room, and without further parley Norbert found himself hurried through the familiar hall into the courtyard. Crossing this, his captors drew him into the loggia, where stood Hendrika herself beating her breast and crying aloud at the fate she had brought upon the son of her beloved master.

Norbert had only time for a look at the broken-hearted woman, but it was a look in which affection was clouded by no reproach. He had not learned in the school of William the Silent all these years in vain.

With rude urgency Norbert was now led down the lowest stairway and thrust into the windowless subterranean room which had served as the secret printing room of Nikolaas Tontorf.

Having searched him for weapons and money, and stripped him of both with many curses, the soldiers told him that the general had said since he was fain to die in his old home he would grant him the privilege by means of a length of good hemp rope at sunrise.

With this grim sentence, they closed and bolted the heavy door.

Norbert groped his way about the well-remembered chamber with strangely mingled feelings. The presses, rough with rust and dust-covered, stood in their former places. Save for them the room was empty. Doubtless it was used now solely as a prison.

How often in his far-off, happy boyhood had he worked at those same presses by his father's side, turning out the pages of the coveted Bibles in the long night watches! And now he stood again within those heavy walls, alone save for memories, under sure sentence of immediate death, a storm-tested, weary, and yet undaunted man.

The slow hours passed. No sound broke the breathless hush of the place save the monotonous tread of the soldier on guard before his door.

A muffled sound of voices indicated when the watch was changed, and Norbert believed this to mark the hour of midnight. Waiting until all was still again save for the steady pacing of the guard, he groped his way along the wall as he had already done before in the darkness, until his finger touched the secret spring in the invisible panel, known now, as he believed, to no living soul on earth save himself.

Instantly the panel slipped aside and access was laid open to the hidden repository of Nikolaas Tontorf's work. The sliding shelves Norbert found to be still heavily loaded with books, doubtless exactly as his father had piled them there at the close of his last night's work. Strange, hidden, and yet eloquent monument to the persistent devotion of the man!

Norbert felt the ropes. He shook them softly. They were firm and stout as ever, for all the silent years in which they had hung useless. Yes, he could dare trust himself to them. He entered and touched the panel behind him, which slipped back at once to its proper place with a soft click of the spring. Then, sailor fashion, Norbert climbed by the ropes to the closet above, and, down on his hands and knees, he felt for the spring which should release him from his prison, though it might be into yet more imminent peril.

Having found the spring, he realized what, for the time being, he had forgotten, that it must be manipulated from without. No pressure from within could serve to stir it a hair's breadth.

The perspiration broke forth in cold drops on Norbert's forehead. Had he escaped the hands of the Spaniards but to bury himself in a living tomb?

It could not be. From the inner lining of his doublet he drew out a stout knife which had escaped the vigilance of the soldiers. Down on his knees again he found the small metal bar of the spring and began the process of sawing it in twain.

A long process it proved to be and full of indescribable suspense, since any moment might reveal to the man on guard below that his cell was empty and an alarm be given. The sickening, mouldy vapors in the narrow, stifling closet, the blackness of darkness in which he was enshrouded, added to the overpowering difficulty of his task.

His brain grew dizzy, breathing became well-nigh impossible, death itself seemed welcome and no longer to be fought, when in some far corner of his brain a sweet, gay voice seemed to sing:

> " If my lover gentle prove,
>   Knightly, brave, and true to love,
> Slave and servant will I be ;
>   Tell me, tell me, am I true?"

"Yes, Jeanne," he murmured, in a choking whisper, "your lover will hold himself brave and knightly for your sweet sake."

In another five minutes the knife fell from his benumbed hand, but it had done its work, the spring was severed.

Noiselessly the panel slid aside, and Norbert, slipping behind a chest, was at once within what had been the inner room of his father's private office. It was dark, but in the chamber beyond, on a small table, a candle was burning. The room had been turned into an officer's bedchamber. The officer, who lay heavily asleep on the narrow iron bed, was Captain Trenchart. His broad, slouched hat and long military mantle were thrown carelessly upon a chair.

Catching up these, Norbert strode across the room so lightly that not a board creaked, opened the door, and wrapping himself hastily in the mantle, and placing the hat well over his forehead, he crossed the loggia and entered the great courtyard.

Directing his steps without a moment's delay to the vaulted entrance at the side, he strode imperiously past the sleepy guard with a muttered word under his breath, which might or might not have resembled the countersign for the night, but which the guard was plainly too indifferent and too accustomed to midnight sallies of the young Spanish officers to care to challenge.

In another moment Norbert had reached the Lange Delft, and now his knowledge of his own native town stood him in good stead. An old, disused canal bed, covered now by streets, led from the Lange Delft straight to the city moat. It had been the favorite haunt of his adventurous boyhood. Diving into its unused recesses, which had apparently been forgotten by the people of Middelburg since he encountered in them no sign of life, Norbert soon made his way to the moat at a point where, below the city wall, no guard was stationed.

Without a moment's hesitation he plunged into the icy waters of the canal and swam, unseen, to the opposite side. A rapid run of a few miles along the dikes brought him safely within the patriot lines, which he reached exhausted, but triumphant.

On the following day, being the nineteenth day of January, Norbert presented himself before the prince, who was at Zierikzee, directing the operations of the siege of Middelburg.

The prince inquired eagerly as to the results of the perilous mission which the young man had voluntarily undertaken in order to learn the true strength and condition of the Spanish garrison.

"The townspeople and soldiers are alike famishing, but five-and-twenty Spanish ships, under d'Avila, lie off Flushing, ready to join the fleet of Romero at the first possible moment. They will then be a hundred ships strong, and if they succeed in carrying through their cargoes of provision, Middelburg will be lost. Mondragon is as brave as a lion, and although his men are dying a score a day, he will hold out while there is hope of relief. We Dutch are not alone in our ability to stand these bitter sieges."

Such was the substance of Norbert's report.

The fleet of Romero, heavily freighted with provisions, still lay in the harbor of Bergen op Zoom.

At the direction of the prince, the Beggar fleet, under Admiral Boisot, at once moved up the East Scheldt and took its position nearly opposite Bergen, whereupon the prince himself, putting out from Zierikzee in his own galley, assembled the officers and men of his armada and adjured them with all the fervor and eloquence of which he was master not to permit Middelburg, the key to all Zeeland, and even now on the point of yielding to the patriot forces, to be wrested from their grasp.

The response was a burst of wild cheering. On the sea, if not on the land, the Beggars felt themselves master. With one accord officers and men declared themselves ready to shed every drop of blood in their veins for the prince and the Fatherland.

Then followed the fierce naval battle of Bergen, in which the Beggars grappled the Spanish ships to their own in the narrow channel and fought with wild and desperate courage with battle-axes, pikes, pistols, and daggers, giving no quarter and asking none, casting every prisoner forthwith into the sea, until twelve hundred Spanish soldiers slain and fifteen ships captured, the enemy knew themselves beaten and retreated into the friendly port of Bergen.

Then from the wet and slippery decks of the
victorious fleet with wild and terrible melody rose
the Beggars' song, and filled sea and sky with its
thrilling echoes :

" The Spanish Inquisition has God's malediction,
The Spanish Inquisition of blood-drinkers' fame !
The Spanish Inquisition will find a meet conviction,
The Spanish Inquisition has played out its game !

" Long live the Beggars ! Christians, ye must cry,
Long live the Beggars ! Pluck up courage then,
Long live the Beggars ! If you would not die,
Long live the Beggars ! shout ye Christian men !"

Back to Antwerp d'Avila, hearing of the fate of
his countrymen, brought his fleet with hot haste,
while Romero coolly confessing that he was "a
land-fighter and no sailor," made good his way to
Brussels, both commanders acknowledging that the
city of Middelburg must be abandoned to its fate.

Further struggle was plainly useless and on the
eighteenth of February the prince received the
articles of capitulation from Mondragon, to whom
he granted honorable conditions, permitting him
and his troops to leave the place with their arms,
ammunition, and personal property.

"The capitulation of the fiery Mondragon, and
the capture of Middelburg," says the brilliant
English biographer[1] of the prince, "marked the
epoch when the Spaniard was forced to recognize
the Hollanders as ' belligerents,' not as rebels, and
the prince as their lawful stadtholder, and not a
proscribed outlaw."

The citizens of Middelburg, glad to shake off the
Spanish yoke to which they had so long ignomin-
iously submitted, took the oath of fidelity to the
prince as stadtholder, and from this day returned
loyally and with undivided hearts to their patriotic
allegiance.

---

[1] Frederic Harrison.

The first man to enter the now deserted house in the Lange Delft on that February day was Norbert Tontorf. Within the beautiful portico he was met by the new burgomaster, the Syndic Heldring, who placed the key of his father's house in Norbert's hands.

"It is the wish of the town council, worthy Mijnheer Tontorf," said the burgomaster with grave ceremony, "that the house of your father, which has by the surrender of the Spaniards become the property of the city of Middelburg, should by it be presented to your father's son in token of the good service rendered by you in the release of our fair city from the Spanish yoke, and in everlasting memorial to the virtues and patriotic services of Nikolaas Tontorf."

Deeply moved, so that words of reply failed to come at his bidding, Norbert received the noble gift.

Then, when he found himself left alone as he supposed in his father's house, a sob in the dark recesses of the corridor called Norbert's attention to the weeping Hendrika. She was lurking in the background, awaiting opportunity to implore pardon for her innocent betrayal of her young master to Mondragon.

"Not a word, not a word, Hendrika!" commanded Norbert imperiously, concealing his own emotion ; "since the end is glorious all is well. It is for you now to bring the dear old home aspect back to this dismal barrack. Stop your tears and get to work."

A few days thereafter, the prince having arrived, and having in person restored to the inhabitants of Middelburg their ancient charter, or *Keure,* and the whole city being wild with rejoicing, another scene of a character not wholly different was enacted in the house in the Lange Delft.

In the Gossaert-Saal, on his own beloved hearthstone, stood Norbert Tontorf, not flushed with triumph, but bearing himself with the humility and gravity which became the son of a line of martyrs, led to martyrdom from that very spot. Before him stood the Prince of Orange, his liege lord and beloved master.

"This house," said Norbert, with difficulty commanding his voice, for poignant memories in that moment crowded thick and fast upon him, "my father's house, my lord, and my grandfather's, has, by the good will of the city of Middelburg, been given back to me. Shall I have a home like this when my master is without a home? Greatly should I shame me to hold as my own such a possession. It is no prince's palace, but a plain burgher's house, but such as it is, freely as it was given to me, I give it herewith to you, whose service is dearer to me than my own life, praying that you will deign so to honor my father's name as to receive it."

With tears in his eyes the lonely prince clasped Norbert's hands. There remained to him that day indeed, of all his vast possessions and ancestral palaces in the Netherlands, not so much as a single roof which he could claim for his own use.

"This house, Tontorf," he said, "is a sacred place. With a reverence and gratitude for which I can find no words, I accept it from your hands as my dwelling-place, my *home* in Zeeland. Not without compensation, however, shall it pass to me from the hands of its devoted, heroic owner, and not without the condition that it shall remain the home also of the son of Nikolaas Tontorf."

XXXV

THE LONELIEST MAN IN EUROPE

GREAT and terrible sixteenth century in which the human spirit, so long slumbering and enslaved, awoke to its sublime though awful destiny of freedom and self-direction !

Few indeed were the spirits, noble and ardent, which, reaching in its tragic course to heroic height and spiritual greatness, were suffered to live out their appointed time !

"*All the country is longing for you as for the Angel Gabriel*" ; so wrote the prince to his brother Louis, "his sword, his mouthpiece, his pride."

Two months had passed since the capitulation of Middelburg. Leyden was closely besieged by the Spaniards, and from the east the gallant Louis, with health restored and his old unconquerable, buoyant courage, was leading a small army to join the forces of the prince in the neighborhood of Delft, whence together they would march to the relief of Leyden. With Louis at the head of the reinforcements were his brothers John and Henry, of Nassau, and Duke Christoph, son of the Elector Palatine ; the two latter youthful knights of two and three and twenty.

Thus the four Nassau brothers were now together in the field, fighting for the freedom of the Nether-lands.

The days of April passed and the prince, from his camp on an island between the Waal and the Meuse, waited and watched with indescribable eagerness for the coming of his brothers.

"*Let me know when you plan to cross the river*, he writes, "*so that I can meet you.*"

Then, having heard rumors of an engagement
with the Spaniards, the following day:

"*I beg you to let me know who of yours are left on
the field or wounded. . . My regards to the Duke
Christoph and my brothers.*"

Three days passed without tidings and on April
twenty-first the prince writes in deepest anxiety
and dread:

*My Brothers: Being in the greatest trouble in the
world at having had no answer from you to the seven
letters I have written since the 10th, I have decided to
send you this messenger. . . Only let me hear your
condition.*"

No answer ever came.

The river had been crossed, the battle had been
fought, and on the field it was the heroic Louis of
Nassau, his brother Henry, and the young Count
Palatine who were left dead in the trampled and
blood-red marshes of Mook Heath, of whose tragedy
the heavens themselves had given fearful portent.

In a suspense which was like slow death to him
the prince, broken-hearted at last, struggled on.
For a time both the households of the elector at
Heidelberg and of the Nassaus at Dillenburg refused to believe that their young heroes were slain,
since their bodies were never found.

Two months after the battle of Mook Heath, a
piteous wail comes from the aged Countess Juliana
of Nassau, that she can still learn nothing of their
fate. Two only of her noble band of sons, William
and John, were left her now.

At Heidelberg the summer, heavy with suspense,
wore slowly away.

On an August morning Charlotte de Bourbon,
with the Electress Amalie leaning on her arm, was
walking on the great terrace of the castle before the
ancient chapel of Saint Udalrich. From the Glock-
enthurm, looming to the east of the terrace through-

the silvery morning mist, could be heard the sound of the great castle bell, slow tolling. At the feet of the Jettenbühl, the crag which descends sheer from the terrace wall, the quaint, gabled roofs of the old town rose through thick masses of greenery, but the lovely Neckar valley and the mountains of the Odenwald were hid from view in a misty curtain.

The face of the electress was careworn and anxious while that of Mademoiselle also bore the stamp of the sorrows which the last two years had brought her in the death of Jeanne d'Albret and the manifold murders of St. Bartholomew. As the Princess Amalie listened to the mournful funeral bell quiet tears were falling unheeded down her cheeks. "My lord has given the word at last," she murmured. "Even he has abandoned hope. Our gallant Christoph will never come back to us."

Charlotte could not command her voice for a little space, but in a moment she said softly :

"Ah, dearest friend, never have I seen a grief more nobly borne than that of the elector."

"Yes, Charlotte," returned madame, "though he has aged full fast under it. He has gone alone now into the chapel to pray for submission to the good will of God."

Bending her head Amalie's lips moved in silent prayer. As the two stood with bowed heads and folded hands, the Elector Friedrich and his daughter Kunigunde joined them, coming from the chapel.

The bell ceased tolling and with trembling lips the young girl murmured :

"Christoph loved the prospect from this terrace more than all else in Heidelberg, father. How often I have seen him leaning on this wall at eventide——" and her voice choked with sobs.

"Be of good courage, children," said the deep, steady voice of the white-haired elector ; "the lad is dead, but he died on the bed of honor. I shall go to him, but he will not return to me. Glad am I

2 A

that he fell in the cause of God! Let us not think
of him alone, or solely of our own sorrow. Think
too, of his noble companions, of Count Louis, in
whom our prince has lost his very right hand, and
of the boy Heinrich, his grand old mother's pride
and darling, so young, so pure in life and heart."

A strange, unearthly calmness was in the quiet
words, a calmness new won in solitary prayer, the
calmness of him who "best can drink his cup of
woe, triumphant over pain."

"In truth," said Amalie, "I fear me the mourning in Dillenburg is yet sorer than here to-day. The
Countess Juliana has had sorrow upon sorrow."

"Let us go to my cabinet, dear wife," said the
elector, taking her hand, his brave eyes dim; "let
us together write a letter to the countess that we
may share our mutual sorrow, and the comfort of
our God."

Together the princely pair with slow steps entered the castle and Charlotte was left to soothe
the sobbing girl, Kunigunde, as her loving nature
gave her a rare power to do.

Then Jeanne de Mousson appearing upon the
terrace a letter in her hand, her face seeming to
speak of new trouble, Kunigunde hastened away
to hide her tear-stained face.

"What is it, Jeanne?" asked Charlotte anxiously. "From whom is your letter?"

"From Captain Tontorf."

"The captain is a faithful correspondent, Jeanne,"
returned Charlotte, to whom Jeanne's great secret
still remained untold. "What news does he give?
How is the prince bearing this latest blow?"

"Mademoiselle, I fear me that even his endurance has failed. Captain Tontorf says he has
borne himself for the past month like a man benumbed by despair, in a silent, grim agony which
has been terrible to see. 'None the less,'" and
she lifted the letter and read, "'my lord has

worked on, never stopping to rest, hardly daring methinks to pause lest he could never begin again. Day and night he has fought for the relief of Leyden. We are in camp between Rotterdam and Delft. I write in my tent. A little more than two weeks ago his highness went with Paul Buys to Capelle and directed the piercing of the great outer dyke in sixteen places, for he is determined to drive out the Spaniards around Leyden by letting in the sea. The good people who will lose all say, *"Better a drowned land than a lost land,"* and so the deed is done. God give it success, for it is the last hope for Leyden !

" ' But success will mean little to Holland if it must lose its leader,' " Jeanne read on ; " ' even the prince is human, and grief, anxiety, and exposure in the flooded fields have done their work. A violent fever has attacked him and he lies for the most part unconscious, wakening only to dispatch a messenger to bid them of Leyden hold out yet a little longer, and then sinking again into stupor. It has gone abroad in the camp that his is no simple intermittent fever, as was at first supposed, but the pest itself, and hardly can Brunynck and I find them who will come near his tent for terror of their poor lives.' ' "

Charlotte had changed color, and her look betrayed deep agitation as she held out her hand and murmured :

" Let me see the letter."

Silently Jeanne handed it to her, but a singular confusion and trepidation were visible in her face as she watched that of her lady.

In another moment, with a swift movement of amazement Charlotte looked up, and pointing to the head of the letter cried under her breath :

" Jeanne, what does this mean ? Tell me instantly ! This letter from Captain Tontorf to you, Jeanne de Mousson, begins, ' *My wife* ' ! "

"And if it is true, dearest lady," said Jeanne, facing Charlotte with firm, fearless look, "it is for your own dear sake that I became the wife of Captain Tontorf, and for your dear sake that I have withheld from you the knowledge of it, lest you should send me from your side while yet you needed your poor Jeanne! Even so you sent Jeannette Vassetz back to France when she confessed that the Sieur George d'Averly had won her heart. Do you think I would have my dearest lady left alone?"

With which Jeanne, womanlike, burst into a fit of hearty and honest crying.

Then the whole story, short, brave, and simple as it was, was told, and Charlotte de Bourbon knew as she had never known before what the love of the Gascon maiden for her signified in its self-sacrificing strength.

"Your promise to Captain Tontorf," said Mademoiselle, as they sat awhile later confronting each other with flushed cheeks and tear-dimmed eyes in her boudoir whither they had betaken themselves, "your promise, Jeanne, bound your husband not to claim you until Charlotte de Bourbon bade him so to do?"

"Yes, my lady," and Jeanne bent her head, her dark eyes downcast.

"Do you love your husband, Jeanne?" The question was asked in the softest of whispers, and the lips that spoke trembled.

Jeanne lifted her eyes then and looking straight into her lady's face threw herself upon her breast, her face hidden there.

"Oh, I do love him, my lady," she sobbed out, "I cannot, cannot help it! I have loved him since the first day that ever I saw him there on our river at home. Forgive me that I do! I will never leave you to go to him, unless you bid me, and he knows I never will. He is too brave and true to ask me."

"But what if I should bid you go to him now, this very day? Would you be glad or sorry? or would you be afraid of a camp of soldiers and a sick man from whom his craven servants flee?" and Charlotte's gentle lips curled with irrepressible scorn.

"Would I be afraid?"

The Béarnaise had sprung to her feet, her eyes flashing through their tears.

"Try me and see!" she cried. "Bid me go and I will show the men who dare to weigh their lives in the balance against the life of the saviour of the Netherlands, that a woman dares more than they! Together my Tontorf and I will minister to the needs of his highness, and if a woman's wit and a woman's nursing can win him back to life, he shall live!"

"Then go, Jeanne," said her lady quietly. "Do not let us waste an hour in needless parley. Take with you the aunt of Jacqueline, Vrouw Van Marle, for a companion, and I will beg the elector to furnish you with a goodly escort. By the grace of God you are a married woman, and a married woman can go anywhere. But for good speed's sake and greater safety, Jeanne, keep your veil drawn, and hide those eyes of yours as much as you may."

"I might wear the costume in which I took my wedding journey," replied Jeanne demurely, "I think that would make me perfectly safe."

"And Jeanne," added her lady, a soft color rising in her cheeks, "will you tell the prince, when he is better, that he is not alone, not wholly bereft and forsaken—that he has friends in Heidelberg who pray for him, who never, never forget?"

"Yes, my lady, I will tell him."

XXXVI

THE PRINCE CONVERSES WITH HIS CAPTAIN'S BRIDE

"WHERE is that glorious Gascon girl, with the eyes?" asked the prince dreamily.

Weeks had passed.

They had brought him in his extremity of weakness to Delft, believing that the air and the better comforts possible there would hasten his recovery. He lay now in a cool, shaded chamber in the old convent of Saint Agatha, always his abode when in Delft, and beside him sat Norbert Tontorf.

The prince was emaciated to a degree from the fever and from their hollow sockets the large brown eyes, dull and lusterless now, looked out with the peculiar pathetic appeal of extreme exhaustion.

"She is coming even now, your highness," said Norbert gently.

A door was opened at the far end of the room and with noiseless steps Jeanne de Mousson entered bearing a tray on which was a bowl of broth for the sick man. She wore a simple gown of a deep blue color with dainty ruffles of white needlework around the open throat and at the wrists ; a trim black satin bodice set off the pliant grace of her shape, and her brown hair was rolled in burnished waves from her low forehead. Norbert watched her with a sudden exultation that her bright, girlish beauty was released at last from the hard, conventual disguise and concealment.

As she stood by the side of the prince's couch, Jeanne's rich and brilliant bloom was fairly startling in contrast with the deathlike pallor of his face.

406

Lifting his eyes weakly the prince smiled at the sight of so much loveliness, and took the nourishment she carefully administered without a word.

Then as Jeanne turned to leave the bedside the prince caught her hand in his feeble grasp and murmured:

"Who are you, my child? and how came you here?"

Hitherto he had been too weak and his thoughts too confused by his malady to care to ask a question save for the city of Leyden,—the one neverchanging anxiety which even the shadow of death could not abate.

At the question Jeanne's cheeks grew yet rosier and she glanced shyly at Norbert, who at once approaching the side of the prince and taking her hand in his, said quietly:

"She is my wife, if it please your highness, formerly the demoiselle de Mousson, who came from the Abbey of Jouarre with the Princess de Bourbon. We were married more than two years since, but the lady's duty to the princess has kept us hitherto apart."

A spark of light kindled in the hollow eyes of the prince and the sorrowful lines about the mouth relaxed.

"By my faith, Tontorf," he murmured with a touch of his natural animation, "it is something late to say, if it please me! I had thought I had given you work enough to have kept you out of mischief."

"We took brief time for our wooing and wedding, my lord," said Norbert laughing, "and until the lady appeared in camp the other night, and my orderly brought me word that my wife asked speech of me, I was like to forget that I was fortunate enough to have a wife. It was the first time that I had so much as given her a kiss, but she had to take it then, I assure you, my lord, for the sight

of her was the first ray of promise or hope we had
had for weeks. God bless Mademoiselle de Bourbon for sending her ! "

"Amen. But I fear the captain does not deserve
such a wife," added the prince, who was smiling
for the first time in months, "since he was in danger of forgetting that he had one. What say you,
Madame Tontorf ? "

"I could not forgive him, monseigneur," replied
Jeanne, with her charming Béarnaise accent, "had
he put me from his mind for any save your highness. I knew ever that I must take second place in
his heart since the first must always be yours."

The prince fixed his eyes full upon the two eloquent young faces, with a smile tender and benign.
He essayed to speak but his voice faltered.

Jeanne seeing that he was weary made haste to
leave the room.

The following day she sat alone with the prince,
Norbert being sent to carry dispatches to Admiral
Boisot. For the water had risen around Leyden,
and a fleet of two hundred ships, manned by the
Beggars of the Sea, and provisioned for the starv-
ing Leydeners stood now but five miles from the
city, just off the great *Land-scheiding*, within which
the Spaniards, still safe from the flood, lay in their
trenches. The prince's order to Boisot was to
carry the *Land-scheiding* immediately at all costs.
In spite of the prostration of his fever, every
detail of the situation was firmly grasped by him
and ceaselessly pondered.

But now as he sat propped in a chair beside an
open window through which the September air
flowed in a warm and vitalizing flood, the heavy
burden of his State cares and even of Leyden's
peril, seemed to slip for the moment from the mind
of the prince.

"Madame," he said, looking into Jeanne's face
as she sat repairing his neglected garments by a

small table, "your husband, who goes yet unpunished, by the way, for the trick he has served us,
said something, methought, as to your coming
hither at the bidding of Mademoiselle de Bourbon."

"Yes, monseigneur," Jeanne responded quickly.
"At the moment in which she learned of the illness
of your highness, Mademoiselle learned also for the
first time that her devoted servant, Jeanne de
Mousson, had become the wife of Captain Tontorf.
My lady is swift to act when she sees need, and
she sent me on my way to Holland even that same
day."

"And you would not have joined your husband
save at her bidding ? "

"Nay, monseigneur. Captain Tontorf had made
me a solemn pledge never to claim me until Mademoiselle of her own free will should bid him."

"Such devotion is rare, madame."

"Such a mistress is rarer, your highness."

The prince was silent, but the deep lines of
wasting sorrow and suffering seemed to fade perceptibly from his face as a new, unuttered hope
stirred to life, new, and yet not all unknown.

Louis, his idolized brother, was beyond the reach
henceforth of earthly hopes or fears.

"I once met Mademoiselle at Heidelberg," he
said slowly ; "it is more than two years since,
shortly before Bartholomew."

"Yes, monseigneur. Mademoiselle has not forgotten. She bade me say to your highness that
you must not feel yourself even yet wholly bereft ;
that your friends in Heidelberg can never forget
you, and never cease to pray for your peace."

"Said the lady so ? " replied the prince quickly.
"A gracious and consoling word." And he fell
into deep reverie.

Later in the day, when he had slept and showed
a noticeable increase of strength and spirit, the
prince said to Jeanne :

"If Leyden is saved, dear lady, we shall be forced to send you and that husband of yours off on a honeymoon to celebrate the event."

"Oh, charming!" cried Jeanne.

"You have heard of a town named Middelburg, in our province of Zeeland?"

"That have I, monseigneur! Captain Tontorf talked to me of nothing else on our long ride from Jouarre. I feel almost as if I had heard the bells of the minster and seen the house in the Lange Delft, where his boyhood was spent."

"I am minded," said the prince, smiling at her eager face, "to condemn the pair of you to solitary confinement for a month or two presently in that same house in Middelburg."

Jeanne laughed with joyous, unconstrained delight.

"I am supposed at present to be owner of that same mansion," continued the prince. "The Spanish occupation has left it dilapidated, stripped, and forlorn. I should like to see what you two could do with it. Tontorf knew it in its original order, and you have your woman's gift of restoring waste places and making a home out of a desert, as you have shown here. Would you care to undertake the task?"

"With all my heart," said Jeanne, with shining eyes.

"It would be my wish," said the prince, "that the house should be, in so far as it is possible, restored to its former condition. I wish to place it under charge and disposal of yourself and of your husband. It will also be my home when I am in Zeeland henceforth, and I ask nothing better for myself than the simple dignity and substantial comfort of an old Dutch burgher mansion," with which the prince fell silent again, while in the busy brain of the young wife by his side a host of happy thoughts were stirring.

Full soon the promise thus made was fulfilled, and Captain Tontorf took his bride to the house once his father's for the promised honeymoon. For October brought deliverance to Leyden, and all Holland thrilled with the tidings that this, the most famous of the great historic sieges, had ended with the Spaniards in full retreat before the incoming flood. The Dutchmen, and the Dutchmen's awful ally, the sea, had come off at last victorious.

The prince, in spite of his weakness, hastened to the long-suffering city, for whose deliverance he had fought his way back to life, and amid a very tumult of thanksgiving he granted its citizens the gift they craved in token of their heroic resistance, the charter of a university.

XXXVII

AT THE KIRMESS

"AH, buy a basket, my lady! Take but a look at this one! See the bright border! *Mais c'est elegant, n'est-ce pas?* All woven by these hands, your highness. See how strong it is, and yet light enough even for your ladyship's delicate hand."

Thus pleading, a Romany woman, with flashing, black eyes and blue-black hair smoothed under a scarlet kerchief tied below her chin, held out a sample of her wares to a young lady who at the moment had entered the motley labyrinth of the open New Year's Kirmess in the market-place of Heidelberg.

It was Charlotte de Bourbon.

She wore a pelisse of puce-colored velvet, thickly sprinkled now with snowflakes, and from the furred hood light locks of her golden hair had been blown by the gusty wind, for it was snowing and blowing furiously. With gay and breathless laughter Mademoiselle and her two companions, the Lady Kunigunde and Jacqueline Tontorf, had sprung within the gypsy's booth for shelter from the storm. They had been enjoying their lusty fight with it, for all three were full of high spirits and the fine elastic vigor of youth and health.

But as she looked at the Romany woman, Charlotte de Bourbon, startled, exclaimed:

"*Voilà*, Kunigunde, can you believe it? This is an old friend of mine; see if she will know me."

She spoke in French; her voice was exquisitely modulated; her blue eyes, in their sunny clearness,

412

showed a child's eager pleasure in the sudden recognition.

"You and I have met before, good friend," she
now said, looking with a frank smile upon the vivid,
sunbrowned face of the Romany woman. "Do
you remember the Abbey of Jouarre? Do you
remember a little billet which you came there one
summer day, three years ago, to deliver?"

"It is the lady abbess herself! God love your
lovely face and forgive me that I forgot it!" and
down on her knee fell the woman, pressing her lips
to the snowy fur border of Charlotte's cloak.

"And your ladyship got safe away from those
terrible stone walls! And you have found a good
home here in Almayne, *n'est-ce pas?* And the gallant knight who sent the billet by me to your ladyship,—he with the yellow hair, the laugh in his
voice, the free heart,—is he too well and happy?"

Charlotte's face changed swiftly.

"The Count of Nassau died on the field within
the year," she said softly.

"*Misericorde!* Never did I see so fine a gentleman as that. May the saints receive him! And
will your ladyship tell me, then, what has become
of the dark-eyed demoiselle who was with you at
Jouarre, at Fontenay—the Béarnaise? She is not
with your ladyship to-day?" And the black eyes
glanced keen inquiry at the faces of Kunigunde and
Jacqueline.

"Ah, the demoiselle de Mousson. She is married
to the man of her choice and flown far from me into
the Low Countries," replied Charlotte, shaking her
head with a wistful smile.

"And in a few short months," said the woman,
with the incredible swiftness of intuition of her
craft, "Mademoiselle will be married to the man of
her choice and will be flown after her! Ah, let me
tell your ladyship's fortune!" she exclaimed im-
portunately.

Wave after wave of brightest bloom tinged Charlotte's cheeks at these unexpected words.

"No, no," she murmured, with a gesture commanding silence, " you have said too much already."
Pouring a handful of small coins into the woman's
apron, she turned from the booth only to meet, to
her increased confusion, the fixed, respectful regard
of a pair of eyes which, unknown to her, had been
riveted upon her face for several minutes.

Against the corner post of the adjoining booth a
cavalier, of foreign and distinguished aspect, stood
quietly leaning, a noticeable man of marked dignity
of bearing.

Why was this unknown personage so steadfastly
watching her? Had he heard that strange, wild
prophecy of the Romany woman? Had he observed
her excitement? Where was Kunigunde? What
had become of Jacqueline? They had been carried
out of sight for the moment by some current of the
crowd. She was alone. She would move on as
rapidly as might be and escape that steady, disqui-
eting gaze. Ah, no; to escape was impossible!
She had passed the spot where the stranger stood,
but with rapid step he was at her side. Saluting
her now with profound reverence, he said in a low
voice and with a slightly foreign accent :

"Have I the honor to speak to her grace the
Princess de Bourbon? Hardly, methinks, can I be
mistaken."

The lady, greatly amazed, bent her head in token
of assent.

A letter, sealed with a large crest, was in the
stranger's hand. Placing it in her own, with another low bow, he continued in the same under-
tone :

"I have just arrived in Heidelberg, your grace,
sent from the Prince of Orange on a two-fold commission—a public commission to his excellency, the
elector, a private mission to Mademoiselle de Bour-

bon. This letter I am charged by my lord and prince to place in the hands of your ladyship at the first opportunity I have of speaking to you alone. I have been in Heidelberg but two hours and count myself fortunate that my errand is already half fulfilled."

With a parting salutation, courtly and deferential, the stranger passed on, mingling with the moving crowd and immediately disappearing from view.

Hardly had Charlotte slipped the letter into the folds of her dress when Kunigunde's voice was heard just behind her, saying:

"Oh, here you are! We lost you or you lost us, it may chance of intention. Who, pray, is yon handsome cavalier who was plainly unable this long time to take his eyes from your face?" and with arch raillery Kunigunde drew Charlotte, who protested that she did not know the gentleman, on into the bewildering intricacies of the Kirmess.

But Mademoiselle had no interest left in the noisy holiday scene, and could feign little. The letter which lay against her heart seemed to set it throbbing with wild pulsations. She was perturbed, confused, excited; but most of all a strange exultant joy seemed buoying her up, insomuch that she scarce knew that her feet touched the ground, and ever there rang in her ears the words of the stranger, "My lord and prince! My lord and prince!" Within an hour, being weary of the crowded Kirmess, the three maidens returned to the *Gasthaus zum Ritter*, where they had left their horses.

The landlord, a privileged personage with the family from the castle, came bustling to meet them as they reached the door with a low obeisance and a broad smile on his face.

"The horses shall be ready in exactly three minutes, mesdames! The gracious ladies have probably not heard of the distinguished arrival at

my hostelry since they stopped on their way to the
Kirmess ? No ? I thought as much ! Ah, it is a
very great lord, indeed, and not only so but a great
poet. The gracious ladies must have heard the
noted ' Wilhelmuslied ' :

Wilhelmus van Nassouwe
ben ick van duitschen bloet."

and the landlord hummed the first staves of the
famous song under his breath with an air of triumphant consequence.

"St. Aldegonde ! " cried both princesses in one
breath.

"The same ! It is Philip Marnix, my lord of St.
Aldegonde, come straight from Holland on an errand
to his excellency your honored father, gracious
Fräulein, from the great stadtholder, William of
Orange."

"Oh, but really ! " cried Kunigunde with fresh
interest. "I have long desired to see him ! And
do you know, sir, the nature of his errand ? " and
she cast a roguish look aside at Charlotte's blushing face. "The self-same cavalier, *liebchen*, who
spoke to you just now," she murmured under her
breath.

"Oh, yes, gracious Fräulein," the host went on
in a declamatory tone. "It is an embassage of
weighty and most honorable character. His lordship is empowered to negotiate with his excellency
for a removal, for a time at least, of some of the
brightest ornaments, some of the most eminent sa-
vants of Heidelberg's glorious university, to the new
foundation at Leyden."

"Is it so ? " responded the lady. "Doubtless
then we shall see the gentleman presently up at
the castle. But my father is even now down in
the town at the university hall, if you had but
known it."

"Trust me for knowing that, gracious Fräulein !

Oh, yes I gave my lord of St. Aldegonde many a point he could not have otherwise obtained. I directed him where to find his excellency and they are doubtless now conferring together."

The three maidens, by this time mounted, galloped up the snowy, trodden bridle path through the naked chestnut wood to the castle, followed by their grooms. Hastily dismissing her attendants Charlotte withdrew to her room in the Frauenzimmerbau and at last had opportunity to take her mysterious letter from its safe hiding-place and to break the lions of its seal.

The signature was William of Nassau, the import of the letter, as a glance sufficed to reveal to the lady, was an offer of marriage in due form.

Charlotte's eyes flew across the lines. It was a letter which well might quicken the beating of her heart, noble, stately, yet loverlike.

With fine restraint, but scarce veiled passion, the prince declared his devotion and begged to learn if it could be returned. "The Sieur de St. Aldegonde will tell you," he proceeded, "that I am at the ebb of all my worldly fortunes and no brilliant *parti* for a princess of the blood of France ; that I am no longer young ; that I am deep in debt, and deeper yet in the difficulties of this stormy time ; that I can promise you no easy and joyous life, but rather invite you to share the fortunes of a man fighting almost alone in a war whose issue is uncertain. Yes, unhappily more than this is true ; I have no palace such as would befit you ; I can surround you with no state and splendor such as you deserve ; a dower-house in Middelburg, a plain burgher dwelling, and nothing to boast of, is all that I can at present offer my bride. However, my heart is yours and I make bold to offer you my hand, pledging you my best service in all good faith, to cherish and protect you while I live if you will do me this greatest grace."

2B

The Sieur de St. Aldegonde, his good friend, the prince added, would answer whatever questions should arise and would plead his cause in all honor and sincerity.

Clasping the letter to her breast Charlotte rose, and lifting her head as if she had been crowned, stood in the sunset light streaming through the oriel window. No words, no sound escaped her lips, but bright tears of exquisite joy and proud humility fell fast down her cheeks.

"My lord and prince!" her heart cried, "thus he stoops to woo me, the poor fugitive, the homeless, disinherited dependent! He hides his greatness, and makes naught of his fame, setting forth the rather all that should bring him down to my poor estate, with matchless art. Has love taught him? Oh, has he loved me long? If I could but know, for I—I have loved him forever, and forever shall I love!"

But suddenly into the rapture of her heavenly hoping a thought sprang which stung her as if it had been a poisonous dart.

Was the prince a free man? Had she a right to this riot of joy?

Until that moment Charlotte de Bourbon had forgotten the existence of Anne of Saxony. Had the prince too forgotten?

XXXVIII

"A SPIRIT, YET A WOMAN TOO"

"WILL the Sieur de St. Aldegonde attend Mademoiselle de Bourbon at once ? She wishes to speak with him in private on a matter known only to himself. She will await him in the east gallery of the Bibliotheksbau."

St. Aldegonde stood in the leaping firelight before the magnificent chimney which gave grandeur to the Ruprechts Hall, musing on the two-fold mission which had brought him to this famous court. The elector had taken him straightway up from the town to the castle, with hospitable tyranny, and he was expecting momentarily a summons to attend him and the electress at the evening banquet.

Turning as he heard himself thus addressed, he saw a graceful girl with serious eyes and quickened, timid breath who had entered the room with noiseless steps, and who stood as if awaiting instant response.

"My Fräulein, shall I follow you ? " asked the good knight courteously, concealing his surprise at the unexpected summons.

A motion of the girl's hand was the only reply, and she hastened out from the hall, St. Aldegonde closely following.

Passing through a chill, gloomy passage which led to the northern end of the great Ruprechtsbau, Jacqueline Tontorf, for she was her lady's messenger, opened a door at its farthest extremity and in another moment St. Aldegonde found himself in the great Gothic library of Heidelberg Castle. The eager eyes of the Holland savant could discern in

419

its dimly lighted recesses the endless treasures of folios, manuscripts, and books of priceless value, treasures of an irresistible attraction to him, the scholar and poet. But Jacqueline's slender figure, gliding swiftly on before, forbade him to linger. She now sprang lightly up a few steps to a door which she cautiously opened, beckoning him to approach.

"Yonder," she said, speaking for the second time, and pointed down a long gallery. It was flooded by the cold luster of the January moon whose light fell through the tall, arched eastern windows. "My lady will meet you at the foot of the turret stairs."

Wherewith St. Aldegonde found himself alone in the moonlit gallery, for the door into the library softly closed upon his girlish guide. Without hesitation he advanced to the massive octagonal turret at the northern end which, belonging to the adjacent structure, the Frauenzimmerbau, in which the ladies of the court had their apartments, abutted on the gallery of the great library. As he neared the small pointed doorway, cut in the thick masonry of the ancient turret, he heard a slight sound above him.

He halted where he stood, gazing at the narrow portal. There was a rustle of flowing silken garments, footfalls on the cold stone stairs as light as the moonbeams, and Charlotte de Bourbon stood before him. Dressed in gleaming white silk for the evening's festivity, her face was white as the light drapery which was drawn about her head and shoulders, and in her clasped hands, dropped before her, she held a letter with a broken seal. Her large blue eyes were fastened full upon the knight's face.

St. Aldegonde bowed low, amazement and something akin to awe making him speechless.

Was this vision the blithe laughing maiden whom he had encountered a few hours since in the Kir-

mess with her blushes over the bold words of the
Romany quean and her deeper blushes when she
received the letter from his hand ?

That was a creature of flesh and blood, with
spirit high and buoyant, a woman joyous, gracious,
wholly human and adorable. This was a being of
another strain, at once queenly and ascetic ; the
princess-abbess of other days, cold and pale and
still, her loveliness touched with a tragic loftiness,
all the nun within her looking in wondering reproach from her startled eyes, all the womanhood
of her betrayed by the trembling of her sweet lips ;
in fine, a woman who believed she felt the first
breath which had ever blown upon her chastity
and that from the lips of the man she loved.

" Is Anne of Saxony *dead*, my lord ? "

The abrupt words, breathed rather than spoken,
had in them a most moving cadence of appeal,
despite their imperiousness.

" She is thrice dead to the man who was once
her husband, your highness," St. Aldegonde made
answer firmly.

The poet in him discerned as by a lightning flash
the movements of the lady's spirit. He divined
from the very accents of her voice that she loved
his lord. Her heart stood ready to surrender to his
siege, but conscience and will had risen to arms.

" If it please you, monsieur, let us confine ourselves to facts. Their excellencies await us both
presently, and there is scant time to deal in meta-
phors. Is the Princess of Orange dead ? Else is
this letter a shame and affront to my maidenhood,"
and Charlotte lifted the letter in her hand as if to
return it to its giver, but in the very act her hand
fell again.

" Nay, gracious lady," cried St. Aldegonde,
pierced to the heart thus to hear the honor of his
adored master attainted ; " let it not be said ! let
it not be thought ! My lord has loved you with a

whole-hearted though silent devotion from the day he saw you first at this court. He plights you a pure and knightly troth, if so you will receive it."

From the lady's eyes slow tears fell and sparkled in the frosty moonlight.

"It was thus I read his letter, but I had forgot ——" and here her voice faltered.

"Forget now and forever, dear lady," cried St. Aldegonde, low and urgently; "it is right to forget! It is kindest, best! And yet a word of explanation is your due. The former wife of the Prince of Orange is not merely a vicious woman, insane by reason of intemperance, as you have doubtless heard," here the gentleman's face grew stern and his voice sank to a lower key. "Far worse than that is her case, albeit the truth has been closely hid, for in her vain, dissolute frivolity she has betrayed her husband's honor and name; she has lived in shameless violation of her marriage vows, and to-day she is as dead in the eye of the law of God and man as though the cell in which she hides her madness were her grave. Her very life is forfeit, her marriage ties are annulled by her crime. For all this ample proof is forthcoming. You little know my lord, madame, if you can dream that he would stain your maidenhood by the offer of a hand which was not free. The Prince of Orange places your honor far above his own desire, his own happiness. Upon this Mademoiselle could even have depended. That she has doubted it, pardon me, shows that she has yet to sound the depths of his princely nature, and of a patience which I dare to think is in nothing less than the patience of God's holy saints and martyrs. For my lord has borne in silence and in secret the consequences of another's sin beyond the last verge of requirement, as your very question proves. Nevertheless, Mademoiselle, he will bear this burden still if such be your decision."

St. Aldegonde paused, his arms crossed upon his breast, his eyes, grave and sorrowful, searching Charlotte's face.

A faint smile was dawning in her eyes, was trembling on her lips. The letter was hidden now in her bosom. Her tense limbs relaxed, her stately head drooped.

"What think you, Monsieur de St. Aldegonde," she murmured, with delicate reserve; "has not my lord and prince merited something better than that at my hand?"

"Mademoiselle, to my thought he has," replied St. Aldegonde stoutly.

"Monsieur says that the prince has—borne me in his thoughts these several years?"

"Yes, your highness. That I know surely from his own lips."

A rosy flush mantled the lady's cheeks, heretofore so pale.

"And yet he has not spoken?" she softly said.

"Mademoiselle," the brave St. Aldegonde made answer, something almost like a sob smothered in his breath, "the dead boy we loved so well, our gallant Louis, the *ewig jung*, loved your ladyship, hoped in time to win you. My lord discovered this, and, as beseemed his nobleness, was silent."

The lady's eyes grew wide with wonder, with awe and tenderness. With a swift, generous gesture she held out both her clasped hands toward the man who had so well known how to plead his master's cause.

"I am not worthy the love of so great a man!" she cried, all the heart of her breaking in pure joy upon her voice, "but tell the prince, monsieur, that my devotion to him outranks his for me in years, for long before I ever saw him, while yet I was in my convent at Jouarre, a lonely girl, shut away from the great world outside, his name was the name of all men living which ruled my thoughts."

St. Aldegonde listened to these words with kindling eyes.

"Nevertheless, I must acquaint Mademoiselle
with the whole truth. There are some things that
should be said, as that, *primo*, my lord is no
longer young."

"Then can my youth be the more welcome gift,"
was the quick response.

"He is poor."

"Then are we the better mated."

"His life is led in a tumult of war and strife and
danger."

"The greater need has he, then, of a peaceful
hearth and home in which to find a refuge."

"He has espoused an unpopular, it may even
be a losing, cause."

"In that he has but shown that he is greater than
other men."

"His is no light-hearted temper, your nobleness;
the prince is a man of many sorrows and acquainted
with much humiliation."

St. Aldegonde's voice trembled.

"In this he is like our blessed Saviour," the lady
made reverent answer.

"And his life—it is never beyond the reach of
his enemies. He lives in mortal peril at every
hour."

"That I know," she said, with a look never so
high-hearted, "and that alone would call me to his
side. Who can tell but God would have me not
only to live for him, but also to lay down my life
for his sake?"

XXXIX

" JE MAINTIENDRAI "

" SAXONY rages, good Philip, and Hesse imagines a vain thing ! "

It was the prince who spoke with mild irony, striding up and down his private room in the old convent of St. Agatha in Delft, booted and spurred, plainly about to depart. St. Aldegonde, who had just entered with a clouded face, was leaning against a table littered with numberless documents and letters. The room was dusty and comfortless, and showed the lack of a woman's care. The prince was sadly missing the good offices of Madame Tontorf. It was April.

"Yes, the landgrave, I hear, is positively foaming at the mouth at the prospect of the divorce of his niece," rejoined Marnix seriously. "You have sacrificed yourself so long, my lord, to screen their family pride, the scandal has been kept so long a complete mystery from the public, that the lady's uncles have taken it for granted you would continue to do so to the bitter end. Not that they ever thanked you for your silence, as far as I have heard," he added, with a trace of bitterness.

"Not they," returned the prince lightly, "but they can curse me fast enough now when I break silence perforce. They deplore and protest, deprecate and imprecate in good German and bad Latin, as you can read for yourself, if you will," and he pointed to the confusion of letters on the table.

"Are the formalities for the divorce yet completed, my lord ? " asked his friend with ill-concealed anxiety.

425

"No, but they will be shortly," was the composed reply. "I have also had letters to-day, Philip, from France, forwarded from Heidelberg. The elector and madame wrote most warmly, as before."

"Ah, yes, they are surely on your side. But what from France ? What says Montpensier ? "

"He sulks in his tent and will say nothing. He has disinherited and disowned the maiden, and with that—enough said. France is non-committal, '*not wishing to mix himself with the affair, as being against his religion.* Catharine de Medici goes so far as to *consider Mademoiselle fortunate in meeting so good a parti, and will not take the marriage in ill part.*"

"Cold comfort that."

"Navarre, however, gives us a most affectionate approval. The son of Jeanne d'Albret will never fail in friendship toward Mademoiselle. Young Condé too is cordial."

"Good as far as it goes," said St. Aldegonde, "but I fear the tactics of the queen-mother are likely to make use of this proposed marriage for further alienation of the French government from our cause."

The prince glanced up sharply at the phrase "proposed marriage" and frowned.

"Oh, probably," he said carelessly.

"Meanwhile I have had this from John, your brother, my lord," and drawing out a letter, Marnix read the hasty, passionate lines : "'*Dear Aldegonde, if you have any love for the prince and for the welfare of the elector, and if you do not want to run into danger yourself, do let this thing be delayed for a time.*'"

The Count of Nassau proceeded to set forth with much force and cogency the disastrous results which would ensue to the great cause of Protestantism and the struggle against Spain if the prince persisted in a divorce and re-marriage which must alienate every German magnate in the empire, save the Elector Palatine.

"The prince listened quietly. He had seated himself now at the table and as Marnix concluded he remarked gravely :

"Yes, John is in despair. I can match that letter with half a dozen here in which he fairly weeps over my imprudence. John is badly frightened, and I am not sure but my good friend Philip is as much so," and the prince smiled slightly at the anxious face before him. "My brother Calvinists here in the Netherlands have their fling too, at me. 'This man,' they say, 'it seems can change his wife and his religion as often as it pleases him.' That is not exactly the *glückwunsch* a man would choose for his marriage," and the characteristic melancholy became more marked in the face of Orange.

"And what will you do about it all, my lord ? " asked St. Aldegonde impressively. "I confess that I believe John right in the matter. This Bourbon marriage will be a bad blunder politically, however desirable to yourself as a private individual."

The prince looked at his friend for a little space with a peculiar, imperturbable smile.

"Philip, what think you I am likely to do about it ? "

The other scanned his face closely and replied briefly : "You will marry the lady."

"Precisely—if she is still minded to have me." Then Orange added with strong, grave emphasis : "You can bear me witness, old friend, *my intention has always been, since God gave me any understanding, not to trouble myself about words and menaces in anything I could conscientiously do without wrong to my neighbor. Truly, if I had paid regard to the threats of princes I should never have embarked in so many dangerous affairs contrary to the will of the king in times past. The time comes when active resistance with the grace of God is the only remedy.*"

" And this is such a time ? "

" *It is even so now with my marriage. It is some-thing I do with good conscience before God and with-out just cause for reproach from men. I firmly be-lieve that I am taking the right course not only for my-self but for the general cause.* John and you will be the first to admit it ere long. Further than this I have nothing to say, believing that I am the best judge of my own conduct. This you can write to the landgrave, to Saxony, to John if you will, but write nothing more. For me, I have no time to write, I should have been on my way to Middel-burg a half-hour since."

Aldegonde bent his head.

Whether fully convinced of the political wisdom of the Bourbon marriage, he could not mistake the iron determination which lay behind these quiet words ; he read it in the compressed lips, in the keen but quiet light in the eyes, in the firmly closed, flexible white hand of the prince as it lay on the table.

He rose from his place.

" My lord," he said, with a smile of whimsical resignation, " you are in love."

" True, Philip. Can you wonder ?

" Not I, my lord, I who have seen the lady."

" Marnix," the prince began in a musing tone, " life has not gone over-easily with me up to this day."

" You are right, my lord."

" What think you," he proceeded slowly, his chin lifted, his head thrown back, a brooding dark-ness in his eyes, " might it not even be pardon-able if once, just once, a man should act to please himself and seek to bind up a somewhat bleeding, and if the truth were known, Philip, perhaps even a broken heart by the touch of a woman's hand— a sweet woman, my friend, with a pure hand and a holy ? What if the man should not even ask, should not even care supremely what the political effect of his action might be? Could forgiveness be found for such a wretch?"

"I believe it could, my lord," returned Marnix, mastered by the charm of his friend's mood.

"Then, Philip," and the prince rose from his chair, the brooding smile still in his eyes, but a strangely imperious thrill in his tones as he spoke, "start on your journey for Heidelberg as speedily as you may! March roundly now in this matter! A man may surely be in haste to see the bride whom he has not seen in three years. Fetch her, Philip, as fast as you may and not disturb her ease. Take the route straight down the river, if you find it safe. It is easier for Mademoiselle, quicker also. And Philip, commend me to my lady as you journey with such good will as you may. Speak me fair, good friend. She will have heard many things hard for her gentle spirit; she may tremble at the life before her, may even shrink at the last from joining her fate to so stormy a one as mine."

"Nay, my lord, Mademoiselle will neither tremble nor shrink."

"Are you so sure?"

"The lady resembles you, my lord, in this particular; she is of an excellent high courage. Also she is very deep in love."

A brilliant smile rewarded this deliverance. Then with a salutation of gay, ironical gallantry, as graceful and spirited as the manner of his youth, the prince hastened to leave the room. St. Aldegonde watched him from the window as he swung his slender, flexible body with one leap upon his horse's back and galloped out of the courtyard on his long journey to Middelburg.

"Adorably stubborn person!" he murmured to himself with a grim, reluctant smile. "Now then, back to Heidelberg!"

XL

THE BOURBON LILY BLOOMS IN DUTCH SOIL

THE Prince of Orange knew the people of the Netherlands better than any man living.

His deeper insight discerned the effect upon them of his proposed marriage, and he builded better than the men knew who prophesied disaster. He saw that in the land itself dwelt the secret of its salvation. Long ago he had learned that the favor of princes was vain, but that in the heart of the common people of the Provinces was stanch and sturdy constancy. It was to this common heart of the people that his marriage most effectually appealed.

What if the German princes took counsel together and said : " If Orange can afford this romantic, imprudent marriage with a dowerless, escaped nun, we need trouble ourselves no longer in his behoof " ? To the harried, worn-out people of the Provinces, whose only hope was in their stadtholder, his betrothal gave fresh heart and courage, and well he knew it! Let the German princes go, then, if they must! A thrill of joy ran through the fainting land. The prince would bring a lovely lady of the royal house of France among them. He would establish a home and a household and plant himself more deeply than heretofore in their simple burgher life and in their stricken cities. This meant that their cause could not, after all, be hopeless. This meant that he committed himself wholly and forever to that cause with all that he held dearest. It dispelled the haunting fear that he was perchance after all a free lance, striking brave blows for the

Provinces to-day, but ready to depart to another land to-morrow and leave them to their fate.

A tenderer sentiment, moreover, stirred everywhere and found frequent expression, for dearer than all they held it that the harsh and rugged lines of their prince's life were to be softened and beautified by a woman's gentleness, and that the anguish of his lonely heart was at last to find noble consolation.

It was therefore with joyous anticipation that the Netherlanders awaited the return of St. Aldegonde, who was known to have set out early in May from Heidelberg with the bride, accompanied by a goodly retinue, as befitted the state of the adopted daughter of the great Protestant elector and a princess of the house of Bourbon.

On the 7th of June a stately barge, adorned with great richness, flower-laden, its mast wreathed with lilies, under escort of a little fleet of sister ships, sailed into the Dutch port of La Brille.

On the deck of the barge stood the lilylike lady, golden-haired, tall and queenly, dressed all in white and silver, around her a little bevy of her maidens, among them her favorite, Jacqueline. On her right hand stood her faithful Christian counsellor, the Sieur de Minay, on her left the prince's advocate, the Sieur de St. Aldegonde.

As the little fleet anchored amid thundering salvos echoing from shore to shore of the wide-mouthed river, a small boat put out from the crowded jetty, and a stately man of middle age, in a magnificent costume of black and gold, with the order of the Fleece upon his breast, leaped to the deck of the barge, and fell on one knee before his bride-elect.

As he lifted her hand to his lips and his eyes full of love and worship to her face, the fervent cheers of the multitude, the blare of trumpets, and renewed salvos from the cannons rent the air.

Let us glance back at the quaint words of the old

chronicler of *La Joyeuse Entrée* of the "serene and high-born princess":

Blaze forth your gladness, you cities of Holland and Zeeland!
You, men and women, blaze forth on every side your joy
In honor of the great prince and of his consort noble and re-
   nowned!
May God, who has accorded them his grace, continue it to
   them evermore.

When the chaste and noble young lady entered the city of
   La Brille,
Each one bade her welcome, and joy burst from all around;
Fires burned on the towers and in the streets both night and
   day in a ravishing manner,
Not a voice of complaining or regret troubled the general ex-
   ultation.

Five days later, being the twelfth day of June, in the year of grace 1575, in the parish church of La Brille, the Princess de Bourbon was united in marriage to the Prince of Orange.

That day, in letters of gold on a banner of white, was borne aloft the significant motto chosen by the prince:

"A single dawning has conquered all my night!"

A BRIEF RECORD OF SEVEN HAPPY YEARS.

[The following is a memoir in the handwriting of Meovouw Tontorf, née de Mousson, inscribed by her as above. This record, preserved in the archives of the Tontorf-Hassalaer family, of Middelburg, has been, by their kind favor, placed in the hands of the writer of these annals, and is here appended.]

IT is the seventh anniversary of my lady's marriage, being the twelfth of June, in the year 1582. I, Jeanne Tontorf, am sitting here in our beloved home in the Lange Delft, known now in Middelburg as the *Heerenhuis*, and being alone, since my good man has not yet returned from Antwerp, my mind runs back over some of the scenes of those years, and the strange events which have taken place under this roof.

I have come even now from bidding good-night to my precious little princesses in their white beds. For the first time, to-night I can say that I am glad that I have no child of my own.

In this room where I write, how well I remember standing with Norbert that April afternoon seven years ago, ere yet we dreamed aught of the purpose of monseigneur. The sun was streaming in through these windows, and we were busily planning how best to order the room for his highness' use, when we heard his own step on the stair and he stood before us, fine and lordly in the open door, whip in hand, in riding costume, plainly just off his horse.

We had not looked for him to come to Middelburg that day, and, believing him still in Delft, our surprise and gladness were the greater, but naught to what should follow.

Never had I seen monseigneur with the commanding, masterful air he wore that day, the while his eyes were shining with a most marvelous gladness. Every vestige of his illness has now disappeared.

"Madame," he said, and a new note of joyance rang in his voice, "you are preparing an apartment for my use?"

I replied that this was our chief concern.

"And for the captain and yourself?" to which I answered, yes.

"But you have arranged no rooms for your lady!" he exclaimed. "How is that?"

My heart almost stopped beating.

"My lady!" I stammered. "Mademoiselle is in Heidelberg."

"Very true, but please God we shall see her ere long in Holland, and surely a room shall not fail her in this house." Then having mercy on our bewilderment: "Yes, good friends, give me joy! Mademoiselle de Bourbon has plighted me her troth by the Sieur St. Aldegonde."

I cried for joy as I never cried for sorrow, and even Norbert's eyes were dim. It seemed too great a grace.

Later monseigneur told us somewhat of the bitter rage and opposition which his proposed marriage had awakened on all sides. I think our gladness touched his heart very deeply.

Well we understood that Mademoiselle's poverty and friendlessness did but appeal with far greater force to his chivalrous heart than all the power and wealth of thrones could have done. And then I knew that he loved my lady. Had I not watched him that evening in Heidelberg at the banquet of the elector? Had I not seen the look in his eyes when he rode away the morning after?

And Mademoiselle! She had always worshiped her dream of the prince from afar, and for three years her whole heart had been his, as well I knew.   How could I wait to see her joy ?   But the time seemed short, so full were we of happy labor in making her home ready for the bride.

The city council of Middelburg voted a generous annual dowry to the princess, and put a large sum of money at my husband's disposal wherewith to equip this house with rich new carpets, tapestry, and furnishings, and thus ours was indeed a delightful task.

Then came the great day, and we went to La Brille in the prince's company, and after monseigneur I was the first to bid my lady *bienvenue.*   I never saw her so royal nor so beautiful as when she stood that day on the deck of the barge, white lilies in her hand, with the prince kneeling at her feet.

No wonder the people went mad with joy ! Their prince, their saviour, who had suffered such unspeakable loss and sorrow for their sakes, who had been stripped for years of home, of wife and child, friend and brother, was at last to find joy and compensation.

But even they could not know, even the prince himself has never known until now, the divine purpose which filled my lady's heart that day, and which never left it : *to guard his happiness, his life, at the expense, if need be, of her own, to ward from him that doom which she had seen written on his brow !*

Ah, dearest mistress, purest soul, how truly hast thou fulfilled thy purpose !

We were at Dort with their excellencies for the great nuptial festivities and then presently, we going on before, the prince brought his bride to Middelburg, and the venerable Burgomaster Heldring received her in the great hall below, which Norbert's family used to call the Gossaert-Saal, but which is now known as the Prinzen-Saal.

How the bells rang out all over Middelburg that day, and the banners waved from the abbey and the Stadthuis windows, and *Gekke Betje* and *Lange Jan* forgot their ancient feud and rang out a glorious carillon in pealing unison.

My lady from the first moment loved our dear adopted country, its deep green fields, its soft skies and pearly mists. She loved the brave, true-hearted people of Holland and Zeeland, their rich and stately old cities girdled by broad slow rivers, and best of all she loved Middelburg and in this house she found her truest home, so she ever said.

Great joy was this to my husband, who has been indeed fairly glorified by this consecration of his birthplace to the use of the two persons whom he most reveres on earth.

But the other towns must share the princely favor and it was almost a year after the marriage before their excellencies took up their constant abode with us here, not very long I think before the death of the good Elector Friedrich, which caused them both such heartfelt grief. They brought with them their firstborn little daughter,[1] Louisa Juliana, just two months old.

Great and stirring events filled the year which followed and many a great edict and manifesto and torrents of letters of State were written in the room where I now sit alone. Greatest of all was the pacification of Ghent, a very masterpiece of diplomacy by which the prince united, alas, for but brief time, all seventeen of these provinces, pledged to resist the tyranny of Spain and to tolerate both forms of religion. (Religious freedom is ever one of monseigneur's chief concerns ; even the Anabaptists share his sympathy and protection.) But the Southern provinces were and remain at heart Catholic ; fickle are they and easily led away, and no union with them has ever proved lasting.

---

[1] This princess married in 1593 Friedrich IV., Elector Palatine, grandson of Friedrich III., guardian of Charlotte de Bourbon. The Electress Sophia, ancestress of the house of Hanover, was her granddaughter, and Queen Victoria, of Great Britain, was thus ninth in descent from William the Silent.

For inflexible patriotism and steadfastness in religion the prince has ever need to look to the Northern provinces. Their union abides firm and stable. We believe it ever will.

It was after monseigneur and my lady had spent well-nigh a year under this roof, that we had a strange and mysterious visitor who spent four days with us that spring, but departed without having accomplished his secret mission. This guest was Doctor Leoninus, a savant and diplomat of Louvain, and he was sent to Middelburg by the new viceroy, Don John, half-brother to Philip of Spain. His purpose was to seek to win the prince to abandon the cause of the Netherlands by every flattering promise of power and wealth which might tempt an ambitious man to withdraw from an endless and hopeless struggle against terrific odds.

My lady confided to me as well as to the Sieur de Minay, always her trusted counsellor, the object of the very learned gentleman's visit and we watched with some secret amusement the obsequious and flattering deference of the guest, in whom Spain was in reality on its knees before the prince, and likewise the cold, dignified courtesy of his host.

Not for one moment did it enter into the heart of monseigneur to give up the cause of this poor fainting, drowned-out land for the sake of his own pardon, or power and exaltation. Nay, not even to recover his eldest son, kept a prisoner in Spain all these years, would he do this, for, as he quietly told Leoninus, he had "*long ago placed his own particular interests under his foot as he was still resolved to do while life should endure.*"

Once he turned, when we were alone, but our guest still prolonging his visit, and said to Madame :

"*Ma mie,*"—it is thus he is wont to address her, —"forgive me ! It has not occurred to me to lay this matter before thee as deserving thy consideration. Thou knowest the mission of Leoninus.

438

What sayest thou ? It would in sooth bring an end to all our troubles."

It was the only time I ever saw my lady angry, but there was no loss, since monseigneur found her more charming than ever in her indignation. So Leoninus was sent back to his master Don John, who wrote to Philip that he could prevail nothing, since the people here are *" bewitched by the Prince of Orange. He is the pilot who is guiding this bark, and he alone can lose or save it. The greatest obstacle would be abolished if he could have been gained over."*

Shortly after this the Spanish troops departed from our land for a season amid the wild rejoicings of the people.

Never have I dreamed of a life so purely happy as the life which was lived by our household under this roof. Perhaps there were times when the Sieur de Minay had longings for our own fair France, albeit he said ever that life without his princess would be scarce worth living, but for me my heart's ease was too full for longing. Norbert being now captain of the prince's bodyguard, was ever in attendance. He and I have our own beautiful apartments overlooking the Lange Delft, and the pervading sense that this sacred place is our home fills us with abiding gratitude, while there has been a yet higher joy in knowing it the actual home of their excellencies. To them our whole united life has been given in a service which we both hold our chief joy and honor.

To see monseigneur and my lady together daily in the sweet habitudes of their wedded life was little less than glory to me. The charm and repose and loving spirit of Madame seemed ever to exert a magical spell on the mind of her husband, through all those stormy and troublous times. Often have I heard him say "What a happy life this is that I live with thee, Carlotta!" and add that she had given him all the true happiness his life had ever known. In every state paper, even, where he mentioned her, it was as "*our very dear and well-beloved wife.*"

However perplexing his cares of State, when he entered his home the wearing anxiety would leave his brow, and in place of the sternness of his mouth, which indeed after the death of Count Louis had become almost grim and harsh, a smile of gentle serenity was seen oftenest. In very sooth, for all his greatness never saw I man more dependent on love, more sensitive to womanly sympathy, than our great stadtholder.

The devotion of the people to my lady was boundless, and their pride in her modest but royal loveliness was often touching to me. She gave their poor, starved hearts and downtrodden lives the touch they needed of beauty and grace and sweet majesty. "Ah," I have heard men say as she passed, "the Bourbon blood is generous and right royal. You can see it in every movement of Madame, in every step she takes!"

Wherever sorrow and poverty entered in, and in truth this was on every hand in those days, there my lady followed with gracious gifts and her own loving-kindness. What wonder all adored her!

Ah, they were blessed years to us, for all the public cares they brought.

Count John of Nassau (I have learned he was bitterly opposed to monseigneur's marriage), after coming to Holland and sojourning in our household wrote that he found the prince "*in excellent health, and in spite of adversity, incredible labor, perplexity and dangers, in such good spirits that it makes me happy to witness it. No doubt,*" he added, "*a chief reason is the consolation he derives from the devout and highly-intelligent wife whom the Lord has given him—a woman who ever conforms to his wishes and is inexpressibly dear to him.*"

My lady completely won his heart, and a brave and generous heart it is. He has given all that he had to the prince's cause, himself with the rest.

Soon after the visit of Doctor Leoninus a second daughter was born to their excellencies under this roof, and great was our rejoicing.

The Queen of England, who had veered around now to the side of the prince, had promised to stand sponsor to our Middelburg baby, and a great christening feast was held here in the Stadthuis, to which many guests, including the burgomasters of Flushing and Veere, were bidden. Later, in Dort, the child, who has always been my especial nursling, was christened and given the name Elizabeth, Sir Philip Sidney, an equerry and favorite of the English queen, standing sponsor.

On this occasion we all were deeply touched by the resemblance of the young English nobleman to our own lamented Louis of Nassau, and the prince and my lady gave him every proof of deep regard, for, indeed, monseigneur says, he sees in him one of the ablest statesmen in Europe. Sir Philip has ardently espoused the prince's cause, and will use all the influence he may with his selfish and shifting queen for our poor Netherlands.

In the autumn of that year my lady took her little children, and the older Nassau children, Marie, Maurice, Anne, and Emilia, who had been brought by monseigneur's brother, Count John, from Dillenburg, and removed her residence for a time to the prince's ancestral castle of Breda, so long in the enemy's hands, but now restored.

The Princess Marie, a charming maiden of twenty-one, came straight into my lady's heart, as did the younger princesses, and it was beautiful to see her motherly and yet more sisterly tenderness to them. "All our children, big and little," is the way she ever wrote of them to their father. The young Prince Maurice is a handsome, mettlesome youth,

with a high opinion of himself, and indeed he has
much intellect and a wondrous masterful spirit.
My husband often speaks of being at Dillenburg
Castle on the night when he was born.

After this, for reasons of State, the prince resided
much of the time in Antwerp, for a year and more,
and there my lady's heart was gladdened by the
coming of the Chevalier de la Noue and other French
gentlemen, who now attached themselves with ardent devotion to the service and court of monseigneur. Deepest joy of all, however, was it that the
inexorable coldness of her father, the Duc de Montpensier, yielded at last to the intercession of our
dear Madame d'Albret's son, the King of Navarre,
who espoused my lady's cause with most earnest
zeal. The Duc acknowledged her again as his
daughter and wrote in affectionate and honorable
terms to her husband and children. Furthermore,
he has issued an official manifesto as peer of
France, which has been published far and wide.
In this he declared his full approval of the marriage
of the princess and his grace of Orange, as being
"useful, profitable, and honorable for our daughter,
and for the state and greatness of our house," and
concluded as follows:

*"Wherefore we request and require the Imperial
Majesty and all the kings, princes and sovereign
potentates with whom we have the honor of being
related and allied, as well as other lords and princes,
our good friends, that if any question, trouble or
quarrel is spread abroad in the matter of this said
marriage, or to the prejudice of the children thereof,
born or yet to be born, be it regarding their estate,
condition, or otherwise, it may please them to take
their honor in hand and to have and receive them
in their good protection, giving them such comfort,
aid and favor as all princes are wont to use, the one
toward the others,"* etc. . .

Thus happily ended the long, one-sided battle between the proud and powerful father and the weak,
defenseless child; and it was the latter, after all,
who won.

Monseigneur the prince had not been slow in dis-
covering that my lady's wise administration of
affairs at Jouarre had given her skill in the direction
of public matters. Every year he grew to depend
more upon her in this sort and she frequently acted
as viceroy for him in his many absences from Antwerp and ever wisely and well.

But Antwerp was never heart's home to my lady
as was this dear Middelburg Heerenhuis, and in
truth I think she ever dreaded it as a treacherous
and turbulent town, her anxieties for the prince
being always keenest when he was there and out
of her sight.

So, after their long tarrying in Antwerp, right glad
was I when in April, two years ago,—it seems not
so long,—a blithe little letter from my dear lady
told me to have the house ready, for they were all
coming to Middelburg for a time.

Great preparations were made in the city to receive the family with pomp and feasting, but methinks no hearts were so glad as ours as we made
ready the beautiful rooms so long unused.

When the first excitement was over, my lady
and I had long quiet mornings together with the
children, and many a stroll through the beautiful
abbey gardens and along the green and curving
banks of the city moat in the spring sunshine, the
babies and their nurses coming after, and all so gay
and joyous.

It was thus we were walking,—how well I remember it,—the broad waters moving swiftly under the April breeze, and the children shouting to
us that the bluebirds were singing and summer
must be near, when, against a trunk of a tree my
lady chanced to notice a placard, fresh printed,

which shone white in the sun, and with never a thought of dread, straight up to it she walked and began to read.

We never knew who placed it there. Afterward they were common enough, sown indeed like evil seed in every city.

For this is what my lady read, her face growing ever whiter :

" *Philip, by the grace of God, King of Castile*, etc., etc., *to all to whom these presents shall come. Whereas, William of Nassau, a foreigner in our realms, once honored and promoted by the late emperor and by ourselves, has by sinister practices and arts gained over malcontents*, etc., etc., . . *and whereas he has taken a consecrated nun and abbess in the lifetime of his own lawful wife and still lives with her in infamy . . . and whereas the country can have no peace whilst this wretched hypocrite troubles it,* . .

" *We hereby now declare this head and chief author of all our troubles to be a traitor and miscreant, an enemy of ourselves and our country. We interdict all our subjects from supplying him with lodging, food, water, or fire under pain of our royal indignation.* . . *We empower all and every to seize the person and the goods of this William of Nassau as enemy of the human race ; and hereby, on the word of a king and as minister of God, we promise to any one who has the heart to free us of this pest, and who will deliver him alive or dead, or take his life, the sum of 25,000 crowns in gold.* . . *We will pardon him any crime, if he has been guilty, and give him a patent of nobility, if he be not noble,*" etc., etc.

Every word of that infamous Ban was burned into my brain as if with letters of fire. It was the closing, craven stab of the prince's ancient enemy, Philip's evil genius, Granvelle, and envenomed with his hideous hatred.

We called for our carriages and drove home in silence. My lady did not cry out nor faint, but her face looked as if carved out of stone and I think from that moment she never doubted what the end should be.

In the portico stood monseigneur as we reached the house. I knew he had been watching for my lady's coming, fearing this dastardly placard had met her eyes, since he knew it to have reached Middelburg. That he had read it I knew on the instant, by the proud way he held his head and by the fire in his dark eyes.

"Come, *ma mie*," he said with a tenderness untellable, and taking her hand he led her into the Prinzen-Saal and I saw him point to the beautiful window on which he had caused her arms to be blazoned, within a wreath of Bourbon lilies, and the motto below, "*Candidior candidis.*"

"My lily!" he said, "my purest, my dearest," and he kissed her on brow and lips.

I closed the door softly, and came away to weep.

Life has gone on bravely in the two years since then and we all have sought to do our part cheerfully, and no one ever heard a murmur pass my lady's lips, but we have wrought as under the shadow of death. The prince has never for a moment faltered or failed in his steady courage, putting the whole matter by, when once he had made answer in a proud and dauntless "Apology."

There have been birth and death and marriage among us, for two little daughters have been born to their excellencies; Count John of Nassau has been married to our dear Heidelberg princess the Lady Kunigunde, and sister Jacqueline has left us to live with them; while the venerable Countess Juliana, our prince's mother, has gone to those so dear to her who died for God and country.

Last summer a great and solemn deed took place, for the estates of the United Provinces by oath ab-

" ' My lily ! ' he said, ' my purest.' "

Page 444

jured their fealty to the King of Spain and declared him deposed forever, by reason of his intolerable tyranny, from the sovereignty of the Netherlands received from his father in the year '55.

God grant that never again may our long-suffering land be brought under that cruel yoke! No one can foresee the end. The Prince of Parma, the present Spanish governor, is a man of craft and cruelty, far abler than Don John, a powerful general, and full of subtle scheming.

The sovereignty of Spain being now set aside, and the Provinces free and independent, monseigneur not daring, however, to believe that they, small and defenseless, could stand alone without the protection of one of the great powers, the protectorate had been offered to monsieur, the Duc d'Anjou, brother to our French king, Henri III., of Valois, and now succeeding his brother as a suitor for the hand of Queen Elizabeth.

Monsieur, who was well pleased to assume the over-lordship of so fair a domain, accordingly marched over the border in August with five thousand gentlemen, and having gained considerable favor, and yet not wholly won over the estates, which were slow to put their trust in a son of Catharine de Medici, betook himself presently to England to woo its frigid and fickle virgin queen.

In November we heard from St. Aldegonde, who was at the English court, that the royal pair had exchanged rings and that the marriage was really arranged. There was rejoicing then everywhere in the Netherlands, since such alliance would give our people a doubly strong defender ; but to-day it seems to me farther off than ever. Since I have seen monsieur I would wager a round sum that her majesty of England, who has the handsomest man in Europe, Robert Dudley, ever at her feet, will never take for her husband the ugly, froglike, weak-kneed youngest son of Catharine de Medici.

It is just four months ago that amid the greatest
excitement, monsieur, with his suite and a great
following of English noblemen, given him as escort
by the English queen, entered Middelburg, having
landed the day before in Flushing, crossing from
Dover, thus ending his sojourn in England, known
there, they tell us, as " Monsieur's Days."

For weeks our city council had been preparing
for the event, and truly monsieur received a brilliant ovation as he entered Middelburg, for every
turret of our Stadthuis and of the great abbey
blazed with torches, the order being given also that
" the great bell shall toll and pitch-barrels shall be
burned on the choir of the abbey, and also before
his excellency's door, and on the market place."

Monseigneur had gone to Flushing to receive the
royal party, and my lady had brought her wee
baby, born in Antwerp in December and named
Amalie for the electress, to join the other little
children whom I had kept all winter here. She
could not await the coming of the Duc in Antwerp,
for monsieur was to bring in his train her beloved
brother, François de Bourbon, the prince-dauphin,
whom she had not seen for all these long years.

He was lodged in the abbey with monsieur and
the gentlemen of his suite, but made all haste to
the Lange Delft, and the brother and sister had a
most affecting meeting, while the cannonading and
speech-making and banqueting went on before and
within the Stadthuis. How we rejoice now that
this long-cherished desire was fulfilled ere it was
too late.

The English gentlemen, the Earl of Leicester,
Sir Philip Sidney, and half a dozen great lords besides, were lodged here in the Heerenhuis, which
had been excellently re-furnished for their use, the
many chambers surrounding the great court, of old
used for the apprentices and the printery of Norbert's father, Nikolaas Tontorf, having been wholly

made over and transformed into goodly order, meet for such illustrious guests.

In the morning following, quite without premeditation, a small levee was held by my lady in the Prinzen-Saal with all her little children. For my Lord of Leicester had begged that he might see the godchild of his queen, our little Elizabeth, and the other children of their excellencies as well. They being fetched, my lady stood with all her babies about her, her brother at her side watching the pretty troop with wondering admiration.

The little Elizabeth, who is now five years of age (she has her mother's golden hair and her father's large brown eyes), wore the diamond and ruby ring sent her by the English queen, and held out her tiny hand in a most diverting manner for my Lord of Leicester and the rest to kiss.

The Sieur de Minay, who is ever in accord with me, says the same—I shall remember my lady forever as she stood there then so queenly, albeit so unconscious of herself. She was ever most fair, most serene when with her children, for only then, I think, could she forget that dread for the prince which wore ceaselessly at her heart. Her color was still exceeding delicate from her late confinement, but the joyous excitement had brought a pink bloom to her cheeks, and her great blue eyes, as divinely innocent as those of her children, were shining with all a mother's rapture of adoring pride.

I saw with what reverence my lord of Leicester regarded her, and, as for his gallant nephew, Sidney, he could scarce withdraw his eyes from her face, and methought the homage of his look rendered more palpable than ever that strange resemblance of his to Count Louis. It is my own fond belief that neither gentleman had ever chanced to see so fair a pattern of all wifely and motherly excellence as was then before their eyes.

I noted François de Bourbon, my lady's brother, as he turned and spoke aside to Sir Philip, and I heard the latter gentleman say under his breath :

"Purer than a nun, patienter than Griselda, prouder than our English queen."

It was then that monseigneur entered, coming from attendance upon the Duc at the abbey, and found the English noblemen thus gathered around his wife and their children. Not less deferentially than they, and methought with a grace that exceeded them all, his highness quietly greeted Madame, and as he bent and kissed her brow, I at least caught the radiance of their mutual glance, and I saw my lady in that moment crowned with a nobler crown than her majesty of England can ever wear.

Then presently monseigneur was fain to carry my lord of Leicester hence to the abbey to confer with the Duc, and with them went the other gentlemen and my lady also withdrew with her children. But Sir Philip Sidney begged me to abide yet a little and keep the Princess Elizabeth in his sight, that so he might the better report her pretty prattle to his mistress. Accordingly I was present while he talked with the Sieur de Minay and with my husband, for as was to be expected, the child was soon overlooked for graver concerns.

"How chanceth it, monsieur," quoth Sir Philip presently, "that his grace of Orange hath attained so rare a height, for verily the man puts greatness away from himself, as a thing for which he hath no relish, and yet seems withal but the greater and more imposing."

"Your lordship," replied the good d'Averly, "the Prince of Orange shows in the highest degree what life can do with a man who by the grace of God has made a glory of failure and a majesty of defeat."

"How mean you, monsieur ? " responded Sidney, his face showing intent interest.

"Your lordship has but to remember," said the Sieur de Minay, " that the prince began life a *grand seigneur*, an aristocrat, a monarchist to the core. His morals were those of the court of Charles V., his statesmanship was that of Machiavelli, learned in the same court ; he was of vast wealth and ambition, and up to the time Granvelle left the Netherlands, singularly successful."

"Where, I pray you tell me, sir," interposed Sidney, "did his reverses begin, for in England he is not reckoned a highly successful man ? "

"They began," returned d'Averly slowly, "when he took into his heart the seed of revolt against political and religious tyranny. It was a seed which germinated slowly, but which has grown to be the governing force of monseigneur's life. It has made him great, but his greatness has been won not by brilliant successes, but by slow stages of deepest suffering. Every ambitious scheme, every flattering hope has been successively crushed and brought to naught, and bitterest of all has been the faithlessness and betrayal of his friends. But it was in the depth of defeat that the true chivalric spirit of the man shone forth, for it was then that he emptied himself of selfish schemes and personal ambitions, put away power and prerogative forever, and sunk himself utterly in the forlorn hope of wrenching this exhausted land inch by inch, town by town, from the tyranny of Spain. Can you name a knightlier deed in the high, ancient sense in which the perfect, gentle knight pledged himself to redress all wrongs, to fight for the defenseless, and never to seek his own good or gain ? Here he planted himself, establishing a household of such noble simplicity as your lordship sees, calling to his side my own beloved lady, a homeless, dependent maiden as great of nature as himself. With magnificent coldness he has rejected the many attempts to win him by promises the most seductive, of power and grandeur, to forsake these poor Provinces, which almost against his own will, he, the monarchist, has welded into a republic. He has scorned alike bribe and ban, and will maintain the freedom of this new-born republic even if it costs life itself. But, even now, who can foresee the issue ? ''

"Monsieur," said Sir Philip, who had listened with deep emotion, "the prince is fighting the battle of freedom not for these Provinces alone, but for the human spirit. He may die, but he cannot fail !"

Five days the great folk tarried here in Middel-burg and then went on in splendid state to Antwerp. My dear husband attended them, while I remained with the children of their excellencies here. Nor-bert has associations so gloomy with Antwerp that he never goes there I believe save with a presenti-ment of evil, and so it was this time ; but besides him all were full of gladness.

Just one month from the day that they entered Antwerp in triumph, the festivities being now over and the prince chiefly concerned in presenting Mon-sieur d'Anjou to his new people in as favorable seeming as might be, the blow, so long dreaded, fell upon us. The Ban at last has begun its work.

On Sunday, March the eighteenth, our prince was shot through the throat and jaw and mortally wounded as all believed, by a mysterious man of vulgar aspect, who presented him with a petition as he passed from dinner with his guests. The assassin was killed on the spot, being pierced in thirty-two places by the halberdiers.

I have heard the whole terrible story now from Norbert, and most amazing is it to him even above others.

While the excitement following the attack was still at its height, my lord, as was supposed, dying, my lady going from one swoon into another, each man looking upon each with suspicion, as a possible

accomplice in a dark plot, and all believing that
Monsieur d'Anjou was at the bottom of the treachery, with another Valois conspiracy akin to Bartholomew, Norbert, as captain of the prince's bodyguard, was called by St. Aldegonde into a close-
locked ante-room. It was next that in which lay
the body of the murderer.

"Hither, Tontorf!" he cried, his hands full of
papers. "Upon your faith, thank God, I can rely!
and you can keep a cool head. Take a look with
me at these dirty belongings of yonder wretch.
They are the contents of his pockets. Let us get
speedily to the bottom of this business and find if
that infernal bullet was French or Spanish."

They spread the collection out upon a table—an
Agnus Dei, a green wax taper, two dried toads,
used as charms, a number of bills of exchange, a
Jesuit catechism, a set of tablets scrawled over
with vows to divers saints, and I forget what besides. My husband scanned the bills narrowly
and suddenly, with I know not what fierce impre-
cation, exclaimed :

"Instantly! let me see the body!"

At the inner door, on guard, stood young Prince
Maurice, white as the dead, but cool and unflinching, directing all that was done. Reluctantly he
permitted Norbert's entrance.

For a moment my husband stood gazing fixedly
at the hideous form of the murderer, a strange sense
of something familiar in his face growing ever
stronger. Then with a swift rush of memory and
a countenance which men say was terrible, he cried :
"It was no French but a Spanish bullet! There
is no Valois plot! I know this fellow! His name
was Juan Jaureguy, and he was sent to do his foul
deed by that Spanish devil, Gaspar d'Anastro!"

With that he burst from the place, called the
guard together, and marched them straight to the
Rue d'Augustin, and to that house of evil memory,

where he and poor little Jacqueline were so long imprisoned, fifteen years ago.

At the door they were met by the man whom I believe of all men Norbert most abhorred, the cashier Venero, the tool whom Anastro used before for his murderous purposes. Except the paramour of Anastro, the members of the merchant's family had returned to their old habitation within the year and quietly established themselves.

"Arrest that man on the spot!" my husband thundered, and pressed his way on into the house, giving Venero in one look a prophecy full stern of the retribution which was waiting on his evil deeds.

In an inner room they found another whom Norbert recognized, the *padre*, Antony, who on the other terrible occasion had absolved Venero before his crime was committed, and who had just performed the same diabolical office for the scant-witted scullion, Juan Jaureguy. Him Norbert remembered as a poor, half-starved urchin about the house. This friar they promptly arrested. For the arch-conspirator, the cold, calculating coward, Anastro, they sought in vain. The crafty Spaniard, too wary to risk his own life, had taken his passport and left Antwerp on the preceding Tuesday, and was even then safe under the protection of the Duke of Parma, who gloried in his deed, which was then fully believed to be successful.

Venero has made a full confession in my husband's presence.

Anastro, it seems, hard pressed and greedy for gold as ever, stimulated by the Ban had entered into a compact with King Philip to take the prince's life within a certain period. If successful he was to receive eighty thousand ducats and the cross of Santiago. He had compounded with Venero and Jaureguy to do the deed, convincing them that the prince deserved death for the crime of *lèse-majesté*. He had fooled the latter into believing that he could

453

render him invisible by his magic arts, as soon as
the murder was committed. He promised to make
both miscreants his sons and to divide his property
between them. In fine, he had played upon their
fidelity, their superstition, and their cupidity until
they were powerless to resist him. And yet he has
gone unpunished, and these poor wretches alone
have suffered the penalty.

Of a surety I can say, our prince is the first gentleman in Europe ! When he was shot, a prayer for
mercy for Jaureguy, a cry that he forgave him his
death, were his first words. Then later it was his
earnest desire that these accomplices be not tor-
tured before their death, while he was far less concerned as to his own recovery than to shield Monsieur d'Anjou from suspicion. As ever, his thought
was for himself last of all, and first of all it was for
our land and its weal ; his sufferings were borne
with an incredible sweetness, and his noble spirit
seemed to conquer even the approach of death that
so he might still live to save his people.

As for the people of Antwerp and of all our cities,
they thronged their streets, crying aloud with sobs
and tears for their prince, their father, their only
shield and succour. Meanwhile, Anastro, safe-
shielded in Parma's camp, was writing exultant letters to King Philip, assuming the full success of his
plot, and greedily craving his reward.

On Wednesday, there being then as it was
thought no hope, all Antwerp held a solemn fast
and the churches overflowed with the weeping people flocking to them to pray for monseigneur.

A week later, and the execution of Venero and
the friar having taken place in the square opposite
the town hall, it was then thought the prince
showed signs of mending. This continued until
April fifth when renewed hemorrhage from the
half-healed wound made a danger graver than ever.
This peril was overcome by means of the pressure

of the thumb of his attendants upon the wound which was continued day and night for more than a week.

My lady, who had rallied as soon as she found there was a ray of hope, could hardly be persuaded to leave her lord for an hour. Her hand was the one oftenest at his service, and it was her love which slowly brought him back to life. But even the strength which love gave her sometimes failed under the terrible suspense, and many a time she was borne away fainting. Day by day I could see her body decline until nought of her seemed left alive save the puissant spirit. But meanwhile for monsiegneur hope grew stronger and became certainty, so that on the second day of May all Antwerp again gathered in the great cathedral and the joy bells rang out over all the city for a general thanksgiving.

The prince was restored. He could even go with the multitude to the cathedral to join in the voice of praise. But my lady? Ah, no, that joy was not for her.

He came gaunt and wasted, but never so imposing, and kissed her ere he left the house. She was standing by a window to watch his going forth.

"*Ma mie,*" he said, with infinite tenderness, "thy cheeks are paler now than mine. While the others praise, I shall pray for thy better health. God be with thee, sweetheart, who hast saved my life by thy love and faithfulness."

"Farewell," she said and smiled, and her smile was of an unearthly sweetness, full of strange triumph and yet sadder than any tears I ever saw in mortal eyes.

Then, the prince having gone forth, my lady turned to me and with a long sobbing breath moaned like a beseeching child:

"Take me now, Jeanne, faithful friend. I can bear no more. Take care of thy poor Charlotte."

Soon we had her in bed and the physicians were sent for and came hurrying back to that sorrowful house, but she was even then unconscious, and in three days the end came.

The murderers did not fail of a victim.

Once only she seemed to know monseigneur and then she smiled in his face that strange smile of ineffable triumph.

"Sweet to die—sweet to die—for thee," she whispered, "it was for this I prayed."

Then the strong man bent himself upon her bed, shaken from head to foot by his agony of yearning.

It was four o'clock and sunrise when she died.

They laid her in the great cathedral, in the Chapel of the Circumcision, where the chimes shall ring forth their music forever over her grave, and all the city and all the land wept that "so beautiful a soul" had left its mortal dwelling.

Weeks have passed since I began to indite this record. It was mid-June then and now it is midsummer, and continually I have been going back in mind to that last midsummer of our convent life, eleven years ago.

Again it is the forest of Fontenay ; Jeannette and I have gone thither with Mademoiselle ; Count Louis is there, the queen-mother, the Majesty of France. Down the vista of the green forest glade again I have seen the girlish figure of my lady, distant and wraith-like, and by her side the noble lord of Teligny. They bend toward each other in earnest speech, but suddenly in the path before me stands the mysterious Romany woman and, as I follow her fixed gaze, I dimly discern other two ; beside my lady walks the form of a goodly knight (a form which to-day I know full well) beside Teligny, a woman, whose face I cannot see, who wrings her hands.

The gypsy at my side is singing now—

> " Sharp speeds for him life's close ;
> Myrtle for her and rose—
> Yet death apace."

Alas, over soon, over well for Teligny, for my lady, has that woful song found fulfillment !

But there was a second strophe, of yet stranger and more bitter boding. Must it too, then, know fulfillment ? Is there another act in the tragedy of these lives ? Ah, to my lord the prince, what shall be the end? I know only that he seems still to stand within the shadow, and that, to my sight, the seal of martyrdom has never left his brow.

THE END.

[In the last will and testament of that very high and puissant lady, Charlotte de Bourbon, Princess of Orange, done on the twelfth day of November, in the year of grace 1581, in the city of Antwerp, the first legacies named are as follows :

" *To the Sieur de Tontorf and to his wife, twelve hundred florins outright and two hundred livres income during their lives in consideration of the good services which I have received from them, and especially from the said wife, who has served me with such care and fidelity for the space of twenty years that I have great cause for satisfaction therewith. For this reason I very humbly beg my lord the prince to have regard to this and to retain the said Tontorf in his service with the compensation hitherto given him, &c. . . I desire that it shall please him also to keep Madame Tontorf in attendance on our children with the customary consideration which I give her.*

" *I leave also to the Sieur de Minay three hundred livres income during his life, besides twelve hundred livres to be paid at one time as I have already ordered, in recognition of the service which he has rendered me, having accompanied me from France into Germany and having stood by me three years in Heidelberg in order to assist me in my affairs ; wherefore I very humbly beseech monsieur the prince, my husband, to give him the use, during his life, of the lands of Montfort, Cuisseaux and Beaurepère, situated in the Duchy of Bourgogne, with honorable maintenance.*"]

www.ingramcontent.com/pod-product-compliance
Lightning Source LLC
Chambersburg PA
CBHW020920020726
47495CB00002B/278